THE DEATH OF JAMES JONES, SORT OF

ADAM R. FLETCHER

1

"No news is bad news," said Bob, my incompetent estate agent. I was in a warm bath, telephone to my ear, peering through my binoculars at the people who had ruined my street and/or life.

"I've not even had a viewing," I said. "And it's been three, perhaps even four months."

"Nout's selling. Not in Radford, anyway." He made a noise like a balloon being rubbed on carpet. "Serious gang problem."

I knew there was a serious gang problem because I was spying on that serious gang, the Robin Hoodlums. Just a narrow alleyway separated the backs of our modest terrace homes.

I feared them. I feared most things.

"We're already giving it away," I protested.

"Yet no one wants it, pal."

We were not pals. I had no pals. As a child, I had a pen pal called Gregory, but he stopped replying at the same time I stopped sending my pocket money.

"What about students?"

"Students don't have any money, James." Bob then

began a series of promises that were vague and/or meaningless. I hung up just as the Hoodlums' back door opened. Twiddling the dial on the binoculars for sharpness, I was able to glimpse the inside of the house, where I saw the shapes of several bleary-eyed urban delinquents, up to nothing and/or no good.

The alley wouldn't be safe to take on my way to work today, I concluded, conclusively. Which meant I'd need to use my front door, which was, inconveniently, inside my lodger and frenemy Cliff's ground-floor bedroom.

Dressed and thoroughly anoraked, I tiptoed downstairs and nudged his door with my foot. I found him snoring melodiously, curled in a ball of hereditary privilege, his eyes closed.

Shallow people sleep the deepest.

I, on the other hand—either hand, since I'm ambidextrous—always sleep with one eye open.

Sometimes one and a half eyes.

His room smelt of Lynx Africa and ignorance. I crept across its threadbare, snot-green carpet until my feet became entangled in the beige jumper of my decoy girlfriend and/or platonic soulmate, Tabby. I fell shoulder-first into the wall, knocking down the poster of a man called Pink Floyd. A homosexual, I surmised, but I couldn't be certain as no matter how still I stand, the canon of popular culture always misses me. Perhaps it's because I mistrust anything less than fifty years old.

Before that, the jury is still out.

Cliff didn't even stir, of course. I righted myself and reached the front door. I was disappointed to discover he'd not engaged any of the extensive security features I'd installed.

Tutting, I stepped out into another bleak, overcast, drizzly Nottingham day.

"Action," said a woman, and I looked up in open-mouthed shock to find a television crew of four, perhaps even five in my narrow front garden.

"Here he is, folks," said a photogenic man holding a red microphone bearing the logo of East Midlands News. "Nottingham's Unluckiest Man 1999—James Jones."

"That *is* unlucky," said the presenter, looking at my face, his mouth turning downwards through surprise and disbelief and out into disgust. A trajectory I watched happen often, every day.

His colleague, a tall man in a baseball cap holding what looked like a giant duster, recoiled, twisting abruptly and smacking into the cameraman, who, clutching his expensive camera to protect it, fell backwards on a loose, slightly up-jutting paving stone.

His head was exposed. He screamed. I screamed.

"Cut," yelled a woman with a fierce bob clutching a wooden clipboard. She seemed to have a directorial function and was staring at me, head askance. "James, can you go in and come out again?"

"I forgot to feed the cat," the presenter said. "I'll be back in a minute."

"You don't have a cat," the director said.

"What's happening?" the man with the duster asked.

"Misfortune," I muttered, having recovered my faculties. I turned and fumbled for my key then fled back inside and slammed the door. After engaging its many locks and chains, I slumped against it, wondering what was happening, and how I could stop it.

I'm a routined individual: it's the only thing that protects me from chance's sharp edges. Yet despite my best efforts, strict protocols, and rigid rules, misfortune had found me once again.

I lifted the letter box. "Go away."

The director inspected the back of the cameraman's head. "Can you work?"

He winced. "I guess."

I reached into the pocket of my anorak, pulled out an aspirin, and flicked it through the letter box. It bounced off the paving stone and disappeared under a bush.

"Sorry to startle you like that," said the presenter, bending towards me.

"He startled *me*," said Mr Duster.

"He on something?" Mrs Director asked in a poor attempt at a whisper. "Was it definitely unluckiest and not ugliest?"

Cliff's snoring intensified. He sounded like a high-end, self-satisfied electric whisk.

"Go away," I repeated.

The presenter rolled his eyes and turned to Mrs Director. "Can we do it through the door? Could be funny, right? If we can just see his eyes, or more like part of his eyes."

My eyes are my curse. No, one of. Whoever said beauty is in the eye of the beholder fibbed. Beauty is just math. I was never good at math. I am not good math. My face doesn't add up.

She shrugged. "Try it."

The presenter cleared his throat and someone said "action."

"James Jones has set the city record for emergency room admissions, insurance claims, and 999 calls." He had a honeyed voice I might have enjoyed in less perilous circumstances. "He was also struck by lightning—twice. *James*, come out."

I had never been struck by lightning. The natural world has no problem with me. It's just humans and—I suppose, if I'm being completely honest—pigeons.

They were sensationalising things.

I didn't need this kind of attention. Sensational attention. Ordinary attention was disastrous enough. It's why I'd made my life so small and inconsequential, to reduce what I thought of as my Misfortune Surface Area. Yet here I was, here they were, at what was almost certainly the end. I noticed how rapidly I was breathing and grew certain that they were a group of undercover assassins and that I was going to die and, even worse, not loudly enough to wake Cliff.

"I didn't enter any contest." I tried to sound more assertive. "And I'm NOT unlucky."

Fifty per cent of this was true.

"Well, you won it," Mrs Director said.

"Come on, mate," Mr Duster said. "It's just a laff."

"Yeah," the presenter agreed. "A thirty-second puff piece for people to enjoy with their cornflakes."

Anger boiled in my chest. My life had always been full of people saying "We're just having a laugh", "Don't be so uptight", and "Eat this worm or I'll punch you in the face".

I wished Tabby were awake. She'd know what to do. Advice was her specialty and/or profession.

"It's supposed to be a celebration," Mrs Director said.

"Yeah," I mumbled. "Or a fatal trick."

"Twat," the cameraman said, putting his heavy camera onto the path and rubbing his head.

"At least take your medal?" the presenter said, lifting it up to the letter box. It was a silver disc on a red-and-blue ribbon. No one had ever given me a medal.

"Keep it."

"Seriously?" the director snapped. "Come out and take your stupid medal, James, or something unlucky really will happen to ya." She had a mouth on her and I respected it. I could never risk an outburst like that.

I checked my watch: 9.02am.

I was late, and I needed help.

I knew where to find it: Nottingham Central Library. But to get there while avoiding these paparazzi and/or assassins, I'd have to risk the rear alley of doom. I closed the letter box and shuffled through to the kitchen and out the back door, stepping into my tiny paved garden and onto the back and—I suppose, also, by the end—front of a snail, which I had no grievance with and which was merely collateral damage on my way to the gate, where I undid seven bolts and rushed out into my almost-certain demise.

2

I moved left up the alley, trying not to break anything underfoot. It was going well until... *crunch.* A vial of vile heroin cracked and perhaps contained, at one time, crack. I know little about drugs. I can't even drink caffeine. It makes me too exuberant. Crisps have a similar effect. I once ate three packs of Monster Munch at a bar mitzvah and vomited into a stranger's shoe.

I was nine, but that's no excuse.

A gate creaked open behind me. I knew which gate and that it had a single green spray-painted star across it: the insignia of my enemy and/or enemies.

"Oi!" said a gravelly voice.

I turned and saw a man looming behind me in the morning mist and/or drizzle.

It was strange to see him full-size and up so close. He wore a green parka with fur trim, unzipped. It too had a star on the back. I saw these jackets all over Radford. He was my height, slim like a runner bean, sinewy and gaunt. He had lank, greying, shoulder-length hair peeking out from under a baseball cap that said *Power to the Proles*.

His name was Robin Hoodlum.

"Stop," he barked, flashing a jagged-toothed smile. His teeth were like tiny shivs.

Rain splashed onto my nose as I worked hard to control the muscles in my face so that they remained firm, betraying no emotion—particularly, but not exclusively, mortal terror.

Should I run?

I could run.

I didn't run. Fear had poured concrete into my shoes.

"Your wallet or your life," he said, taking two steps towards me. I looked up at the landing window on Tabby's floor. She wasn't there. No one was there. No one was coming. I looked back at him. There was vacancy in his eyes. They were empty hotels. I edged backwards until my heel nudged a large pebble and/or tiny boulder.

I whimpered and was, perhaps, fatally stressed. "What do... err..." My eyes roamed. I had no plan. "You do when you're stressed?"

He took two steps closer, put his hand at the small of his back, and pushed out his hips. There was a disconcerting click. "Heroin."

He was just a metre away now. I could see that the skin around his eyes was tight and cracking. He smelt of sausage rolls and insobriety.

Maybe if I kept him here long enough the paparazzi would find us? That would give them something worth filming, something that showed just how unlucky I really was. "I... err... What's in your wallet?" I stammered.

His head tilted left. "What?"

"It's just, you know, you're a mugger. So, you've seen a few wallets in your time, right? That must have an effect. Best practice and whatnot?"

His top lip scraped across those sharp bottom teeth. "Not a big fan of that word, *mugger*." He raised his chin to a height that suggested nobility. "I think of myself as more of an economic redistribution artist." His voice softened as he relaxed into the topic and began to move and bob. "*Yeah*. Sort of modern-day Robin Hood. Hence our name. Although my name is Robin, coincidentally." He kept bobbing. It was as if he were afraid of being trapped in a straightjacket of his own words. "Yeah, we rob from the rich and give... to ourselves, mostly." He half-stepped left, then right. He was, literally, shifty. "Lot of artistry to this job, actually. People don't realise that. It's not all smash and grab." He weaved then uppercut the air. "Though that's where I shine."

My back was to my escape route. "But you're the boss, right? Shouldn't you be above stealing wallets in alleyways?"

He lifted his hat and scratched at his grease-soaked hair. "Flat hierarchy," he said. "Robin Hood was the original Marxist in many ways, wasn't he? You read any Marx?"

"The jury's in," I said, then regretted it.

"Sorry?"

"On Marx. And no. What's the gist?"

"Well." He cleared his throat then spat on the ground between us. "Class struggle. We proles rising to crush you bourgeoisie. Summat like that, anyway. Bit wordy. I'm more a man of action. Or verbs, at the very least. Nouns are for nonces."

I nodded. "I'm a man of inaction. They French, this bourgeoisie?"

He laughed gruffly. "No, sunshine. You're the bourgeoisie. It's the middle class, basically. It's all about capital, innit?"

"London?"

He went cross-eyed. "You joking?"

"It's not really the time. And I'm not middle class."

He looked up at my modest three-storey home, identical

in size and shape to his and/or the one he was squatting in. "Homeowner though, aren't you?"

"The bank owns most of it. I pay them back slowly, and with great interest. Or Cliff does."

"Who's Cliff?"

"And I'm only on the property ladder's bottom rung because my uncle Alexander died, and as the last person alive in my family, I got a modest inheritance." I tended to either say absolutely nothing or babble manically when stressed.

"Lucky then, wasn't it? Wish I had that kind of luck."

"Not for him. He was eaten by a crocodile."

Robin licked his lips. Everything about his body language suggested that he was a hungry cat and I was a cowering, defenceless, squeaky mouse. "No crocs around here."

"This was in Scotland."

"No crocs there either, last I heard."

"Yeah, there are. They made a movie about it. *Crocodile Dundee*."

I hadn't seen the movie, but they gave so much away on posters at bus stations you didn't need to.

I noticed I was losing him.

He shifted from foot to foot. "Yeah, anyway, I split everything with my merciless men. After costs, of course, and let's not forget marketing, and sales, and heroin, and my modest personal expenses." He frowned and rubbed the back of his neck. "I think I'm coming down with something."

I edged backwards another half step.

"Wallet and phone—NOW."

"I don't have a phone. They're a fad."

He cocked an eyebrow. "You're weird. You on summat?"

"Boss," said a voice from behind him, "you need to—"

Robin turned his head back towards his gate and this was it and I spun and scampered up the alley and fortunately I'm a fast runner as necessity has sadly dictated and I got a lucky break when Robin tripped over that large pebble and/or tiny boulder and I soon hit the T-junction and swerved left into a wider passageway that would spit me out onto the top of Cromwell Street.

My street.

I ran and ran. It was exhausting, but then I'm easily exhausted. I once fell asleep on a log flume. By the time I woke up forty-five minutes had passed and my fingers were webbing.

"Oi!" he shouted, and I could hear his footsteps but he was losing the race and I could see the familiar light of my street and a parked taxi.

But then...

Up ahead...

I heard whistling.

I knew that whistle.

I feared that whistle.

I saw her arm. A large, flappy chicken wing of an arm dipping into a bulky red Royal Mail postbag. She was on the path of the house next to the passageway's entrance.

My postwoman, Pat.

We'd gone to high school together. When I went to high school. She was a big part of why I stopped going. She is a monster.

I skidded to a stop.

I was trapped.

If I went back, I was his. If I went forward, I was hers.

I'd stopped in front of someone's door. I didn't know there was a house with the bad luck to open directly into these cursed alleys. I considered knocking and asking for safe harbour, but this was Nottingham. We only harbour grudges. And the odd fugitive. No, the house probably belonged to a sadistic cannibal. Or a non-sadistic cannibal. Or and/or even worse, a student.

Next to its front door was a wheelie bin. I didn't stop and I didn't think. I simply popped the lid and pulled myself in, aided by a fence post and finally happy to have such narrow shoulders. The smell inside was overpowering. But then, I'm easily overpowered. I was once pushed into a canal by an apprentice barista.

Beneath me was a full-but-not-firm bag of rubbish. There was a strong stench of rotten bananas and fresh maggots. It was hot and damp and pitch-black. In a life full of indignation, I decided this was a new low, or high, depending on how the indignation scale is calibrated.

I pulled the lid closed just in time, leaving a narrow gap so I could hear and/or breathe.

"Did that loser run this way?" Robin asked, between wheezes and coughs.

"What loser?" Pat replied.

"Face like a wonky heroin owl?"

"Ferdinand?" she asked.

"Who?" He coughed twice more. "Shit. I'm out of shape."

"Why you up so early?"

"LATE. Late is what it is. I haven't slept in... what day is it, Pat?"

"Tuesday, duck. Wild night? Who was the lucky lady?"

"Speed. Her name is speed, and it's been a wild three days. I'm on a cloud. I'm a bullet. I'm invincible."

"I get like that on peanut butter sometimes."

"What you got for us?" he asked.

"A couple of winners, for sure. There's a credit card in this. Maybe a passport."

"SWEET."

"And my cut?"

Robin sucked air between his teeth. "Come by Friday."

"You're late paying."

"Been busy."

"I deliver your mail too," she said.

"That a threat?"

"It's a fact, duck."

"A threatening fact?"

"It is what it is."

"Vague?"

"Don't push me, Robin."

"Don't tempt me, Pat."

They parted. I listened as their footfalls grew quiet. Like yogurt left in the sun, the plot had thickened: Pat was working with the Hoodlums.

Twenty, perhaps even twenty-five seconds passed.

Other than the overpowering smell of decay and the intense physical discomfort, I was growing used to life in the bin. It was safe, other than from germs, from which I was under an aggressive, sustained, probably deadly attack.

Footsteps. Light, fast, closer to a skip.

I sank deeper into the rubbish, closing the lid.

"Psst," said a voice.

I ignored it. It couldn't be talking to me. No one knew I was here.

"Psst. Psst. yoU." The voice broke into a temporary squeak. "In the bin..."

Other people were probably in other bins nearby.

"James," he said.

James is a very common name. It was why I'd picked it when changing mine.

"James Jones."

Jones was the second-most common surname.

"Nottingham's Unluckiest Man, James JONes." The voice rose then fell an octave this time. It sounded as if puberty wasn't finished with it yet.

"I come in peace."

I lifted the lid a crack. "That's probably what all murderers say."

"I want to help."

Other than Tabby, no one on earth and/or other planets wanted to help me. The lid was yanked open, and it flipped and juddered off the wall behind me. I squinted up into the light adopting an attack stance, which is difficult in a bin and consisted of me angling my hands at a ten-and-two position in front of my eyes, ready to chop out.

It was ill-conceived.

"Come out, buddy."

I appraised this doughy individual. He was in a puffy red jacket that reminded me of a life vest. He had thick black eyebrows that almost met and a wide, expressive face on an oversized, baked-potato head. His brown eyes were alive, alert, and enthusiastic, and his ratty, patchy beard looked stuck on with glue—it hung mostly below his chin like a neck curtain. His cropped hair was overgelled and glistening in the faddish style of the moment.

His hands were in his pockets.

"Err..." I said, and then at once regretted it, for it didn't move things forward.

"Can I help you out?"

"I'm... fine."

"You're in a bin, buddy." It was more of a *bud-eeee*. His accent marked him as a foreigner: he was from Birmingham.

"Just chilling in there, are you?"

"...Yes?"

His large, lumpy face was warm and non-judgemental.

He wafted a hand in front of his flat nose and its two wide nostrils. "The smell's mingin'."

"What's mingin'?" I asked.

"The smell."

"No. I mean the word?"

"Sorry?"

We had only just met and yet already lost each other.

"You get used to it," I said. "The smell."

"Why are you holding your nose then?"

I realised I'd been unable to sustain my attack stance.

"It's fine," he said, with a flick of his wrist. "You're hiding, buddy. I watched the whole thing from me taxi."

He nodded towards Cromwell Street and then, as I turned, thrust his arms into the bin, gripped me at my armpits, and yanked me out. My feet caught on the lip of the bin. It tipped over with a thud and then there was some crunching and, if I'm not mistaken, the clang of several bottles before my feet connected roughly with the ground and I was free.

"Thanks," I said, shaking bin juice from my hands. I slipped a wet wipe from the stash in my anorak pocket and cleaned myself as best as I could.

The man waited, smiling, looking as if he did this sort of thing all the time and that getting into a bin was an act of bravery rather than formidable cowardice.

I kept checking over his shoulder to be sure Pat and Robin weren't coming back.

"I know who you are. I'm here to help you," he said, like a doctor returning with good news about a lump.

I brushed rubbish from my trousers. "I doubt that."

"Why else would I be here then, buddy?"

"To kick me while I'm down?"

He looked around then whispered, "I know your secret."

Did I have any secrets? I probed my memories.

Yes, I decided. Many. I'd better find out what he knew, so that, at the very least, I'd know it too. He puffed out his chest, and then, as if beginning a performance for which he'd long practised, said, "As you've no doubt guessed, I'm Morpheus."

I glanced over my shoulder, checking to see if I had a viable escape route to Cromwell Street.

"Right now, you're feeling a bit like Alice tumbling down the rabbit hole?"

He was enjoying himself, but I didn't know why.

"It was a bin," I corrected.

"I can see it in your eyes. They're huge. Are you okay, actually? You on summat? *Speed*?"

"They're always like that."

"Oh... well." His voice deepened. "Do you believe in fate?"

"I believe it's my fate to suffer pointlessly then die tragically young. Does that count?"

He pulled a small blue box from his coat pocket. "You're here because you know something. You feel it like a splinter in your mind. Do you know what I'm talking about?"

"There's a splinter in my mind?"

"Yes. You feel it when you go to work, when you watch TV."

"I don't own a TV."

He frowned. "What do you watch movies on?"

"I don't watch movies."

He tugged on his ratty, tatty, unconvincing facial hair. "You telling me you've never seen *The Matrix?*"

"No."

"Then this whole thing must be really—"

"Confusing."

He tugged harder. "But it's so iconic! And we're right at the end now..." He squeezed the small blue box and something white fell out.

"Are they Smints?"

"Shh." He put a Smint in each hand. "You take the blue pill and the story ends." He looked at his left hand. "You wake up in your bed and you believe whatever you want. Or you take the red pill." He nodded to his right hand. "You stay in Wonderland and I show you how deep rabbit-bin goES."

He'd squeaked again. He looked embarrassed and cleared his throat. "Goes."

This man was insane, as were the vast majority of Nottingham's residents. But was he dangerous? I almost missed Pat and Robin, for they were so obviously, traditionally villainous. He was just intensely baffling. I decided it was probably best to humour him, rather than confront his delusions directly.

Tentatively, I reached out and took the pill from his left hand, opened my mouth, and pretended to drop it in.

He looked down and away and also cut to his core and so I turned on my heels and ran for Cromwell Street knowing that TV crew and/or no TV crew, I wouldn't stop until I reached the library.

3

Apart from the heat and dust and, I suppose, the strength of the midday sun, there's no meaningful difference between Nottingham High Street and an African savannah.

Both are wide.

Both are wild.

Both are full of sharp-toothed predators.

But only one has the former chemist and present-day purveyor of sandwich-based meal deals: Boots.

I stood outside Boots on Market Street, my back to the glass, sliding slowly sidewards.

The drizzle was relentless. Three hundred and sixty-four days of the year, Nottingham drizzled. On the other, it rained cats and dogs.

The enormous town hall dominated the horizon like a democratic Death Star. Death was on my mind, I suppose. I looked down at my watch: 9.32. The day was still in nappies and yet I'd already survived attacks from a local TV and/or assassin crew, Robin of the Robin Hoodlums, and a lunatic, barely pubescent, Sminting taxi driver.

Something was afoot. I needed help.

The library was a walk of two, perhaps even three high-street minutes down the hill and right onto Angel Row, which, even at this early hour, would be crammed full of devils and sinners. Crossing Nottingham City Centre at any time of the day was like running a gauntlet of thugs, organised crime, disorganised crime, gypsies, fortune tellers, hobos, chavs, bankers, wankers, rugby flankers, stand-up comedians, sit-down drunks, the mentally ill, the physically ill, psychopathic pigeons, suicidal toddlers, pan pipers, and students.

It was students I feared the most. Students were social grenades, completely self-absorbed, perennially high, never knowing where they were, how they'd got there, or where they were going next. They were just sure they felt good and that tomorrow would be better than today.

They were wrong, of course.

The only way to survive in this feral city was to hide. The best way was in plain sight. That's why I often wore a red British Heart Foundation medium-visibility jacket and carried a clipboard. If anyone got too close, I shouted, "Tenner for your ticker?" which was a magic incantation guaranteeing two metres of personal space.

Unfortunately, in my haste to escape the nightly news, I'd forgotten my backpack with this special urban camouflage.

My eyes caught the board outside a newsagent.

NOTT HAS HIGHEST CRIME RATE IN COUNTRY

This I already knew. At least the headline wasn't about me. I slid further along the shop window. I sniffed and smelt shoe polish. Along came a young man and woman, pinkie fingers intertwined, wearing matching Barclays bank uniforms. They were fresh faced and in love, or at least significant lust, certain tomorrow would be better than today.

They were also wrong, of course.

I let them pass and then fell in step between them and a senior citizen on an absurdly slow mobility scooter. Not ideal cover, but I felt sure criminals and/or low lives and/or *Big Issue* salespeople would see her as the easier mark.

After several tense minutes, the glass-fronted library bloomed into view and the tension I was carrying dissipated. The electronic doors swished open, and I knew that I was, briefly, safe.

4

Every day, on and off the high street, a relentless, dog-eat-dog battle is taking place between life's winners and losers, insiders and outcasts, bullies and wimps, wealthy and destitute, beautiful and ugly, aligned and maligned, suave and stuttering, smooth and lumpy.

During that battle, libraries are a safe space where the world's misfits can rest, shelter, and research all the things trying to kill us.

I rode the lift to the top floor. There, moving through the cramped aisles of books, I headed towards the quietest, dankest, darkest section of them all: poetry. Having a poetry section in a cut-throat, duel-heavy place like Nottingham was like having an orchid garden on death row: possible but superfluous.

I turned out of the central aisle and met two sad, neglected rows of oppressively rhyming lyric, at the end of which were two rectangular tables pushed together against the large frosted-glass windows. Six of the eight seats were occupied, but not by anyone daring to make eye contact with anyone else.

At the centre of the table was a tiny triangular hand-written sign: *Motley Misfits*.

I approached. The heater above us stopped whirring and—I suppose, also—heating. "James," said Peter, smiling warmly. "The only face in the world I still recognise." Peter was an ageing biker with extreme facial blindness and an endless supply of leather waistcoats.

"I wasn't sure about coming," said Annie, a mousy, middle-aged woman with short, prematurely white hair who never single-guessed when she could double. "Is it okay that I'm here?" She tugged on the end of her cardigan's sleeve.

Our host, Hugh, cleared his throat with a loud "Mm-hmm."

Then he did it again. "Mm-hmm."

Then again.

Then again. "Mm-hmm. Mm-hmm."

It was a chronic, albeit benign, compulsion and/or condition.

"Definitely," said Peter, who was very agreeable, despite not knowing who he was agreeing with. I took off my anorak and put it over my chair as a new shape entered the row. It was a woman of perhaps six feet and an inch with luminescent white skin and long, fiery red hair in an all-directional tangle. She strode towards us, the heels of her Doc Martens thudding on the tiled floor. She was wearing leather trousers. Her trench coat swished. I could tell from the length and/or power of her stride that she was not one of us.

"Knee a pony," she said. "Bloody good turnout for poetry." Her voice was deep, almost husky. She sounded like a late-night radio host telling a ghost story.

"Mm-hmm. Poetry?"

She held up a faded flyer. "A Posse of Poets?"

Annie leapt up from her seat. "Bugger, I'm in the wrong

place. That's so... *me*. I wanted Motley Misfits." She rushed to button her cardigan.

"Mm-hmm." Hugh nodded to the sign on the table. "This is Motley Misfits. The poets disbanded last year. Some kind of stanza feud."

Hugh was in his seventies. His head was as bald as a polished cue ball. He was a fan of tweed and elbow patches and had been a history teacher before being bullied to the point of a breakdown by his students during a fraught semester on the Tudors.

"Kid a squid," this interloper said, rolling her green eyes. "That's poets for you. So bloody melodramatic." She turned her head and I glimpsed a tattoo of a coffin on her neck. A skeletal hand reached out of it.

"I was a poet once," said Steven, a young, obese, baseball-capped compulsive liar addicted to computer games, pornography, and Marmite.

She pushed out her lips. "Anything I might have read?"

"Probably. I was quite famous."

"I dated a poet once," said Linda. Her nickname was Short Story because they never were. She had social blindness. In her late forties, she dressed for the age she wanted to be: eighteen. Her hair was dyed a striking blonde, and she dripped with both silver and make-up. She must have put it on with a trowel. She paused her knitting. "He was very romantic. Swept me off my feet, literally, with a shopping trolley. He was on something at the time, but I didn't mind. Never met a man who could—"

"Mm-hmm," Hugh interrupted.

"Do we know each other?" Peter asked the imposing Goth. "I'm not good with faces, you see. Other than James's. It's a disability. Or should be."

"I don't think we've met," she said. "I'm Esmeralda."

"Beautiful name," said Linda. "I was going to call my—"

"Perhaps some overlap," Hugh said, "between the poets and our good selves."

Esmeralda made a sucking noise in the corner of her mouth. "Who exactly are you all?"

"A group for the ignored, exiled, and overlooked. Mm-hmm."

"Spunk a monkey," she said, and tucked a chunky strand of hair behind an ear pierced six times with increasingly large silver hoops. "Yeah, might be *a little* overlap."

Hugh gestured at the empty chair, the one with its back to the row of books she'd just walked. The last any of us would take because it posed the greatest risk of being sneak-attacked.

"You're most welcome to join. Mm-hmm."

She looked over her shoulder. Her backpack was pink and covered in spikes and looked like an instrument of torture and/or a candyfloss hedgehog.

"I guess... well..." She hesitated then sat.

"Excellent choice, Esmeralda," said Peter. "I've no problem with names. Never forget a name. It's just not much use if you don't have a face to put to it."

"Mm-hmm. The first rule of Motley Misfits is that here, you will be seen but not judged, mocked, heckled, head-locked, Chinese-burnt, or wedgied."

"Reminds me of that time I wore a burka," said Linda. "That was back in, what was it, 1967 or perhaps 1968? Must have been '67 because I started that job at NatWest and anyway it gets hot under there and long story short, it's a right bugger to drink champagne let me—"

"Splendid," said Hugh. "I mean, mm-hmm."

I noticed Esmeralda staring at me, her head tilted as if studying a painting she didn't necessarily enjoy but was sure held a secret message.

"Mm-hmm. Who would like to talk today? Mm-hmm."

"Good idea," said Peter.

I pinched my hand tightly over the next twenty, perhaps even twenty-one seconds during which no one volunteered. I wanted to speak and ask for their help but, like everyone in the group, was cautious of the limelight.

"A few words?" said Hugh. "Anyone?"

"I guess I could say a few things," said Linda, pausing the creation of what was rapidly becoming a purple sock. "About the nature of things and whatnot?"

"You spoke last time. And the time before. And that. Mm-hmm."

Peter tugged on the zip of his waistcoat. He'd made the mistake of growing a goatee. The silence would have been heavy were we not all so used to carrying it.

I opened my mouth.

I closed my mouth.

I coughed.

"Mm-hmm."

"I agree," said Peter. "Absolutely."

"A... thing happened," I said, looking down at the tabletop. "Well, two things. Maybe three things. Depends how you define a thing, I suppose, mostly."

"It sure did," Peter agreed.

"I bloody knew it would," said Annie, squirming in her seat. "Do you think more things will happen?"

"I did the thing," Steven confessed. "It's my fault. I'll do it again as well, I'm sure." He lifted his baseball cap off, swept back his hair, and slipped it back on.

"Mm-hmm," Hugh prodded.

"Yes, right." I stumbled on. "So, my name is James, sort of, and I'm a misfit."

"Hi, James," the group murmured, except for Esmeralda, who wasn't aware of our ways and scripts and formalities.

"You belong here," the group said, in unison.

I took a deep breath. "Thanks. So, this morning, at my door, a camera crew from Nottingham Evening News tried to crown me Nottingham's Unluckiest Man 1999."

"Chew a kangaroo," said Esmeralda.

"Of course," said Peter. "I mean... no. I mean... what?"

"Bugger," said Annie. "So that's a new thing to worry about."

"I had a crown once," said Linda. "In my mouth. A dentist from India put it in. In Kerala. Or maybe Rajasthan. Bloody hot out there. And the food. The monkeys are wild as well. Weird that it's also called a crown—"

"Mm-hmm. Why, if I may ask, did you enter?"

"I didn't, Hugh. I don't need that kind of attention. Sensational attention. Or any attention, really."

"How did you win if you didn't enter?" Esmeralda asked. "This is all super confusing."

"Mm-hmm," said Hugh. "Or it's a nefarious plot. Do you have, perchance, a nemesis?"

My eyes darted up. I did a quick count. "I have sixty-one neme..." I faltered. "Nemeses? Nemesi? Depends how you plural a nemesis, I suppose. But just one chief nemesis. My neighbour and gang-kingpin-crime-lord Robin Hoodlum."

"I've heard of him," said Steven. I tried to read his face to see if this was true, but he was inscrutable, with narrow-but-piercing brown eyes that slid frequently left and right but never up and down.

"Me too," said Hugh. "And his violent gang of flim-flam men."

"Wait, sixty-one?" Esmeralda asked.

"I have one hundred and twelve," said Peter. "Although I guess I'm easy to trick because I never see anyone coming. Or I see them but—"

"Thirty-four," Linda lamented.

"One," said Annie, looking dejectedly at the floor.

Why had I thought I could find help here? These people had problems as big and/or even bigger than my own.

"Bugger me," Esmeralda said. "You people are..." She shook her head. I spotted another tattoo. A large, ornate owl on her forearm. Tattoos had always confused me. Wasn't life scarring enough?

"It's not only that," I continued. "I was also hiding in a bin and a chubby, spike-hair taxi driver offered me a red pill and a blue pill that were actually Smints."

Esmeralda laughed loudly then bit down on her bottom lip. "Sorry. Don't mind me."

"Follow the white rabbit," said Steven irrelevantly.

"I had a rabbit once," said Linda. "Did I ever tell you about my rabbit Napoleon?"

Someone entered the aisle, obviously lost. "Self-help?" they asked.

"Down a floor," said Hugh.

"Certainly is," said Peter.

"What's this?" the man asked.

"Poetry."

"Yuck."

"Mm-hmm."

"I took the blue pill, of course," I added, when the man was out of earshot. "Well, it was white, but still."

"Who *would* take the red pill?" Annie asked. "I don't want to know how deep the rabbit hole goes. I don't want to be in the bloomin' rabbit hole at all."

Hugh rubbed his shiny head. "Did you, I wonder, do anything to bring this upon yourself?"

I briefly revisited the past few weeks. I hadn't broken my routines. "No."

He rubbed faster, as if hoping to summon a genie. "Somewhere you're exposed. Audit your life."

"I used to be an auditor," said Linda. "I once audited the Queen's estate, matter of fact. And, I mean, really, just the silverware alone. I spent a full week counting cake forks."

"Don't accept the award," said Peter. "Unless you want to. But best not to want to. Maybe you have to? Even then..."

"Lie low," said Hugh. "Draw your enemy out."

"Or enemies," Annie said.

"Or you could run away?" Steven suggested. "Take on a new identity? I'm on my fifth."

I noticed a badge on Esmeralda's trench coat, which was resting over her chair. It had a dog with the word *bitch* beneath it. A series of connected memories played unbidden in the VCR of my mind.

"When I was growing up," I said, "before my parents were crushed by a falling piano, we had dogs. The first was a cocker spaniel called Mac. It was a pedigree. Everyone in the commune and the surrounding town admired that dog, even though the people from the town hated the commune and threw chips at us from their car windows. The dog lived a charmed, almost aristocratic life then died peacefully of old age."

I paused to push down a feeling and give Hugh an opportunity to clear his throat.

He didn't take it.

"My parents replaced Mac with a dog from a shelter."

"Mm-hmm."

"A mongrel called Buster. Gold, where Mac was royal blue. Buster's eyes bulged, like, well, my own. His face was flat and tilted right. He was two years old when we got him. We were his third home. He was a friendly dog. Didn't bite people. Didn't wet the bed. Didn't scratch the sofa. Yet, everyone hated him—"

"Mm-hmm."

"Shortly after we got him, I ignored my parents' rule about staying on the commune and walked him to the local green. There, some boys were playing football. I already knew better than to ask to join them, so I simply observed and let Buster off his lead so he could explore the field and/or woods and find interesting things to urinate on. I don't remember how much time passed before I heard a loud, piercing whine. Then urgent barking. Then rapid whimpering."

Story is powerful and had rendered the group mute, for perhaps the first time.

"I ran and searched. When I found him in the woods, he was in a crumpled, bleeding heap. A large dog and/or small lynx had attacked him. I scooped him up and ran all the way back to our caravan. On the way, while dying, he repeatedly and enthusiastically licked my face.

"No dogs ever attacked Mac in his entire glorious life. Yet they attacked Buster every time we looked away. There was something off about him somehow, and other dogs knew it. Just as you would have known it. He died from that attack, of course. He died because of who he was."

I let that sink in.

"I am a Buster and the world will stop at nothing until I am destroyed."

There was silence.

"I can't recognise dog faces either," Peter lamented.

"That reminds me..." said Linda, but then faded out.

Annie pulled a balled-up tissue from her sleeve and blew her nose.

"This is SO much better than a Posse of Poets," said Esmeralda. "How often do you meet?"

"Mm-hmm," said Hugh.

"Mm-hmm," Peter echoed.

"Mm-hmm," I agreed.

Conversation dropped and no further advice was forthcoming. I'd killed the mood by delivering a story that sliced too close to the collective bone. We were hiding here together for a reason. Other than Esmeralda, we were all Busters. They could sympathise with me. This was something, but it was also very little and/or wouldn't keep me alive.

I looked at my watch: I was very late for work.

"Can you—*we* become Macs, though?" Esmeralda asked, as I stood and zipped up my trusty anorak.

"No," I said, darting down the aisle towards the lifts. "We can't."

5

The elevator pinged, and I stepped out into the blue sea of empty cubicles. It's easier than you'd think to be forgotten in a midsized insurance company. Insurance is not a passion of anyone on the face and—I suppose, also—other body parts of this earth. It's simply a job people do until enough time has passed that they do not.

Accordingly, they may not notice and/or care when a fish-eyed new colleague is there one day, shifting nervously in his seat, failing to participate in basic banter about recently televised football matches, and necking cans of Vimto until...

Poof, he is gone.

I was that fish-eyed new colleague. I'd arrived for my tenth day of employment and found a note taped to my monitor informing me I was being relocated to the fifth floor. I hadn't known there was a fifth floor. Even the lift seemed put out when I asked it to go that high. I then discovered all the floor's cubicles empty. But there was a note on one, near a draughty fire exit.

This is you, James.

That was nine months ago. I am sure I have been forgotten. This is perhaps the only reason they'd not fired me. For I'm not a model employee. A model employee would, I imagine, have a less rich—and so distracting—inner life. This would allow them to focus on the tasks at hand, and other body parts, I suppose.

I soon reached my cubicle, a heavy stone of dread in my stomach. I took off my anorak.

As perhaps everyone does in times of stress, I like to look at a recent bank statement. I pulled a clean, crisp statement from my trouser pocket: £2612.

That was an entire year of frugal living, a lifestyle to which I am accustomed. Seeing it, I felt my heart rate decrease. I folded it in two then slipped it into the back of my imitation-leather wallet.

Perhaps my weird morning was just a blip? A series of unlikely events followed by a pleasing period of mundanity?

I sat down and switched on my personal computer. It whirred and clicked and, at one point, even beeped. I disliked computers but knew the Y2K bug would eradicate them in a month's time. I reached out and stroked the felt of the cubicle's dividing wall. Cubicles had a bad reputation, but I found them calming.

I'd personalised mine with the following:

1) A family photo.

Since all my family are dead, my photo was of Tabby in a fluffy grey jumper smiling timidly near the bookshelf in her bedroom, looking away from the camera as if she feared it would steal her soul.

2) A laminated quote.

You don't have to be crazy to work here, but it helps.

You don't have to be crazy to work at a midsized insurance company, just in need of money, the pursuit of which has driven many people insane, I suppose.

3) A projectile.

I knew from my careful observations—made from behind the large potted plants near each floor's elevators—that my colleagues often visited each other's cubicles to waste time, inquire about the status of reports whose deadlines drew near, and flirt. This could be awkward and so, during it, they enjoyed having something to do with their hands. For this reason, I kept a sponge American football on my desk. No one had ever come to my cubicle to waste time, ask about a report whose deadline draws near, or flirt.

I squeezed the football sometimes while talking to myself.

Each day, I did a few hours of work evaluating calamities that had befallen our policyholders then passed the rest of the day lamenting and/or fraternising with a talking desktop paper clip.

I clicked my mouse. He appeared, a cheeky grin on his face, asking me what I wanted to do today. None of the options presented were *Forget it ever happened.*

Ping

The elevator doors opened.

Instinctively, I ducked.

People only visited my floor if they were lost, cleaners, or employees having illicit affairs, for which there was a well-suited stationery cupboard.

I peeked over the cubicle wall and saw a man turn from the aisle into a nearby bank of cubicles. "James?" he shouted, uncertainty writ large on his face. "You up here?"

I spun my swivel chair and there was an unfortunate creaking sound as it tipped to the side, causing me to trap my knee against a filing cabinet. Yelping, I stood. "James?" I said. "I mean. No. I mean. I am James. Yes?"

"Ah, there you are." He walked down a strip of carpet towards me then stopped midstride, his mouth forming an O. "*Right.* Yes. They said." He tugged on his tie and sniffed.

His brown hair was fluffy and his skin loose and his face inexpertly shaved. There were patches on his neck. His face was very forgettable. I was jealous.

"There a funny smell around?" he asked. "Sort of rotten?"

The bin incident.

No one had mentioned it at the library, but then, anything goes at the library.

"Maybe?" I ventured.

"Scott," he said, holding out his hand. "We met when you first started."

I looked down at his hand then up at his face. "Germs."

"Oh. Err..." He retracted it. "Right."

It was actually intimacy I feared. "Weak immune system."

"Sure." He didn't believe me. "I sent you some emails. Quite a few, actually."

"My email isn't working."

"Did you talk to IT about that?"

"I talked to a paper clip."

He reached for the football sitting on top of my empty in-tray and gave it a soft lob from one hand to the other, misjudging its trajectory. It fell into the photo of Tabby.

"Oh shit, sorry." He jumped to catch the photo before it crashed to the floor. He picked it up and set it back upright. "Beautiful... frame."

I brushed a crease from my trousers and noticed a brown stain, almost certainly from that close encounter with my neighbour's rubbish.

"How can I help, Scott?"

"Right. *Right.* It's time for your review. Past time, actually. I was going to do it in my office." He looked around. "But since we're here and, well, no one else is. I mean, unless you're busy? With the paper clip?"

They had found me.

It was over.

He freed a swivel chair from the next cubicle over, not even waiting for my answer. My throat tightened. I thought of Japanese water torture, where they hold people under a dripping, boiling-hot tap. The irregularity of the dripping—and their inability to prepare for it—drives them crazy. In many and perhaps even all the ways I am that prisoner and the tap is life.

I put my hand in my other pocket and rubbed at a small strip of bubble wrap. I sat down.

"Why is your chair bubble-wrapped?" he asked, scooting nearer until our knees almost touched. I wished he were here to ask about a report whose deadline drew near, or flirt, instead of to fire me.

"Not sure," I lied, for I had bubble-wrapped it.

"You could have just taken another one?"

There was a chumminess about him, and I didn't care for it.

"It's fine," I protested.

"Do you... Are you... Your eyes..." He looked away. He looked back. "This is difficult."

I stared at the creases in Scott's chequered tie, zoning out.

"James?" he said, snapping me back to the here and now and all its sharp consequences. "We've made mistakes, obviously." He gave me a sympathetic smile that he didn't mean and I saw straight through.

On his lap were several yellow manila folders. "Do you know what the company's claims approval rate is?" he asked, opening the top folder, looking from me to it, then from it to me, before flicking through several pages which slipped from his hand and tumbled to the swirly brown carpet.

"Damn it." He scrambled to pick them up, but their order was now muddled and several had slid under the filing cabinet. He pushed his chair back, got on the floor, and tried to retrieve them before sitting back down and sighing.

Why is he dragging this out?

"And do you know what your personal claims approval rate is?" he asked, when he'd restored order.

This was something I'd not asked the paper clip about.

"Because I do." He fumbled through his folders and pages as patches of red broke out across his neck. "I did... It's..." He spun a piece of paper around. "*High* is what it is."

"You're firing me for that?"

He handed me a piece of paper. It was a claim I had approved four weeks earlier. A Mr Samuel Warwick. *Subsidence.* Many of our cases were subsidence. The ground doesn't really like to be built on for long.

I read it, or simulated reading it.

"Eighty-two per cent" he said, finally and with some relief. "Your rate. Why did you approve this claim? His policy doesn't cover subsidence."

"Yes, it does."

I remembered the case. The photos. Several frantic, pleading phone calls.

Scott took the paper back and scrutinised it. "Well, then this obviously wasn't subsidence, was it?"

"What was it then?"

"Landslip? Heave? An act of God?"

"God wanted his conservatory to collapse?"

"I think..." he said, looking beyond me in a way that made me worry he was about to give me advice. "What did you study, James?"

"A bit of everything."

"Where?"

"The library, mostly."

His nose twitched. "We sell something more important than insurance, James."

Very little is more important than insurance. It's a life raft in a stormy sea of random, choppy cruelty.

"We sell peace of mind, James."

"Mr..." He looked down at his papers again, having already forgotten the policyholder's name. "*Warwick* had nearly twenty years of peace of mind from his policy before he built that impractically heavy, shoddily constructed conservatory. Twenty years of peace of mind is excellent value, don't you think, James?"

He closed the folder.

"Don't," I pleaded. I'd been fired often, but it didn't get easier. "I have a mortgage to pay."

Cliff paid the lion's—and I guess also several other animals'—share, but Scott couldn't know that. He was correct. I did tend to side with the policyholder. I knew how much terror existed in the world. It was why I worked in insurance. I wanted to do good. To help the little guy. I just, well, often became distracted and overwhelmed by the practical matters of hiding from a world that so despised me.

He drew a long breath. "How long have you been at Holloway, Holloway, and Holloway?"

My back spasmed. It was the flamboyance of the name. Names mean something. It was why I'd legally changed mine. "Nine months."

He glanced back down at his folder. "We've overlooked you, obviously. We've not given you the supervision."

"You exiled me."

"Perhaps you exiled yourself?"

"That makes no sense."

"Some of your old team"—he hesitated—"they said they

find you a little... that you derail things. Them, meetings, computers, elevators." He wafted a hand dismissively. "They're stories. Wild exaggerations, probably."

"But..."

"But what?"

"Oh, I'm just used to buts. Big buts."

He frowned. "Is that a joke?"

"It's not really the time."

"Do you actually *want* to work here, James?"

"I need a job."

His teeth scratched his lip. "I feel you're not listening."

"I have a mortgage to pay."

"That's not the..." His hand became a fist. "That's not the right answer."

"It's insurance."

He tidied the folders, then tossed a loose thumb upwards. "Management have decided." Management didn't even sit above me. We were on the top floor. "Restructuring. New direction. I'm sorry." He gave me what he clearly hoped was a compassionate smile.

"Which is it?"

He froze. "Err... restructuring in a new direction? Nothing personal, of course, mostly. We'll pay you for the rest of the month." He stood and ushered me towards the elevator with an open hand. "You'll get a good reference. *A* reference."

I tried to stand but my head had become impossibly heavy and dropped forwards into my hands. My life was falling apart. Again, I tried to get up, but the room was spinning and my eyes wouldn't focus. Scott saw my hesitation, went to the next cubicle, picked up the phone, and made a call.

I was unemployed. A vagrant. A sponger. Someone

forced to plunder my savings before dying destitute and homeless in a below-average alleyway.

"Come on," said Scott. "Don't make this difficult."

It was already difficult.

Nothing happened for a minute, perhaps even two.

Ping

The elevator doors opened.

A tank of a man came towards us, arms folded across a formidable chest. Were they expecting me to make a scene? I have never, ever made a scene. I don't have that kind of interpersonal goodwill to waste.

"All good here?" the security guard said with a grunt. He had tiny ears, which is irrelevant when you have gargantuan biceps. The lanyard on his belt said *Security*. "Ready to go?"

"It's not... It's not fair," I stammered, even though I didn't believe in fairness.

"I'll walk you out," he said, sharply.

"It's fine." I took hold of the top edge of the cubicle wall and climbed to my feet even though the world was wobbling like jelly in a hurricane.

"You don't look fine, pal."

"No. *No*." I stumbled past him, grabbing my anorak from the hook along the way, and made for the elevators. He followed. I hit the button and the doors opened and I tumbled in and fell against the back wall and/or mirror. Scott was clearing my desk.

"Would you mind standing in front of me?" he asked.

"Why?"

"Security."

I just wanted all this to be over with. I wanted to go home and lie on Tabby's bed in her mountain of cushions. I moved around and in front of him, which inadvertently obscured his access to the pad of buttons. He tried to reach around me but his enormous bear fingers missed G.

"Balls," he said.

I moved left half a step, as he moved left too. This time he hit 2.

"Let me," I said, but I was in a state of confusion and accidentally pushed 3 as he was hitting cancel A shrill alarm went off, signifying that we were dawdling. The elevator wanted to work. It still had a job.

Its doors juddered then closed.

Its doors opened.

The alarm went off again.

BING

"Fifth floor," said a pleasing, automated female voice, unaware we had gone nowhere.

The doors closed.

The elevator descended.

BING

"Fourth floor."

The doors opened. A moustached man with a cart and a mop appeared. "Going up?"

"No," my escort said, and reached around me to hammer the close-door button.

"They don't work," I said, as the doors slid back together.

"Just because the company shit-canned you," he said, gruffly, "there's no reason to be rude about the cleaners. They're real people, you know?"

"The button. They're placebo. Tabby told me."

"Tabby?"

"Never mind."

The doors opened.

BING

"Third floor," said the voice. A man looked up from a large mobile telephone. He saw my face and grimaced.

"Going down?" the security guard asked him.

The man spun in a circle. "No, no. Just waiting for someone."

The doors closed.

The doors opened.

The man was there again. He had called the lift back too soon. He turned and then darted out of view saying he'd forgot to feed his cat.

The doors closed. "You weren't in a rush, were you?" the security guard asked. Then he laughed because what could I be in a rush for?

"Your eyes..." he said. "Should I call the doctor?"

The doors opened.

BING

"Second floor."

Three people stood before us in mid-conversation. "Going down?" a woman with thick eye make-up asked.

"Yes," I said.

"No space," said the person she was talking to, who was looking at me, slack-jawed.

Mr Security pointed to all the space on our right. "There's plenty of room."

"There's NO Space," the person repeated, pulling her companion's arm back when she took a half step forward.

"What's that smell?" the third person, a man in a charcoal-coloured suit, asked. They consulted. The alarm sounded.

"Yeah, we're going to wait for the next one," the woman in thick eye make-up said. "Thanks anyway."

The doors closed.

"What's going on?" the security guard asked.

"Nothing," I mumbled.

BING

"First floor."

The doors opened.

No one was there.

The doors closed.

The alarm sounded.

"Oh, come on," he tutted. "Shall we just take the stairs?"

"It's the same," I said. "Risk-speaking. If an elevator breaks you die, but it's very unlikely. People fall down the stairs all the time, of course, but the range of injuries really runs the whole gamut. It's not a death sentence with effective handrail usage."

"What?"

"Effective handrail usage."

"You're... I think I'm coming down with something."

"Sorry."

He frowned. "Maybe I ate something bad?"

"Yeah, maybe."

"Do you smell that?"

"What?"

"Rotten banana."

The doors opened.

There was no one there.

The doors closed.

He let out a long sigh. "Is it always like this?"

"Lifts?"

"What an ordeal," he said, when we finally stepped out at the ground floor, into the bright atrium. I took in its smell for the last time: industrial cleaner and fastidiousness.

He held out his hand. "All the best."

"Germs," I said, before running out to the high street and a nearby cash machine: £2612.

The highest it would ever be.

My throat was dry and scratchy, but I couldn't buy a Vimto because I could no longer indulge in such financial frippery. I sat down on a bench which was free in both senses of the word. Above me, a pigeon was in mid-flight heading for a discarded kebab on top of an overflowing bin. How long before I would eat discarded kebab from a bin? The pigeon saw me, swerved, crashed head-first into a telephone pole, then hit the ground with a loud, disconcerting thud.

It squirmed, attempting to right itself, which probably would have worked had it not been for the rubbish lorry. There was an audible crunch as the massive wheels pulverised the pigeon's bones.

I decided it was the lucky one.

6

After hiding for a few hours in a nook near the library's small Amish section, I edged out of the city centre onto Maid Marian Road to meet Tabby at the offices of the Citizens Advice Bureau. She was in her usual spot, behind the desk on the right, and seeing her there, in her usual-yet-exquisite reasonableness, buoyed me to no end.

Tabby.

Ta

Bee

A gesture of thanks and a command to be who I am by the only person who doesn't judge how little that is.

Tabby in the morning, in fluffy white slippers, drinking lukewarm Earl Grey tea and worrying about Labradors in Romania.

Tabby at work, pushing up her large gold-rimmed glasses with thick lenses, dispensing sage advice to other people to distract herself from herself.

Tabby at night, curled up on the purple couch in her room reading self-help books or period romances where people gossip about each other's headwear until they eat a rotten peach and drop dead at age twenty-two.

Tabby, my friend of almost two decades. My oldest—and also only—friend.

She was poring over the bank statements of a haggard woman with a tight perm and a fierce, cartoon witch's face. "HE WOULDN'T DARE," the woman screeched.

"Here," Tabby said, her voice soft and patient, pointing with the end of her Biro at a bank statement. "Here he took money. Here too, Maureen. This is Betfair. Betfair is gambling."

"THE ROTTER!"

"My advice, and I can help you do it if you like, is to cancel that card immediately. You can probably get the money back if you act straightaway. And I'd also recommend you go to the police and press charges."

"I'll cut off his balls, that's what I'll do. And then I'll fry them and serve 'em to him."

Tabby spotted me hiding behind a rotating display of informational pamphlets. Like the library, Citizens Advice was also a safe haven. Unfortunately, my problems were far beyond the scope of a fold-out pamphlet.

The woman continued. "In my day—"

"Maureen."

"That's the problem with—"

"Are you listening? MAUREEN?"

"If it's not one thing, it's the bloody other."

I slid along the wall to Tabby's right, covering my face with an orange leaflet about overcoming bereavement (people, not jobs).

Maureen was lost to her indignation. I bent down to the height of Tabby's desk and whispered, "I too need advice."

"In my day," Maureen repeated, "we knew the value of money because we didn't have any, or even shoes, and we ate wallpaper paste to survive, yet nowadays if you serve a meal with less than six ingredients people look at you like you've just landed from Mars to insult their family."

Tabby leaned over as if she'd dropped something. Her glasses slipped down her button nose. Without them, she was little more than a well-read mole. "I've been giving you advice for years. You've never taken a word of it."

"But today everything, and I mean everything, is going wrong and I don't know what to do."

"THE EGRET," Maureen yelled. "Stealing from your own grandmother."

"I'm busy being ranted at."

"You should have finished five minutes ago."

"I'm not good at saying no, but if you wait outside, I'll solve this troublesome case quickly, improving the life of a cantankerous, foul-mouthed senior citizen, and then come find you?"

"Can't," I said ruefully.

"Let me guess, roving gang terrorising the high street?"

"From down near Iceland, yes."

"Schoolkids?"

"Worse. *Students*."

"I suggest you stand in the corner, then. The leaflet on identity theft is a pretty thrilling read."

"If anyone stole my identity, they'd soon give it back."

Eight, perhaps even nine minutes later Tabby appeared beside me, coat thrown over her arm, a narrow smile on her usual, I've-just-seen-a-ghost face. While mine asked many probing questions people weren't ready to answer, hers was the facial equivalent of muzak: my favourite musical genre.

"I'm off, Jill," she shouted.

A woman with chunky red bangles and matching earrings emerged from the back office. "We still need someone to do the Saturday afternoon shift, Tabs."

"I have plans."

"I know, Tabs, I know. It's just, well, I've asked everyone else, haven't I?"

"But I have plans."

"Be a doll."

"I can't."

I knew how this would end. Give the world an inch and it will come back and demand one, perhaps even two miles.

"I can't."

"Yeah. I know, Tabs."

It was a stalemate. We stood in silence until Tabby sighed. "*Fine.*"

Jill whooped. "You're just a star, Tabs."

"Uh-huh."

"*Tabs*?" I repeated, as she tugged me towards the door.

"The street clear?"

I took position at the large, dirty windows and did a quick sweep of developments. Opposite, by a municipal bench, a clique of mice ate chips and, I think, a battered sausage. To our left was one of those street-sweeping vans with the swirling brushes that blow the rubbish everywhere, driven by people prone to sudden, untelegraphed swerving, so you can't pass no matter how large a pantomime gesture you give about your geographic intentions.

"There's a pocket of civility on our right," I said. "We'll barely even have to run."

7

Tabby pulled on the brass door handle of Albert's Public House. The door scraped along the uneven pavement then stuck firm, leaving a gap just large enough for us to slide in sidewards.

Inside, it smelt of dandelions and despair. It was quiet, but not too quiet.

I like the quiet.

It's easier to hear my enemies.

It was dark.

I don't like the dark.

It makes me bump into things with my weak shins.

Inside, I could make out the harsh contours of a man best left in the shadows. He was standing behind the bar holding up a wine glass in the light of a rapidly blinking fruit machine. Deeming it too clean, he smudged it with a dirty rag that had been hanging out the back of his trousers, put it on the rack by the beer taps, and inspected another.

"Hello, Albert," Tabby said, as we passed him.

"Hello yourself," he replied, without looking at us.

Albert's was our local. It didn't have a sign because anyone who didn't know about it wasn't welcome.

Anyone who did know about it, well, they weren't welcome either.

Still, they came in droves.

Ostensibly, it was an Irish-themed pub on narrow, threatening St James's Street. But the only thing Irish about it was the green on the walls, and that was moss. No one knew where its landlord and namesake had come from, how old he was, how long he'd been here, and more importantly—since he seemed to hate it so much—why he hadn't left.

I got little enjoyment from it, but then I got little enjoyment from anything, so it's possible I was a poor judge of enjoyment and/or pleasure-proof. Tabby and I mostly drank there for research purposes. It was very hard to pass for normal if you didn't spend time around the common man, studying his affects, mannerisms, and faddish fashions.

Not that there are normal people in Nottingham. There is just normal *for* Nottingham.

You also couldn't do anything wrong at Albert's because everything you did was wrong, as far as Albert was concerned, which made it less confusing and/or personal to be humiliated here than anywhere else.

We took our usual spot in the corner below a chalkboard that read *hope not*.

Looking around, I noted that baggy was in, as was plaid, and inexplicably, even dungarees. The nineties couldn't end soon enough.

Made heavy by the weight of a day I was keen to forget, I slumped low in my seat. About a dozen people were seated along the tables furthest from the fireplace, which was bellowing smoke. Albert was burning books again.

We were early. It would be rammed in an hour or two. A man in a high-collared rugby top approached the bar. I craned to hear. "Bitter, please."

Albert put down a bottle of gin he was diluting with Lucozade. "I'm not bitter. You bitter."

"Sorry?"

"Why are you sorry? What you done?"

"*Okay*. How about an ale then?"

"Everything ails me."

The man tried to look beyond Albert's shoulder. "Stout?"

"I'm trying to lose weight."

Albert's had only two alcoholic drinks: Beer (no further name or classification provided, and brewed on the premises —in most pubs this would be a selling point but here it was both a badly kept secret and why the disabled toilets were permanently locked) and Cocktail (which came in three sizes: small, medium, and large–small was a pint). Albert decided its ingredients on the spot. The man in the rugby shirt was growing exacerbated. He didn't know where he was or why it wasn't working like the other places it was pretending to be. "What do you have then?"

"Beer or Cocktail."

"What type of beer?"

"Beery beer."

"Forget it," he said, turning, scooping up his coat, and striding out into the night, shaking his head.

"Smells a bit like bin," Tabby said, as Albert came over with our usual order. We got better service than most as Tabby had helped Albert with some problems with his neighbours, the government, his ex-wife, his current wife, and his future wife. He never acknowledged knowing her and/or being in her debt, but he was perceptibly less hostile to her and no one else got table service. He put a pint of Cocktail in front of her and plonked a can of warm Vimto somewhat near me.

"Why you staring like that?"

"I'm not staring," I said.

"You blink?"

"I blink."

He scowled at me for a few moments, growled, then walked away.

"So, what happened?" Tabby asked, as I picked at the label of the can that was two years out of date.

"I lost my job."

"Again?"

"No, I only lost this one once."

She squinted, I think. It was dark. "What happened?"

"They tried to give me a medal." I belched. "Sorry. It's the fizz. Is it radical honesty or dishonesty this week?" Tabby was always testing some fad self-improvement framework she was sure would change her life.

She took a tentative sip of her Cocktail. "Malibu? And it's honesty. What medal?"

"How did radical dishonesty go?"

"Not great, to be honest. I have to be honest, I suppose? Even if you want to tell people what they want to hear, you have to know what they want to hear, which is harder than you might guess."

"Tell me about it." A satisfying amount of label came away in my hand. "Oh, your jumper was in Cliff's room. On the floor. You'll need to fumigate it now. There are more bits of old chicken down there than the average KFC."

Cliff's name was like a wet fart in the pants of our conversation and I regretted evoking it. Colour flushed into her cheeks. "Was it?" she asked.

"Near his bed, yes."

"Why were *you* in his room?"

"Routine surveillance. What is your face doing, Tabby?"

"My face?" She pulled back as if trying to see her own face.

"It's doing things," I said. "Are you wearing lipstick?" She touched one finger to her lip. "Wait," I said, having noticed that her normally fluffy, wind-swept, permed brown hair was ironed and flattened. I didn't know if she was flourishing, exactly, but she was definitely wilting less than normal.

My blinking grew rapid.

She looked away.

"Why are you looking away?"

She looked back. Her Coke-bottle lenses magnified her eyes to almost the size of my own.

"Why are you looking back so guiltily? Now you're going red. You've gone red. You're red, Tabby."

"Stop commenting on what my face is doing."

"Then control your face."

"I'm not... I'm..." She drank deeply from her Cocktail.

"It's radical honesty week. You're blushing, Tabby. Why are you blushing?"

"I'M SEEING CLIFF," she blurted. "I didn't want to tell you yet because it's not serious." She folded her arms. "But there it is. I suppose. *Sorry.*"

I took a slow sip of Vimto. I burped despite my best intentions not to. The table next to us grew louder. "Nah, you're more like Phoebe," a woman at it said.

"What? I'm obviously Chandler. I'm the funny one, ain't I?" her friend replied.

I didn't know what a Chandler was. The world was confusing and I'd never been able to shake the feeling that after starting promisingly, they'd put too stuff in it. I had a lot of sympathy for the Amish. If only I could grow a beard, do hard labour, or even soft labour. Not that the Amish would be accepted in Nottingham, a place where you could be viciously attacked for wearing the colour purple.

Time passed. I couldn't say how much, as there seemed to be something wrong with its machination and it was clanking and/or stuck. I took another sip of Vimto and let it splash around my teeth, hoping the sugar would sweeten my disposition.

"Are you listening to what I'm saying?" Tabby asked, when I was quiet for too long. "To the words of it?"

I drummed my hands on the tabletop. She reached over to take one of them. I pulled it away. "Ferdie."

"Don't call me that."

"James, I mean. Did you hear what I said?"

"Of course you're seeing Cliff. We live with Cliff. He pays most of our rent."

She took another sip of Cocktail then licked her thin-but-now-shiny lips. "Or maybe Archers?"

"The radio drama?"

"Don't play dumb."

"I don't play," I said, taking a deep and perhaps slightly melodramatic intake of breath, "but I still lose."

"We're together," she said, accompanied by firm, unrelenting eye contact. "Cliff and I. In a sort-of-relationship type thing."

Despite being obscured by a cardboard cut-out of, I think, an aardvark called Alf, the jukebox came alive.

It was the end of the world as we knew it, but I did not feel fine.

My focus wandered to the fruit machine, whose buttons were being inexpertly tickled by the drunken, exuberant, carbohydrate-ravaged fingers of three burly men holding non-specific beers.

"Why do people play fruit machines when they know they'll lose?" I asked.

Tabby looked over at them and sighed. "They're designed to addict you. The amount of addicts we see at CAB..." She shook her head. "Ban them, that's my suggestion."

"But they also know that, right? That they're playing a game they can't win. It's confusing. All of it, really."

Suddenly, all the lights on the machine flickered in sequence and music played and a robot's voice said "JACKPOT, JACKPOT, JACKPOT." The men slapped each other and bumped chests and looked excitedly down into the tray, but no money was dispensed.

Albert walked over and handed them a bunch of grapes. "Fruit machine win fruit."

I considered ordering an alcoholic drink and I would have, were it not the world's leading cause of death, random acts of violence, and embarrassing personal incidents involving nudity. I'd need my wits about me if we were to make it home. After 9pm, Nottingham City Centre was indistinguishable from WrestleMania, which Cliff watched and hooted and hollered at as if it were real and not sweat theatre.

Tabby reached for my hand again. "Ferdie."

I pulled it away and smacked my palm on the table. "My name is James. James Jones. Sort of. And you're my..." I tried to find a fitting word for what we were. *Platonic soulmate* didn't feel like something you said out loud.

"Sister, more or less," she said.

"I tell people you're my lady-partner."

"Yes, but that's a cover, so they think you're normal. I tell them you're my brother."

"You don't have my eyes, or face, or posture. And single people are strange. They attract attention."

Her finger flicked between us. "WE are strange."

"You aren't strange. You give people advice professionally."

"I dispense pamphlets."

"You own cushions, for god's sake."

She spread her hands out on the tabletop. "Look. Nothing needs to change. Well, nothing important. I'll still be there for you. Like always."

How could she know where she would be? She'd be busy. Busy with his needs. He had ousted me. "AND CLIFF?"

Albert looked up from the machete he was sharpening. He didn't look up often. Two people had tried to order in the last few minutes and he'd simply pretended not to see them. "Cliff hasn't suffered like we have suffered," I said, more quietly. "Like we suffer."

"Well, he has you as a landlord," she said with a laugh, covering her mouth and nose. "Perhaps that's what I like about him. He's less, I don't know... damaged?"

"Well, he's not an orphan, like us."

"I'm not an orphan."

I rolled my eyes. "That's a technicality. This is a lot, Tabby. It's heavy. And you're telling me about it *today*? After I lost my job. I don't have a job, Tabby. I am possibly soon-to-be completely destitute." I'd not even told her about the TV crew and near mugging and crazy Brummie Sminter.

"As opposed to partially destitute? You'll find another job."

"I don't interview well."

"You have savings. You haven't bought anything full-price in a decade."

"I still regret that ham." I downed what I had left of my Vimto. "Why do bad things keep happening to me?"

The song changed. Nothing compared to Tabby. That

was precisely the problem. Not that I had much to compare her to. She was my only friend.

She shot the jukebox a look of daggers. "How does it always do that?"

"It's its job."

She took a deep breath. "Have you ever thought about therapy? Jill at work started going recently, and she's a changed person. It's night and day. She's dying her hair. She placed a lonely hearts ad in the paper. Only creeps because, well, this is Nottingham, but still. She baked scones recently."

"I don't need therapy," I said, indignantly. "I'm not the problem. Everyone else is. And the cost of it? Who do you think I am? Bill Gates? I don't even have a job. Which I think I've mentioned."

"The best investment is an investment in yourself."

"Don't Tony Robbins me."

"I've been talking to my therapist—"

"You have a therapist now, too? Who even are you?"

"I've been trying to tell you that for weeks. You've been so distracted, what with spying on the Hoodlums and re-bubble-wrapping your room."

"Don't make this all about me. It's not my fault. None of it. I didn't choose to become an orphan. Or to end up in that awful place with you. Or to live directly in front of a ruthless criminal enterprise that has destroyed our home's resale value and/or our community and/or lives and/or other things I've forgotten because I'm very stressed and distressed because you're abandoning me for Cliff."

She groaned.

"CLIFF!" Once again, I'd lost control of the volume of my voice. I rose until I was almost standing, my thighs brushing the underside of the table. I could feel lumps of hard gum. Some students at a nearby table turned towards us, sensing spectacle.

"I'm going to go," she said, reaching to the floor for her handbag. "You need some time with this. Shall I get you another Vimto?"

"I can't risk another Vimto right now, Tabby."

"Right, of course." She stood and brushed the creases from her modest black trousers.

"I'm..." She tucked the chair in behind her. "Sorry."

The song changed. I put my head in my hands.

I didn't need to hurt myself today to see if I still felt.

8

Twenty, perhaps even twenty-one minutes later, I staggered out of the bar. The streets were full and the threat of revelry hung heavy in the winter air. Several people sang. One swayed. A dog urinated. Darkness was wrapping its tentacles around everything. I needed to be quick.

And I needed Tabby. I was a bonsai plant: I took a lot of delicate care to keep alive and, beneath my spiky exterior, offered very little. Tabby understood this yet put in the work regardless. I feared that if I lost her, I'd lose myself and/or my life.

I staggered up St James's Street to a Lloyds Bank ATM, the nearest cash machine, as the conversation and its revelations swirled around my head like a bad-news dust storm. The machine released a statement, and I stared down at it.

I blinked.

I gulped.

I blinked.

I held it up to a streetlight: £0.00.

A grenade burst in me and I ran down the road to a different machine, on Mount Street. I did not take care to remain out of sight and/or danger, so much so that I tripped over an extremely inebriated and—according to a sign around his nether regions—soon-to-be-married man handcuffed to a lamppost wearing just a Santa hat and who called me a name I will never repeat.

Another machine. Another statement: £0.00.

My mind broke from its leash and ran away. It didn't have to run far before it crashed into Robin Hoodlum and his merciless men. I didn't know how they had done it, but I knew they had. Probably with Pat's help.

It rhymed with twanker, the name.

I scrabbled over to the nearest bench. A woman saw me, got distracted, and fell over a bollard. Her friends laughed uproariously. A gaggle of students approached. They reeked of cheese, having consumed a week's worth of calories at Pizza Hut's all-you-can-eat buffet.

I was exposed and looking for a place to hide when there was a long, loud *toot*.

I swirled in a circle.

Toot, toot, toot

A taxi.

TOOOOOOOOT

It was him. Mr Matrix.

He pulled up alongside me, the passenger window lowering with a *whirr*. "PSST," the madman said.

I ignored him and walked away.

"PSSSSSSSSST," he repeated, reversing beside me. "Something is happening to you."

Things were always happening to me. Bad things.

"I know what it is."

This I doubted.

"I think?"

And he also doubted?

"Get in."

I stopped. "Go away."

"Give me five minutes and you'll never see me again."

"Yes, because I'll be dead."

Over the brow of the hill, a collection of sturdy, proud women neared. They were blocking the pavement and spilling down into the road. Nottingham Trent's female rugby team prowled these parts. They were part women, part praying and/or preying mantis. I turned back and straight into four strutting youths in green parkas, hoods up, crime on their one-track minds.

I was trapped.

I was wedged.

I was the meat in a sandwich of inner-city peril.

"Get in," he repeated. "You can trust me."

The only person I trusted was Tabby. Wait, did I still trust Tabby?

One of the women burped loudly, and the group cackled and grunted and one pointed and I had a vision and/or premonition of being robbed of my virginity in the carpark behind Carphone Warehouse.

I opened the back door of the taxi and looked inside for booby traps. The seats were black and leather and showed minor-but-appropriate scuffing. A fluffy dice hung from the front mirror. There was a crisp packet in the rear footwell —quavers.

I quavered slightly. I got in.

He pushed a button and there were whirring sounds as all the windows dimmed. "Good cHOIce," the lunatic said, with a squeak.

The doors locked. My body flooded with panic. I reached for the handle. The door didn't open.

"Let me out," I said, as I strapped myself in. My body and mind, long estranged, were now shouting at each other in different languages, from different hemispheres, in different—

"Most people never use the seat belt," he said, grabbing the end of my broken chain of thoughts. He was sitting sidewards in the driver's seat so he could better talk to me through the Plexiglas.

"I know risk," I said, ominously.

"That why you're such a hard man to convince?"

"Unlock the doors."

"Will in a second, buddy."

"The windows?"

"For your protection, of course." He bounced as he talked, excited, like a dog just off its leash.

"Who are you and why are you following me and/or going to kill me, kidnap me, and/or both?"

He pulled a laminated Nottingham City ID down and handed it through the small slot used to pass fare and—I suppose, also—change. The picture was of a man at least thirty years his senior.

"Jamal Sidekick?" I read aloud.

"Me dad. I'm Ricky. Ricky Sidekick."

I handed the ID back, unsure of what it showed.

"We Sidekicks have been around forever." A wistfulness overcame his voice, and he began looking beyond rather than at me. "You don't always HEAR about us because we're the guy behind the guy. We're facilitators."

"Sidekick is not a real surname."

"Is too, buddy."

I didn't have the energy to argue. "Fine. What do you want, Ricky Sidekick?"

A bus pulled up beside us, unable to reach its stop because Ricky was blocking it with his taxi. Or his dad's taxi. Or a taxi he'd stolen. The bus driver hammered the horn and made a hand gesture about milking a cow.

"Alright, alright," Ricky said, reaching down to the stereo. "I'll just put some getaway music on." The theme song from Star Wars—Cliff's favourite movie franchise—burst from the speakers at an impossibly loud volume. Ricky hit the accelerator, and the car lurched forwards a few metres, clearing the bus stop. He then jumped onto the brakes. The tyres let out a puny screech.

"That was fun." He switched off the engine. "Never been a getaway driver before."

We hadn't left first gear.

"That wasn't really a getaway."

"We got away though, right?"

The bus pulled into its stop as its driver mouthed the word *twat*.

"Why are you driving a taxi if you're a sidekick, assuming that's a real thing, which it isn't?"

"Not much sidekicking to do lately. I'm in between heroes, I guess. Although we don't use that word anymore. Frowned upon in our circles. You call someone a hero and they can only disappoint you."

"What do you call them then?"

"It was frontmen for a while, but that miffed the feminists. Nothing much has stuck since." He reached around and pointed at a zip on the back of his seat. "Pull it. No, wait." He fiddled with the stereo. "Something espionage-y, I think."

Some new, no-doubt iconic music began at a tinnitus-inducing volume.

"Bond," Ricky shouted. "James Bond."

"You're coming on strong. We just met."

He turned the volume down. "Shaken not stirred?"

"I'm a bit of both, I'd say."

"You really never? None of them?" He laughed. "Wow." He pointed at the back of the seat again. "Pull it."

"I will not."

"Pull it."

"Fine." I yanked the zip down to the floor. There was a crisp, satisfying sound as the leather folded back and a shelf popped out. Wigs, make-up, moustaches, and fake badges hung on hooks.

"Disguises," Ricky said, snapping his fingers in a modern way that had to cause arthritis. I didn't know what to say. I said nothing. He looked disappointed.

"So," he continued, "this morning I dropped off a film crew at Cromwell Street. Broke a few laws getting them all in the back there, but I got it done. I get things done. That's ME. They told me about you being Nottingham's Unluckiest Man."

"That's sensationalised."

"It got me thinking..." He stared out the back window as if thinking were an exotic place far away, perhaps across a calm lake. "I've spent months holed up in this taxi looking for my next superhero, right? And all I've found is drunk students, bankers in flash suits, and ordinary plebs trying to avoid the drizzle that never stops in this cursed city." He focused on me again. "I haven't, like, met a single person who can fly or read people's minds or is secretly a ninja."

His lunacy was greater than I had imagined. I rubbed the bubble wrap in my pocket against my leg and tried to disassociate.

"But then, well, it's much harder to be good at something than to be bad, right? And *super* doesn't necessarily mean *positive*. It can mean *especially* or *particularly* or *large*, like in *super*market. See what I'm saying? And you're Nottingham's Unluckiest Man?"

"Apparently."

"Which makes you special."

I shook my head.

"And blind people, they have good hearing, right?"

He was having a close encounter with madness.

"Apparently," I offered, as a crumb of agreement.

"So, what I'm wondering, buddy, is if you're unlucky, what if you're also something else? Something useful, even? Maybe I should be focusing on finding raw specialness and moulding it?"

"Or you should focus on your day job, which at least you can't be fired from."

"It's also, like, proper boring and meaningless."

"You should try insurance."

"You work in insurance?"

"I got fired today. Which is a problem because either there's been a bank error or someone has swindled me out of my life savings."

He grinned from ear-to-ear. "Mega!"

"Don't grin. Did you do this? Are you involved?"

"It's stronger than I realised. I found you just in time."

"I'm not a superhero, Ricky Sidekick."

He raised a hand. "True or false."

"False."

He tutted. "I didn't start yet."

"True?"

"It's not..." He sighed. "Let me..." He sped up. "Trueorfalse. People think of you as a loser?"

"True."

"You're weird?"

"People think I'm weird."

"You don't have many friends?"

"True."

"And no girlfriend?"

I remembered the loss of my decoy girlfriend and/or platonic soulmate, which caused a fresh stab of pain in my chest. Was I broken-hearted? No, broken-hearted people were literally dead. I was certainly hurt and/or disappointed. Just because Tabby hadn't been my girlfriend in the conventional, squishy, squelchy sense didn't mean she could abandon me. And especially not for *Cliff*.

"True," I conceded.

"You're an outsider?"

"True."

"You're annoyed at the world?"

"It's more annoyed at me, but true."

He flicked his wrist in another joint-destroying click. "I'm hella good. That's like ten right in a row! You're jilted, rejected. A misfit?"

Does he know about the Motley Misfits? How long has he been following me?

"Dude, this is textbook superhero shit. They're *all* weird outsiders." He bounced in his seat. "So have you got, like, any unique skills or abilities?"

I took a moment to think. "No."

"Come on. Don't be modest."

"I'm good with bubble wrap."

He didn't seem to know what to do with this. He stared up at the taxi's roof.

"I'm ambidextrous," I said, remembering.

"Huh?" He probed that for usefulness. "So you can, like, throw daggers equally well with both hands?"

"No."

"Punch?"

"No."

"Write?"

"No. It's more like either left or right. But I can clean my teeth with both hands."

"At once?"

"Why would I? That doesn't even—"

"No," he said. "Everyone is good at something. Think harder."

"I assure you, I'm bad at everything."

He licked his lips. "The Nothing? That's not bad, as a brand, kinda poetic. Got a bit of a nihilism kick to it."

"Stop, Ricky Sidekick."

"If anyone needs to stop, it's you being so modest."

I'd given him the answer but he didn't want to hear it. "I guess I'm not that bad at hiding?"

"Invisibility," he said, rounding generously upwards. He spread his hands in a sort of rainbow. "Night Shadow? Inspector Invisible?"

"Stop it."

"Sorry. It's a bad habit. Oooh... BAD HABIT. That's dope. For like a nun hitwoman?"

I pulled the door handle. Nothing happened. "Unlock the door."

"Wait." He raised his palms. "Where would you be right now without me?"

"Five minutes further down the road, assuming I dodged those alcoholic nymphomaniacs and Robin Hoodlum's narrowly post-pubescent merciless men."

"What does that tell you?"

"I've wasted five minutes?"

"I'm more than a taxi driver, buddy. I change lives. I deviate destinies. I enable..." His young mind groped for another alliteration.

"Egos?" I offered.

"Epochs," he said, his eyes glistening.

"Yeah, well, I took the blue pill, remember? I like things how they are."

He snapped the fingers on both hands this time. "And that threw me at first. I mean, who'd take the blue pill?"

"People who want to be left alone?"

"Bing-freaking-go! And isn't that exactly who the world needs? Look at politicians, right? You wouldn't trust them to organise a fight at a football match, never mind run a whole bloody country." He seemed really proud of all his lines of reasoning. "No, whoever says they want to be in charge, whoever invites that kind of risk, danger, glory, limelight, well, they've outed themselves as unsuitable for the job."

I thought back to the men playing the fruit machine at Albert's. There was some logic to those lines, however wonky and fanciful. "You think I'm special?"

"Yes. And I get why you don't. But you've probably never really tested yourself, right? If you've spent your life hiding in bins and wherever else. You might be like Mozart if Mozart never got the chance to try out a piano." This was a surprisingly ancient cultural reference for Ricky. "Or Spiderman if he had, like, arachnophobia."

"I have arachnophobia."

He'd stopped listening. "And when I come to find you, right, you're in the middle of a crazy adventure, hiding in a bin from a postwoman and the man who ruined my life."

"People hide in bins all the time."

"They don't."

"Wait," I said, his words registering. "Robin ruined your life too?"

"Yeah. He was in prison with my dad. There was a fight. My dad got injured and can't drive anymore. Now we have debts and I'm stuck in here when I should be at uni or, like, NASA."

I felt for him. Nottingham is sticky like that. "He ruined my street. Several streets, actually."

"Someone should do something about him and his gang."

"The police, you mean? I call them all the time. They're useless."

"No," Ricky said, ominously. "Someone else."

"The army?"

"Nah."

"The SAS?"

"No."

"Neighbourhood watch?"

"Maybe?"

"Well, who then?"

"Someone," he said. "*Someone.*"

"YEAH, BUT WHO IS THIS SOMEONE?"

He tutted. "It's us. I was being cryptic, wasn't I?"

"Ah," I said. "Sorry. That went over my head. But also, no. I'm the last person who should do anything about anything, really."

"No, James. You're special."

I knocked the back of my head against the headrest, considering everything Ricky was saying. That I could be more than what I knew I was—especially after a day like this—was seductive and, despite my inner remonstrations, wooing me.

"It's true things always happen when I'm around," I said. "I seem to provoke things, or repel things. People, really. I'm not sure because I'm usually hiding. It's just better for everyone that way."

He rubbed his chin. "Have you ever tried standing out?"

"No."

"Do you want to?"

"No."

"Is doing things your way working out well for you, then?"

The past twenty-nine years scrolled through my head in a blur of perpetual disappointment. "I'm still alive, so there's that."

"That's a pretty low barrier for success."

"For you, maybe."

He flicked his wrists again. "What I think we should do,

and I'd be there to help you, of course, as your official sidekick—"

"No."

"Try it my way," he said. "Just once. We can start small."

I thought of Tabby and her kindness and softness and predictability and expansive slipper collection. If I was exceptional in some way I'd not discovered, would that win back her attention? Or my savings? Or help me find—and keep—gainful employment? Then I could get a new home somewhere prosperous and with a modest garden I could fill with Amish gnomes.

I rubbed my temples. "How small?"

"Tiny. I've had this sick idea. Just me and you. A controlled environment. Perfect to probe you for, like, supernatural abilities and that."

"I don't know."

He pulled out a business card and pushed it through the slot. "I need a day for the finishing touches, tops."

"Can I get hurt?"

"Nope."

"Can anyone else get hurt?"

"I don't see how, buddy."

"Promise?"

He waggled his little finger. "Pinkie swear."

I sighed. "Give me a lift home and I'll consider it, Ricky Sidekick."

Transcript of a call between James Jones and the Royal Bank of Inverness

Recorded Message: Welcome to the Royal Bank of Inverness's customer support hotline. Your call is important to you. Existing customers, please press one. Potential customers, please press two. Impersonating an existing customer? Please press three. Impossibly angry about the way your life has turned out and want to rant at someone whose fault it isn't? Please press four. For an outsourced call centre where the staff's only knowledge of English comes from *Die Hard*, please press five.

One

Recorded Message: Thank you. If you have your account number at hand, say *Tibbles*.

James: Say what?

Recorded Message: You said *Sichuan*. Transferring you to our Sichuan branch.

James: No... Tibbles. Tibbles. TIBBLES.

Recorded Message: I'm sorry, I didn't quite catch that.

James: Tibbles.

Recorded Message: Would you like to be connected to the next available operator?

James: Finally. I mean... Yes.

Recorded Message: Did you say *Tibbles*? Thank you. Please enter your account number now.

**One*
Nine
Four
Six
Five
Two
*Three**

Recorded Message: Tibbles.

James: HELP HELP HELP OPERATOR.

Recorded Message: Thank you. You will now be connected to the next available operator.

HOLD MUSIC: *I AM THE ONE AND ONLY*

Recorded Message: All our operators are busy at the moment delighting other customers. Please hold or call back at a quieter time.

HOLD MUSIC: *YOU CAN'T TAKE THAT AWAY FROM ME*

Recorded Message: All our operators are busy at the moment delighting other customers. Your call is important to us.

James: It's not though, is it?

Recorded Message: Still in the queue? Be sure to ask about

our premium support hotline. Your satisfaction is our satisfaction.

James: That doesn't even make sense.

Recorded Message: Royal Bank of Inverness, the bank that can and will and does and already did.

James: Who even writes this stuff?

Recorded Message: Tibbles?

James: No.

Recorded Message: Did you say *Tibbles*?

James: No!

Recorded Message: Are you sure you didn't say *Tibbles*?

James: I DID NOT SAY *TIBBLES*.

Recorded Message: Tibbles. Connecting you now.

James: Aargh.

HOLD MUSIC: *CALL ME. CALL ME BY MY NAME. CALL ME BY MY NUMBER*

Recorded Message: Sorry, but all our operators are busy at the moment delighting other customers. We can't wait to hear from you.

HOLD MUSIC: *YOU CAN'T TAKE THAT AWAY FROM ME*

James: FORK YOU!

Gregory: That's rude.

James: Hello? Hello? Is someone there?

Gregory: I'm a real person. My name is Gregory. I collect stamps.

James: I wasn't talking—

Gregory: Do you know what it's like to work in a call centre?

James: Loud, I suppose? I wasn't talking to you. I was, err, talking to my cat.

Gregory: WELL FORK YOU TOO. MOTHERFORKER.

James: How dare you! I'm a customer.

Gregory: Oh, did you hear that? Sorry. I thought I'd covered the receiver. I was talking to the office cat.

James: There's a cat in a call centre?

Operator: Yeah, Tibbles.

James: Can we start over, Greg? Actually, you sound kind of familiar... no, never mind.

Greg: *Gregory*. Okay, fine. So, thank you for contacting Royal Bank of Inverness, the bank that does yes. Do you consent to this call being recorded today for training purposes?

James: Yes. I'm recording it as well.

Gregory: Sorry?

James: For my own training purposes. I'm trying to learn to be more assertive.

Gregory: No one ever asked to do that. I'm not sure that's allowed.

James: Aren't you the bank that says yes?

Gregory: *Does* yes. Yes. I mean... no. I mean... *maybe*?

James: And you're recording me?

Gregory: I didn't consent, though.

James: Do you consent?

Gregory: I need to talk to my supervisor.

James: Pretend I didn't say anything.

Gregory: But you did.

James: I'm not recording.

Gregory: What's that slight hiss?

James: I'm, err, entering a tunnel?

Gregory: With your cat?

HOLD MUSIC: *I AM THE ONE AND ONLY*

DIAL TONE

James: NOO!

10

I spent the next few days at home hiding from all the bad things that had happened and might still be happening and any new ones trying to happen.

Then it was Wednesday. Every Wednesday morning, I visited Nottingham Central Cemetery and the graves of my dear dead parents. Conveniently, it was opposite my home, behind a large brick wall. Were it not for some substantial trees, I'd be able to see the family plot from my first-floor bedroom window. I'd kept up this Wednesday ritual for over ten years. It wasn't quality time exactly, mostly, I think, because my parents were dead.

Also, because the Hoodlums controlled the graveyard and so it was full to the brim with drug scoring and for-profit fornication. I wanted to move my parents somewhere safer but that would mean a lot of paperwork and, also, they were dead, so their hearing was poor and they had little to fear, corporeally.

I went early.

I took them things. My father enjoyed Terry's chocolate oranges and I left those for him. Out-of-date ones were four-for-a-pound at the market. I doubted they were still edible, and one once triggered my Geiger counter, but he didn't mind, on account of the fact he didn't have a working digestive system.

Because he was dead.

I couldn't remember what my mother had liked, beyond my father and me and hypochondria and so I didn't take her anything at all.

I would tell them about my life and sometimes ask them questions about what I should do.

They never answered.

They were dead, you see. Very dead.

This week we had a lot to talk about.

Cliff wasn't in his room, so I left via the front door. He probably slept in Tabby's bed. As I closed said front door and engaged the first of several locks, I heard a voice that made the hairs on my neck, arms, legs, toes, and spine stand to attention.

"FERDIE!"

My former high school bully and postwoman, Pat.

I considered darting back inside, but then we'd get no mail. Perhaps there would be something from the bank. Or my former employer. Or whatever the hell Nottingham's Unluckiest Person was.

I swallowed and turned to see a wide-hipped, uniformed figure thudding down the path, flapping an arm. "Ayyup, miduck."

I was no one's duck, although I often had to duck. "Leave them on the step."

She broke into a wide, unhinged grin. She was all mouth, like a chatty hippo, and waved as if I were a ship far away at sea. "Ferdie, my little Ferdie!"

I trudged towards her and stopped a metre away.

She stepped closer.

Then closer.

Then closer.

I could feel her hot breath. Breath she was always out of. It smelt of corruption and the popular child's sweet, Chewits. In her hand was a small clump of letters and a rolled-up newspaper. She'd crimped her dyed blonde hair. Mud-coloured roots were showing.

"Knock knock," she said.

I kept my mouth clamped shut.

She tutted. "It's a joke, dum-dum. *Knock knock.*"

As she spoke, spittle leapt from her lips towards me.

"Who's there?" I mumbled.

"Sorry?"

"Sorry who?"

She rolled her eyes. "No, I mean I didn't hear you there, Mr Mumble. Captain Mumbleface. The Mumble of Mumbleton mumbling free. Speak loud. Speak proud. And stand up properly, Ferdie. You always look so damn pitiful."

"That's not my name."

"*Is so.*"

"Not anymore."

She rolled her eyes. "Knock knock."

"Who's there?" I repeated, with 8 per cent more gusto.

"Better."

"Better who?

"No! I mean. Ugh. I'm going to start again, okay? Knock knock."

"Who's there?"

"Pat."

"Pat who?"

"Pat, who wants to congratulate you!"

A space opened in which I was supposed to laugh. However, this wasn't a joke, legally speaking. She thrust the rolled-up newspaper into my stomach and I folded forwards. "Page twelve."

"You don't deliver newspapers. That's not your job."

She tipped back onto her ankles. "Ooh! Bright one we have here. Very astute, in't he everyone?" She looked around at an imaginary audience. "Knows a paperboy from a postwoman. No, *Ferdie*, this is a special delivery, and it's just for you."

Who would write about a stupid, sensationalised award I hadn't even collected? I reached for the newspaper, but she snapped it back. Another sadistic grin ripped across her face. She tried to flatten some of her messy fringe then tucked the newspaper under her armpit and took a pack of Chewits out of her pocket. She ripped at the edges of the wrapper. She whistled. I tapped my foot. She held up a Chewit as if it were an emerald. Her cavernous mouth fell wide and open and she threw it in. She chewed loudly. More spittle pooled. All the while, she stared into my eyes. Few people dared to hold eye contact with me: I unnerved, I startled, and I promoted unease.

Not in her, it seemed. I think she knew me too well.

Satisfied, she sighed, unrolled the newspaper, and cleared her throat. "This is in the, err, what's it called. The, you know, big text."

"Headline."

"Right. Headline. Thank you, Mr Reporter, sir." She adopted a news-broadcaster tone and read from the front page. "NOTT AGAIN FOR NOTT'S UNLUCKIEST MAN." Her eyebrows bounced. "You see what they've done, don't you, Ferdie? Very clever..."

"They're going to kill me," I said. "That's what."

"Don't be melodramatic," she said, and cleared her throat again. It reminded me of Hugh.

"James Jones, twenty-nine, of Cromwell Street—"

"How dare they put the street in? That's an invasion of privacy."

"I know a thing or two about those," she said, and laughed. "At least they didn't include the house number." She returned to the paper. "Was yesterday crowned Nottingham's Unluckiest Man! A dire run of mishaps and misfortunes continued for this new local celebrity when he was fired from city insurer Holloway, Holloway, and Holloway."

"That's confidential! This was you, wasn't it? You did all this. You nominated me."

She feigned surprise. "I don't know why you'd think that?"

"Because you're evil."

"Evil? Little moi? Petite... *me*? What when we go back more than a decade? I just want your talents to be recognised, is all."

"You want to see me suffer."

"Exactly. That's your unique talent. No one causes and revels in suffering like you do."

"I'm ordinary."

"No, you're a weirdo. An ugly, fishy weirdo. And the world doesn't like weirdos."

Wait until the newspaper hears I lost my life savings, I thought.

"Wait until they hear you lost your life savings," she said.

"How do you know about that?"

"About what?"

"My savings?"

"What about your savings?"

"You just said it."

"I said what?"

"That I lost my savings."

"You lost your savings?"

She was slipperier than an eel in a lubricant factory.

She had stolen my money, or facilitated its theft, I was sure of it. Well, fairly sure of it. I had to do something. I had to fight back. I rose half a foot. "How dare you!"

She snickered, and it escalated to a full roaring cackle. She leaned forward and poked a chipolata finger at me. "Remember who you are." She turned the finger and shoved it up my left nostril.

"Argh!" I fell back in shock, or tried to. She wrenched me forwards. "Who you'll always be. Who everyone knows you are. You are nothing. No one."

She whistled, removed her finger, and wiped it on my cheek.

"Well, anyway," she said, her voice soft now, as if we'd finished a pleasant conversation about the weather. "Best be getting back to me round. Lovely to see you."

It was drizzling, as usual.

She turned.

She stopped.

She turned back. "They were overpaying you."

"How do you know that?"

"I know everything. I am everywhere. Also, I read your payslip. The envelope got damaged somehow, I guess. Your P45 was in there too. Arranged that quickly, don't you think? Talking of damaged, do you remember that time at school when me and Reese and Staines put your head—"

"My mail."

She looked down at the pile of letters in her hand. "Oh, these aren't yours."

"Then where are mine?"

"I've already delivered them," she said. "To your neighbour."

I didn't know any of my neighbours, what few were left on this road, and they didn't know me and I had no intention of changing that.

"Which neighbour?" I'd send Cliff. He'd probably already had carnal relations with them.

"That's the million-dollar question, isn't it?" She clapped twice. "Ooh, it's like a treasure hunt!"

And with that, she lumbered back down the path, having bested me once more. "Say hi to Cliffy for me," she shouted.

I went inside and collapsed to the floor. This couldn't continue. I had to change something, anything, to break this spell of bad luck. I couldn't just hide. That was all I had done and still there was all this.

I waited five, perhaps even six minutes for Pat to leave and then went back outside. I considered getting a bank statement but knew that would no longer comfort me. I paced up Cromwell Street towards Alfreton Road, slipping my hand into my pocket, where there was a rectangle of fresh, unpopped bubble wrap, which I rubbed against my outer and—I suppose, also—inner thigh.

I turned left and then left again into the overgrown graveyard. I tucked my trousers into my socks to avoid ticks as I passed the once ornate and now sad, neglected headstones falling at odd angles of disrepair.

The wind whipped up and I attempted to fold myself against it, my head down near my armpit. I passed the grave of a boy who had died at the age of seven. His name was illegible but began with an *A*. My life had also ended at age seven, when my parents died.

I turned right in the furthest row and stopped halfway down, at my family's plot. I looked down at the tombstone.

Theodora and Augustine (1952–1977)

They lived free.

They died young.

They loved the piano.

The piano didn't love them back.

Survived by their beloved son, Ferdinand.

Next to them was the last resting place of my uncle Alexander, eaten by that peckish crocodile. I bent down, made the sign of the cross even though I'm not religious, and pulled a Terry's chocolate orange from my anorak pocket and placed it before their headstone, brushing aside a needle and a used condom with a stick.

"I miss you," I said. "I wish you weren't dead and/or hadn't died when I was so young and needy."

There was no answer.

Because, well, you know.

Was there an empty plot here for me? What would they write on my gravestone?

Here lies James Jones, sort of (1970–?)

He was inhibited.

He died young.

He loved bubble wrap and Vimto.

Nothing and/or no one loved him back.

"I'm having a tough time," I said. "It's been a really hard week. Last week wasn't great either, come to think of it. I don't know what to do about it all, actually. It feels like the wolves are circling and maybe even howling and are definitely hungry. I'm at a crossroads although I'm afraid both roads lead off a cliff. No, not that Cliff. Did I tell you about Cliff? He stole Tabby. Also, someone stole my savings. And I lost my job. I guess that's been coming for a while and might even have been my fault. I get distracted. What was I talking about?"

I waited for an answer.

There was no answer.

You know why.

I wished, just once, to visit them in the company of good news. I thought about Ricky. I'd been thinking a lot about Ricky.

He'd been right about one thing. "How I'm living isn't working, Mum and Dad. Hiding is counterproductive. Misfortune finds me anyway. I need to change approach, don't I? Shouldn't I?"

I waited for an answer.

There was no answer.

DEAD DEAD DEAD DEAD DEAD DEAD DEAD DEAD DEAD THEY ARE VERY DEAD.

One day I would die too. Perhaps today, the way things were going. But before I died, I wanted to try being better at living.

I stood. "Yes," I said. "Thanks, Mum and Dad. I couldn't agree more."

I turned, walked, and thought I heard a distant lock open.

Transcript of a call between James Jones and Nottinghamshire Constabulary

If you'd like to report a crime, please press one. If you'd like to commit a crime, please press two. If you're currently being murdered, please press three. If you'd like to become a snitch, please press four. If you'd like to snitch on a snitch, please press five. If you've a uniform fetish and are looking to party, please press six.

**One*

PC Cuffs: You a'right, duck?

James: Err, is this the police?

PC Cuffs: Depends who's asking, don't it?

James: Someone who'd like to report a crime.

PC Cuffs: Victim or perp?

James: Do perpetrators report their crimes?

PC Cuffs: Rarely, but we remain hopeful.

James: I'm the victim.

PC Cuffs: Don't call yourself that. Tony Robbins—

James: Can I just report the crime, please?

PC Cuffs: I know you think you want to, right, but you

don't, see? Because if you do, see, that's more work for me and the boys down the station, see, and there'll be a whole mess of paper and before you know it, the whole bloody days ruined, int'it?

James: But there was a crime. My neighbour, Robin. He's a gangland boss. He nearly mugged me in an alleyway. They're stealing identities. They stole my life savings, I think.

PC Cuffs: Do you have any evidence?

James: I have a very strong hunch.

PC Cuffs: Well, that changes everything, don't it? I'll tell the chief right away, I will. He'll probably suggest skipping the trial altogether, see, what with this being such an open-and-shut hunch, I mean, case.

James: Great.

PC Cuffs: That was sarcasm.

James: Oh. Well, isn't it your job? Finding the evidence, I mean?

PC Cuffs: You know what? Every day I come in here and I work these bloody phones, see, and it's *restraining order this* and *he's threatening me with a corkscrew* that. I listen to it, I do, and try to sympathise, I do, see, but it just feels like, I don't know, why can't you all just get along?

James: In Nottingham?

PC Cuffs: What's that got to do with it?

James: Do you live in Nottingham?

PC Cuffs: Mansfield.

James: My condolences.

PC Cuffs: So why don't you move then, if it's so bad?

James: No one wants to buy my house because of the Hoodlums and perhaps also because it's narrow and the back faces them but the front faces a graveyard.

PC Cuffs: Hang on.

HOLD MUSIC: HE CAME INTO HER APARTMENT. HE LEFT THE BLOODSTAINS ON THE CARPET

James: That's in poor taste.

HOLD MUSIC: SHE RAN UNDERNEATH THE TABLE. HE COULD SEE SHE WAS UNABLE

James: To sympathise?

HOLD MUSIC: YOU'VE BEEN HIT BY, YOU'VE BEEN STRUCK BY...

James: He's not smooth. Hello?

PC Cuffs: I'm back, duck, and don't you know, it's the

darnedest thing, see, because I've just looked through all the drawers and I can't find me tiny violin.

James: What?

PC Cuffs: To play you a sad song.

James: This is outrageous. I want to speak to your supervisor. You're here to serve the public. I pay your wages.

PC Cuffs: That old bloody chestnut. You're not the only one who pays taxes, you know? I do too, yeah. So I also pay my own wages then, don't I, see? So I guess I work for myself then, don't I? Which means I can pick what work I want to do, can't I? And I've decided I don't want to deal with your neighbourly bloody squabbles.

James: It was my life savings.

PC Cuffs: Talk to the bank.

James: I've tried. Their telephone support is a nightmare. Look, this is a straightforward case. If you put this one particular house and maybe a postwoman called Pat under surveillance, you'll solve it quickly.

PC Cuffs: A postwoman called Pat?

James: Yes, I know. Names mean something.

PC Cuffs: How many of Nottingham's finest should I send out, then, to surveil this postwoman Pat?

James: I don't know, four?

PC Cuffs: Four of our best crime fighters?

James: Two then?

PC Cuffs: Two of our highly trained boys in blue?

James: One? I mean, if they're so highly trained.

PC Cuffs: What's your name, then, if names mean something? Simon Sucker? Paul Patsy?

James: It's James. James Jones. *Sort of.*

PC Cuffs: What do you mean *sort of*?

James: Well, it's not my birth name.

PC Cuffs: Using a fake name, are you? Bit shifty, that. Seems like we should come investigate you?

James: No, you should investigate my neighbour, Robin Hoodlum, leader of the Robin Hoodlums, a vicious gang of merciless men terrorising all of Radford and perhaps the entire city and/or the wider East Midlands.

PC Cuffs: How do you know so much 'bout him, anyway?

James: I watch him through my binoculars when I'm in the bath.

PC Cuffs: Blimey. That all you do then is it, in the bath, staring at another man through your binoculars?

James: Sometimes I take notes.

PC Cuffs: You like to watch, do you?

James: It's how I stay alive.

PC Cuffs: It's how you harass and stalk and spy on your neighbour. What's your real name, James Jones, *sort of*?

James: I'm innocent.

PC Cuffs: We'll be the judge of that. Tell you what, I'll report them both, shall I? The forms are right here, see. We'll do his so-called strong-hunch money theft *and* your harassment and stalking and who bloody knows what else?

...

PC Cuffs: Shall I do that, shall I?

...

PC Cuffs: Hello, you still there? *Hello*?

DIAL TONE

12

Two days later, carrying mild-yet-heavy dread, I alighted a double-decker bus in West Bridgford. I couldn't remember the last time I'd been so far from the squalor of downtown. I found myself in a clean, bright, and perhaps even prosperous suburb. It had been so long since I'd seen prosperity, I no longer trusted myself to identify it.

Overhead, three pigeons sat on top of a bus shelter with malfeasance in their eyes. I shuffled on before they attacked me.

While taking care to stay in the shadows, I looked with jealousy at the quiet streets and imposing, often-detached homes and occasionally peeked over a creosoted fence to admire the ponds, trampolines, gnomes, and other baubles of family living.

All of this would have been stolen in Radford, or arsoned, at the very least.

Yes, it was a different world. A better, fairer world, or so it seemed until I had to hide behind an ice cream truck to avoid a coven of schoolgirls singing a pop song glorifying violence. No one's baby should be hit one more time. Or at all. I'd been hit plenty and, coincidentally, often by schoolgirls.

After losing my way twelve times, I found the address on Ricky's embossed business card, on which his job title was listed simply as *Maverick*.

While I knew little of architecture, I could identify immediately that his home—or more likely his parents' home—was a bungalow. There were several windows and a small porch with a stained-glass-effect panel door that I didn't find compelling and reminded me of a church, although I'd never been inside a church, other than the time I was chased into one by an entire female polo team. My parents refused to enter places of worship. They were anti-authoritarian, which makes it surprising that they'd joined such a strict alternative-living community.

Ricky's home had a small square overgrown front garden with several unruly bushes pushing out onto the path. There was a sign on the gate warning of a dog, which didn't concern me because every house in Nottingham has a sign warning of dogs, a common tactic for keeping burglars at bay. My own home warned of a dog, a cat, and an aggressive turtle.

Apprehensive, as per usual, I took a deep breath to steel myself, gave myself a small-but-barbed pep talk, high-fived myself as a final pick-me-up, then walked up the path and rang the bell.

Nothing happened.

I considered ringing the bell again but was afraid this would look too confrontational and/or like I was a salesman of Bibles and/or God.

Time passed like clockwork, I suppose. At some point I decided I'd squandered enough of it that I could ring the bell again.

I rang the bell again.

The door flew open and a man with a face full of thunder and/or other power-weather elements stared down at me, nostrils flaring. He looked very much like Ricky only drained of his enthusiasm and then left in the sun to harden, like a conker.

"WHAT?"

"Ricky?" I mumbled at the ground.

"At work," he growled, but then his gaze swerved up and over my left shoulder to Ricky's taxi, or perhaps more likely *his* taxi, parked out on the street. His nostrils widened even further. You could have bathed in them.

"RICKY!"

When there was no answer, he hit a button on the wall. A chime rang and the porch light switched on and off semi-rhythmically. He blinked once, slowly, looking at me. "What's the matter with you?"

I wasn't sure where to start, so I nibbled my lip until Ricky's voice crackled through a nearby speaker. "Yo, Pops?"

Ricky's father began to berate him in a foreign language. I didn't speak it but have been berated so often, I've developed a finely tuned sense for it. I took several small steps backwards.

"Dad. Dad. Dad. Dad. *Stop*. Dad." Ricky tried and after about two, perhaps even three minutes succeeded, and his father ceased his tirade. "White boy," he said gruffly, before turning and lumbering inside, leaving me on the doorstep. Not that I would have gone in, not without seeing Ricky and getting a bit more of a feel and/or scope for the place.

I stood and did nothing, albeit unconvincingly, until Ricky appeared from a side gate and cut across the front garden and in front of the bay window, a spring in his step, whistling what was almost certainly the theme music from a movie I'd not seen but that was an important brick in Hollywood's titillation industrial complex.

"Welcome to the first day of the rest of your life," he said, redundantly, as every day was the first day of the rest of your life, including the day you died. Seeing Ricky, and seeing that Ricky was happy I'd come, I had an unfamiliar feeling. I wasn't sure what it was, but I welcomed it. I think, maybe, it was pride.

Ricky believed in me. I didn't want to disappoint him. I was done disappointing myself.

"Bad time?" I asked, as he reached past me and shut the front door. He was wearing a thick, very cuddly black jumper and jeans three sizes too large. There was something of the mascot about him. I could imagine him enthusiastically greeting people at the entrance to an amusement park.

"Nah, fella. My dad's just, well, more invested in me being a taxi driver than a sidekick."

I felt a sharp tug of guilt for the time I was taking up foolishly exploring the idea that I was something I was not: something special.

"But he was a sidekick, right?"

"Yeah, for decades. Maybe that's why he's disillusioned with it."

"Why did he stop?"

"He followed the wrong guy. He was charismatic but the bad kind. Turned out to be a Ponzi, basically. A SEX Ponzi." He cleared his throat. "Then prison and that fight. He won't even go to Radford anymore."

"I wouldn't want to fight him."

Ricky shrugged. "You ready for this?"

"Yes," I lied. It was hard to be ready when you didn't know what you were getting ready for.

He gestured across the front of the house with his forearm. We made our way to the gate Ricky had come through and arrived at a staircase that led into the home's basement.

"My tricked-out pleasure palace," he said.

I felt a pang of trepidation. Very pangy, trepidation. I realised I'd forgotten to tell anyone where I was going. If I didn't escape Ricky's "tricked-out pleasure palace", how long would it be before Tabby learned of my demise? Especially with her being so distracted by advice, period romance, and, I suppose, present-day romance?

Would she be better off without me? Probably.

Would I be better off without me? It seemed likely.

So then there wasn't actually that much at stake.

"It safe?" I asked.

"I built it myself, pretty much."

This was what I'd feared. Looking down the stairs, I saw wires sticking out from a wall. The whole place looked to be a major tripping hazard.

He started down the six stairs. "Come on then, buddy."

I descended a single step. Nothing exploded and so I went down one more. The pattern repeated. It took me some time to reach the bottom, where Ricky was unlocking the door with his fingerprint. He looked back to see if I'd seen him do this and/or was impressed. I wasn't but pretended to be.

Inside, which was pitch-black, he fumbled to his right and picked up a large remote control with glow-in-the-dark buttons. It wasn't like the one Tabby used for her television. This one was four times as large and held five hundred buttons, perhaps controlling all facets of his life.

He hit the lights. The space seemed to be two rooms, but the door to the rear room was closed. This room was large and square and full of what I was sure he was going to say were *projects* but that looked more like unsuccessful prototypes for nuclear fusion. The ceiling was low. Everywhere the eye went, it met cables. There was the smell of aniseed and ambition. In the corner was a leather La-Z-Boy. I was sure this was his bed.

"Too cold?" he asked.

"It's fine."

"I'll warm it up one degree." He hit a button. A TV in the corner flicked on to something called MTV.

"Dang." He hit the same button and the lights flashed then cut off. "My bad."

He shook the remote. An alarm sounded. He hit a switch by the door marked *Switches get stitches*. Everything went out. A fan powered down with a hum. "I'll just reset it."

There was a loud beep as the power returned, and in the low light, I could see Ricky's cheeks had gone a mighty shade of crimson. I turned from him to a table that held a stack of stapled papers.

"What's this?"

"Screenplay."

"What's it about?"

"This guy who has amnesia so he can't, like, remember anything, and he has to solve a case backwards. So the whole film is sort of backwards."

Ricky had some out-there ideas. Out there in a way that made you not want to let them back in. "What's it called?"

"Memory Lost."

"The whole film is backwards?"

He frowned. "I was sure it was a good idea at the time. Take one. A memento."

I picked it up, let it hover above the table, then put it back down as Ricky walked deeper into the basement towards the rear door.

"This is my best idea ever!" he shouted. "Yeah, it is. It's

going to get me out of this basement and out of that damn taxi."

"I thought *I* was going to do that?"

"Oh. Err. Yeah. Sure?"

Had Ricky already lost faith in me? I followed him and we stopped at the door. He turned, fanned a circle with his hands, and said, "Have you ever wanted to be a spy?"

"No."

"A secret agENT?" He coughed after his latest squeak. "Secret agent."

"No."

"An assassin?"

"No."

"An all-action movie star?"

"No."

"On an incredible, time-sensitive, all-or-nothing, save-the-world mission?"

"No."

"Humanity's only hope?" He pulled at a clump of his aggressively gelled hair, easily spiky enough to pop a balloon.

"No."

With each no, he shrank a size.

"An international man of mystery?"

"No."

"A national man of mystery?"

"No."

"A local man of mystery?"

"No."

"A dinosaur hunter?"

"Is that...?" I rubbed my weak chin. "That's not a thing, is it? I just want to be left alone, mostly. Or rather, I did. But it doesn't work and so now I'm here, but I don't really know why. I'm spiralling and/or clutching at straws, and the straw might break my back. I'm confused, really, I guess, idiomatically or metaphorically or otherwise."

He shrunk further. "Anyway, I think other people want that. To have a sick experience like that. To feel that adrEN-ALine." He flushed with embarrassment again.

I'd had several sick experiences, often involving tuna.

"To feel that adrenaline," he repeated, in a more commanding, adult voice.

I didn't have the heart to tell him that they didn't.

"So what I've done is, well..." He bit his cheek. "It's hard to explain. Basically, what if I told you that on the other side of this door is a series of quests. You've one hour from entry to solve them all. If you do, you'll be released."

"And if I don't?"

"You'll be stuck in there forever." He howled like a wolf at the moon.

"No," I said, edging back towards the stairs.

"It's not real." He leaned closer. "I can get you out whenever. There are cameras. I can talk to you too, and give you clues. *Wicked*, right?" He flicked his wrists again in that annoying way. "You get three clues. What do you think, buddy? I call it a Rescue Room."

I tugged at my anorak's sleeve. "Have you put a lot of, well, time into this?"

"Yes."

"And money?"

"All my money."

It was my turn to bite my cheek. "Any of it refundable?"

"No."

"Ah."

"You don't like it?"

"I just, well." I shuffled on the spot. "It's probably a little too revolutionary to be grasped immediately."

He cheered at this notion and fumbled in his pockets for the key.

"Let me summarise," I said. "You think people will pay money for you to lock them in your basement?"

He nodded. "Damn right I do."

"For one hour, while you watch them on CCTV as they solve puzzles?"

He stood tall. "Yeah."

"While pretending they're dinosaur hunters?"

"Yeah."

"And asking you for clues to release themselves?"

While the malaise had begun with me, it proved contagious. His hands dropping to his sides. "Yeah," he whispered.

"I'm excited to try it," I lied. I was merely determined to do something radical to try and break my run of misfortune, and this was something.

He brightened. "Really?"

"You bet," I said, which was more noncommittal than it sounded since it was about him, not me. I don't bet. Betting is for people who don't understand statistics and how they're stacked insurmountably against them. Not only does the house always win, if you play long enough, they win your house.

"Let the games begin," he said, taking out the key, throwing it up in the air, and catching it.

13

After a delay of fifteen minutes—during which Ricky rushed around trying to put out the fires of his various overconfidences on the other side of the closed door—he decided the Rescue Room was ready for its grand unveiling.

The door opened. He stepped out. It seemed as if his entire face was twinkling. "THE BIG MOMENT," he said, sweeping his hands in a circle then stepping to the side and gesturing me in.

I put a blueprint for a robotic vacuum cleaner back onto the cluttered workbench.

"I hate hoovering," he said, as an explanation for it.

"Does it work?"

"You bet your life it does. *Will.* It's in the theoretical stage. I've a ton of really epic ideas in that stage. It's an exciting stage, you know? Would you like to invest?"

"My life savings have been stolen."

"Ah." He clicked and then pointed at me. "Right. My bad."

"Plus, I already have a Tabby. She likes to hoover."

"What's a Tabby?"

"Why is it pitch-black in there?" I asked, from my tiptoes, looking over his shoulder.

"Suspense."

I gave an involuntary shudder. "I'm not a big fan of suspense." I was already a long way from my comfort zone, and while in some ways that was exciting, in other ways it was probably horrifically suicidal. I glanced around. "How about you do the room and I'll watch from the cameras. I can give you clues if you like?"

"Nah, buddy. Only I know the puzzles."

"Let's go in together then? With the lights on."

"You can trust me," he said.

"I do. Of course." I didn't, of course, which he needn't take personally since I didn't even trust myself.

"I'll go first," he said, turning and walking in.

I followed but stopped at the threshold.

"I'll put the light on," he said, in the soft tones of compromise. "But you have to close your eyes until I say."

"Okay," I said, pretending to close them but then actually leaving them open a devious crack, through which I watched him grab me and yank me inside before I could react.

"Wait!" I shouted, as he slammed the door in my face.

"Boo-yah," he said, from the other side.

"You tricked me."

"Ha! I'm just getting started with that. Open your eyes."

"I never closed them."

"Then who tricked who, buddy?"

"Well, I'm in your basement torture prison."

Dim lighting came on overhead and I spun in a slow circle to get my bearings. A large display on the opposite wall flashed: *60:00*

59:59
59:58

59:57

"Welcome to Jurassic Lark," Ricky said, his voice distant and crackly. The ceiling was blanketed with glow-in-the-dark stars. The floor was covered with half an inch of sand and dotted with large fake rocks and extensive, thick, and—I suppose, also—fake green foliage. Eating from a tree on the far side of the room was an orange brontosaurus. It had a target painted on its back. Literally.

"Clock's ticking," he said, and then gave a maniacal, villainous laugh I was sure he'd practised. I looked around for the source of his voice. "Where are you?"

"Up here," he said. Hanging from the ceiling was a purple pterodactyl, wings spread. Its eyes lit up red when Ricky spoke. "Bitchin', right? Now, explore everything."

The opposite motto of my life.

I was afraid to move or touch something in case it electrocuted me, caught fire, or asked me a trivia question. Rooted to the spot, I roamed the room with my swivelling, generously proportioned eyes. In the middle of the room, under the pterodactyl, was a camping chair and a fold-out table. Behind that was a giant, glowing mock waterfall of blue fairy lights. On the wall next to that was a map with square gaps in it. On my right, in line with the camping chair, was an exercise bike poorly disguised as a sitting triceratops. It didn't push the paper-mâché envelope. Between that and the wall was a large tank, in which a mechanical crocodile swam back and forth and looked tremendously pleased with itself.

"Are crocodiles dinosaurs?"

"Basically, buddy."

Above the tank, lashed to some netting, was an enormous papier mâché Tyrannosaurus rex in midbite. "Did Tyrannosaurus rexes actually exist?"

"Of course. Haven't you seen *Jurassic Park*?"

I didn't bother dignifying that with an answer. Ricky's imagination couldn't be faulted. I just wasn't sure yet about the rest of him.

The air in the room was oppressively still, and I feared insufficient for the full hour, and so I breathed through my nose. I spotted a rifle near my feet. I felt both confused and threatened in equal measure. I was in this mess because a man—or perhaps very-senior boy—had found me cowering in a bin and concluded I was a superhero, or superhero-adjacent. The world is random and sometimes it goes wrong, yanking innocent, ordinary people like me—minding their own business, trying not to get mugged for the seventh time—onto wild new paths and/or straight into walls.

"Explore," Ricky demanded.

"I am."

"You're standing still."

"With my eyes."

"Try your body, buddy."

There was a yellow-and-black-striped cable that ran between the bike and the fish tank. That seemed strange. I walked over and tapped the triceratops's back and/or seat. Nothing happened. I tapped the fish tank. It seemed sturdy. The crocodile gnashed its teeth at me.

"This is you exploring?" he asked.

"Yes."

57:00

56:59

56:58

"You can touch things."

"I need a clue."

"That was a clue."

"A more specific and/or helpful clue."

"As if."

"But I don't know what to do."

"Interact with things and don't be so bloody shy about it. Touch, lift, pull, *RIDE*."

I looked at the triceratops. "I don't know how to ride a bike, never mind a triceratops."

"Who doesn't know how to ride a bike?"

"My father was about to teach me, then..." I faded out.

"It's not that kind of triceratops."

"I have balance issues."

"It's freestanding."

"That's what *you* think."

I walked to the chair and table. On the table was an envelope Ricky had attempted to age with dirt and fire. "I need a clue."

"You don't need a clue."

"I'm not good at puzzles."

"Explore things. Open things. *Read* things."

I picked up the envelope and shook it like a maraca. That didn't help so I put it down. I picked it up again. I put it to my ear. I didn't hear the ocean. I put it down again. I nibbled my lip. I picked it up again. I decided it really was an envelope and that I was probably supposed to open it. I turned it over and tried to slide my fingers under the flap. They didn't fit. Ricky had obviously glued the envelope tightly in an attempt to encumber me. I ripped at a corner but found the stationery impossibly thick. I put it in my mouth and bit.

54:00

53:59

53:58

I flipped the envelope over and this time managed to get just a little of my pinkie under it. I slid it along and felt a sharp prick. Blood sprayed from the deep papercut. Light-headed, I sat down on the camping chair. A whoopee cushion exploded from under the seat. In shock, I leapt up and knocked the table with my knee. It fell on its side and hit a dinosaur egg, which rolled over a hidden switch, which dropped a model stegosaurus from the net above me which I, instinctively, fearing for my life, grabbed by the tail and launched across the room in the direction of the tank and the T-rex. The spikes of the stegosaurus's tail cut the webbing holding the almost life-size Tyrannosaurs rex easily. It crashed forwards, smashing the tank with its head.

This room was no stranger to cable either, so water cascaded down from the tank to mix with electricity, its natural enemy. I climbed up on the chair as the fizzing started and the lights cut out and the crocodile snapped its way towards me and I was plunged back into total darkness. Really the worst kind of darkness.

"Did I win?" I asked, redundantly.

I heard Ricky chastising me, himself, and life in general on the other side of the door. I didn't mind being chastised. It was familiar. As he did so, I stared up at the ceiling starscape wishing Nottingham had stars.

The panic of my predicament—coming to a unfamiliar place to participate in a strange thing—had subsided and, to my surprise, been replaced by calm. It was over. I was alive. It hadn't been that bad. Far better than what I'd imagined happening, anyway. I suppose the thing about anxiety is that you spend a tremendous amount of time in a jail cell of your own specific, callous creation. When you actually do come out into the real world, while awful, it can't compare with the scope and/or wickedness of your imagination. I decided that maybe I had as much to fear from my own mind as I did from the world, and that doing things was a positive new direction for my life or what little was probably left of it.

There were more sounds—swearing, skulking, sulking, and even searching, possibly of the soul—before the heavy door opened and there he was, shining a torch in my face, blinding me.

"Shit off," he said.

"That's about the measure of it."

"This was... I did..." The torch's beam swept the room. "Seriously, James?"

"Sorry."

"I don't even know where to start."

"I know the feeling," I said.

"It feels like you didn't really even get the concept?"

I shrugged. "Dinosaurs?"

"Did you think of riding the triceratops?"

"Why would I want to ride a triceratops?"

"How about that map on the wall? Did you notice there's pieces missing?" The beam swung over to the wall and was jiggled for emphasis.

"I'm not into maps. I've never been anywhere. Other than Mansfield, once. But that's a sad story and I don't tell the story because then I'll be sad, or at least sadder." I was babbling, embarrassed that I'd so easily destroyed his room and/or hopes and/or dreams.

"I guess life doesn't always find a way," he said dejectedly. "Did you look in the brontosaurus's mouth? There's something taped there. It's part of the map, and also a key."

"Not much use, part of a map."

"Perhaps it belongs to the larger map on the wall? If you lift that boulder over there, you'll find another part of the map."

"Odd place to... *oh*."

"The map is actually of this room, or, well, the Lark, you'll see, if you turn it upside down. And there's an *X* here on the floor, under the waterfall."

"The hidden switch."

The lights flickered and then came back on. I could now

see how creased his brow had become and how wide his nostrils were flaring. The age gap between his father and him had shrunk to nothing. Anger ages.

Ricky entered the room and righted the table. I climbed off the chair and sidled past him, splashing through the puddles to be nearer the door, in case I had to beat a hasty and/or overdue retreat. He walked towards the tank, stepped over the broken glass, got on the triceratops, and pedalled. "This would have opened the lid to the tank," he said. "And then you could have fished something from the crocodile's mouth, perhaps with the end of the rifle?" He got off and walked to the far side of the room, where the crocodile was repeatedly banging its head on the wall. A good visual summary of how I felt inside. He took something from its mouth.

"This key unlocks the first aid kit in the corner," Ricky said.

"There's a first aid kit in the corner?"

"It has the parts you need to restore your time machine."

I had not seen a time machine. "Do you mean a clock?"

"No," he grunted. "You're a time traveller."

"I thought I was a dinosaur hunter?"

"You're both. You went back in time to..." He sighed. "Forget it. You needed two keys. The other was in the stomach of the stegosaurus."

"Obvious in hindsight," I said, edging ever closer to the door. I had no idea whether Ricky's disappointment made him violent. He wasn't particularly intimidating, physically, but I'd once been bested by a grieving twelve-year-old in a pet cemetery whose foot I stood on, so I knew from experience that age was just a number when it came to violence. I'd been at the cemetery to visit the graves of Mac and Buster. Buster's had been vandalised again.

"Did I fail or did the room fail or was it both?" I asked, hoping it was the room.

He pondered it before saying, "The room," but through gritted teeth. Then his voice changed, taking on an unfamiliar accent. "Our scientists were so preoccupied with whether or not they could, they didn't stop to think if they should."

I couldn't believe any scientists had worked on this. They should have known better and/or had better things to do with their time, such as anything.

"I'm actually proper gutted," he said, and kicked the crocodile in the face. "Although, I guess it could be a framing problem, maybe? Like how I introduced it? Or it's just"—he swept the room with his gaze—"a lame idea."

It was always better to fail privately rather than publicly, and all at once, rather than in dribs and drabs. At least I'd given him this gift. "I thought I stood a good chance too, what with my ambidexterity."

He laughed. "Are you sure you're ambidextrous?"

"Yes. My father was as well."

"It just seems like..." He looked away.

"It's okay if you're jealous that you're not ambidextrous. You have many other good qualities, like your enormous self-belief and your taxicab."

"It's not that, buddy. It just seems like you're terrible at most things." He froze. "That harsh? I don't want to be harsh."

"No, no, it's fair."

"So, is it possible that you're not ambidextrous? That you're just so cack-handed, it doesn't matter which hand you use for anything?"

He was lashing out. He needed to be careful because while old me would run away whimpering, perhaps new me might stay and try and strangle, stab, tickle, or bubble-wrap him, which I'd be able to do it equally well and/or badly with both hands.

I didn't answer and seconds passed and then Ricky kicked at shards of broken glass. "If only that robot vacuum cleaner was non-theoretical," I said. "We should go outside now before something else goes wrong."

"What else could go wrong?"

"I'd rather not find out." I shivered, wishing I'd worn both my anoraks. I took a few more steps towards the door, my shoes squelching.

"We can't give up," Ricky said, following me out. "You have something. You did almost nothing here," he said, looking back towards the Lark. "I mean, frustratingly little, just tried to solve some puzzles, and yet look at the outcome? It's proper real, your power." He rubbed at his cropped hair, getting gel on his large but inexperienced hands. "It's like you're a MAGNET for misfortune."

If my life had a common thread, however tangled, it was that.

I swept a hand down my torso. "You still see something you want to mould?"

"You bet I do. You have a power. It's not quite what I thought it was. But it's there, and it's, well... powerful."

"You're delusional."

His chest inflated. "That's what they say to all mavericks. What we need to know is, do you generate misfortune or attract it? Like, if you get close to people who are suffering, can you take it away from them?"

I shrugged. I'd never really thought about it because I was busy just trying to stay alive and/or out of the way. "Everyone around me is always doing much, much better than me. That's true."

"I've woken up excited every day since we met," said Ricky.

I gasped. "That's... really?"

"Fo shizzle."

"I'm not even sure what real shizzle is, but..." My toes curled. "Thank you?" I was so overwhelmed by this compliment that I was willing to overlook how thin the evidence for his theory really was.

"Yeah," he said. "If I'm right, if you can do that"—he tipped back his head and howled—"that would be epic. That would be a game changer. We could really get out there and do some good."

"But then I'll have it? Others' misfortune?"

"Bingo."

"But then *I'll* have it?" I repeated.

"Uh-huh," he said. His eyes had glazed over.

"I don't want it, Ricky."

"They don't want it either. That's why we'd be helping them."

"Yeah, but who's helping me?"

He winked. "Me. I've got your back."

"Then I'm..." I began, but he was staring off into space, lost to me, and I feared also to logic, running wild with his old friend possibility.

A cold breeze whipped through the basement from the open door out to the stairs. A copy of Ricky's screenplay blew off the table to the floor. I'd seen enough.

"Ricky?"

There was no answer. It was my turn to click my fingers, despite its risks to my joints and tendons. "*RICKY?*"

He came to with a slight judder. "Yes, buddy?"

"I'm going home." I walked to the exit, buoyed to be leaving alive and/or with all my limbs. I ascended the staircase until I felt a tug on my arm. I turned.

Ricky's eyes were wide, and there was wildness in them. "We NEED to do another test."

"I—" I began really quickly, but not quickly enough because he anticipated it and cut me off anyway.

"A *small* test."

"Idontwantto," I said really quickly, before he could interrupt me.

He raised his hands higher. "Nothing dramatic. Just you standing near people."

"*Okay*, okay. You need some time. Take a day or two."

"I don't know, Ricky," I said, but I was already thinking about the home I was returning to, where I was stuck, unemployed, almost destitute, where I'd have to listen to Tabby and Cliff copulate and/or the Hoodlums celebrate and intoxicate themselves with my looted life savings. Whatever it was Ricky and I were doing, however stupid and madcap, it did have the virtue of being extremely distracting. And it got me out of my head, which was a dark place. And nothing bad had happened to me here, if you ignored the stress, anxiety, and wetness of my socks. Ricky had a lot of mopping and sweeping in his future, but he was a ball of energy that needed a wall to bounce off. I'd almost done him a favour by destroying the back half of his pleasure palace and/or Lark. I also liked the idea of reducing people's misfortune—even though they'd never reduced mine and, if anything, swerved out of their way to make things worse for me and/or point and/or laugh while I was judged, mocked, heckled, headlocked, Chinese-burnt, and wedgied.

And so I said "Maybe" really quietly, and that was already more than enough.

14

"Cliffffffffff," I said, at the breakfast table, as he twanged his ukulele for the hundredth time in eight minutes. While I didn't care for Cliff, I found it pleasing to elongate his name for stress-relief purposes. "Can you refrain from that? I need to concentrate."

He looked up from his ukulele, a simpleton's guitar. "You're eating a crumpet."

"I'm not concentrating on that."

His stupid, shaggy blond hair fell over his wide forehead and symmetrical ears and he glanced at me with a smoulder: his one facial expression. He was wearing a fluffy green jumper made of something show-offish, probably hemp. All he wore on his lower half was a pair of black boxer shorts that he'd stolen from a man, I think German, called Calvin Klein.

He looked down at his ukulele again, twanged all of its two, or perhaps even three strings, sang an off-key, "James", stopped, played another mini-cord, stopped, looked up, smouldered, then let go of the strings. "My mind has gone blank. That's weird."

"Is it normally full?"

"Don't be a meanie, James." His American speech was long and slow, like a tired worm.

"Don't be..." I said mockingly, but faded out. My mind knew that I was very angry at him and yet my body couldn't entertain the spirit of that anger. He was just, well, Cliff. Being angry at him was like being angry at a puppy covered in honey wearing a pink ribbon at sunset. Yes, he'd stolen my decoy girlfriend and/or platonic soulmate, but he was also paying most of my rent at a time when I had no money.

He looked back down at his instrument, ready to give song creation another whirl. "Not much rhymes with James, does it?"

"Shames? Blames?" I offered.

He strummed a few chords, tried to frown, succeeded only in smouldering downwards, and sang, "It's James. DEE-DUM-DUM. You don't wanna see him play ball-games. DEE-DUM-DUM. It causes him shames. DEE-DUM-DUM."

He looked up, fluttering his eyelashes in the pursuit of praise.

"DEE-DUM-DUM," I said flatly. "Do you really do this professionally?"

He pursed his thick, rubbery lips. "Sort of."

The workings of his business were mysterious to me and, I think, him. He brushed hair from his eyes, but it fell back perfectly. While I still couldn't grow a beard, Cliff was effortlessly shaggy. He was like a fisherman's fisherman.

"Why do you never seem to work?" I asked.

"It's a... streamlined operation."

"What does the operation do, exactly?"

"I sell a ukulele course by mail order. Or someone else does. I presented it, though."

Ukuleles didn't interest me beyond being something

whose name was better than the thing itself, like *crevice*, *curmudgeon*, and *palaver*.

"People pay you for this?" I asked.

"They do," he said, but he couldn't hide his own surprise.

We were silent for twenty, or perhaps even twenty-five seconds.

"Cliffffff, would you say I'm a person of high moral integrity?"

His eyes moved skittishly. "I don't know, James." He hesitated. "Maybe?"

"Yesterday, on your personal computer, I discovered on the Internet superhighway that I received an email from a man in Sudan. He said I was someone of high personal integrity and that he had a business opportunity for me."

"Sudan?"

"I know. And to think, I've never been anywhere."

"You went to Mansfield that time." He looked down, strummed, and sang. "M-a-n-s field. A field of men. He went there once and he didn't go again."

He bounced his blond eyebrows in an invitation for positive feedback.

I returned to my crumpet in silence.

"It's a trick," Cliff said. "The Internet is full of scams like that."

"Oh." I put my plate down. "I wanted to believe it, being new to the Internet superhighway and/or also in a desperate situation."

"That's how they get you."

"Have they got you before then?"

"Me?" he said sheepishly, as Tabby appeared in the doorway in his stars-and-stripes dressing gown, fluffy white kitten slippers on her feet.

"Morning you two," she said through a yawn. The Hoodlums had set fire to a pub on their road at some point in the early hours, probably because it stopped paying them protection money, and half the city's fire engines had arrived to fight it, ostensibly, as through my binoculars I'd seen several firefighters toasting marshmallows in its flames. The night had not been restful. Few were. She moved to the counter behind Cliff, took off her glasses, and wiped them on a tea towel. "You okay, James? I've been worried about you."

I frowned. "Why?"

"Because it's the habit of a lifetime." She approached the table and kissed Cliff on the top of his head.

I let out a sharp yelp. "Sorry. Don't know where that came from. I'm fine, mostly, perhaps?"

"You lost your job."

She didn't know the half of what I'd lost.

"And your life savings."

So she knew two-thirds of what I'd lost, or maybe three-quarters. It was too early in the day to remember precisely how many losses there had been in the past week. She filled then plugged in the kettle. "I also heard you on the phone the other day." I remembered that Tabby's chamomile personality could lull you into a false sense of security and/or privacy.

The kettle shook and gurgled. It must be nice to be a kettle. For your point and function to be so narrow, well-defined, and easily achievable.

Each day you boil.

Boil. Boil. Boil.

There was a sudden spark and then the power and lights cut out, causing Tabby to leap a full foot in the air.

"Blimey," she said, upon landing.

Cliff went to the fuse box, and I made a mental note to

have more respect for kettles and their distant cousins, toasters.

"I'm gagging for a cuppa," she said impatiently. "What's the forecast for today?"

"Drizzle," Cliff shouted from the hallway. "The Hoodlums are probably growing dope again."

"That reminds me." Tabby's voice rose in excitement. "Yesterday at work, this student came in. I saw her and thought, you ring a bell, you know? Anyway, she gets talking, she's late on some bills, wants to move but has a bad credit rating because someone stole her identity and ran up debt in her name. All the while she's talking, and while I'm giving her some excellent advice, I'm trying to place her."

"Probably a CAB regular?" Cliff guessed, now back at the table. The kettle had resumed its task.

"No, she had all her teeth. Seemed, I don't know, *with it*? Anyway, she showed me a bank statement and I saw her address: Portland Road."

The Hoodlums' road.

"The plot keeps thickening," I said.

"What plot?" Cliff asked, inanely. If there were a plot, it would outrun Cliff quickly. The best he could hope for would be to trip it up as it passed, becoming embroiled in it that way.

"The plot to destroy my life and/or kill me," I said. "That plot."

"Pat's involved," said Tabby. "I know it."

The room grew icy cold.

Thunder crackled in the distance.

A sleeping kitten was decapitated.

"I know it too," I said. "I saw them together, plotting."

"Pat the crazy postlady?" Cliff asked, still wedged in the middle of a conversation for two.

"We went to school together," Tabby clarified. "Well, when we went to school, right, James?"

"I always forget how far you two go back."

"She was the school bully," Tabby added, as the kettle gurgled and burped. She readied a mug.

"One of," I corrected. "I don't want to talk about it."

Tabby continued anyway. "Pat had a particular problem with James. As did her whole gang. And the other students. And the teachers. And the headmaster—what was his name, James?"

"I forget."

His name was Mr Watson.

"And Janitor Jim," she said, sitting down at the table. "He used that mop for everything but mopping."

"Were you bullied as well?" Cliff asked Tabby.

She nodded softly as she said, "More in the group home than at school."

"Guilt by association," I said. "But I don't want to talk about it."

Tabby dipped her head but not her eyes.

"Don't look over the top of your glasses at me."

"It's not good to bottle up the past. Shame grows in the dark."

This was almost certainly a line she'd stolen from legendary peddler of pith Tony Robbins.

"You're thinking of mould and/or mushrooms. Were you bullied at school, Cliff?" I asked, already sure of the answer.

"Me? No."

"How about at college?"

"No."

"University?"

"Nopes."

"On the high street?"

His eyes narrowed. "Who bullies people on the high street? There's so many people around."

"Exactly, Cliffffff."

"Adults don't bully other adults," he said, incorrectly and/or idiotically.

"High school never ends. Only the uniforms change."

He shrugged and somehow made the action look heroic, perhaps on account of his sculpted shoulders. "Pat keeps trying to seduce me. At least I think that's what she's doing. Says she wants private ukulele tuition."

I swatted the air. "Not every woman wants to fornicate with you, Cliff."

"I never said they did."

"No, but you think it."

"We should go to the police," Tabby said, blowing on her tea, "for all of it. Yes, good idea, Tabby. Shall we do that then?" She looked around expectantly.

"I've called them at least five times. They're overwhelmed and/or incompetent."

"Well, someone needs to do something," she said.

Everyone was certain that action improved things rather than made them worse. It had to be a delightful way to live, until it got you killed.

She got up and fixed herself some Weetabix. Cliff practised his song about Mansfield, which Tabby praised excessively. Love affects other senses, not only sight. She then began simultaneously reading a self-help book called *The You of Your Dreams, Now* and thumbing an already well-thumbed period-romance paperback called *Forbidden Mounting*.

"Why are you up so early, anyway, Cliffffff?" I asked.

He flashed his white teeth. "I want you to take me to that group."

"What group?"

He laid his ukulele down delicately. "Rejects United."

I rolled my eyes. "There is no group called Rejects United."

"You know, that one you were part of, Tabs."

"Tabby is part of many groups. She's committed to self-improvement. Or self-delusion."

"The group for introverts," Cliff clarified, as Tabby gulped her mouthful of Weetabix down.

"I quit them," she said. There was just a hint of milk above her top lip. "Too much wallowing. Remember when I planned that trip to the zoo and no one came, James? Annie claimed she was allergic to grasshoppers, which I just don't think is a thing, really, is it?"

"They're not introverts, Cliffffff. They're people shunned by life, toiling on the social fringes. They'd dream of being merely introverted."

"Yes!" He clapped. "Those dudes!"

"Motley Misfits," said Tabby, then returned to her books.

"That's no place for you, Cliff," I said.

"Why not? I'm good with people."

"Exactly," I said with a sneer. "There are many tragic cases there."

"Are they weirder than you, James?"

I considered each of them in turn.

"Not really," Tabby said, before I could reply. "James is just an acquired taste."

"Weirdness has many forms," I agreed. "Just like a... job centre." The comparison was more literal than I'd intended. I was obviously still worrying about my lack of employment.

Cliff's voice softened. "It'll help me understand you and Tabby better, though."

Tabby blushed. "Sweet."

"No," I snapped. "It will just confuse you."

"You can use my computer this afternoon."

"Think bigger," I said, but my resolve was melting. After all, I'd long wished Cliff would check his too-numerous-to-count privileges. This would be a good first step. And I needed to look at job postings and furiously email some banks and—I suppose, also—the police.

"The next two afternoons?"

"A week."

"Deal," he said.

"Two weeks!" I countered.

"That's not how negotiation works."

"Put on your shoes, Cliffffff."

15

Five minutes later, I found Cliff peeking out from behind his bordello-red bedroom curtains at the street. Concern had cut lines into his forehead. "No sign of Pat."

"Huh. So you do know what it's like then? To hide and cower?"

"I know what it's like to want to avoid Pat."

"Imagine the world was full of Pats?"

He shuddered.

"That's the world in which I live. In which all misfits live."

We left through the front door, which was a perk of our nascent friendship and/or amnesty in our long-established feud.

"Shall we walk or take Aggie?" he asked, as we passed his beloved custard-yellow hippie wagon. It was hanging half off the curb and over a double yellow line. I checked the windscreen, but it had received neither ticket nor criminal attention. At the very least, a family of four should have moved in by now and claimed squatter's rights. Cliff was jammier than an elephant in a swimming pool of elderberries.

"We'll walk," I said, because I once let Cliff drive me to Superdrug to buy fungal cream, and I try not to repeat my mistakes. While most people drive understanding that you can't be in multiple places at once, every action has an equal and opposite reaction, and you go left around a roundabout, Cliff drove with only absolute certainty in the universe's desire to bend to *his* every will and spontaneous, unindicated lane change.

I pointed at the car's roof. "Why is your surfboard still up there?"

"I'm a surfer, duh."

While it had a tremendous number of open drains, Nottingham was a long way from anything with waves. "Yeah, but you're not though, Cliff."

He shrugged. "You don't have to surf to be a surfer. Like how you don't have to provide heating to be a landlord." He gave me a pointed look.

"You're on the ground floor. It heats itself."

"Heat rises, though."

"Not in Nottingham. Here it just lurks menacingly."

We shuffled on as the clouds darkened. All my immediate neighbours had moved out, or rather been chased out by the Hoodlums. Their homes were boarded up. I slipped on some wet leaves then narrowly avoided a large dog poo. Cliff saw neither but missed both easily. As we passed 2 Cromwell Street, the nearest inhabited home to mine, a young woman in a gold dressing gown—probably a student, judging by the bulging hedonism bags under her eyes—ran out and quickly, casually, simulated throwing rubbish into her green wheelie bin.

"Hey Cliff," she shouted, making a hand gesture that suggested he should call her. He smiled and waved back, midstride and/or bounce. He walked like a man on the moon who also owned the moon.

"What is it women like about you?"

"Well." Bounce, bounce. "I'm like a... cool dude, I guess?"

"If you have to append 'I guess' to the end of something, it's not true."

"No," he said firmly. Bounce, bounce. "I *am* a cool dude." Bounce, bounce. "I mean, I'm fun. I'm easy-going. I'm... breezy."

"Is that what women like? Breeziness?"

He pushed some hair from his eyes. "Don't you think?"

"I have precisely zero practical or theoretical knowledge of what they like, Cliffff."

"Hmm." His brow furrowed. "Well, I'm also an entrepreneur. Maybe it's that?"

"You're a mail-order ukulele teacher."

"And I'm American. Exoticism is always good. Helps you stand out."

Standing out might work for him, but the past week and/or my entire life had shown me it didn't for me. No matter what Ricky believed. Several days had past since the Lark and I had agreed to meet him later for our second and almost certainly last test.

We picked our way down the hill of Wollaton Street, approaching the high street. Cliff continued walking in the centre of every pavement like a large, proud, bouncy ship, forcing the world to swerve from his bow or perhaps stern. Depending on how you side a boat.

At the next junction I stopped, removed my backpack, and pulled out two British Heart Foundation medium-visibility jackets and clipboards. "Put this on and hold this."

Cliff regarded them as if they were something stuck to the bottom of his shoe. "Why?"

"They're a shield. These simple uniforms help protect us from the city's miscreants."

"No way, dude." He glanced around to see if anyone was looking. "Super nerdy."

"Tabby wore them with me sometimes."

"No," he said, pushing them away and bouncing off down the road. I looked at them and then, feeling self-conscious, slid them into my backpack and hurried after him.

"What you doing?" he said, as I emerged from a narrow gap between parked cars in which I'd taken temporary cover.

"Walking to town, obviously."

"You're scuttling."

"I don't scuttle, Cliff. And stop smouldering at me."

"Come out from that phone box," he said, a pedestrian crossing later.

I opened the door and whispered, "I'm just waiting for that rowdy group of plumbers to pass."

"They aren't rowdy, dude."

"One is whistling."

He yanked the door open. "It's weird. You're drawing attention. I mean, it's 1999. Who still uses a phone box?"

"Mobile telephones are a fad."

"You're a fad," he said, pulling me out by my arm.

We turned onto always-busy Market Street. We were in the lion's mouth and/or den. My heart rate rose appropriately. Outside of the post office, in the safe harbour between a parked van and three bright-red postboxes, I ducked for cover.

If Cliff really wanted to get to know Tabby and me better, I'd show him the world as we saw it. I poked around the edge of the postbox and called to him. He trudged back. I swept my hand across the gritty urban vista. "What do you see?"

"Err..." His face blanked. "The high street?"

"Yes, Clifffff, good."

He tried to walk off again.

"STOP, Cliffffffff!"

Cliff stopped but was not happy about it. "What now, dude?"

"Look more closely." I mimed binoculars. "There are a hundred small daily dramas playing out around you in this rich tableau of human suffering. So come back here and look again and then tell me, specifically, what you see. *Pay attention.*"

He pouted, took two steps back, and cocked his head. "This got something to do with the Misfits?"

"Everything, Cliffffff. Everything."

"Fine," he said. He swept his gaze slowly from left to right. "Err... I don't know, dude, like, people and stuff?"

"Talk to me of the people, Cliffffffff."

He turned in a slow circle. "O-okay. So, I guess there's like, well, that woman over there by Dorothy Perkins? She's smoking hot."

"Anything else?"

"That jewellers. I dated a girl there briefly. I'm having some flashbacks that are, well, making me a little hot under the collar." His eyes roamed. "Oh, there's a sale on at GAME. I want to get the new *Pro Evo*. And I need ukulele strings. How long have we got?"

"Not long enough. Anything else?"

"That alley."

"What about it?"

"I threw up there once after a foam night at Ocean. Epic."

"Anything else? Any hazards, for example?"

He rubbed his stomach. "I'm hungry. That's dangerous. I get really hangry, you know?"

I nodded. "Anything else?"

"Boots. I could definitely go for a meal deal. Chicken and bacon."

"Tell me, Cliffff, is your heart rate elevated?"

"No." He frowned. "Why would it be elevated?"

I lowered my voice and body. "What about the homeless person sitting on the other side of this bank of municipal postboxes?"

He peered round the corner. "He's just sitting there, drinking from a can of Special Brew."

"So, he's inebriated, is what you're telling me?"

"It's a strong drink."

"So, it's 9am, and he's drunk?"

He blew a raspberry. "Probably, yeah?"

"Drunk people are dangerous."

"Nah, they're just funnier." Cliff's blue eyes were twinkling. He was actually enjoying himself. He was always enjoying himself. It was irksome.

"What does he have?" I asked.

He rubbed his chin. "What does he have? I don't know? Scurvy?"

"He's a man who lives on the high street, Cliffff. That tells me two things: he's extremely tough, and he has nothing to lose. *Nothing*. There's nothing more dangerous than a man with nothing to lose."

"What about, like, a terrorist?"

"Shut up, Cliffff. Okay, look again. What about that gang at your"—I turned and calibrated to his body's metaphorical clock—"2pm?"

"Those schoolkids?"

"That gang of violent, delinquent youths, yes."

"They're trading stickers."

I followed them with my eyes. "Or pretending to?"

"They're in uniform. They're going to school."

"Are they not getting awfully close?"

"Probably because they're going to GAME and we're an easy shortcut across the road."

"And now?" I stepped aside to widen the space for the three of them to pass between us. One could fit, but the other two had to wait and pass single file. Cliff stayed where he was, provoking a direct confrontation.

"Sorry mate," the second boy said, as the corner of his satchel brushed Cliff's leather jacket.

"No worries," Cliff replied, beckoning the third through the gap with a sweep of his right hand.

"Have a good one," the third boy said.

Cliff turned. "See? Nice boys."

"The first one had menace in his eyes."

"I'm pretty sure that was astigmatism."

"If anyone's stigmatised, it's me. Check your wallet."

He patted the pockets of his white chinos. "It's still there."

I got out the medium-visibility jackets and the clipboards. "Are you ready to experience the high street as it could be?"

He turned away. "Nah."

"Then I will not take you to the meeting, Cliff," I said, sincerity burning in my eyes.

"Fine." He wafted a hand. "I'll go on my own."

"You don't know where it is."

"It's at the library." He pointed in its general direction. I didn't believe he'd ever been to Nottingham Central Library, never mind its poetry section.

"The library is large. And these people don't want to be found. Or don't know how to be found." My shoulders dropped. "Or are cruelly overlooked. It's complicated. And sad. Mostly sad."

Five, or perhaps even six seconds passed.

"*Fine.*" He gestured for me to hurry and hand it over.

Dressed in our urban camouflage, we walked down the hill to Market Square. We were scarcely in the pedestrianised zone when a woman approached near a shop selling cut-price—and, I think, also quality—jewellery.

"Hiya." She was wearing a bright-green duffel coat and yellow earrings of elephants that I think were supposed to communicate that she had been to Africa and found it largely agreeable. "I'd like to donate, I would. I've been meaning to for ages and I saw you here and I thought, well, that must be fate, mustn't it, really? You know what I mean? The heart is important. So, I guess what I'm saying is, stick me down for a tenner a month will ya, me lovely?"

As she talked, she stroked Cliff's arm. He didn't even shudder.

Finally, she saw me. "This man bothering you?" she asked.

Cliff howled with laughter.

"Because the police station's just over there." She pointed.

"It's cool," he said. "It's just James."

She flinched. "He gives me the willies."

"We're on a break," I said, and pointed to the nearest comparable charity collectors. There were a dozen in sight, plaguing the conscience of the early morning commuter.

"That was—" he said, as we carried on down the road, only to be interrupted by an on-rushing senior citizen with a blue rinse perm.

"COOOO-EEEEYYYYY!" She smiled, her blocky dentures visible. "Lovely to see a young man out early, doing good."

We were two young men. A fact that had escaped her. "You've certainly stolen my heart, young man. Lovely looking man that you are, too. Sort of... breezy, aren't you? Fifteen pounds a month, that okay? No, make it twenty. I only have a small pension, but you have to do your bit, don't you?"

"Out of forms," Cliff said, brushing her off gently. "Thanks, though."

"Oooh, an American. Yankee doodle I-don't-mind-if-I-*do*. Such a lovely accent. So... *loud*."

"This is fun." Cliff was beaming. "Is this what you thought would happen?"

I had a sudden debilitating headache and stopped to rub my temples. "No, Cliffffffffffff. It is not what happens to me. Or happens to the people we're going to meet. That you're not ready to meet. That you'll never understand. That your existence mocks, actually."

"Hey," he said, with another cock of his already cocky head. "I'm just walking here."

"Walk faster," I said.

* * *

The library smelt of moths and maybes. We took the lift. I was tired. Tired of it all. "Remove your urban camouflage."

"Where are we going?" Cliff asked.

"Poetry."

"Nottingham Library has a poetry section?"

"Exactly."

On the top floor, we walked down a series of narrowing corridors as the lights grew darker and the books dustier and the visitors increasingly dishevelled before becoming non-existent.

"Now, Cliff. For the group to accept you, you're going to need to be flawed in some irredeemable way."

He nodded. "I can be that."

He had zero doubt, as usual. It was maddening.

"I used to have a stutter," he said. "That enough?"

I stopped near a display of books about tractor maintenance. "You stuttered?"

Cliff's speech, while often punctured by the American blights of *like* and *dude*, was as smooth as creamy peanut butter.

"Y—y——yeah. I even had to go to s—s—s—speech therapy for it for a few years. Kids used to make fun of me, chase me around the playground, tie me to trees, like, you know. Kid stuff."

As he stuttered, his face screwed into a tight yet testosterone-soaked rag. It was a convincing performance, and I suppressed the desire to praise him. Life had praised him enough. "But you said you weren't bullied?"

"Bullied? *Nah*. Just kids being kids. Even when my arm got broken. You know, horseplay."

"That doesn't sound like horseplay."

"Well, it involved a horse. Surely I need more than a stutter? People don't become outcasts just because they stutter."

"You have no idea how fickle the world is, do you?"

"Ss———s-s-s-s————u-u-ure. I do—oooooo."

"Sufficient," I said, and we carried on, turning a last corner in New Age to move out into the wilds of Poetry.

16

"Morning," I said to the motley group of misfits huddled in our usual corner. You didn't prefix things with the word *good* here, since you knew it hadn't been. It was, however, morning, and that was a fact no one could deny, although I wouldn't have put it past Steven to try.

"Salutations, James," said Hugh. "Mm-hmm."

Annie arrived just after us. "Am I late?"

"You're not late," said Hugh, checking his pocket watch.

"Definitely not," said Peter. "You're bang on time."

"It's just so *me* to be late."

"It is very you, yes," said Peter.

She froze. "Is it? Really?"

"You're perfectly on time," Hugh said reassuringly.

Peter nodded. "Couldn't agree more."

"I'll be on time next week," Annie said, taking the chair next to Cliff, her hands trembling.

I'd not introduced him. "This is..." I said, gesturing with my palm then paused. To call him a friend would be to rub their noses in it. I thought about calling him my enemy, which was more truthful but would have revealed how I felt about him. Was this still how I felt about him? And if it's true that you should keep your friends close but your enemies closer, it's probably a strategic mistake to let your enemies know you're doing that. Thinking about all this took so long that everyone grew uncertain as to whether more words were coming.

"C-C-C-C-C-C-C-Cliff," Cliff said, finishing my orphaned sentence. The group nodded sympathetically. He was in. Cliff—not good at looking downtrodden and ineffectual—smiled beatifically before relaxing into one of this trademark chin-down-eye-up smoulders.

"Delightful to have you here," said Hugh.

"I agree completely. Always nice to see a new face," Peter said. "Which I do... all the time." He ran a hand up and down in front of his own. "Face blind."

"Mm-hmm."

Esmeralda arrived, her long trench coat swishing behind her, clutching a bag of donuts and humming to herself. I hadn't thought we'd see her again.

"Morning all." She sat, tucking some locks of her formidable, wild red hair behind her ears. "I work at Dunkin'. These are yesterday's but they're still good. Well, as good as Dunkin' ever are."

She took off her jacket, revealing a tight black T-shirt of heavily made up gender-fluid vampires. She unrolled the brown bag and pushed it to the centre of the table. "Do your worst. Or your best."

Linda opened her handbag and took out her knitting project—a black scarf. "I always do both at once," she said. "Otherwise, life's a frightful bore, don't you think?"

"I work at Dunkin' too," said Steven, leaning over and pulling out a mangled, sugar-crusted lump with pink glazing.

"Oh yeah?" Esme said. "Where?"

"The counter, mostly."

"What days?"

He pulled his baseball cap low. "All the days, pretty much."

"I've never seen you. Who's your boss?"

His eyes flitted left then right. "Jim."

"Do you mean Jack?"

He chuckled. "Don't get me started on Jack."

"Mm-hmm."

Peter turned to me. "Nice to see you again, James. Such a relief to still recognise one face. Strange it's yours and not my wife's—"

"I once dated a chef," Linda said, pausing her hypnotically clacking needles. "And he said the pastry from the middle is saved and it's a special delicacy chefs keep for themselves and it's called, I forget now, a bunghole?"

"This is a reality TV show in the making," Cliff whispered.

"This is our lives," I said, forgetting to whisper in response. I cleared my throat. "Sorry."

"Mm-hmm," said Hugh. "Let's begin. Who wants to hold court today?"

Silence, as usual.

"How about you, Esmeralda?" Hugh prodded. "I'm sure everyone here is frightfully keen to get to know our newest regular member."

"Flunk a skunk," she said, mouth half full of donut. She swallowed. "Member? It's only week two."

"Second week," said Peter. "Spot on."

"Even so," said Hugh with a reassuring smile.

She rubbed the sugar from her hands and put the rest of that donut onto the table. "Well," she said with a dismissive shrug. "Fuck it."

I fidgeted in my seat, hands under my bottom, sensing

that intimacy was looming on the horizon like a Mongol horde.

"There's not much to say, really, is there? I'm new in Nottingham." She back-pedalled. "Well, not strictly. I grew up here, sorta." Her gaze wandered. Cliff went in for his second donut. "I'm a misfit, I suppose. Am I though?" She pressed her lips together. "*Fine.* I am. *Good.*" She nodded sharply, the matter solved. "I used to fit in, mind. Or I stood out, but in an acceptable way. Actually, that was kind of my job, standing out."

Cliff regarded everyone and the library and life itself as if it were all a lovely dream.

"People can be cruel," she said. "Or they can be nice but then they're dying." Her nose twitched. "I should go back a bit, I guess? I was always very loud and confident. Like at school and that? A kind of 'it' girl. I could see the arc that my life would take, you know what I mean?"

She looked around at faces that really wanted to agree but couldn't.

"Yes," Peter tried, then crumpled and faltered. "No."

"S——sss——sure," Cliff offered.

Esmerelda viewed them both with suspicion then carried on. "I knew I'd go to uni in London and then become, like, a really spectacular artist with something original to say about the human condition. I'd summer in New York and winter in Rio. I'd take lovers everywhere." She licked her lips. She was wearing black lipstick. "Both men and women. Life would be an all-you-can-eat sensual buffet. And, prod a cod, I would indulge. But then things happened. Unexpected things. Life, I suppose? First my mum died. She was crushed by a block of masonry that fell from a shoddily constructed balcony. So yeah, that was a blow."

A thunderbolt fired across my chest. I'd been just ten

metres from my parents when that piano had tumbled from a giant stack of scrap and debris and compacted cars. I pinched myself on the wrist.

"I started to self-harm. I was in London, but in London everyone wants to be seen but no one wants to watch. I grew increasingly desperate. I became a performance artist, believe it or not, Ripley." She laughed at the memory. "I beheaded a chicken in front of four people in a loft big enough for a hundred. I sat handcuffed to a chair naked for eight hours, a marker pen on string around my neck. No one came. Well, one guy by accident, looking for snacks. He wrote *WHY* on my forehead. Not even a question mark. Still gets me, that."

"Mm-hmm."

She smiled at Hugh. "Exactly. So, I was running out of money. I was running out of time. I was running out of self-belief, which is the worst thing to lose."

I nodded even though she was wrong. The worst thing to lose is your life, or an eye, or both eyes. I closed my eyes, sinking deeper into the awe I felt. How had she found the confidence to do all these things? Why was she telling us about them so unselfconsciously?

I wasn't the only one enraptured.

Linda was frozen midstitch.

Annie had removed her hand from in front of her mouth.

Steven had stopped lying and/or eating.

Esmerelda stared down at her hands. "That arc I thought I was on, well, it curved wildly away from where I wanted to go. No one wanted my poetry. My dad, who's my best friend, he was diagnosed with ALS. He needed a carer, so I packed up my little hatchback and left London to come back here, to a place I've never even liked. A place where it's really hard to belong."

These last two statements received an enthusiastic round of loud-but-silent nods.

"Now, if I'm not cooking donuts, I'm watching a man I love decay to the point where he will asphyxiate. It's hard to deal with that, you know? To come out in the world after it and be, I don't know, breezy?"

I shot Cliff an accusatory look as Esmerelda folded her arms across her chest. "So yeah, that's me, I suppose."

I clapped and narrowly avoided saying "bravo" before I realised no one else was clapping. They did turn, however, and glare at me and so I stopped abruptly, very late into a clap, which now resembled a self-high-five. "Sorry," I said. "That was..." I faded out. She had really thrown herself at life. It had given nothing back, but that was not her fault. That was its callous nature.

"Marvellous," said Peter. "I couldn't agree more."

Esmerelda raised an eyebrow. "With what?"

"Every word."

"I couldn't do half of what you've done," said Annie, wiping away a tear with her sleeve. "Good for you."

"I sacrificed a chicken once," said Steven. "I was working at Bernard Matthews at the time but that doesn't make it better."

"Talking of addiction," said Linda. Had we been talking of addiction? Steven was addicted to lying, that much was true. Linda put her knitting on the table. "I once got pulled over. I think it was on a Tuesday? They said I was speeding, but it was a matter of a mile per hour, maybe two. Which isn't much between friends, is it? Anyway, long story short, the policeman climbs out of his car and we have a friendly chat and instead of a ticket, he gives me his number. The next day I call it and it's disconnected."

"Mm-hmm," said Hugh.

"For you," Linda said, handing Esmeralda the finished black scarf.

"Aah, ain't you sweet? My colour as well," she said, trying it on.

I closed my eyes, dumbfounded, high on her pain and in admiration of her honesty. I even considered eating one of her donuts, but since the chain of custody was broken, I couldn't be sure she hadn't filled it with anthrax. Cliff had eaten two without dropping dead, but we were not of the same constitution.

"Thank you, Esmeralda," said Hugh. "That was stupendously... *honest.*"

"Call me Esme."

The rest of the meeting was uneventful. Hugh told Esme she'd always have a place here. Annie invited her over for tea but then refused to say where she lived. Peter told a story about how he'd ended up in Nottingham, and how it had taken him twelve years to go from hatred to indifference. Steven said he had developed a cure for ALS and things got heated and one member threw a donut before Hugh restored order. We discussed having a New Year's Eve party, but all agreed it was too anxiety inducing to host and little better to attend. Peter handed around a flyer about facial blindness which called on the government to make it an officially recognised condition—one that would afford him preferential parking and an emotional-support peacock.

I took comfort in being around these people. I didn't need to study them like I did the inebriated strangers at Albert's because I was one of them: a cautionary tale.

I signalled to Cliff that it was time to leave. By the lifts, as I was rummaging through my bag for our British Heart Foundation medium-visibility jackets, Esmeralda appeared by my side, zipping up her trench coat. I left the disguises in the bag, rezipped it, and put it on.

"Howdy," she said. "Hi, I mean."

I felt a tight, unexpected pain in my loins. I'd probably stretched something on the fast walk here trying to keep up with Cliff.

My hands were clammy. I looked at her, opened my mouth, but no words came out. What could I say to a woman who had once stripped naked and allowed strangers to write on her body? What could I say to a woman who had moved several hundred miles, alone, to our nation's capital? What could I say to a woman who had survived multiple ear piercings?

"Do you live around here?" she asked.

I used all my powers of concentration and managed a quiet, burpy, "Maybe."

Her left eye closed. "Do you move a lot? Are you in the circus?"

"Yes," Cliff interrupted. "We live in Radford."

"You live together then?"

"Don't remind me," he quipped.

"Your stutter?"

"O——oh. Comes and g———goes?"

"Right." She turned back to me. "Coffee?"

Cliff had done it again. He had seduced her, somehow, without even trying and now she was trying to get to him via me. I should have predicted this. "It's stimulating enough," I said. "Life."

She looked at Cliff. "Is he joking?"

"He's rarely joking."

"They have their uses, I suppose. Bully avoidance and whatnot."

She laughed at something private and in her mind. "Well, I mean, other less-stimulating beverages are allowed, of course." She was looking at me but obviously still addressing Cliff. I waited for him to answer. He stood there uselessly as she tucked another clump of hair behind her ear and tapped her right boot.

"I've got to get to work," Cliff said, then smirked idiotically for some private reason.

"I..." I looked at my watch. I had forty-five minutes until I had to meet Ricky. It was not worth going home, I'd spent enough time in this library, and my three favourite benches would already by jammed with vagrants, vagabonds, and teenage Vanessas with prams. Here was someone new I needed to study, if only to learn what threat she posed to my life's non-fragile non-equilibrium.

"A Vimto," I said, "is possible."

17

I craned my neck forwards, and peered left then right. The street outside the library was clear of danger. "Okay," I said, turning back to the entrance. "Now." She'd vanished. "Esme?"

"Over here, duck."

I looked back out at the street. Esme was outside already, looking down at me as if I was playing a game whose rules had been lost. "What'cha doing, kiddo?"

"Basic surveillance."

"Ah," she said, turning to follow my gaze to where a pigeon was strutting in front of an aggressively chromed hairdressers called Cut&Dry.

Tabby cut my hair but never punned about it.

"Who you afraid of?" Esme asked.

"No one," I lied, but then remembered where we'd met and/or had just been. "Everyone."

She smiled, and her tongue poked out from between her teeth. "I'll protect you, duck," she said, and turned, striding, back straight, chest forward, like a loud, proud, Gothic peacock. I scampered after her. Her stride was twice mine.

"How about Starbucks?" she asked.

"They don't serve me."

"What do you mean?"

"I went there once with Tabby. They pretended not to see me. And her. But I think that was because she was with me."

"Who's Tabby?"

"This way." I gestured. "I know a bench."

"I'll make sure they see us. People usually see me just fine."

"Well, you're tall." She was a head taller than me, although much of that might have been her confrontational shoes. "And your hair is on fire."

"I should hope not."

"Metaphorically."

I turned to make sure the pigeon wasn't following us. It had vanished, but I knew it would return and probably not alone. A taxi beeped. I jumped then exhaled in relief when I saw it wasn't Ricky. He would be a lot to explain.

"What did you think of the meeting today?" I asked.

"Eh," she said. "I'm still trying to wrap my head around this whole Misfit thing. Is Hugh, like, in charge?"

"It's not a group with leadership material. He's the oldest, I suppose, so there's that."

"Did he found the group? Is he, like, the original Misfit? Misfit zero? Good poet names, those."

We walked up Long Row and then onto Pelham Street, passing the back of Squares, which was a bar and not a shelter for the socially inept, as I'd discovered at high personal cost years earlier.

"Misfits have been meeting at the library for generations, or rather, hiding there together alone," I said. "No one's sure when the first two misfits actually spoke to each other. It might have taken several years and/or decades."

Esme tipped her head back and laughed. "Great, that is.

I can imagine them moving slowly ever closer but not quite making eye contact, never mind conversation."

"Come this way a bit," I said, as we drifted apart non-metaphorically by a sausage stand called ONLY BANGERS.

"Why?" she asked.

"There's a large awning coming up on this side, near Wetherspoons."

"Oh, I love a large awning." She winked but skipped a step towards me as a young woman passed us pushing a pram that was aping a sports car. Her hair was pulled tightly back and gave her face a note of alarm. In the pram, where there should have been a baby, there was a hot-pink bowling ball. A rat ran between us and then swerved towards the sausage stand. Over by Burger King—which I'd recently discovered was not actually burger royalty—three youths in school uniform were tripping up a smaller and so more-defenceless youth.

"Oi," she shouted, and shook her fist. "Leave him alone, you scrotes."

We entered the part of the city known as the Lace Market. I sniffed and smelt boot polish and prosperity. This had once been the most prosperous area in the entire country. It was a shame lace had turned out to be such a fad. Markets had stood the test of time, however. There were no markets here, although at several strategic points the Hoodlums were selling stolen things from the boots of cars that were likely also stolen.

I spent the walk puzzling over Esme's behaviour towards me. In particular, her lack of repulsion. It couldn't only be about Cliff because at the first Misfits meeting, she didn't know he existed yet she'd spent a significant amount of time scrutinising me, and without pity and/or disgust. The only logical conclusion was that she was a professional lady-swindler trying to win my confidence and/or love to steal my life savings. What was unfortunate for her and—I suppose, also—me was that the Hoodlums had already stolen it.

"So what bench?" she asked. "We've already passed, like, fifty."

"It's hidden behind several thorny bushes, in the corner of a church's cemetery."

"Oooh." Her eyes widened. "Sounds promising. Any poets buried there?"

"I should hope not. It's near a solicitor's that I think is a front. A lot of sketchy characters, and I don't mean artistically."

I stopped near the entrance to an NCP car park. A busker was playing a song about walls. I didn't share his certainty that they were worthy of wonder. Or that anyone was going to be the one who saved me.

"Now, to reach it, we're going to need to walk down a very narrow lane. It doesn't smell good, but it's safe, Esme."

"Or we could just go to, like, Costa?"

"This is safer."

"You're strange, J."

I took a step back and tumbled off the curb, falling on my behind. She helped me up. Had I really just been given a nickname? I'd had nicknames before, of course, but never insult free. My cheeks burnt with pride. Even my ears felt hot.

She smiled warmly. "There are worse things than strange."

We soon reached the lane. I let her go first since she was armed, even if it was just with a spiky backpack and commanding height. We walked single file down the lane. The church stood on our left, visible above a brick wall topped by iron railings. While it would be a stretch to call

God a fad, it was disappointing his followers had so dwindled in number when he had such excellent real estate.

"Shame it'll be a yuppie wine bar in a few years," Esme said over her shoulder. We reached the entrance to the church's grounds, and she stopped. "Where now then?"

"Turn left," I said, and followed her through the open gate. "Now right." The grounds were peppered with gravestones, most in disarray. The problem with having died a long time ago was that there were ever fewer people in the here and/or now to care.

"There is no right," she said, as I took her by the arm and dragged her between two bushes into a teeny-tiny clearing next to the wall. Plenty big enough for us both, as long as we sat up straight and stayed close.

"Err, so this is a grave," she said, pulling thistles from her hair. I had sat on it often, but now, appraising the space through her eyes, had to admit it was probably a sarcophagus of some kind, and not an official bench.

"Convenient height and/or location though."

"Very secluded." Her eyebrows bounced and she ran her hand across what little of the cold slab we weren't sitting on. "Bring all the girls here, do ya? Anything could go on here and who'd know? Makes me kind of hot." She fanned herself.

"You could take off your coat, I suppose?"

"I could take off more than that."

"Yes, but it's December."

"Yeeeeah." She looked up and sighed. "And what with the drizzle?"

"Are you officially a Goth?" I asked. "Or do you just dabble?"

Her face scrunched. "I suppose I am... yeah. Why?"

"The tattoos. The leather. The spikes. The lipstick."

"No, I mean why do you ask?"

"What's it about?"

If we'd had the luxury of a middle distance, she'd have stared into it as she considered her answer. Instead, she was forced to stare into the non-distance of the bush's backside. "I think, although it sounds like a paradox, you're most alive when you're most aware of death."

"I'm always aware of death," I said, taking two cans of Vimto out of my backpack.

"Ta. Ain't had that since I was a kid."

The cans opened with satisfying hisses. We were side by side and our thighs almost grazed. I noticed that my heart rate was elevated and irregular. It was hard to make eye contact. It had been easier when we'd had the high street to distract us from each other. I looked down at the ground. Which was one of my all-time favourite places to look, anyway.

"I make you nervous, don't I, J?"

There it was again. Just one letter but a stifling amount of bonhomie. I didn't deserve it. Black lipstick was smudged on the rim of her can.

"It's okay," she said. "Cute even. Most guys these days they're so cock-of-the-damn-walk, you know? But then they get it out and they've no clue what to do with it." Her shoulders bounced when she laughed. "They're all talk, is what I'm saying. There's too much talking in this world," she continued, undermining her own point. "Too much fakery."

I couldn't take it anymore. "Why are you being nice to me?"

"You're interesting."

"No, I'm not. I'm weird."

"Yeah, but that's what makes you interesting."

"And unemployed."

"And I work at Dunkin' Donuts. Big deal."

"But I'm—"

"Not someone people are nice to?" she guessed.

"Someone they throw cans at," I said, cradling my Vimto as if it were a warm cup of Bovril.

She laughed again, loud and expressive. "You're funny. Although I don't think you realise it."

"Look." I sighed. "I don't have money, Esme. If you're a swindler, I mean?"

Her head tipped back but then hit the wall. "Ouch! A what?"

"A hoodwinker?"

"If only."

"A femme fatale?"

She fluffed the back of her hair. "I'd like to think so."

"Did your mum really die from falling balcony masonry?" I asked.

"Who would lie about that?"

"Steven. He said his parents drowned in a ball crawl."

"Really? Ha. I was seven and there. It was a freak accident."

"I was there too."

"I don't think you were."

"No. I mean. Never mind."

"I was nearby, playing in a flower bed. Did yours really die from a falling piano?"

I gave a crisp nod. "A one-in-a-million. But one-in-a-millions happen all the time. I'm not good with statistics, although I used to work in insurance. Our commune was next door to a scrapyard with a famously poor reputation and there might have been an issue with breaking and—I suppose, also, if we're being completely honest—entering. Not to mention theft. I'm not sure, I was young, and in retrospect, probably the wrong person to have been made lookout."

Her face froze then cracked. "That's part of why I

wanted to go for coffee actually." She raised her can and burped. "But Vimto's also fine. Few people know what it's like. I only lost my mum. I don't know what I would have done without my dad."

"Suffered."

"Good thing there's the Motley Misfits then." She smiled. "Your story last week. It moved me, I guess. That sounds kinda lame, but whatever. And not only the parent thing. It's part of why I felt okay sharing my story. It was brave."

It was an act of desperation but she couldn't have known that and so I understood why she believed what she believed, which is about the best we can hope for in each other, I suppose.

The church's bells rang out. "Bugger," I said, jumping up. I was late to meet Ricky. "I have to go."

"Hot date, J?"

"It's December."

"See you around?"

I picked up my backpack. "You'd have to look hard."

"I know your bench." She ran a hand across it. "Sort of."

"It's one of many. No, one of four."

"You're a source of intrigue," she shouted, but I was already through the bush.

18

I tumbled into the passenger seat, and found Ricky throwing Bombay mix into his gaping bear's mouth. "'Sup, player?"

"What?" It was like we spoke different languages.

"What's going down in the hood?"

"I don't know? House prices?"

We were not in the hood. He was parked at the edge of the Lace Market, outside an arthouse cinema.

"True that," he said, fishing around in the glovebox. He lobbed something at me and I was so shocked, I didn't have time to drop it. It was a translucent earpiece. "Nearly forgot." He went back into the glove compartment. "Put this on too." He held it out—a black Casio watch with electric-blue trim.

"Digital? Yuck."

"It's the microphone for the earpiece. Mega, right?"

"Why do I need these?"

"So I can give you instructions. For when you're stopping crime."

"What? I thought I was just hanging out and trying to suck people free of their misfortune."

He munched loudly on another handful of his mix. "Still, no reason you can't do all that while stopping crime, right? Crime involves misfortune," he said. Bits of food flew from his mouth. "And all superheroes stop crime."

"You never mentioned stopping crime. I don't know how to stop crime. I've often been a victim of crime, I suppose."

He stroked at his patchy, wannabe beard with his greasy snack hands. "Did you learn anything from that?"

"That crime pays and being a victim costs?"

"Can you, like, channel that frustration?"

I removed my analogue watch and slipped on this new one. "Into a sort of motivating vitriol?"

"Now we're talking."

"I usually channel my frustration into quiet lamentation."

Ricky's nostrils twitched. "Solving crime this way isn't so different, really."

"It's more direct?"

"Yes, buddy."

"How's your basement?" I asked.

"Nearly dry. Look," he said, uninterested in the change of subject, "it can be a minor crime. To start. You know, your classic cheeky shoplift, loiter, or jaywalk. Then, once we learn how your misfortune superpower works, and we've busted some small, local riff-raff, we can take on the big boys." He winked. "And I think you know who I'm talking about."

"Al Capone?"

"He's dead."

"That'll help then."

"Think in the now."

"The Mafia?"

"It's Nottingham, not Napoli."

"The triads?"

He chuckled. "No. The Hoodlums, of course. The people who ruined both our lives."

"Did they? I had sort of already ruined most of mine. Or my parents had by dying. The Hoodlums ruined the last bit though, that's true." I started counting on my fingers. "They made me hide in a bin. They stole my life savings. They mugged me and/or near mugged me several times. They burgled us twice, although only Cliff's room as Tabby and I have fortified ours. They definitely ruined my street. And that ruined the value of my home. That's quite a lot, I guess."

"There we go." He made a mock gun with his hand and fired. "We're on the same page."

"But they're well organised. They're also about twenty people. All of them violent and unburdened by scruple."

"We're two people," he said, as if it were comparable.

"Why am I going out there on my own, then?"

"What? I mean, I'm helping from the tAXi." His voice ran over another high-pitch speed bump on the road to maturity.

"Batman's Robin didn't wait in the car though, did he?"

He took a deep breath. "I'm more of an Albert."

"Prince Albert?"

"The old butler dude with the gadgets."

I looked down at the plastic earpiece I was rolling around in my hand. "It just seems like I'm taking all the risk."

"All the risk?" He checked his reflection in the rear-view mirror. "You're the one with the special powers."

"Don't sidekicks have special powers? How do you become a sidekick, actually? Is there like a school or something?" We'd rushed into this project on a wave of his enthusiasm and/or my desperation. There was still a lot I didn't understand about his wrong world-view.

"What do you think this is, buddy, Harry bloody Potter?"

I'd not read the hit memoir of the child potterer, so couldn't comment.

"No," he continued. "There's no school. It's a dynasty kind of deal. You learn it from your dad, you teach it to your kids. It's about reading people. I have to know what you want before you know what you want."

I wanted to be left alone.

"You want to be alone," he said. "But you're no good alone. You need to be in the world, although I don't know why yet, and it's my job to keep you there until we figure it out."

I nodded, staring out at the street through the fogging windscreen. He was more perceptive than I'd realised. "No crime-stopping," I said.

He let out a long sigh. "Okay, buddy."

I enjoyed his *buddies*.

Two pensioners on mobility scooters argued about who'd first seen a parking space. One was wielding a golfing umbrella as a weapon. It disheartened me to think that life might not become more genteel as I aged.

"I'm a little scared, Ricky. The Rescue Room was such a fiasco. My entire life up to and—I guess, also—including this point, has been the same."

A switch seemed to flick on within him. "'My mumma always said life was like a box of chocolates.'"

It surprised me that people from Birmingham called their mothers Mumma, but I let it go. He'd never talked about his mother before, perhaps because she said things that were so patently untrue.

"It's certainly not a Bounty," I said, after brief contemplation. "I suppose in some ways it's a Curly Wurly because it swerves around in a lot in disastrous, horrible, twisty directions. It's definitely not an After Eight. If you go out after eight in this city, you won't live long."

"You never know what you're going to get," Ricky said. He was doing an impression of some kind. There was a hint of the bumpkin.

"It tells you on the label."

"Mumma always had a way of explaining things so I could understand them." A new urgency overcame him. "'Listen, you promise me something, OK?'" He reached for my arm. "'Just if you're ever in trouble, don't be brave. You just run, OK? Just run away.'"

"There's no risk of bravery, so that's one thing you don't need to worry about."

He snapped out of whatever nonsense trance he'd entered. I let out a sigh and/or groan.

"No! No!" Ricky said, his head shaking. "Sighs and groans are not how we're going to begin our second mission." He rifled through the glovebox again.

"Let me guess? You have some epic music you want to play?"

"Damn right." He pulled out a CD called *Shaft: The Motion Picture Soundtrack*. "Something rousing."

A song built. Its singer had a deep voice contrasted by high-pitched backing-vocals that reminded me of Ricky's voice in all the moments it was undermining him.

He sang along to the song's chorus, grooving from side to side in his seat. "*Shaft!* Sing it with me." He clicked his fingers as the chorus looped. "Come on, James. *Shaft!*"

"Are they saying *shaft*? Like... elevator shaft?"

"Yes. It's the guy's name." He bobbed and weaved. "*Shaft!*"

"Is he a good guy, this Shaft?"

"Yeah, but with sharp edges."

"Does he shaft people?"

"Only if they get in his way."

As the song faded, Ricky tapped the steering wheel several times. "Roused?"

"I'm not sure I'm rousable."

He grabbed me by the shoulder. "YOU CAN DO THIS." He shouted.

"I bruise easily." I said, still unsure exactly what I was supposed to be doing out there beyond subjecting people to, well, myself.

He loosened his grip. "I AM YOUR SIDEKICK AND YOU CAN DO THIS."

"I'm anxious."

"ME AND YOU. YOU AND ME."

He'd be in the taxi, safe. "Are you listening to me?"

"WE WILL MAKE IT. WE WILL MAKE IT BETTER. THE WORLD. BETTER IT WILL BE. YOU FEEL ME?"

"Yes, let me go." At least if I was out of the taxi, it would be easier to run away from him, if he stayed this annoying.

"ARE YOU READY?"

"Probably not, no," I said, as I opened the taxi's door and stepped out, sucking in a lungful of indifferent, mildly poisonous Nottingham air.

19

I walked along the pavement, huddled into myself for warmth. The wind was strong and westerly and I regretted not having been born somewhere exotic and warm, such as Surrey. I passed Screen Room, Britain's smallest cinema, which had only twenty-two seats, if its posters were to be believed. As omens went, its presence felt important-yet-obscure: did it mean that our exploits would one day become a movie? A bad movie only twenty-two people would see? That's the flaw with omens: they're open to interpretation, which makes them useless for orientation.

I hurried on.

"*Alpha, Delta, Tango. Confirm receiving signal, Papa, Eagle, Buddy?*"

"Err," I said, unsure if I needed to push something or have my watch right up to my ear. I tapped its screen.

"*Ow! Fuck! Don't touch it. It's sensitive. The Russians would kill for this technology. You don't need to lift your wrist. My uncle Sanjay invented it. He's got a stall down the market. Sells brushes. Well, unless you know the password. Okay, so, mooch about a bit, see if anyone's doing any dirt.*"

"Gardening?"

"*CRIME. I mean crime. Jesus.*"

"Misfortune, Ricky. I'm just going to stand next to someone suffering misfortune."

I wished I were still hiding with Esme at the church. I wished I believed in God, or some kind of higher power, but I'd seen no evidence the meek would inherit the earth. The meek probably wouldn't even be named in the will. If they made it to the wake, it would be to hand out vol-au-vents. I wasn't a superhero. I was, mostly, an idiot. Perhaps even a superidiot.

But this wasn't how Ricky saw me.

I wanted to be what he thought I was. And so I walked, watching closely, as was my nature. A pigeon—that same pigeon, I was certain, because of its cocksure nature—was sat on the awning of a shop specialising in leather bedroom and/or dungeon accessories. I stared it down, letting it know I'd seen it and knew it was up to no good. It cooed, feigning innocence, but its eyes were cold, dead marbles. I made a shooing gesture with my arm, and as it swooped down towards me, I turned and ran but it gave chase, forcing me to swerve and cower behind a mother pushing a baby in a pram. The pigeon wasn't expecting such extensive evasive manoeuvres and when it dropped its payload, it was the baby who was hit, frontally. The mother screamed and called the pigeon a word I will never repeat.

I carried on down the road as if nothing had happened. I felt sorry for the child because it wasn't its fight but at the same time took solace that its mother would likely be carrying numerous poop-removal paraphernalia.

It rhymed with brothertrucker, the word.

The pigeon swirled triumphant loops in the sky.

"*What was that all about?*" Ricky asked.

"Nothing."

"*Does your power involve pigeons?*"

"They have the power, not me."

A man in an expensive tailored suit was eating a ham and I think cheese sandwich in a metal chair outside a bar called Vodka Revolution, which might have been a reference to the Bolsheviks, I couldn't be sure. They'd been too sure, I think. Tabby and I had watched a documentary about them a few weeks earlier, when life still made sense and/or was nonsensically cruel in familiar ways.

"Everyone's doing just fine here," I said to Ricky.

"*Yeah.*" His voice crackled. "*Prosperous area.*"

"Maybe we should go to Radford?"

He whistled. "*So much misfortune,*" he said. "*Where are you even going to start?*"

I fell off a curb and stumbled into the road.

"*Careful, James. Focus.*"

"Sorry," I said, shaking out my right ankle which was stretched but not strained. I turned sharply back onto Carlton Street.

I looked up the small hill towards Pelham Street, where I'd enter the pedestrianised zone. My stomach was heavy with uncertainty and Vimto. I wanted a different life but knew that wanting things was the first step on a one-step path to disappointment. Was a path a path if it had only one step? I wasn't sure.

When had I last been sure? I wasn't sure.

I swung my careful gaze looking for misfortune. Instead, perhaps predictably, I found crime: two schoolchildren, in uniform, kneeling at a bus stop, spray-paint canisters in their small-but-already-misdeed-mangled hands.

"*That's a crime,*" Ricky said, having spotted them too.

"A minor one. And we agreed no crime-stopping."

"*It's vandalism.*"

"Barely."

"*Bust them.*"

"They're probably very violent."

"They're just babbies. They're like eight."

"I've tangled with eight-year-olds before. They're freakishly strong and utterly convinced of their own immortality."

"Okay," he said. *"Fine. It's a bit beneath us anyway, graffiti. We'll let it go. Wait for a bigger crime, like a kidnapping. A lot of misfortune in kidnapping. Although maybe just your presence here is already stopping people committing crimes? Maybe you're solving crimes right now, in fact?"*

What I *was* doing, in fact, was walking, albeit not like how I usually walked, which involved skulking in the shadows, margins, and peripheries of this city. Pressed, ducked, tucked, and obscured. No, I was walking like normal people walk, which is, mostly, in the middle of the action, completely oblivious to the horrors happening around them to people with large noses, crooked teeth, body odour, acne, monobrows, or fat thighs.

A man thudded into my back. "Sorry, pal. I don't know how I didn't—" He froze in shock as I turned to face him. "Everything okay?"

"Yes."

"You on something?"

"Err, life?"

He gave a brisk nod. "That'll do it. Gotta run, forgot to feed the cat."

"It's working," Ricky said, as a white van honked and its passenger hung from the window and made a hand gesture at me about an overflowing champagne bottle. *"People are responding to you."*

"Negatively, yes."

I carried on towards the centre since everyone there needed help of some nature. *"I can't go much further,"* Ricky said, trailing in his cab as I neared Wetherspoons.

I stopped at the entrance of an alley between the army surplus store and the calendar shop.

I'd seen something.

The alley was long and narrow, as they always are, I suppose. At the start of it, just fifty centimetres from my brown imitation-leather shoes with Velcro, someone had made a home for themselves. It was a primitive affair consisting of a tangle of mattresses, sleeping bags, and other bedding under a roof of cut-up blue IKEA bags strung together with thick white string. I couldn't see the man living in it, but I could tell he was there by the folds and lumps.

Outside was a folded piece of cardboard. One word was written on it: *HUNGRY*.

Behind him, at the end of the alley, was a door, before which stood a large bin, a heap of rubbish bags, and several loosely stacked cardboard boxes. Above the door was a CCTV camera pointed directly at me and/or him.

This man was experiencing extensive misfortune. I waited and watched. One, perhaps even two minutes passed.

"*Anything changing?*" Ricky asked.

"Yes," I said, looking up. "The drizzle has intensified."

The man turned in his bedding.

"*Now what?*" Ricky asked.

I waited another thirty, perhaps even thirty-five seconds. There was no change in the man's predicament.

"I'm going to reduce his misfortune," I said, "but a tiny bit more proactively."

Just a minute's walk up the hill was Greggs. Nowhere was the relationship between calories and cost as favourable as at Greggs.

"He told us what he wants," I said. "I don't need to

spend more than a pound to make this man's day. I'm off to Greggs."

"Should we spend money, buddy? Superheroes don't give people money. Maybe we should just wait longer?"

I was already speeding up the hill because I was buoyed by the kind civic act I was about to commit and because I didn't want Ricky to talk me out of this and into something more traditionally heroic, like rescuing someone stuck up a tree, or under something heavy, or needing martial art skills such as jew-jitsu.

They were out of sandwiches at Greggs, so I procured an enormous slice of pizza laden with cheese and tomatoes for the princely sum of eighty-seven pence. It took some time to get served because all the cashiers pretended to be busy. At one point, seven people were cleaning a single coffee machine. Getting served required elaborate hand-waving and remonstrating and then simply leaving the money on the counter, but I got it done. I carried the pizza back with a warm, perhaps even smug sense of satisfaction and put it down before the man's makeshift home.

Ricky was still parked behind me. The Bombay mix was out again, I noted.

The man was still hidden in his bedding. He didn't move.

I picked the pizza back up.

I put it down, louder. The paper crumpled.

No response.

I picked it up.

"*Just leave it there,*" Ricky said.

"It's Nottingham. It'll be gone in twenty seconds." I needed to get his attention. I cleared my throat.

No movement.

I cleared my throat again. What was the etiquette here?

The man needed a bell. "Hello," I said. "I got you some... err... food?"

The bedding began to move. Then there was a cough. Then another cough, deep and phlegmy. The lumps moved and then, like an egg, cracked, releasing a man who sat up, furiously rubbing his long, scruffy, matted ginger hair. His face was covered in freckles. His eyes were bloodshot.

"You allreet?" he asked.

"Sorry?"

"I'm sure it's not that bad."

"What isn't?" I asked.

"Wotjowunt?"

"He was difficult to understand because he had few teeth and/or was a Scotsman."

"Do you need help?" he asked.

He was making no sense. I thrust the bag out. "I got you some pizza."

"Oh, did you, aye?" he said, without gratitude. I thrust deeper, my arm now at full stretch.

"Cheese on there?"

"Is it legal to sell pizza without cheese?"

He winced. "Lactose intolerant."

My arm dropped back to my side.

"Gotaneee without the cheese?"

"You could take the cheese off?"

"Yeah, I could."

"I shook the bag and lifted it back towards him. "So?"

"Seeps through though, dinnae?"

Surely it was better to have a stomachache than hunger? This wasn't going badly so much as weirdly. I couldn't tell if his misfortune had increased, decreased, or remained unchanged. A dog poked its head out of a navy-blue sleeping bag and gave a delightful, soft whimper. The man rubbed its head affectionately. "Get anything for mah dog?"

"I didn't know you had a dog."

"It's on the sign."

"Is it?"

"Yeeee-ah."

I pulled my sleeve over my hand and picked up the sign. There was a crude black lump next to the word *HUNGRY*. "That's a dog?"

"What else would it be?"

"I thought it was a squiggle?"

"Why would I draw a squiggle?"

"Art?"

"You taking th' piss, pal?"

The greasy pizza bag was leaking its contents onto my hip. As a mini-protest at the man's ingratitude, I was no longer holding it strictly horizontally.

"*What's going on?*" Ricky asked. "*You getting his life story?*"

I raised the bag again. "Give it to the dog?"

He wetted his lips loudly. "Gives her terrible wind."

"Well... at least you're outside then?"

His jaw set. "That's insensitive, pal."

"Just looking on the bright side."

"Of homelessness? Aye, there's a bright side, and a cold side, and a wet side. There's all the sides, and let me tell you, pal, they're shite." I looked over my shoulder, unsure what to do. "Do you think I want to be out here?" he continued. "That I'm happy living in an alleyway under some blankets and a couple of IKEA bags?"

"I just wanted to do something nice."

"Ah bet ye did. You're a real hero, ain't ya? Everyone just wants to do something nice, don't they?"

"I'm sorry." I stepped back.

"Everyone's sorry, aren't they?"

I considered running. "Forget I said anything, or did anything."

"Everyone wants to forget, don't they?"

My intentions had been good but it wasn't enough; it was never enough. I was making his life worse. *I* was the misfortune. I had always been the misfortune. How had I let Ricky convince me otherwise? "I'm going now."

"Go," he said and looked away. "Just like everyone else."

I started walking then realised I was going in the wrong direction. I turned back. "Everyone turns the other way," he yelled. I now had to pass him again. "Passing me by, are you? Just like life."

"Can you stop that?"

"Being homeless? No, I can't. Little tip, mate. Just give money. I have a much better idea what I need, you know? Dinnae have to be much, mind. A few quid and I'm set for the day."

"A fiver, maybe, if ye'r flush. Or it's payday. A tenner, well, that goes a really long way, aye. I was given a tenner once. That made mah week, that did. I still remember it."

I stopped. He was stroking the dog's head. "She probably remembers it too. Had a whole tin of food, steak and gravy, didn't you, Lassie?"

I was still holding the pizza slice. I pulled my wallet out slowly with my other hand. The man smiled. The dog smiled too, or so it seemed. The only thing in the wallet was a single ten-pound note extracted that morning from a secret stash in my mattress.

"I've only got a ten," I whispered to Ricky.

"*Give it to him,*" Ricky said. "*If you can make a man's week for ten pounds, that's a bargain.*"

It was easy for him to say. It wasn't his ten pounds. I pulled out the note, folded it over, and handed it down to the man. "Tenner for your ticker," I said. "Sorry again. About, you know, everything."

He nodded. "You're alright, pal, you know? Even if you're dead scary looking and mumbly and sad. Folk should give you a chance."

"How do you know they don't?"

"Just supposing, ah suppose." He stood and shook out his legs. He was wearing blue jogging bottoms crusted with layers of dirt and grime and what looked like Tipp-Ex. His oversized green hoody bore the logo of Holloway, Holloway, and Holloway, my former employer. Seeing it made me flush with annoyance, firstly because the name of the company was so stupid, and secondly because they had fired me for reasons that—if I allowed myself moderately creative personal accounting—were unreasonable.

The man blew twice into his hands to warm them up. "Can you watch mah dog, real quick?" He moved off the bedding and onto the street.

"No."

He jerked to a sudden stop. His eyes narrowed to slits. "Just for a minute, like?"

"It's a bad idea."

"I just want to get a coffee to warm me up. And a tin of dog food. Allreet?"

"That's long enough."

"For what?"

"Bad things. Misfortune."

"*Do it,*" said Ricky. "*It'll be fine.*"

"You're going to do bad things to mah dog?"

"Not me, no. Other people."

"Who are these other people?"

"I don't know yet."

"Are you high, pal?" the man asked me. "Your eyes..."

I considered this. "No, I'm sort of low, actually. Maybe

even rock bottom. I've lost, well, several things. Sort of nearly everything, I suppose."

He scowled and looked at his alleyway home and then back at me in a way that encouraged me to compare his standing and my own.

"Perhaps more of a lower middle, now that I think about it," I conceded. "But it's still better to take the dog with you."

"Cannae." He frowned. "Arthritis."

"Leave her on her own then?"

"Nah, folk have been complaining aboot her."

"Really, why?"

"Violent."

"You want to leave me alone with your violent, arthritic dog?"

"She's only violent if you pick her up."

"Good to know."

"Or stroke her."

"No danger of that."

"Or get too close."

"Good—"

"Or too far away. Right so, anyway, cheers. You two have fun." He skipped off down the road before I could protest. The dog was a mangy, bony grey greyhound. It looked up at me then lowered its head back to the sleeping bag. Was it a Buster or a Mac? A Buster, if this was its fate. Not that I believed in fate. I had once been to a fete but that was by accident when I was looking for a carpet warehouse.

The dog whimpered pitifully.

"Sorry," I said.

"*You apologising to me?*" Ricky asked.

"No, to the dog."

"Why?"

"For whatever is about to happen."

I looked over each shoulder, without knowing why, and also up at the sky, for falling pianos and other such hazards that could undermine my ability to care for a dog lying in a pile of bedding. I watched the homeless man, who I decided to call Al because he lived in an alley. Al walked towards the town hall. As he left, I made an executive decision—which wasn't my nature, since I'm not executive material, or even middle-management material—and put the pizza down on the ground. Then I ripped the bag open.

"There you go, girl."

The dog sniffed the air. I stood awkwardly. It lifted its head and slid forward, stretched, and then licked the pizza once, twice, three times. Then it did a dog frown and pushed it away with its nose before turning and climbing back into its makeshift bed.

How dare this dog.

Sure, this pizza wouldn't have passed muster in Sicily, but this was Nottingham. Nottingham was a long way from Sicily, I was sure. Not sure how far, precisely, but at least three hours. I looked down at the dog and then up at the road.

"*Come back*," Ricky said. "*The dog will be fine*."

"I made a contract with that man, even if it was only orally and he didn't really wait for me to sign it with confirmatory words."

Nothing happened for thirty, perhaps even forty-five seconds.

A police van pulled up in front of Ricky's taxi. A sturdy uniformed officer got out and approached me. "'Ello, 'Ello, 'Ello," he said, with bowed knees and a lift of his hat. "What do we have 'ere then?" His chubby cheeks shined as if polished.

"That always how you greet people?" I asked.

"That's the standard police greeting, sir."

"With bowed knees?"

"First thing you learn, sir. You're loitering, sir."

"What?"

"Afraid so, sir."

Typical. You couldn't get help for a dozen daily quality-of-life violations in Radford, but in salubrious parts of the city, the long arm of the law grabbed you for just standing still, watching another man's mangy dog.

"I'm not loitering," I said. "I'm just watching this dog."

"*Po*tato, po*tato*, sir."

"Sorry?"

"Your dog is it then, sir?"

"No."

"A stray is it then? Well, we'll do something about that." He turned and spoke into his radio before adding a final "Sir."

"Don't do that. It's mine. *Yes*. Sort of."

"Best you take it with you then, sir."

I looked nervously back up the road but Al had disappeared. "Can't."

"Won't?"

"Can't."

"Must," he corrected. "We've had some complaints, you see, sir. From the owner of the alleyway, about you blocking his exit."

"This isn't... I don't live here. This isn't my house."

"I'm not judging you, sir. How you live is up to you. How you smell is, well, I understand it's difficult, sir, that's all I'm saying. But you and your dog must move, right now." He pointed down the high street. "Radford is over this way, sir. Perhaps you'll find a more suitable place there to bed down?"

"I'm not homeless."

He scrutinised my face. "I also know a clinic."

"I don't need a clinic."

"Animal Welfare has been called, sir. Best be quick about it before they get here, no?"

"She's got arthritis."

"Carry her then, sir."

"Good idea." I moved closer. The dog growled. "Can't."

"Won't?"

"*Can't,*" I said, exasperated.

"Well, well, well then, sir." He tipped his hat again. "Bit of a quandary, sir."

"*Abort,*" said Ricky. "*Papa, Tango, Foxtrot. Abort.*"

A bright-blue van parked in front of the police vehicle. On the back door, in white paint, it said *ANIMAL CONTROL*. A wiry young man got out of the van holding a long metal rod with a hoop at its end. The policeman turned and walked a few steps towards him. I looked around and up and then down and, having analysed the situation thoroughly, decided it had too much me in it. I ran the few steps to the taxi, where I got in and slouched down in the front seat.

"What'cha doing?" Ricky asked.

"It was getting out of control. I thought maybe it would fix itself if I left."

"You've barely left."

"Why don't *you* go help him and his dog?"

"I'm just the sidekick."

"Shouldn't you be by my side then? Not always hiding in the taxi."

"I am LITERALLY by your side, buddy."

"Now, yeah. But not when I was out there trying to stop them from impounding Al's dog."

The policeman turned in a circle. "Where did? There was a...?"

"Who is Al?" Ricky asked.

"Alleyway guy."

"How do you know his name is... Oh, I get it. *Clever*."

There was a loud bark, then a whine, then a whimper. "We could go together?" I said.

"I'm allergic."

"To confrontation or dogs?"

"Dogs, mostly."

"But what if they put it down?"

"It's not an it."

"What if they put her down?"

"That would be terrible."

"We should do something about it, no?"

"No doubt."

The dog catcher approached the greyhound cautiously, metal rod and hook primed to swipe, and then it happened and he had the dog by the neck and was yanking it towards his van as it growled, putting up all the fight it had in it, which wasn't much.

The policeman got back in his van and drove away. The dog catcher got out a mobile phone. "Found it. Jesus. *Fine*. I found her or him. I'll be back in twenty. Shall I pick you up something from Greggs? Slice of pizza, maybe? Yeah, no problem."

He bent down and picked up the slice still in its ripped bag as two men wearing branded polo shirts came out of the side door of the army surplus store. They walked to Al's home and scooped up all his bedding, carried it to the large black wheelie bin, and dumped it inside. They then covered it with the full bags of wet, dripping rubbish.

"Too late now?" I asked.

"I think so."

"Shame though."

"Sure is, buddy."

"We've failed again, haven't we?"

"It's looking that way."

I put my head in my hands. "I think we did, you know?"

"What?"

"Shaft him."

"Let's bounce," said Ricky, turning on the engine. There was a loud thud on the window. I turned to see Al knocking on it with a tin of dog food. Steak and ale. "Where is she?"

"I... It's... complicated."

Ricky put the taxi into gear.

Al peered at the backseat. "She in the taxi?"

"She's... I warned you."

"What have you done with mah dog?" He grew frantic, banging ever louder with the tin.

"It's not... Ricky?"

"Hello, buddy," he said. "You a'right?"

"Buddy yourself. Where's mah dog?"

Ricky pushed the button to dim the windows.

"The police were here," I said.

"And?"

"Animal Welfare," Ricky added.

"I was gone like five minutes?"

"It escalated," Ricky said, "quickly."

"WHERE IS MAH DOG? Get out!" Al shouted. He was still carrying the tin but it was clear it had become a weapon.

"Err, can't," I said, and locked the doors. "They took it. Animal Welfare. There was nothing I could do."

He raised the can to head height.

"Drive, Ricky. NOW!"

Ricky accelerated just as Al brought the tin down. The wheels screeched beneath us and we lurched forwards and were away and around the next corner and Ricky squeezed all the power and acceleration he could get from first gear before shifting to second. Al chased and chased but was losing the race and threw the dog food tin and it bounced off the roof with a loud thud, likely denting it.

Ricky jumped a red light and then did four laps of a mini-roundabout while screaming in delight. "Hell of a chase that."

We re-entered Radford. It was another world. Here you stood out if your coat had all its buttons. A lady of the night and—I suppose, also—day walked out of the cemetery opposite my home, heading towards Tesco Metro for her drug of choice, probably Hobnobs.

Ricky parked outside 12 Cromwell Street. The road was calm and empty but for a few plotting pigeons on a telephone line, a feral badger feasting on the carcass of a fox, a flasher in a plastic mac heading towards the local high school, and a Hoodlum was setting fire to a milk float. The milkman was just about visible, running towards the bottom of the road.

It was good to be home.

I looked down into the footwell. There was a collection of comic books and DVDs of a superhero and/or heist nature. "This is why I hide, Ricky. It's just better for everyone. I don't take misfortune away, I amplify it, even more so in high-stress situations. I don't want to hurt people. It's not their fault. They don't deserve... *me*."

Ricky fiddled with the stereo. "I'd love to disagree, but that Al fella has had a pretty tragic day and I guess we have too and all we tried to do was help."

I rested my head against the window.

"How would you rate your common sense?" he asked.

I took a deep breath. "There's no official scale for that, as far as I know."

"But do you think it's, like, above or below average?"

"The thing with common sense is that it needs to be fed

by common experience. I haven't had many experiences, really. Not normal ones."

He nodded so I continued. "The experiences I have had are mostly weird and/or tragic. That makes them hard to learn from. I have little idea how to behave and very often, instinctively, make the wrong decision. I made several of them here. I could have read Al's sign properly. I could have just left the food. I could have not insulted him by making that inconsiderate remark. I could have refused to look after his dog. I could have told the policeman the truth. We could have stopped the animal control guy. I could have had the common sense to not have listened to you in the first place and saved everyone all this suffering. It was no better in the Rescue Room. I didn't get into the spirit of that at all. I didn't investigate things like you said. I didn't understand that a partial map is asking to be filled. I panicked at the sight of blood and threw a dinosaur at another dinosaur."

Ricky clicked his fingers, a mad glint in his eye. "You have uncommon sense."

"Uncommon sense?"

"Yeah, you know it's the opposite of—"

"I got that. You're making it sound like a strength. I know you want it to be. But it's not. And it's not like I can just do the opposite of what I think is right either. People are too complicated. The opposite of the wrong thing is not the right thing. Not looking at someone is wrong, but staring is also wrong. Asking no questions is wrong, but too many is equally suspicious. Being late is always bad but so is being too early."

"Interesting." Ricky nodded several times then reached for the steering wheel. "It's like with driving. It's not that driving fast is dangerous and slow is safe. Slow is safe only up to a point. Then if you drive slower, like my mum, bless her, it becomes *more* dangerous because you're not behaving as everyone expects."

He pressed play on the stereo.

"I don't know what to do with all this, Ricky. Or maybe I do. I was doing that thing already. The thing is nothing. The thing is hiding."

The words didn't seem to register with him.

"Just look at the speed and severity with which Al got shafted by you. It was majestic. There's something special here, buddy. I just don't know how we can use it for good."

"I feel terrible about that man's dog."

"Me too," he said. The song's intro built.

BAD BOYS BAD BOYS

"Maybe," he said but then stopped.

WHAT'CHA GUNNA GO?

"What?" I asked.

WHAT'CHA GUNNA DO WHEN THEY COME FOR YOU?

"Nothing," Ricky said, but he had his idea-face on: a glazed-over mixture of concentration and constipation.

BAD BOYS BAD BOYS

"We've just assumed that you're a good guy, right?" he said. "But what if you're a villain or even a supervillain? What if we're not supposed to stop crime and alleviate misfortune but *cause* it?"

WHAT'CHA GUNNA DO?

"A villain?"

"Yeah, a force of evil."

"Evil?"

WHAT'CHA GUNNA DO WHEN THEY COME FOR YOU?

"A baddie like, you know, the Penguin."

"They're not evil, just a bit rapey."

"No. *The* Penguin."

"There's more than one, Ricky."

He slapped his forehead.

I considered what he was saying. The world had long been cruel to me. Had I ever tried being cruel back? Not that I could remember.

"Evil," I repeated, trying the word on for size. It was a big word for an averagely sized man. "I don't think I have the sort of casual callousness required to be evil. And I've no interest in blowing up the moon like a comic book villain. I don't really ever see it because I don't go out after dark, but I like that it's there and making the tides come in and out and stuff. It's a good thing, I think, the moon."

"I agree wholeheartedly."

"And wouldn't I feel less guilty about the dog, were I evil?"

"You can be evil and really love dogs, like that Hitler fella."

"I guess."

I thought about all the people who had crossed me, or tried to, but there were too many and so I thought about just the most egregious ones. Robin and his Hoodlums, mostly. Then Pat. I imagined Robin standing at the edge of a remote cliff completely free of witnesses and/or consequences and perhaps waving my bank card around like a tiny flag. And then I asked myself, could I push him?

Yes, I decided.

In fact, the thought of his untimely death and what it might do to local housing prices buoyed me no end. And while this test had been another disaster, during it, I'd been out and in the world, not at home lamenting everything I'd lost. Sure, this had been a fiasco, but what if the goal was to create a fiasco? That had to be easier. Doing good? Righting wrongs? That was tricky stuff. Giving was hard but taking was easy—Robin and his Hoodlums proved that. Destruction was much simpler than construction, its boring, bookish older brother.

"Make a list of causes," Ricky said. "Things you hate about the world. Things you want to change. People who've crossed you. Then we're going to go get revenge, one by one. Oh, are we going to get revenge, buddy. We're going to tear this motherlicker down. We're going to bathe in the blood of our enemies."

He had run away with himself again. He stared out into the distance. He was a natural plotter and hatcher. A pigeon defecated on the windscreen. It was white and yellow and eerily reminiscent of a Cadbury Creme Egg.

"Sorry," I said, nodding towards the mess.

"Not your fault."

"Even if it turns out we're good at being bad, we're not going to be ready to take on the Hoodlums now and/or probably ever, Ricky."

"Let's see."

"Ricky," I said, grabbed by a sudden thought. "What if *we're* our own worst enemies?"

"Sorry?"

"Nothing."

"So you're in then?" he asked.

I tapped my cheek. "Potentially, maybe. But only if you promise that this is the last test and that rather than tearing it all down, we first rip it a little bit at the corner?"

"That sounds good," he said, but I think he was lying.

20

A few days later, I was in the kitchen getting a warm glass of water. Cliff emerged from his bedroom looking pained, which I'd never seen before. Seeing him didn't pain me, I noticed. He was growing on me, like a benign but financially lucrative abscess.

He sat down at the kitchen table. "Got a minute for your old pal Cliff?" he asked.

"It's been a hard week full of failure."

"You're used to that though, right?"

Compassion was not one of his strengths. Unlike strength.

I sat down. It was dusk and the fading light cast a depressing shadow over half the table.

"You've been in a relationship for a long time before, right?" he asked.

"I've never been in a relationship. A woman did hug me once, outside of Laser Quest, but she wasn't my type."

"What's your type?"

"Forgiving."

He laughed as if this had been a joke.

"I have little by way of role models when it comes to love," I said. "Why do you ask?"

"Oh, you know. I'm just thinking about me and Tabby, I guess? She's not my normal type, but it's going great." He smiled beatifically.

I was happy for him. Was I happy for him? I wasn't sure. I knew I would have been happier for him if his happiness had not come at the expense of my own, seeing as how he was stealing my supply of Tabby, someone upon which I had built quite a dependency, although perhaps less in recent years since she went off to discover herself. And I had been busy here what with bubble wrapping and fretting and whatnot. I was also beginning to wonder just how much of her time he could feasibly take up, bearing in mind how simple he was. Just as no one regretted getting a pet turtle because they required so much maintenance.

"I'm not bored," he added. "I usually get bored with them. Women. Often the same night. Sometimes within the hour, if we've already had sex."

I took a sip of my water. "Yes, but Tabby's complex and multifaceted and has a brain. Not to insult the women you usually go for."

His brow furrowed. "That is kind of insulting actually, dude."

"You didn't meet her in a discotheque toilet queue, is what I'm saying. Your relationship is built on friendship and also proximity, which is mandatory for friendship, I suppose? I'm new to friendship. I may have a new friend now, actually."

"Do you mean me?"

His arrogance was startling. "No, Cliffffffff, I do not mean you. How long have you and Tabby been... well... lust buddies or whatever?"

He ran a hand through his shaggy locks and stared off

into the distance, at least as much as was possible in a kitchen-diner in which you'd be brave and/or foolish to swing a dead cat.

"It started when we got drunk at Jill's fancy-dress party."

"That was months back." I'd been busy re-bubble-wrapping my room that night. Not that I'd have gone otherwise.

"Yeah, I guess." Cliff's time horizons extended only sixty seconds in any direction. I guess it made sense to live in the moment when all your moments were as pleasant as his.

"Do you ever worry she'll get bored with you, like she did with me?"

He paused. He blinked. He paused. He blinked. "Bored with me?"

It was as if I were speaking Mandarin.

"That's your problem," I said, tapping my cheek. "That's it exactly. Yes, Clifffffff, *Exactly*."

"What?"

"You can't appreciate what you've never considered you might—and almost certainly will—lose."

I remembered Esme and the Goth desire to be stroked but not grabbed by the cold, bony hand of death.

"Huh," he said, taking the idea for a slow walk around the sandpit that was his mind. "I usually just go with the flow. I'm like a shrug brought to life."

This was more insight than I'd expected from him. "Do you ever think about the worst thing that could happen happening, and how that might make you and/or those around you feel?"

He put his finger in his ear and twiddled. "Is that a thing people do?"

"Yes, Clifffffff. All the time. It's how they stay alive and/or appreciate that they are alive."

He reached over and flicked the light switch. The bare bulb lit up the small room. "Yeah, I guess you are very good at maximising your own distress. You have a very vivid imagination."

"Only for peril. Try it with me. Imagine you're, I don't know, making toast with peanut butter."

"Okay," he said, but his eyes glazed over. I banged my fist on the table. "No, Cliff! I need you to really picture yourself there. Close your eyes. It's morning. The sun would be shining if the sun ever shined here. The birds would be singing if birds here knew how to sing rather than just squawk belligerently. You're hungry, Cliffffff. Perhaps even hangry. You're standing in the kitchen scratching your back."

"It's morning?" he said.

"Okay, not morning, it's mid-afternoon. You've just woken up. You're hungry. Perhaps even hangry. You're scratching yourself. Now, it's the first time you've eaten peanuts that day, right?"

His eyes rolled upwards. "I suppose, yeah?"

"Well, what if you've developed a lethal peanut allergy overnight?"

His eyes rolled back down and brought his eyebrows with them. "That's not a thing. That's not how allergies work."

"Have you ever thought about how everything that's a thing, Cliffffffff, once wasn't? Take, for example... I don't know, smallpox? For almost all of human history, *not a thing*. Then, suddenly, BIG DEADLY THING, Cliffff. Bubonic plague, not a thing. Suddenly, REALLY BIG REALLY DEADLY THING! Thing that kills everyone. *Dead*. So, you didn't have a peanut allergy yesterday. Because not a thing, right..." My adrenaline was pumping now, lifting me from my seat. "BUT THEN,

SUDDENLY, THING, CLIFF! THING THAT MEANS YOU CAN NO LONGER BREATHE! And not only that," I said, calming down a little. "Unlikely events can occur together." I knew this from personal experience. I'd lost my savings, my job, and Tabby all in one day. Well, I found out I'd lost them on the same day. The seeds had been sown earlier.

"So what if, while struggling for breath and close to death, you slip on the small puddle of water near the sink from the leaky tap that I've been meaning to get fixed for a year, perhaps even two, and you stumble, gasping, tipping, tipping and..."

I opened a drawer then let my voice sink to a whisper. "You prostrate yourself on this kitchen knife." I thrust one in his direction. "Which sinks into your non-metaphorical heart. Which stops."

"This..." He grimaced. "Is this really what it's like to be you?"

"So, you die." I threw the knife down on the table and rubbed my hands together. "But that's not the end, Cliffff! No, you wish that was the end. Because who finds your body?"

He fidgeted in his seat.

"Tabby. Her first proper boyfriend—dead. Blood and peanut butter everywhere. She's traumatised. She'll never love again. I've got to keep your deposit for industrial cleaning."

He dropped his head into his hands. "Jesus."

"And all just because you wanted to make toast. Nice one."

His lip trembled. "Is this why you've covered everything in your room with bubble wrap?"

"How do you—"

"And why you scuttle everywhere?"

I put my glass carefully into the sink. "You're welcome, Cliff."

Pulsing music—loud enough to make the knife rattle—shook the room suddenly. We covered our ears. We knew where it was coming from. I also knew what the rest of my evening would entail: binoculars, a warm bath, being fobbed off by the police and/or my bank.

"I hate them," I said, in a voice just shy of a shout. Ricky was right. We had to do something. "WHERE'S TABBY? IT'S SCRABBLE NIGHT."

"SHE'S..." He waited for a break in the music. "I'm not supposed to say."

"SO WHY TELL ME YOU'RE NOT SUPPOSED TO SAY?" I yelled as the music returned.

"SHE'S MEETING HER DAD."

"WHAT?" I got up and paced the room, which was, at most, three paces wide. "WHY? WHEN?"

"HE CALLED HER LAST WEEK. ASKED TO MEET UP."

Fortunately, I was already wearing my shoes, which I never took off, even while in bed. "WHY DIDN'T SHE TELL ME?"

"SHE SAID SHE KNEW WHAT YOU'D SAY."

The music stopped. We relaxed. "Well, why aren't you there with her?"

"We're not really at that stage. The parent-meeting stage."

"It's not about you, Cliffffffff. You and your stages. She needs support."

"She's a grown woman."

What he didn't know, what he couldn't know, was that the age we are when our parents abandon us is the age they find us on their return. He'd never had his development arrested, or his faith in humanity tested. He wasn't like us.

Nor could he become like us. I doubted he could even understand us, no matter how many Motley Misfit meetings I took him to, or precious life wisdom I shared with him in this small kitchen.

"Where are they meeting?"

"Albert's, I think."

I threw open the front door and ran.

21

I yanked on the door to Albert's and bumped straight into a face I'd not seen in ten years. The biggest change was the nose—now a swollen, bulbous, alcoholic one set in a blotchy red face in which every second blood vessel was broken. He looked as if he'd aged thirty years. His ears were cauliflowers.

"Ferdinand," said Craig, Tabby's so-called father.

I tipped back onto my heels and he gave a snorting, derisive laugh that became a rattling cough. His body had fared badly too. He was all stomach now and looked like a barrel with arms. He was whiter than a swan but even more violent. I was too shocked to say and/or do anything and so I just stood there, frozen, sad-eyed, my mouth making a small o.

"Long time no see," he added, and coughed again, this time into his fist. His hands were shaking, and it wasn't from fright.

I was looking at excess. I was looking at addiction. I didn't like the way it looked, nor the way it was looking deep within me and finding me lacking.

"I'd have been fine with it being longer though," he said.

I tried to say something but was still stuck, twelve years old again and powerless. He knew it. And he enjoyed it. "I'd say you look prosperous but..."

I looked down and away.

"You here for her then?" he asked, but he knew the answer.

I turned around to see if I could go back out but a group of students were coming in and I was jammed between him and them and so made to move forwards into the bar. He puffed out his already over-puffed chest and barged into me as I passed.

"Good chat," he said, sarcastically, and then laughed as my feet tangled and I fell forwards but caught the corner of the fruit machine, just staying upright. I shuddered then moved towards the bar. The lights of the jukebox were spinning as music serenaded the drinkers.

The singer was wrong. Boys did cry. I was choking back a tear of my own.

"Vimto Valery," Albert yelled, and the revellers at the bar turned and laughed. I swallowed the embarrassment and tried to pick a path through the crowd. My frustration, my anger, my humiliation: it wasn't important. I looked around for Tabby and found her alone at our usual table, wiping her eyes with a balled-up tissue I'd seen her pull from the sleeve of her crisp, white work shirt.

Above her, the blackboard said THIS IS YOUR LAST WARNING.

I sat down, Albert following me over. He put a pint of Cocktail in front of Tabby and grabbed the empty one. "Might never happen," he said.

"Already has," she replied, picking up her spectacles.

He put his finger deep into his ear. "Might not happen again?"

She sat straighter. "No. *No* it won't."

He moved across to a nearby table of Holloway, Holloway, and Holloway employees. I recognised them but they'd forgotten me. Their ties removed and their top buttons undone, they were huddled over a newspaper crossword. "You want cross word, you came to the right place," Albert said and/or threatened.

Tabby was staring into space. I reached for her hand. "What happened?"

"Why are you here, James?" She said, without eye contact.

"You know why."

On the circular table was a folded letter with the logo of British Gas. She pushed it towards me with one finger. It looked like a bill. I unfolded it and read the address, which I recognised from an arson claim I'd approved at Holloway. It was a high-rise on the outskirts of the city.

"Other side," she said. I turned it over.

Tabatha,

I'm pleased you've grown into a competent, employed adult with a career ahead of you at the Citizens Advice Bureau. This is because of work I did in your early years. Things are not going well for me through no fault of my own. Time to repay your debt. Below are my costs for you from ages 1 through 11:

Clothes: 2,498
Food: 5,550
Rent: 10,290
Childcare: 14,412
Play items (e.g. Mickey Mouse bicycle with stabilisers): 3,611
Total: 36,361

It's only fair.

Your Father

P.S. Why are you still living with that freak Ferdinand?

I bit down on my lip until I could taste blood. "That cruddy motherpucker."

"I know."

The song changed. It didn't matter how many times I said please. I'd not get what I wanted. I wanted him gone from our lives.

"This is a new low," I said. "Even for him."

Tabby nodded, sipped from her drink, then shuddered. "Prosecco and... parmesan?"

"And why the trucking truck does he value his childcare so highly?"

She put the drink down and pushed it away, her lips pursed as if she'd sucked a lemon. "I can't believe I let him do this to me again."

I didn't want her to beat herself up. That was life's job. "Well... I mean... he is your father."

"In biology, yeah."

When Tabby was eight, her mum had been at the stove cooking pork chops. As they sizzled away and Tabby was drawing on the floor, Beverly turned, went out to the hallway, put on her coat and walked out, never to return.

A few years later, Beverly went walking again and must have got really lost this time because she ended up spread across the windshield of a train. Craig, already both a prodigious tippler and a believer in the value of corporal punishment, spiralled. The state took Tabby into care. Which was where she met me. Over the following years, like something you can't flush, Craig reappeared from time to time to stink up Tabby's and/or my life.

"People don't change," she said, dabbing her eyes. "They just grow older and meaner."

"I'm sorry."

"You're lucky your parents are dead." She froze. "I didn't mean that. It just... It just came out. I'd *rather* he was dead."

I slumped lower in my seat.

"I really thought this time maybe he'd changed and he wouldn't be such a giant prick. His skin, Ferdie—James. I don't think he'll make it many more years. I see people like him every day at work. There's only one bit of advice you can give them and they never take it because their life has only one thing in it. They're not going to give that up. I think this was one last desperate attempt for a payoff to get the money he needs to drink himself to death."

"Are you going to give it to him?"

"No."

"You don't deserve this. You are good. You help."

She took off her glasses and dabbed at the make-up running from the corners of her eyes. "Who deserves anything?"

"What do you think about the Amish? As an option, I mean. For us?"

"How did you—" she said, then stopped. "Cliff?"

"You should have told me."

"You would have stopped me from coming."

She rested her hand over mine. Colour spread into my cheeks. Fortunately, it was too dark for anyone to notice. A man at the bar in a red shirt was doing increasingly theatrical mimes to try to get a pint. It looked like he was trying to land a plane with just his elbows.

"Why did you meet him here?"

She went in for another sip while holding her nose. She shuddered then set down the glass heavily and pushed it further away this time. "Oh god. What's the opposite of a grower?"

"A shrinker?"

She chuckled. "This was the first place that came to mind. And I didn't want to go anywhere that I have happy memories, in case he ruined them."

I looked around, scanning faces of merriment and menace. People at a nearby table clinked glasses. A young couple in a dark corner were attempting to trade tonsils near a table of six students, perhaps a support group, comparing how fat their mothers were. One was supposedly so fat that she had more rolls than a bakery, which I thought was unlikely. Certainly not more than Greggs. A homeless man I'd often seen outside the launderette Wishy Washy was drying his socks on a stick over the fire, Albert was burning crisp boxes today. In the far corner, two women were swaying, each with an arm around the other's shoulder, singing along to the music. At least I wouldn't have to worry about the weather on my wedding day. Cutting Craig out was the good advice Tabby wouldn't take.

"I have happy memories here," I said, "studying people with you. It's a weird place but there's something honest about it. Even if it's brutally so. Do you have thirty-six thousand pounds?"

"I work at Citizens Advice."

While most of their positions were voluntary, Tabby was high enough in their hierarchy to be paid a living pittance.

"Would you give it to him if you did?"

"Of course not." She scrunched his letter into a ball and

threw it under the table. "It's done. *Over.* Will never happen again."

She was kidding herself. To pull a stunt like this, the man had to be desperate. Desperate people don't give up easily and/or ever.

She smiled, albeit meekly. "Take my mind off this. How was your day? Did you get pooed on by a pigeon?"

"Very nearly, actually."

"Attacked by a toddler?"

"There was a ferocious little guy down by Mothercare. He was in an orange dungaree with beavers on it but he wasn't fooling anyone. He was out for blood. Did I tell you about my friend Ricky?" It felt good to say the word *friend* even though that friendship would be over soon when we didn't find a use for it.

"Good for you," she said. "A friend who isn't me."

"Or Cliff."

"Are you and Cliff friends?"

I shrugged. "Ricky thinks I might be special. That I might have superpowers, or superdisabilities. Something super, anyway. We're running experiments. All disastrous. Which might be the point. I'm not sure. It's mysterious."

She laughed and her eyes lit up and I felt something stir within me. My life had little, but it had her. And she was worth a lot. Maybe not objectively, at like a public auction, but subjectively, to me. And I was reminded that—with the exception, perhaps, of bubble wrap popping—there is no greater sound than the woman you care for laughing, and that I would do a lot and/or almost anything to protect it.

22

I slept badly that night, hunted, haunted, and—I suppose, also—harangued by Craig's bloated face. He would be a reoccurring problem in our lives because Tabby was too nice and patient and pathologically helpful to break contact with him.

He needed to be stopped, once and for all.

I sat up, the morning light floating in through the curtains, taking a moment to stroke the bubble wrap that covered my mattress and greeted me like a soft, forgiving friend.

I popped.

I felt better.

I popped

I felt better.

I ran a bath. Lying in it, trying not to think about how easy it would be to slip, hit my head, and drown, I wondered if Robin was still gleefully spending my life savings. How much money was hidden in my mattress? A few hundred pounds, I estimated, as I ran my hands through the foam in the bath, lifted bubbles to my nose, and then blew. I hung my arm out of the tub and grabbed my binoculars.

Their kitchen was empty.

The blinds were down on the first floor.

I noticed cracking in their brickwork and wondered if they had insurance. I craned my neck back so I could see the top floor.

There he was. At the window. Also holding binoculars. A cigarette hanging loosely from his mouth. Topless. Ghostly white and deathly skinny. Watching me watching him.

I yelped.

I panicked.

I dropped my binoculars and they splashed off my chest into the water. I slid down after them in a rash attempt to hide. Where could I hide? My enemies were everywhere. And my allies? They were...

Cliff.

Of course. Cliff. A new ally. We were a weird threesome now, instead of a weird twosome. He was actively seeking to know and be part of my and Tabby's world. That was what the conversation in the kitchen had been about. It was my duty to help and/or train him. To be of use to us, he had to be made more scared of life, love, and loss and less flippant about all our fates.

I got out of the tub, got dressed, and crept down to his room. He was snoring away, as per usual. He'd probably been up late playing ultra-violent computer games. I unfurled a roll of my magnificent, extra-strong-and-long, industrial-grade bubble wrap. Was it strong enough to secure an entire man? Especially one as lumberjackish as Cliff?

I had wrapped myself in it often enough, privately, to think that yes, it just might be.

I took his hands, pushed them together, and bound them with tape. He was on his side, so I crouched to the floor and looped the roll of bubble wrap under the wooden bed frame, retching as I brushed crusted socks, a crusted playboy magazine, and a crusted meatball sandwich, got up and leaned over him, pulled up the sheet as it brushed the wall, before tugging it back across his body, then looping it back under the bed again.

My whole body throbbed and/or prickled.

I felt intensely powerful.

I did like being a bad guy and suddenly felt excited about the third test with Ricky.

I did another loop of wrapping.

I taped.

I did another loop.

I taped.

It was noisy but Cliff didn't move.

Staring down at my trap, I was giddy enough that I let out an uncharacteristic whoop, followed by an unbecoming holler. He was completely at my mercy. I regretted not wearing my balaclava as I picked up the saucepan and wooden ladle I'd brought through from the kitchen. I held it about six inches from his restful, peaceful, beautiful idiot head.

THWACK

THWACK

THWACK

He screamed and his body jumped slightly in the air, his legs kicking out, which was when he discovered I'd restrained him in a cocoon of industrial-grade postal supplies.

"James! What the fuck?" His voice was full of panic.

"DOOM DEATH DESTRUCTION," I bellowed. "DOOM DEATH DESTRUCTION."

He flailed like a fish in a hot pan.

"What are you doing?"

THWACK

THWACK

THWACK

"You're a lunatic!" he said, scrabbling for his life. "Let me go. James. PLEASE?"

I increased the speed of the thwacking.

THWACKTHWACKTHWACK

"DOOM DEATH DESTRUCTION."

THWACKTHWACKTHWACK

"DOOM DEATH DESTRUCTION."

THWACKTHWACKTHWACK

"You can't stop it, Cliffff. Jeopardy can arrive at any moment. Especially a vulnerable moment like when you're sleeping."

He ripped at the little bubble wrap he could reach with his nails.

THWACKTHWACKTHWACK

"DOOM D—"

"Stop thwacking."

"The thwacking never stops, Cliffffffffff. Not in my and/or Tabby's world, which is now your world."

He stopped resisting. His body went limp. He bit a bubble and it popped, and he laughed and so he bit more. "This is quite fun. Feels nice."

"I know, right? DOOM DEATH—" I paused. "You are trapped, correct?"

Pop

Pop

"For now, at least."

Pop

Pop

He giggled, and with that giggle, the lesson I was imparting slipped away. I bent low and close to his ear.

THWACKTHWACKTHWACKTHWACK-THWACKTHWACKTHWACKTHWACK

"DOOM DEATH DESTRUCTION!"

THWACKTHWACKTHWACKTHWACK-THWACKTHWACKTHWACKTHWACK

"DOOM DEATH DESTRUCTION!"

THWACKTHWACKTHWACKTHWACK-THWACKTHWACKTHWACKTHWACK

I dropped the saucepan on the floor and walked out.

Causes I Could Really Get Behind: A List by James Jones:

1. Widen all lanes, alleys, passages, corridors, and toilet stalls to at least three metres, rendering them unattractive for nefarious undertaking.
2. Ban all technologies, foods, fashions, and hairstyles less than fifty years old.
3. Bully all bullies to a level of tyranny equal to or greater than that which they have inflicted.
4. Conduct all job interviews with blindfolds.
5. Expand the traditional definition of beauty to include that which has been, until now, not included. Focus on oversized amphibian eyes and weak chins.
6. Construct a Great Wall of Mansfield, encasing the city entirely.
7. Pulp all self-help literature, beginning with the work of serial huckster Tony Robbins.
8. Create a national Amish Appreciation Day.
9. Issue a restraining order against Carlsberg Craig, Tabby's so-called father.
10. Imprison, either officially or unofficially, Robin Hoodlum and his accomplice, Postwoman Patricia Eldridge. See also 3.
11. Diaper all pigeons of an adversarial nature.

24

"Here he is," Ricky said, as I let myself into his office, lab, and taxicab for what was almost certainly the penultimate time, "the Jekyll, the Jackal, the Joker."

We were parked out Citizen's Advice, I'd just had lunch with Tabby: a baked potato, cheese and beans. Humble, but effective. "I guess I'm bringing the metaphorical fire and fury," I said, settling into the passenger seat. Only Cliff knew just how much fire and fury I was packing today.

"What'cha wearing?" he asked.

"Nothing," I said, slipping off my British Heart Foundation medium-visibility jacket. I rolled it and stuffed it into the top of my backpack. I ran my hand along the edge of the passenger seat. I would miss this taxi dearly. It had become a safe space.

"I'm feeling good about this test," he said. "You've shown such a talent for destruction, and it'll be way more fun to be villains."

I felt exactly the same way. "There's just one thing, Ricky. I can't go to prison. That's my red line."

"Understood."

"I wouldn't do well incarcerated. I'm a soft-scoop man

in a hard-as-nails world and I value my freedom, even though I just spend it fruitlessly fretting. Speaking of which." I handed him a piece of paper. "Here's my list of causes."

He read it aloud. "Widen all alleys? Jesus. That's ambitious."

"Easier than the Great Wall of Mansfield, I'd think."

"Mansfield again? What's your problem with the big M? It's a fine place. Bit rough about the edges, sure."

"When did you last go there?"

He jogged briskly through his memory. "Jeez, back when my parents still spoke to each other. Ten years, maybe?"

"Let's go there. You take a walk around. I'll wait in the taxi."

"Nah, we're busy being evil."

"We'll fit in well then."

"We need to focus," he said, putting the list on the dashboard. "What's the plan?"

I tipped my head back. "You're the ideas man. Don't tell me they're my remit now as well? Because if they are, we're really in trouble."

He pulled out his phone and checked the display. "Yeah, I've been a bit busy, buddy. Financial trouble, you know? And if it was down to me, I'd do something big. I'd blow up the Hoodlum HQ, do a jewel heist, or assassinate the Pope. You feel me? But that's me. So I thought I'd wait for your list of causes."

"You would do them?" I said, making the sentence drip with sarcasm.

"Fo shizzle."

There had been a lot of talk of shizzle, in all in various forms, but I was still confused what any of them were. I stepped over it. "Don't you mean I would do them and you would wait in the taxi?"

He rolled his eyes. "We've been over this already. I could be out there trying to get all the glory. But I'm not, am I? I'm in here, directing things. I'm the Steven Spielberg, the Ridley Scott, the Stanley Kubrick."

"Who—"

"Famous directors."

"Ah. How old are you, Ricky?"

"Seventeen."

"SEVENTEEN! No wonder we barely speak the same language and you wander so in pitch."

"I look older, I know. It's the beard."

"And the jowls."

He checked his face in the rear-view mirror. I retrieved the list from the dashboard and we sat in silence for one, perhaps even two minutes until lightning flashed in the dark, usually notionless sky of my mind. "There a print shop around here?"

"On the Trent cAMPus, yeah."

"Take us there, Jeeves. I've had an idea."

He reached for the key then stopped. "Is it evil?"

"It's beyond devious."

He grinned. "Attaboy."

Forty-five minutes and one exasperated print-shop employee later, I left the shop with two hundred circular stickers bearing the word *LIES* in a popular youth font, comic sans, and as many bookmark-sized manifestos. Ricky had elected to go pick up a few fares so he could afford a family kebab night he didn't seem excited to attend. On returning to the street to wait for him, I ducked behind a small wall next to the Student Union Building.

Around me, clusters of students passed the time doing ordinary student things: boozing, hazing, happy-slapping, and sexually harassing. I could see the brand-new four-floor Boots Library gleaming in the... drizzle. Did it have a poetry section? Not that they'd let in uneducated riff-raff like me. I once applied to Nottingham Trent to study risk management but was rejected after the interview. I harboured no resentment towards them, however, and wished them well, in hell, where I hoped they were having a nice time, rotting.

Ricky pulled up. I crept back to the taxi clutching my plastic bag of print-shop goodies and wearing a wide, perhaps self-satisfied smile.

"Were you hiding behind that wall?"

"What? No. I was doing up my laces."

He looked down at my feet. "They're Velcro."

"I get in a lot of unexpected footraces." I thrust a manifesto at him. "Check this out."

He took it reverently, as if it were made a precious metal. He read, then turned it, found the other side empty, turned it back over, then winced. "The Tony Robbins thing again?"

I nodded. "Indeed."

"Who is this clown, anyway?"

"Be happy you don't know."

"You're going to put these inside his books?"

"Oh yes." I nodded much faster. "And other self-help books." I threw my head back and cackled.

Ricky waited until I'd finished. "That the entire plan or just, like, a teaser?"

"If we've learned anything from the previous tests, it's that I don't need to do much to cause chaos."

"True. True." He pressed his lips together. "It's just..." He looked away. He looked back. His mouth opened. His mouth closed. He was obviously pained by something, and it pained me to see it. "Is it evil enough, is what I'm wondering?" he said finally. He handed the manifesto back but the reverence was long gone.

"It's a promising start," I said, taking it from him. "Strongly hints at future evil, no? At being a thing that might really escalate?"

He tugged on a few strands of his terrible neck-drape beard and looked out the windscreen at an impractically dressed student in an orange miniskirt. He put on the windscreen wipers for obvious weather-related reasons.

Whip-whap

I had to win him over. It was my turn to rouse. I raised my chin and inflated my chest. "I think it could be a thing that might even, possibly, one day, get a little out of control. Become a revolution, even, maybe? Vodka or not. Perhaps even a coup, and I'm not talking about chickens."

Whip-whap

Ricky turned to me after the student had entered the library. "What are you talking about?"

"I'm not sure. It's the excitement, I think. It *is* refreshing to be bad."

Whip-whap

"Your manifesto. It's..." He searched for a word. "Subtle. And I've watched enough Adam Sandler movies to know that you don't win over the masses with subtlety. You gotta get up in their face and really batter them with your point."

Whip-whap

"The best evil is subtle, I think." This wasn't what I thought. I was ad-libbing because I'd spent seventeen-pound-fifty of my dwindling mattress money on printed materials. I'd thought very little about evil other than how to best hide and/or cower from it. "Sure, you can come out with guns blazing, metaphorically, and that's effective. Efficient even, I suspect. Sends a powerful message. But isn't it better not to menace too directly? To merely sow the seeds of mistrust and uncertainty in people's imaginations, so that they menace themselves?"

Whip-whap

"That sounds about right," he said, after a long pause and some nervous facial-hair pulling. Anyone could see that his lumpy face was full of doubt, and he began lowering and raising his window electronically, which, while impressive technologically, was an unneeded distraction and/or letting the rain in.

I gave it one last shot, clicking to get his attention. "And all really evil people, well, they had to start somewhere, right? They didn't just murder someone or overthrow the government. Not right off the bat. No. They built up to it." I was enjoying myself, a testament to the convivial atmosphere that had developed between us, which I found ripe for spitballing. "First they, I don't know, interrupted someone at a brunch. Then they jumped a bus-stop queue. That gave them a kick. So they tripped up a cat. Then, before they knew it, they were moonwalking on a priest's grave."

It was my turn to bounce in my seat. "From there? Well, it's a hop, skip, and a jump to ransacking a village and bathing in the blood of your enemies, isn't it?"

Ricky's nose wrinkled as he considered it.

Whip-whap

"I guess that's... true, yeah?" he said, very slowly.

"So?" I prodded.

He raised his window a final time. "Okay, I guess?"

"Great!"

And just like that, we were off to Waterstones.

Whip-whap

A Manifesto:

This book lies.
You are who you are.
You cannot change.
It is what it is.
I'm sorry it's not more.
But it could be less.
Get on with your life and/or give up.

26

"I'm in," I said, as I entered Waterstones. A prickling sensation rippled up and—I suppose, also—down my spine. Just as when I'd thwacked Cliff, it felt good to be bad, or, at least, prickly, which, if not good, was good-adjacent.

"*He's in,*" Ricky repeated, redundantly, because it sounded cool. The shop was doing a brisk trade. I sniffed and smelt apple sauce and chumminess. The average Nottingham resident graffitied more books than they read, so most of the clientele were clustered around the calendars, cookbooks, and assorted non-book knick-knacks.

Trying to look innocuous, I casually, while fake-yawning, picked up a book about Persian cuisine. I flicked through the pages and—while the photography was impressive—had to agree with Maureen, Tabby's recently swindled and/or advised citizen: there's no reason a dish should contain more than six ingredients. At the group home, we ate chips five nights a week. There appeared to be no chips in all of Persia. I put the book down, sure that even if pomegranates were real, they were a fad.

I turned and saw that a small man in a tight black Waterstones shirt was staring at me from over near the tills.

Since people regularly stare at me, I saw no cause for concern but still bent down and pretended to tie my non-existent shoelaces.

I stood up.

There he was.

He'd appeared as if by magic.

Not so much up in my face but in my chest. Licking distance. He was five foot three, or perhaps four. His face was narrow and sharp and there was dirt on his cheek. He had too many teeth. His jaw jutted out. He had angry dark-brown eyes that commanded respect and a thick brown beard that crumbs wouldn't dare get caught in. If there were a school for angry leprechauns, he'd have finished top of its class.

"We - got - a - problem - here?" His voice was low and measured, and he left gaps between each word. Everything about this man screamed menace.

I tried to stay calm and turned my head slightly in case my earpiece was visible. "Sorry?" I said, softly.

"Do - we - have - a - problem, you - and - I?"

"Erm?" I nibbled my cheek. "I have some? People have said. I don't know about you." With each word out of my mouth, his piercing, empathy-free eyes narrowed. "N-no," I stammered. "We're fine."

"You - don't - look - fine, is all?"

"That's kind of rude."

"*Is it starting already?*" Ricky asked. "*Unbelievable.*"

The man tossed a thumb back towards the rest of the store. "What you looking for?"

"I guess... I suppose... a book?"

"You - don't - know - then?"

"A book." I nodded. "Yes."

"Uh-huh. Genre?"

"Self-help?"

He looked me down and then up and cleared his throat. "Should have guessed."

He made a sucking sound with his mouth, and I had the sense he was evaluating me and whether I'd passed whatever test this was. He flicked his head backwards. "Left past the life-size Jamie Oliver."

"Thanks." I stumbled away as fast as I could.

"*What was all that about?*" Ricky asked.

"No idea."

"*We been rumbled already?*"

I glanced over my shoulder. He'd gone. "I haven't even done anything yet."

I took a deep breath, rubbed some of the bubble wrap in my trouser pocket, enjoying the tight, crisp pop against my leg, and tried to relax into the delicious muzak rippling out of the overhead speakers.

All I wanted for Christmas was the destruction of my enemies and perhaps a quick bath in their blood. Didn't even need to be a whole bath, really. If push came to shove, which it so often did, I'd settle for a cat wash in the sink of my enemies.

Feeling a little better, I snaked my way through the crowds and a section devoted to trivia-based stocking fillers. Then I spotted him, this Jamie Oliver character, who, thankfully, held a book with his name on it. His name was everywhere, I now noticed. He also did cookbooks, apparently. He looked like he enjoyed a chip.

I checked around me again and decided that the metaphorical coast was clear. Nottingham was a long way from the non-metaphorical coast, of course, which was perhaps why you never saw mermaids.

The pockets of my anorak bulged. "I prickle," I said, then regretted it, as I moved towards a table at the entrance to self-help whose job was drawing attention to the New and Notable. "Putting plan in operation," I said, while pretending to be enthralled in some gibberish calling itself *The Power of Now*.

"*Damn right you are, fella*," said Ricky.

Carefully, being sure I wasn't under surveillance, I yanked a sticker from my pocket, surreptitiously removed its backing paper, then stuck it onto the cover, re-titling it *The Power of LIES*.

The prickling intensified dramatically, becoming a slinky of electricity that slithered down from the dull brown hairs atop my head to the in-grown hair on my left big toe.

I looked around. I saw no one. I put the book down. "First book stickered."

"*Baller*."

Inside its sky-blue cover, I slipped one of my bookmark-sized manifestos. "And manifestoed."

Then I did it again.

And then again.

And then again.

Tony huckster Robbins's *Unlimited Power* became *Unlimited LIES*.

Rich Dad Poor Dad became *Rich LIES Poor LIES*.

LIES to Win Friends and Influence People

The Alchemist LIES

The 7 LIES of Highly Effective People

Who Moved My LIES?

The LIES of Positive Thinking

Men Are from LIES and LIES Are from Mars. (This one wasn't my best work and if anything, I regretted the usage of a second sticker.)

I felt a rush of power for the second time that day. I was standing up for what I believed in, soaring far above and beyond this place and time, exalted.

"It's glorious, Ricky."

"The revolution starts here," he agreed.

I was defacing private property, bringing down a billion-pound industry built on LIES and false hope.

"I think you were right," I said. "I was born to do this. I'm doing my life's work. The way I feel, Ricky, we can think seriously about destroying the Hoodlums and/or the moon."

"Pukka," he said, and I knew he was clicking and/or throwing gangster signs and the thought of it made me smile.

A hand clamped onto my shoulder. "Who - is - Ricky - then?"

I tried to turn, but the guy had my neck with his other hand and held it straight. "You're - mine - now," he growled. "You sick little puppy." He took the hand from my shoulder and yanked out my supposedly invisible earpiece.

"Who are you?" he shouted into it.

I could hear Ricky's voice faintly. *"Who are you? Where's James?"*

"I'll ask the questions. Who sent you?"

"No one."

"Mossad?"

"Who's that?"

"IRA? Tamil Tigers? WHO DO YOU WORK FOR?" Not satisfied with the answer, he then dropped the earpiece to the floor, and stamped on it. "I - think - we're - alone - now," the guy said to me, as he moved his hands under my armpits, turned me in a short, sharp circle, and dragged me, seemingly without effort, towards the rear of the store. I felt like a cheap plastic chair on a lawn.

"Help," I whispered.

As we moved from self-help, a man and a woman—long married, I suspected, by how much they resembled each other facially—approached the New and Notable table and casually browsed it in the futile pursuit of personal betterment and/or ignoring my plight.

The male half of the couple picked up a book. I strained to listen. "*The Power of LIES*," he said. "That sounds interesting."

"Does as well," said the female, "and it's two for one. So does this one over 'ere about alchemists. Bunch of bloody crooks. Good someone's finally exposed 'em. Let's get them both, shall we, duck?"

I wriggled to free myself. It didn't work. "Keep wiggling, little piggy. I like it when you wiggle."

Something was happening again, and I had lost control of that thing again, and was entirely at its mercy, again.

It would not be merciful.

"You're leaving here in a wheelchair, pal—I was special forces," he said. We'd reached some hitherto unseen door near Erotica and he threw me through it and I landed in a confused heap in a nondescript corridor next to a whiteboard holding a staff chart written in green marker pen. There was little to recommend about the handwriting.

I was in shock, disbelief, and fear. How had this man, this pocket-sized man, so effortlessly moved and/or bested me? He was practically foaming at the mouth. Short men had the most to prove, I supposed. He'd more than proved himself to me, so I hoped he could now move on with his life and/or not end mine.

He stepped closer. "This is assault," I said, holding my hands up to keep him back. "Call the police."

He licked his lips. "Damn right it is."

"Call them!"

"You think they'll come here? For you?" He reached down, knocked my hands away, grabbed a fistful of my anorak, and dragged me along the floor into a small, windowless room. He left, slamming the door shut, then locked it from the outside.

I sat up and checked myself for injuries. How had this happened? What about my famed stealth skills? *It was the enjoyment*, I decided. I'd lost control of myself amidst the prickling. The room had a metal table and four chairs. It was sterile.

I don't know how long I was alone in it, on the floor, rubbing my head and feeling sorry for myself, but if I had to guess, if you put a gun to my head and really squeezed me for an inkling, I'd say it was five, perhaps even six minutes.

The angry, compact security man returned.

"You can't do this," I said. "Let me go."

He held aloft a copy of *The 7 LIES of Highly Effective People*. "And you can't do this, Sandra Bollocks. Sit down," he said, pointing at the red chair on my side of the table. "And turn out your pockets."

"No," I said. "I know my rights." I didn't know my rights. "This is totally over the top."

"And this"—he waved the book in my face—"this is below the belt."

He slapped his palms down on the table and stared at me, baring his teeth. It was brave of him to bring height into it. Many things were below his belt.

"You can't drag people around. Or lock them in rooms. This is kidnapping."

He tipped his head back and laughed. "Don't talk to me about kidnapping. What's happening to you, it's a walk in the park compared to what I *want* to do. I was in Kabul. I once killed a man with a spoon."

"Witches?"

"What?"

"The cabal."

"No, cretin. *Kabul*. Afghanistan."

"Ah," I said. "Not much of a traveller. I went to Mansfield once. Tabby and I ran away from the group home. A Mansfieldian man stole my shoes and threw them up a tree. We slept in the park that night. I didn't like it, too much was different. Also, my socks were wet, and I had a severe case of the sniffles. They grounded me when we got back to the group home, which seemed unnecessary because I'd decided I didn't want to go anywhere else anyway. They also beat us, but that was to be expected."

I was babbling. It was my nerves.

The security guard looked bored and/or horrified. "Did I ask for your life story, PJ Larvae?"

I sat down as he had asked. He sat opposite. We were eye to eye.

"That's just one sad chapter," I said. "I'm trying to... I mean, I guess... I'm a human. Like you."

"You're trying to make me pity you. It's a trick and a transparent one."

"I'm just babbling."

He pointed at his face. His movements were jerky. "Is this the face of a man you should underestimate?"

"I'm not underestimating you."

"Yes, you are. You came into MY place of work, in the daytime, and you took a steaming shit on the rug, didn't you?"

"I didn't know you worked here."

"Oh, well. That makes it worse, almost." He sighed but somehow made it violent. "Do you think I want to work security at Waterstones?"

It was a job. I didn't even have a job. There wasn't much glamour in it, but this was Nottingham—anything with glamour flew south, like a migrating bird.

"No?" I guessed.

"Yet here I am. Makes you think, doesn't it?"

"Err... yes?"

"Makes you think how many rungs I must have fallen from Kabul to here. Probably makes you wonder why, doesn't it? Who I might have crossed? Who might have crossed me? What corners I might have cut?"

I turned out my pockets.

"Bingo," he said, as I dropped a stack of manifestos and stickers onto the table. "B-I-N-G-O."

"I'd barely started," I said. "They're just stickers. They come off."

He ripped some of them up and threw them at me. They swirled in the air. "It's disrespect, that's what it is. Sticky disrespect." He turned, pulled a corded phone off the wall, and stabbed at the number eight. "Boss. Got something in here you need to see. *Pronto.*"

I don't know how long we sat there together in angry silence, but if I had to guess, if you put a gun to my head and really squeezed me for an inkling, I'd say it was two and a half, perhaps even three minutes.

The door opened. A lanky, thin drip of a man entered. He wore a cheap navy polyester suit two sizes too big. His name—according to the tag on his chest—was Chris, STORE MANAGER. He was, perhaps, nineteen years old.

The security guard licked his lips. "Real live wire we got here, Boss."

Chris, STORE MANAGER, picked up a manifesto. He read it then put it gently down. He picked up a sticker, peeled off the backing, put the backing paper carefully back on, then took a long breath. "Have you even read *Rich Dad Poor Dad*?"

"No," I confessed.

"Well," he said, sounding more disappointed than angry, "it changed my life."

"How?"

"The magic of compound interest, that's how."

"That's not magic, it's... I'm not sure."

Chris, STORE MANAGER, tipped back in his chair. "What are you trying to achieve with this nonsense?"

I put my head in my hands and rubbed while considering my options. While most people thought honesty was the best policy, having worked in insurance, I knew honesty was a bugger to get any kind of payout from. And even if I'd wanted to be honest, I wasn't sure what I'd say. What were Ricky and I doing? I think we were trying, mostly, to distract ourselves from the bleakness of our existences.

"Out with it, Susan Saran-don't."

"Err..." I stopped rubbing and peeked out from between splayed fingers. "My friend sort of bullied me into being a villain. This is... I'm being a bad boy, I guess? I don't know... It's new. It was kind of thrilling. There was some prickling, even. But then all this..." I dropped my hands to the table.

A vein throbbed in the security guard's neck as he ground his left fist into his right palm. "He's high as a freaking kite, Boss."

"Calm down, DJ."

"I'm not high."

"Look at his eyes. He's a tweaker. He's giving me the heebie-jeebies."

"That's normal," I said. "I give them to everyone."

"Has he actually stolen anything?" asked Chris, STORE MANAGER.

"What's a tweaker?" I asked. I'd been called many things, including, memorably, salmon-spazbucket by a Hare Krishna outside Bargain Booze, but never a tweaker.

"No, Boss," DJ conceded. "Not that I can see."

"And the stickers come off?"

I nodded. "I paid extra for that."

"You're just weird, mate," DJ growled. "An ugly little frog man."

He shouldn't keep bringing height into it, I thought, before realising that *I* was, once again, bringing his height into it. I did the same with Pat and her weight. And so-called Jamie Oliver and his love of chips. And Chris, STORE MANAGER, and his ill-fitting suit. And Ricky and his pathetic, ludicrous beard. You'd think someone so harshly and superficially judged by the world would be more generous to others, yet this wasn't the case, I was coming to understand. *It's deep in us, I guess. Whatever it is.*

"I'm going to have to run this past Head Office," Chris, STORE MANAGER, said.

DJ jumped up as if electrocuted. "Not those pencil-pushers. They've no idea what it's like out here in the trenches of literature. It's a word war, we're its foot soldiers, and we're losing."

Chris, STORE MANAGER, hesitated then picked up the phone.

"These books are all lies," I said as he dialled. "They won't make you rich. They won't make you friends or help you influence people. You're selling false hope to the gullible. We're all stuck as we are."

He frowned but hung up the phone. "Then why are you trying to change?"

"What? I'm not."

"You're trying to be evil."

I hadn't noticed the contradiction.

"And anyway," he continued, "self-help isn't about change, per se. It's about releasing the authentic person already inside you. The person you were born to be. There's a book you should read by Tony—"

"You were born to be the manager of Waterstones?"

"Yes," he said without hesitation. "I believe I was."

"I wasn't born to do this," DJ snarled. "I was born to do much, much more. How about I take him out to the alley, Boss, rough him up?"

He looked down his nose at DJ. "You're not working the fairgrounds anymore. This is Waterstones. We're respectable. Middle class."

DJ cracked his knuckles. "Say - the - word, Boss. THE W-O-R-D."

Chris, STORE MANAGER, narrowed his eyes and looked at me. "Have you learned your lesson?"

"Absolutely," I said, without knowing if it was true.

Chris, STORE MANAGER, stood, hung his head, shook it slowly, and said, "Put him in the book then kick him out."

He left. We sat, DJ and I, him staring at me or rather into me, making strange, loud noises with his mouth as if he were chewing glass. Eventually he tired of menacing me. "Your lucky day, Goldie Prawn."

"Not really."

"I could make it much worse?" He turned to a small cupboard with sliding doors.

"Err... no, that's okay."

He took out a Polaroid camera and snapped my picture without asking. "Not that anyone's going to forget that face," he said, lunging across the table. He picked me up by my middle and carried me back through to the shop entrance on his shoulder. Customers turned and one cheered and I went very red as I bounced with each of his fast, hostile steps. It was like riding a tiny donkey. Not that I'd ridden a donkey of any size.

At the entrance, he shouted to a cashier, who ran out from behind the counter and held the door open for him. "Good riddance," he said, as he launched me into the street. I landed on my hip and let out a loud, unbecoming scream.

A few people looked and snickered, but a man lying in a crumpled heap, rubbing his hip, confused, sad, thankful not to have lost his life to a psychopath who claimed to have killed a man with a spoon, in a pool of his own stickers and manifestos didn't raise even a heckle on Nottingham High Street.

27

I hobbled, my pride and body bruised, back to Ricky, my delusional, fairweather, self-proclaimed sidekick. He was relaxing, as usual, in the driver's seat, eating a small pie while rocking in enjoyment, throwing gangster signs to rap music. He jumped to turn the stereo down as I opened the door, concern etched into the cheeks and forehead of his youthful face. "I looked for you *everywhere*, buddy. What the hell happened?"

I sat, sighed, and rubbed my bruised hip. "If you looked for me everywhere, you would have found me, no?"

"Well, you're here now," he said, and put the small metal pie tray into a plastic bag at his feet. "How'd it go? Badly, I'm guessing, since you're all scuffed up and your eyes are bulging more than normal. I promise I swept the entire shop like five times, but there was no sign of you or that madman."

"This was really, really stressful, Ricky."

"Who was he? He sounded mean."

"DJ, the security guard. He locked me in a windowless room and threatened me, and the manager nearly called Head Office."

Ricky looked impressed. "That escalated quickly."

"I've rarely experienced slow escalation."

"How many books did you deface?"

"Nine," I mumbled. "Maybe. But they sold better because of it, Ricky. You might have been right about that whole subtlety thing."

His shoulders dropped. "So I guess we're not criminal masterminds?"

"It doesn't seem like it. But I am banned from Waterstones."

"Was it at least proper thrilling to be evil?"

I blinked slowly, taking a moment to collect and reflect and, I think, mourn. It had been, but the thrill was so much briefer than the awful consequences of it. Each test had been a miserable, useless failure. I was a bit proud that I'd tried something new and exciting and could tell my (dead) parents, Cliff, Tabby, and perhaps even Esme about it, but it made no sense to keep doing this, knowing that these attempts would never lead to anything positive, pleasant prickling aside.

I picked at my trousers. The knees had significant-but-not-fatal grazing. "Life's thrilling enough already."

Ricky nodded. "You got humbled by a security guard at Waterstones, a man with no training or power. It's not an encouraging start. Maybe you're not a natural villain. You'd be caught before you got an outfit and catchphrase never mind an island lair shaped like your face."

I lowered my head. "What gets me, though, is that I didn't do that much wrong this time. Not like with the Rescue Room or Al the homeless guy. I didn't even have time for my uncommon senses to lead me astray."

"No?"

"DJ was on to me so fast. As soon as I entered the store, really. He'd decided I was no good and/or up to no good. Yet there were plenty of other people around. I was just a man browsing cookbooks, as far as he knew. So why did he react so strongly to me? And treat me so harshly? It was like I was... destined to fail."

"This is getting a bit woo-woo, buddy." He reached into the plastic bag. "Want a mince pie?"

"I can't risk a mince pie right now. The chain of custody."

"Sorry?"

"Ricky, you know how when some people walk into a room it lights up?"

"Yeah." He grinned. "My uncle Sanjay is like that. Charisma on a stick."

"When I enter a room, the opposite happens. There's a kind of general dimming. People check their watches, or now, their mobile telephones. Someone says something about needing to get home to feed the cat." I raised my hand to stop him interrupting. "And that's best-case scenario, Ricky. *Best case*. It's more likely that someone will ask me aggressively what I think I'm doing in that room. Or just grab me and throw me out and slam the door in my face."

"Come on, buddy. You're exaggerating, no?"

I remembered Cliff and how I'd tried to be mad at him after I'd learned he was dating Tabby. It hadn't been possible. I knew why now: beauty disarms. And, therefore, the opposite also had to be true: a lack of beauty *arms*.

"I think it's about how I look and move and think," I continued. "People want symmetry. And confidence. And normal-sized, less-penetrating eyes. And faddish, modern, cropped hair, like yours. They expect the people they meet to want to take up space. They don't expect someone scuttling and hiding in a medium-visibility British Heart Foundation jacket."

With each line I was crumpling deeper into my seat.

"It's like I start every social interaction at a disadvantage I don't have the common sense or charisma or looks to overcome."

I raised my hand higher to hold back the disagreement building in him. "I provoke people, Ricky. I bring out the worst in them. Sometimes they pretend they're on my side, but they never are. It was no different with the homeless man or the policeman, or my ex-boss, Scott, and I suppose even the film crew back when all this started."

"You're a *provocateur*," he said, in a poor foreign accent, undercutting the severity of what I was saying. This should have annoyed me, but I still appreciated how generous he was in his descriptions of me.

"In the exclusively negative sense, yes. We're just wasting time and giving ourselves false hope with all this nonsense." I gestured at nothing in particular, but he knew what I meant. I meant him and me.

"I wouldn't say that," he said, but pulled his mobile telephone from his trouser pocket. He inhaled deeply, gathering his strength for a lengthy rebuttal. Ricky wouldn't just give up on us. He was down, visibly so, but not out. He needed us. And perhaps I needed him. And so, I settled in for the hard sell of test four.

Instead, all the light drained from his eyes. He ran a hand through his hair, and it got stuck halfway. "I'm wrong about my whole good versus bad theory and sidekickery and everything really, aren't I?"

I hesitated then nodded.

"Then I'm stuck in this taxi?" He banged on the steering wheel with both fists. The horn went off. Several people looked and/or scowled and he raised his palms in meek apology.

"Unless you've got any other great ideas or inventions that don't involve me?" I said.

"Hmm." He considered it. "I was thinking of becoming a penetration tester. That would be pretty sick. You think there's any need for that in Nottingham, though?"

"Pornography? Aren't you a bit young and not traditionally dashing?"

"No, it's like a for-hire spy, basically. People pay you to break in and test their security and stuff."

"That's not a real thing."

"*Is.*"

"In Nottingham? The only high-value thing we have is the motorway that takes you to other places."

Ricky's mouth opened and then closed and then opened. "Maybe."

"And you're quite large and lumbering."

"So?"

"And memorable. You've a memorable energy. You don't blend."

His eyes hardened. "Neither do you."

He turned away, and we sat in angry silence. I wondered if I'd too quickly dismissed his latest pie-in-the-sky notion.

"I invested in this new singing-fish thing," he said, almost apologetically. "Big Mouth Billy. It's a trophy catch that sings. I'm the exclusive UK distributor."

A small, wet wave of sadness crashed over me. The silence returned. Ricky stared up at three small birds twittering on a power cable. "What if you could say anything to anyone? I was thinking about a service to broadcast short messages."

I blew a raspberry. "The harassment, Ricky, it would be endless."

He seemed to have halved in sized during our conversation. Enthusiasm inflates a person, I suppose, and I'd robbed him of it.

"Yeah, you're probably right. Just another dumb idea," he said with a sigh. "I'm sorry. About everything."

"It's not your fault."

"I convinced you."

"I made myself convince-able."

Two young men sporting neck tattoos strutted past in the green parkas of the Hoodlums.

Ricky scowled at them. "You're just an odd duck with boggle eyes and terrible luck and common sense while I'm a humble, brilliant taxi driver's son forced to toil my days away in the family business. And the police won't help us. And the city's gone to shit. And the Hoodlums have won. And there's no justice for people like us."

I cleared my throat. "That's about the measure of it, yes."

He looked away then snapped back. "'Someday a real rain will come and wash all this scum off the streets.'" His accent was now a sort-of bargain-bin Cliff.

"It rains every day, Ricky. It's drizzling right now. It's not enough."

"'I got some bad ideas in my head.'"

"Yes, but you're young."

"'You talking to me?'" The accent had become Italian, or perhaps Italian American.

"There's no one else here."

He puffed out his chest. "'You talkin' to me? You talkin' TO ME?'"

"We've clarified this."

"'Well, I'm the only one here, so...'" He grinned. "Travis Bickle."

"Who is Travis Bickle?"

"*Taxi Driver.*"

"A movie?"

"A great one."

"Does he get in a pickle?"

"Sure does. A murderous pickle."

"My least-favourite kind of pickle."

Conversation faltered. Goodbyes are hard. It was why I'd always been so restrained with my hellos.

"I feel a bit like that character at the three-quarter mark of every story who's failed and thinks all hope is lost," Ricky said.

"All hope is lost. But it was lost a long time ago, if that's any consolation?"

"Not so much."

"I enjoyed it," I said. "The parts that weren't terrifying. I'm glad you found me in that bin."

"Lift home?"

"It's fine. I'll walk."

He nodded. "Bye, James."

"Bye, Ricky Sidekick." I reached for the door handle then stopped. "Wait. There is one last thing I need you to do."

28

Climbing out of the taxi, I felt sad and heavy, like a depressed piano. Everything I touched caught fire, metaphorically. I'd always known this and yet I'd let Ricky convince me otherwise. That was over now. I would miss Ricky. New friends were rare.

I remembered Esme. She didn't seem to mind how little I offered. Did we have friend potential? Outside of the Misfits and in the real world, even? I had given her a can of Vimto, so there was that. We weren't an obvious match on account of the fact that she was reasonably normal, brave, and devastatingly direct. Yet it seemed like she was in a desperate and/or lonely situation and had reached out.

I slipped on my medium-visibility jacket and walked to Dunkin' Donuts.

"Drama a llama," she said, leaning on the counter with her elbows. The shop was empty. It was weird to see her in a conventional uniform that covered her many distinctive physical and—I suppose, also—attractive qualities. She looked like a caged bird of paradise leaning there, her wild red locks threatening to split her tight orange hairnet. She had forgone her black lipstick. Behind her was an enormous wall of brightly coloured racked donuts. The special was cinnamon espresso, allegedly.

It was all a bit much. I felt like that pauper, Charlie, lured to the chocolate factory under false, competition-winning pretences only for a management position to be foisted upon his naive shoulders. Anyone could see those Oompa-Loompas were on the verge of unionising and were going to make his young life hell.

"You been volunteering?" she asked, when I said nothing for longer than was conventional and/or expected. "Good on ya."

"Oh..." I thumbed the jacket I'd forgotten to take off. "Sort of." Liars need good memories, and while I had an excellent one, it was clogged with trauma. I took it off. "No, actually. I don't volunteer. This is urban camouflage."

"Squirm a worm," she said, and laughed. "You're a dark horse and that is, generally, the best kind of horse."

"Do you make those up on the spot?"

"The donuts?"

"The rhymes."

"Of course I bloody do. You want to try?"

"Fling a..." My eyes roamed. Time passed. I gurgled. "No animals rhyme with fling, apparently?"

"Yeah, sometimes easier to work from the animal backwards, I find."

"Cow a"—my lips moved rapidly as I brute-force-tested verbs—"smow. Smow a cow? Oh, that's rubbish. I'm not good at doing things on the spot. Or after careful planning, really. Other than making nemeses. I made a new nemesis just now, actually."

She squinted. "I'm starting to wonder if donuts are my nemesis. Do you want one?" She turned to them. "On the house, I guess?" She looked back at a smaller room with its door open. Did she have a boss? Do you need a boss to sell donuts? It didn't seem like something that would benefit from too many layers of organisational bureaucracy.

"Sure," I said. "If you'll split it with me on a bench of my choosing?"

"What with all that drizzle? It's December, J. How about we go get sozzled indoors?" Her head kinked. "Spoons?"

My eyes circled as I did a quick mental calculation. It was early afternoon so the students and the alcoholics—and there was significant overlap between the two groups—would be sleeping one off while the after-work crowd would still be at their desks sending each other virus-filled chain emails. And nothing felt as threatening with Esme around.

"I guess I could use a Vimto."

She looked up at the clock. "I've still got a good hour to go."

"That's okay. I know a place to hide. Several, actually."

Wetherspoons Public House was basking in the glory of a recent royal-blue paint job. Six different signs outside advertised that they had Sky TV and, presumably, weren't afraid to use it. It looked like the sort of place where every meal was in a deal and anything edible was breaded, including bread.

While nervous about entering an unknown pub, I tried my best to present a calm, stoic front as I held open the door for Esme so that she'd have to enter first. Inside, there was a long copper-heavy bar flanked by enormous televisions showing tiny men racing large horses. I wondered if DJ had ever been a jockey?

Esme strolled up to a free spot at the bar, hands deep into her trench-coat pockets. "Fine day for it, right?"

"Drizzling," said the barman, a stocky character with an anchor tattoo peeking out from the rolled-up sleeve of his blue Wetherspoons-branded shirt. A tea towel hung over his shoulder. "What you 'avin'?"

"Pint of non-specific," she said. "Dealer's choice."

"Spitfire," came the reply. "It's on special."

"Lovely."

"Vimto, please," I said.

He ignored me and poured Esme's pint. "One pound twenty, luv."

"Oi," she said, and then turned to me. "Vimto for my man here."

He squinted. "Who?"

"You taking the piss?" she asked.

He sniffed and looked away. "I think I'm coming down with something."

"Vimto," she repeated.

"We don't have it," he said, reluctantly. "And it's for kids."

"Sparkling water then?" I said. "Slice of lemon. No, wait, hold the lemon."

He didn't look at me, but he did grunt, which was, at least, some form of acknowledgement. Esme paid although it was almost free.

"It's different to Albert's," I said, as we slipped into a booth by the bar. A man in a flat cap on a stool had fallen asleep cuddling his beer. The ceilings were low and the floor had a swirly green-and-blue carpet that I felt sure was under-appreciated by the customer base, the average age of which was pushing seventy and so they probably all had cataracts.

"Friendlier, you mean?"

"Brighter," I said. "Sportier. But also flatter, somehow. Like they left its lid off."

"It was like he didn't see you," she said, watching the barman from the corner of her eye.

"No, he just didn't want to."

"Do you think face blindness is real?" she asked.

"Peter? I don't know. And why my face but not his wife's?"

"Distinctive," she said. "Yours is not a face you forget. You know?" She leaned forward. "You know what I mean, James, right?" I pulled back. She stroked the owl tattoo on her arm.

I glanced at it. "Why an owl?"

"My spirit animal."

"Sheep," I said, "for me. Maybe a naked mole rat."

"I have a thing about eyes. Large eyes." She widened hers in an imitation of an owl. "You'd have to try really, really hard not to find beauty in a pair of eyes, no matter who owns them." Her tongue left her mouth. "The bigger the better. I've got a thing about licking eyes, actually. It's called worming. It's a sort of fetish, I guess?" She licked her lips.

That same unselfconsciousness was in play again. I wasn't ready for it. Sparkling water whooshed up my nose and I coughed and spluttered and it sprayed out and onto my trousers.

"You okay?"

"Wrong hole," I said.

"You sound like my ex-boyfriend."

"Sorry?"

"Nothing."

I became even more self-conscious about my massive eyes and the seat got hot beneath me and I wriggled and time passed just about, but not really, as I searched for a plausible but safe subject change to drag us up from the sexual gutter. I considered the Amish but they had to be at it like rabbits, what with all those sturdy, woodworking, dungareed children.

"I thought I had special powers," I said, hastily. "Or my friend did. Now he doesn't and I don't either."

Esme leaned back. Then forward. Then back. Then downed a third of her beer. I had confused her enough that she'd stopped telling me about her fetishes, so I filled her in on what had happened at Waterstones. Then I looped all the way back to how I'd met Ricky. We'd already revealed so much of our stories at Motley Misfits that it didn't feel strange to continue in this honest, candid vain. Throughout, she laughed and smiled and winked and seemed to enjoy my eccentricities rather than finding them threatening. She also never said she felt unwell, asked if something smelt bad, or told me she had to feed her cat.

"How was your day?" I asked, when I'd run out of both steam and anecdote.

She shrugged and did a duck impersonation with her lips. "Had a lunchtime date with this fella I met on the Internet."

"You can meet men on the Internet?"

"Yeah, online dating."

"I thought that was about calendars?"

She paused. "Have you dated lately?" She lifted a hand from the table and then dropped it again. "Actually, you know, I'm just going to assume no. Well, lucky you, is all I can say. I'm thirty-five. I know, I don't look it." She looked left then right then blew a kiss at no one in particular. On the screen, a tiny man crossed a line first on his horse (also dark) and it made many people happy, especially the man. The horse seemed indifferent.

"Weird things happen in the dating market at my age," she continued. "Men have all the power. And that's something I don't like. And Nottingham isn't exactly a hotbed of intellectualism, let's be honest. You're giddy if the guy uses full stops. They're always just braggarts, psychopaths, and investment sodding bankers. Today's was an investment banker, actually." She stopped to take another enthusiastic swig of beer, burped, then wiped her mouth with the back of her hand. "Barely understood a bloody word he said. It was all derivative of derivatives. No one listens, James. You know what I mean? And worse than that, really, is that they're boring."

"Boring can be good."

"Tell me what I just said?"

"But you've already said it?"

"Do it."

"Erm..." I played back my inner tape. "Weird things happen in the dating market when you get into your thirties. Men suddenly have all the power. It's really horrible out there. And Nottingham isn't exactly a hotbed of intellectualism, let's be honest. You're giddy if the guy uses full stops. Should I go on?"

"Plough a cow," she said, and grinned. "Oh, fixed the cow one for you. You might have missed a *practically*, maybe, but otherwise, that was pretty much perfect."

She was making a point, but I wasn't sure what it was and whether it was sharp.

"What you doing Thursday night?" she asked.

"Sudoku," I blurted, then regretted. I only had loose Sudoku plans.

"I'm performing. Only poetry, mind. But I think it's about time I get back on the stage."

Here was further confirmation: she was no Misfit.

"Where?" I asked.

"King's Head."

"Will it rhyme?"

"Maybe, baby."

"What is it you like about poetry?"

"It's..." She tapped the tabletop. "Well, I like any honest attempt to express the craziness of all this, really, you know?" Her eyes wandered around the bar. "Just the weird bat shit nonsense of all of it, I suppose? Poetry doesn't have a lot of rules, really, despite what you might think, and that creates a space and sometimes, although it's rare, someone can fill that space with something really, really fucking wonderful."

"That sounds... nice, actually?"

"So?" she prodded.

"Uh-huh."

"Do you want to come then?"

"Just me?"

She stroked the edge of her pint glass. "Bring who you like."

"I'll think about it," I said. "The poetry."

A shape appeared to my left and hovered. It whistled. The shape was corpulent and cleared its throat loudly before letting its mouth gape. I looked up. My heart plunged deep into my stomach.

She was sipping from a pint of cider. "Well... well... *well*. Of all the people I thought I might see in here, you were *very* low on the list, Ferdie."

"This is a private conversation," I said.

"Last I checked, sunshine, this was a public house. What you got there? Sparkling water?" She rolled her eyes. "Classic."

"Who's *she*?" Esme asked.

Pat looked Esme over. "Who are you, Night of the Living Dread?" She turned back to me. "She your therapist, Ferdie?"

She didn't wait for my answer before making her next guess. "Social worker?"

"N—"

"Probation officer? Life coach?"

"No."

"Actually"—Pat tapped the end of her nose with her index finger—"no, you look familiar. Do you... work the toilets at Walkabout?"

Esme's hand balled into a fist.

"Bin lady?" Pat guessed. "Part-time prostitute?"

Esme stood. She was a head taller than Pat but a third as wide. "You should think carefully about what you say next, bitch. Just as I'm thinking carefully about the fun ways I'm going to stop you being able to say it."

If Pat felt threatened, she wasn't letting it show. She looked down at me. "If you're with him, darling, it's you who should think carefully." She snorted. "I could tell you some stories."

I hung my head, waiting for it to be over. The man next to us had smelt blood and was awake now, watching the show.

"We all got stories," said Esme. "But it's only his I'm interested in. Now take that stupid grin away from me before I wipe it off your face."

Pat rolled her tongue around her mouth. "Got a mouth on her, ain't she, Ferdie? Shame you'll never get to use it." She laughed and turned and lumbered off towards the fruit machines.

Esme sat down, saw me slouching and/or ruing, and grabbed my chin. "Keep your chin up, J. *Always*."

"Okay," I mumbled.

"Now, who was that?"

I sighed. "No one."

"And why did she call you Ferdie?"

"I am him, *sort of*."

Another tiny man on another enormous horse defied

long odds: twenty-two to one. What were the odds of Esme and me remaining friends? Much, much longer. It wasn't that I offered nothing. It was that I offered less than nothing. I was a net negative. Always had and would be. Now, because of me, Esme was being insulted in public. This had been a mistake. All of it. You can't outrun your past. You might create a small distance, enough to lose sight of it briefly, but it's still there, chasing you, and the second you let up, it will destroy your present and any hopes you had for a future in which you'd be different.

I slipped out of the booth. "I have to go," I said. "Sorry."

29

I crashed into Tabby's room, needing comfort and/or distraction. Alone, I would only mope and lament. "This was a day I would like help forgetting."

She and Cliff were on the couch, balled in a tight knot of attraction. Tabby's perm looked even more frazzled than usual. There was a strong air of relaxation in the room. Cliff was smoking marijuana or heroin or something that was on fire and in stick form and hanging from his mouth. He puffed and then passed it to Tabby.

"Tabby!" I screamed. "No!"

They both giggled. "You should try it," she said. "It's fun. Makes you giggly."

"Everything is fun until you end up in an alleyway without any trousers giving sexual favours for Happy Meals."

The laughing grew quite raucous—so the drugs were already ravaging their systems. I moved closer and peered into Tabby's eyes, whose whites were a shade of deep red that signified love, illicit narcotics, and/or both. My close attention only made them laugh harder. I hadn't known that drugs made you laugh like this. It didn't sound that bad, as a characteristic of a thing. And if Tabby—a woman who oozed reasonableness—was doing them, could they really be that dangerous?

"You know how you're teaching me things?" Cliff asked, a glint of conspiracy in his eye.

"The thwacking?"

He held out his heroin hash stick, which was now a pitiful nub. "It's time you let me return the favour."

"ARE YOU MAD?"

"Get him," Cliff said, and they leapt on me, sweeping me off my feet in the non-romantic, non-metaphorical sense. They wrestled me into submission, which was made easier by my bruised hip. Tabby held my jaw open and her foreigner accomplice blew smoke into me.

"I tingle," I said, thirty, perhaps even thirty-one minutes later, as I lay like a starfish on that fluffy purple carpet. "I'm tingling. Do I have shingles? Do shingles tingle? Or at least mingle?" I held my hand up to the light, turning it, mesmerised. I noticed how smooth and youthful and unblemished by labour my skin was. This was something I'd lose if I converted to Amish-ism. I still thought often of the Amish. I craved to be a simple man in a world I understood, one without whimsical modern indulgences like microwaves and MRI scanners. Sure, God would heckle me from time to time, but if I was going to be heckled by anyone, I'd probably want it to be God.

Or Tabby. She and Cliff were curled up on the cream three-seater couch. A tumble of in-love limbs. There was a pleasant shimmering haze inside my head as my brain dropped down through the gears. The colours in the room had put on make-up and were planning a party. "What will happen next? Will I hallucinate snakes?"

"I don't know," said Cliff. "Just roll with it."

"Rolling? Yes, excellent." I rolled back and forth. "Carpet. It's like hair for a room." I stared up at the fairy lights surrounding Tabby's mirror. "Twinkle," I said, with great profundity.

"Twinkle," Tabby repeated, ruffling Cliff's hair, which was unnecessary because it was self-ruffling.

"Does anyone else find it troubling that so much of the word *heroin* is hero?" Cliff asked.

"IS THIS HEROIN?"

"No."

"We should have done this sooner," Tabby said.

"Become junkies?" Cliff asked.

She dropped her head onto his shoulder. "Exactly."

He reached down to pass me another one of his self-rolled crack sticks. I sucked on it and then coughed wildly. I thought of Craig then pushed the thought away.

"Hold it in," Cliff schooled.

I took another drag and this time held it until my cheeks expanded and my throat burnt and my insides were an organ fire.

"Better. Just about."

"Is this how you always pass the day?"

He nodded. "If it's a good day, yeah."

"It has got much to recommend about it," I said, noting that all the complexities of existence had melted to reveal what had always been there and would be there and I guess was the core essence of everything. "Ice cream?"

They murmured in agreement.

"I've never eaten ice cream. As an adult, I mean. I once ate it as a child, but it was a trick and other kids had put glass in it."

"He broke a tooth," Tabby said. "It's actually a really sad story."

"I think I've got some Phish Food," said Cliff, "but I'm heavy. Pull me up?"

"It's doubtful," I said, rising unsteadily onto my knees. I lunged forwards, grabbed Cliff at his middle, and pulled him down towards the floor. It was a close replica of how DJ had winched me from that windowless room, but I am not DJ, and so I simply pulled Cliff onto me in what became an impromptu laughing fit and/or sumo bout.

Needless to say, I lost.

Slowly, he scrabbled to his feet and, with those long, soft steps, padded out to the landing.

"Hold the handrail, Cliff."

"Awww," said Tabby. "Sweet."

I rolled over so I could look up at her. "Shouldn't you be at work?"

"My dad came in yesterday."

I sat up. "Why?"

"Asked for one hundred pounds as an advance." She looked away and lowered her chin.

"How dare he." I thumped the carpet, which took it well. "What did you do?"

"Clammed up, mostly. Some fidgeting." She fidgeted. "Went very red. Made some excuses."

"Did you give it to him?"

"I only had a fifty. I gave him that then hid in the back until he left. Which is not what I'd have advised anyone else to do, but there we are."

I closed my eyes.

"What if he keeps coming in?" Her speech had accelerated.

"Tell him no."

"I've tried that."

"Tell him louder."

"It's not... I can't. That's why I called in sick today. Although I guess I will be sick if we smoke too much more. Then it won't be a lie, at least."

"What is it?"

"Just some weed."

"*I'm* a weed."

"You're not."

"You're a good egg, Tabby, fundamentally and/or metaphorically." I made the shape of an egg with my hands. "You don't deserve him."

"I think you mean figuratively? I had to help Cliff out of your packaging prison earlier." She pushed up her slipping glasses. "It was funny but also kind of weird. Even for you. Are you—"

"We have to do something," I said. She was trying to change the subject. I was not the problem. "We have to make him stop."

Cliff reappeared at the door, his face wide and welcoming like a... happy canyon. "You need a minute?"

"No," we said together, and so he sat back down clutching a small, frozen lidded pot. I sat up, leaning on the sofa with my elbows and keen to get back to the innocence of my illegal high.

"Open sesame," Cliff said, as a silver spoon of intense wet coldness brushed and—I suppose, also—entered my narrowly parted lips. I gurgled in surprise as the spoon's contents melted to reveal a dense, sugary nirvana. "What is this elixir?"

"Phish Food."

"Are there actual real-life fishes in it?"

Tabby and Cliff giggled.

I giggled.

The pot passed between us. "Fine," I said, about the co-mingling of our germs. "Fine."

"What's fine?" Tabby asked, as I lay back down on the carpet. It was like sinking into infinity.

"Everything, mostly. Will I pay a spect—speck-spect-tack." The word *spectacular* had become hilly and I had to detour around it. "Will I pay a high cost for this tomorrow?"

"No," Cliff said.

"Maybe," Tabby countered.

"MORE FOOD THAT IS PHISH."

"What's next for you then, Harry Hedonist?" Cliff asked.

"Esme," Tabby said.

I sprang up. Had I told her about Esme? Had Cliff? Was there anything to tell? Remembering what I had and hadn't told people had been less of a problem when I did nothing but hide and the only person I spoke to was myself and, perhaps, Tabby.

"Fiery woman," I mumbled.

"Not bad on the eye too," said Cliff, "in an Edward Scissorhands kind of way."

"We live opposite a graveyard," Tabby scoffed.

"It would be quiet," I said, "were it not for all the fornication."

I reached out and touched a thick navy scarf that had fallen off the edge of the sofa. It looked like one of Linda's. It had never been in the navy. That was a lie. I put it over my eyes. I couldn't see. I wrapped it around my neck. It was like being cuddled by a felt cobra.

"It's better to be a woman." I said, stroking it.

Tabby peeked over the edge of the sofa. "Men wear scarves."

"Not in Nottingham."

"Floyd," said Cliff, getting up and putting in a CD. Loud music wailed. It sounded like threshing machines squabbling in 1979's California. Each song lasted twenty-seven minutes, during which Cliff kept his eyes closed and tapped his foot. I was having difficulty with size and perspective. I'd fallen down a technicolour well.

"How old is this music?" I asked.

"Thirty years or so."

I tried to conjure a snappy quip but found I had turned around too many times in my mind and was humour-dizzy. "I've always liked you, Cliffy."

"That's not true."

"Who are you to tell me who is the truth of the things!" I stood but swayed. "I am the man who knows about the... *things*. The thinkers of the thoughts. The haver of desires?" I reached for the tub of ice cream but Cliff pulled it away and my footing betrayed me and I collapsed and realised I was sleepy.

The phone rang.

"Ring my bell!" I yelled. "Don't answer. They'll hoodwink you."

"They won't," Tabby said. "But it might be work."

"This is no time for advice." My voice boomed. "Was that advice? If so, ignore it. No, take it!"

She put the phone's receiver to her ear. "Hello?" While we heard only her side, I knew with whom she was speaking by how heavy her voice became. "Oh. No, well? Maybe. We're. No. I—Yes. I know I said that. No. I. It's not fair. No. Right, yes. No. I'll—I'll—I'll call you."

Tabby hung up. Her lip quivered.

He would not ruin this. Who she was becoming. Who she already was. She wiped away a tear and, all at once, I knew what I had to do.

30

I slept for a tremendous amount of the following day. So much of it, in fact, that when I woke up, night had fallen, making a real splash of it. My mouth felt as if like it contained an entire towel. My head was as heavy as an anvil. In an attempt to lighten it, I took a large number of aspirin.

There was a plastic bag from Ricky waiting for me in Cliff's room. I packed several things and, full of trepidation, left the house and boarded a public bus. On the seat next to me, I placed both the plastic bag and a giant, full duffel bag.

I rode the bus to Hucknall. An inebriated man in a launderette had once told me it was named after a red-headed singer, but I couldn't be sure. He'd also said life was a roller coaster, which I agreed with broadly. The previous day had certainly been that. I'd spent all of it whizzing and lurching, ascending and descending, from the immense, prickly high of defacing the books to the plunging low of my encounter with DJ then the hurtling, drug-powered ascent of getting actually high with Cliff and Tabby, not to forget the pleasant time listening to Esme overshare bedroom secrets before Pat arrived and ruined everything.

Now I needed to be bad again.

I got off the bus. Squalor hung heavily in the air. I picked my way through the shadows of an estate of social housing. Kneeling between two parked cars, I checked the AA Ordnance map I'd packed. The wind whipped up, and I tucked my chin into my chest. Several high-rises punctured the night sky, which was black and starless, what with all the pollution.

A posse of delinquents loitered near a housing block's entrance, listening to violent urban poetry playing from a rectangular boombox. I didn't know who this Warren G person was, or if he really had the credentials he claimed, but I could agree that perhaps more regulation was necessary.

I worked a wide circle around them, utilising an unlit corner, a parked mobile dog-grooming van, and a chunky lamppost. I moved quickly, quietly, purposefully, even though anguish and uncertainty were weighing me down and each step felt as if it was into wet cement, in socks.

Reaching my target, I stared up, in awe, at all eighteen floors of brutal, sharp-edged concrete. If I'd seen anything that needed the soft, reassuring embrace of bubble wrap, it was this place.

I poked my head into the gloomy stairwell, sure I couldn't trust the tower's lift. The stairwell smelt of urine and underprivileged ghosts. Mercifully, it was empty. I began my slow trudge upwards, stopping at each floor to listen for sounds from those above.

Thanks to Ricky, I knew the layout, and a little of what to expect. I needed to talk to the man in apartment 402 and I needed him to listen, even though he was an angry, violent individual who despised me and/or found me pitiful. I would reason with him, and if that failed, threaten and scare him. I would show him I wasn't someone to mess with.

Unfortunately, I was someone to mess with. I was someone *everyone* messed with, especially, but not exclusively, pigeons. This would be a dramatic change of role for me, although two recent auditions—Waterstones and the Thwacking of Cliff—had suggested I enjoyed the depraved side of life.

This time, I'd made sure I had a specific, detailed plan and goal, and had worked to minimise all variables.

This time, I'd use my tried-and-tested weapons of choice and, if I'm honest, pleasure.

This time, if it blew up in my face, which it almost certainly would, I'd fail doing the right thing. Even though the costs might end up being high, I would be happy to pay them. I had nothing to lose. Well, only myself.

So nothing that mattered.

"I need to do this. I need to do this. I need to do this," I repeated as a sort of mantra, I suppose, leaving the stairs and finding six flats to my left, six to my right. There was a view out to the city's dump.

I sniffed and smelt bonfire and bewitchment. I dropped and army-crawled towards flat 402, staying below each apartment's front-facing kitchen window.

Flat 398 smelt strongly of marijuana: I was high again today but on self-righteousness.

Flat 399 had two full trash bags outside: I remembered that time I hid in a bin. I was done hiding.

Flat 400 had a sign warning of an Alsatian: my bark would no longer be worse than my bite.

Flat 401 had loud music of a reggae persuasion. I paused to try to relate this to my predicament but failed. It did make my head bob, slightly, so there was that.

Flat 402 was the home of Tabby's father, Craig. I didn't need to find a way to tie it to my predicament because it was my predicament.

Putting my eyes to the frosted glass of his front door, I saw the shapes of what looked like junk mail letters and takeout flyers. A distant television squawked, its light flickering into the narrow hallway. I took a moment to compose myself but found my throat had become a narrow, ineffective straw, like in a fast-food milkshake.

I lifted the letter-box flap and peered inside.

At the end of the hallway, in the living room, was the edge of a human foot and/or leg. It was motionless. The TV was showing sport. Sport didn't interest me. It was just people confusing good genes with high skill.

I had neither.

I closed the letter box, shuffled to my right, and sat with my back to the wall below the kitchen window. Should I have asked Ricky to help me? He wouldn't have been of any, of course, but he might have been company to enjoy during my demise. I could have asked Cliff, but he would have said he and Tabby weren't at that stage. The kidnapping and threatening stage.

From my duffel bag, I removed a can of Vimto, took a swig, and felt the sugar flood my brain. Then I pulled the balaclava down over my face and got up and slowly lifted the letter box of another man's front door and I had obviously completely lost my mind but there we are.

31

I saw them dangling there.

Ricky had been right. The door was locked but the keys were in it. From my bag, I removed a specially modified litter picker. A handle ran up to a small gripping hook, adapted so that it could rotate 360 degrees with the press of a button on the handle. This part of the plan was all Uncle Sanjay. He wasn't a man I would cross, nor a market stall I would ever visit.

I would never have believed it could be so simple had I not tested it on my own front door. I had supplementary locks, of course, because my home was a fortress. Craig's was not. There was nothing to steal here. And the person guarding it was always drunk.

I slipped the device into the letter box. Gripping it with two hands, I moved it right and down into position. It took a few attempts to get a good grip on the key. Satisfied, I pushed the button on the handle and the pincer grip turned, taking the key with it.

There was a very satisfying click.

I pulled the device out and pushed down on the door handle slowly. It gave. The carpet beneath it rustled. I took a very, very deep breath, stepped in, and closed the door quietly behind me. The hallway smelt of vindaloo and vehemence and I took a few steps towards the living room.

I stopped.

I listened.

I carried on, passing the grubby kitchen full of takeaway boxes and stepping over unopened letters, Chinese takeaway leaflets, an empty gin bottle, and a kebab wrapper from which sauce was leaking in the shape of a top hat.

The prickling returned with a vengeance. It felt as if I were made of sparklers. I licked my lips. Rarely do we do something that we can't take back. Almost all lines crossed can be re-crossed or rubbed out. Or they turn out not to be lines at all, merely markers between the old and new.

Not this. I had broken into a man's home.

I peeked into his bedroom. It was sparsely furnished, the bed unmade. A pornographic magazine lay open on the floor surrounded by about fifty-six cans of Tesco Value lager.

I shuffled on to the living room and then, unable to stay quiet, let out a loud gasp at what I saw. Craig was slumped over on a white lawn chair before an old, battered television. His head was lolling precariously on his left arm, which was on the narrow armrest.

That wasn't why I'd gasped. I'd gasped because at some time in the distant past, Craig had placed empty bottles in a row along the far wall and this collection now wrapped the room in a giant anaconda of inebriation. The only space left empty was a narrow path a foot wide, running from the door to the chair. This was not an apartment. It was a nest.

It was also an unforeseen complication.

I lingered in the doorway, listening to his loud, rasping breaths. He sounded like a power tool draining of battery.

This was no way to live, and I knew a thing or two about how not to live.

I walked that narrow path, watching as I planted my feet, making sure not to clip any of the bottles. His tongue hung from his mouth like a dog's on a hot day.

Uncertainty was flogging me. I tried to steel myself, balling my hands, reminding myself I was here for the person I loved and/or depended on most in this world. I bent down and opened my bag and removed a large reel of bubble wrap and two deluxe tape-dispenser guns whose wheels had been oiled—the office-stationery equivalent of a gun's silencer.

With little space to work, I put a triple layer of tape around his hands and forearms then unfurled a metre or two of bubble wrap vertically into the air and swished it around his upper torso and the chair. He stirred and so I sped up, working the next layer of wrapping and tape. I took a moment to stroke a sheet across my face before wrapping his lower body and taping his ankles tight against the plastic chair. What I was doing was both calming me down and thrilling me up. Attraction is weird and multifaceted. Some squeaking was inevitable, but I had practised at home, since the Thwacking of Cliff, and I'd truly mastered the one-handed dispense.

I worked quickly and methodically.

Then I stepped back to check my work, which was when I caught a bottle of something called hooch with my heel, which clattered into a WKD, which clinked violently against several empty red wine bottles, which tumbled into bottles of harder spirits, and soon the whole collection was tumbling around us like glass dominoes.

Craig lurched upright and awake. "Oi!" He jerked his hands upwards, but the tape held.

I darted round and round him, my head bowed, both my

tape guns firing, trying to avoid scattered bottles while doing two more quick laps.

"Fuuuuuuuck," he screamed, his eyes wide and confused. "HELP!"

I stood before him and held the sharp blades of my tape gun to his lips. "Scream and I will cover your mouth and/or your nose and you will have a really, really hard time breathing, mostly."

His eyes screamed in alarm and confusion. "What are you doing?"

"Imperilling you. Imparcelling you. Both, I suppose?"

"*I'll kill you,*" he growled.

I'd used two full reels of tape. He looked like something that would emerge from a pond in a 1950s horror movie. I crossed my arms and snarled in an attempt to look menacing, before remembering I was wearing a balaclava. Craig began biting on the tape and bubble wrap. This was understandable but foolish, for he was greatly underestimating the quality of these materials. I could have shipped him to Australia like this.

"I don't have money."

"I'm not here for your money," I said, repositioning my balaclava, realising I'd forgotten to widen the eye holes, which was why it was so hard to see.

Craig let out a long, deep howl of a laugh that ended in a rattling cough. "I know those eyes."

"No, you don't."

"And how you move. You scuttle, *Ferdinand.*" He let out another menacing howl. "You are so far out of your depth, you little shitkicker."

"Who's Ferdinand?" I said. "What a stupid name. My name is Jam—" I stopped, but it was too late. I had foiled myself, which was only just better than soiling myself. When committing a crime, it's imperative not to tell the victim your name, especially when they know your name. Both names. Criminality 101. Not a course I'd taken because I'm an abider of rules, although I once failed to return an interesting library book about Amish fashion through the ages. The fine was daunting, but, on reflection, still worth it.

"You're a loser," he hissed. "A virgin. A man-boy."

I'd heard worse before breakfast at the group home. I'd experienced worse, too. There were some... It's hard to... Children aren't always believed. And so they are alone. And that they stay.

I slipped my guns into my bag. "I just want to talk."

"We're going to do more than that," he snarled, and rocked the chair left and right. He was no longer scared of me. The swinging motion continued until he tipped and landed hard on his left side and the chair leg snapped and bottles skidded off in all directions.

"Argh," he moaned.

"You're confused because it seems soft," I said, of the bubble wrap, "but it's impossibly strong. I get it imported. It comes from Leamington Spa."

"You're a freak."

His head was resting against the dirty carpet. I moved round, kicking bottles out of the way. I wanted him to look at me. He lay there, his left cheek pressed to the floor, his eyes wild and darting. I bent down and poked my finger into his face. "You're not in a position to insult people."

"Fuck you, Ferdinand."

"Who is this Ferdinand?"

He sighed and stopped wriggling. "What do you want?"

"Just to talk."

"We could have done that without this." He flicked his head backwards, as much as was possible in his state.

"You wouldn't have listened."

"I would."

"You're violent."

He cackled. "Yes. And I know where you live."

"Then you probably also know how I live?"

"Sadly?"

"Paranoid, and accordingly booby-trapped."

"The only booby you'll ever know. I'm going to rip your ugly head from your scrawny neck."

"This isn't about me."

"I'm making it about you."

"It's about *you*." I pointed at his face. I felt fantastic. I was a cleaner of slates. A righter of wrongs. A... flipper of fates. Why had I waited so long to do this?

"Get on with it," he snarled. "This hurts."

"Tabby," I said. "Your so-called daughter."

"She *is* my daughter."

"I want you to promise to never contact her again."

"No," he snapped.

"Yes."

"Or?"

"Or... else?"

He howled with laughter again. I'd hoped a lifetime of being threatened would make me a talented threatener, but this was not the case.

"Or else... what?" he asked.

"Do I seem like someone with much to lose?"

"No, Ferdie. You seem like someone with little to offer."

"That's not... those things can both be true."

"She's my daughter, shitbird." He coughed. It rattled around in his chest.

"You gave up those rights."

"You weren't there." The remaining colour in his cheeks drained away.

"It doesn't matter."

"You don't have kids." He grunted. "You don't know what it's like."

"I don't have kids because I wouldn't want to inflict someone like me on them. It's a shame you didn't have the same foresight."

"You couldn't have kids because you repel women, and men, and probably animals too."

"Only pigeons, actually."

"That's..." He hesitated. "When her mum left? That gutted me, that did. Gutted Tabby, too."

"And you took it out on her."

"Kids need discipline."

I wagged my finger. "Parents want obedience. You're not her father. You gave up those rights when you put her into care."

"The state took her away."

"And why did they do that?"

"Fuck you," he spat, leaving drool hanging from his mouth. "I did my best." He tried to turn his head away from me but there was nowhere to go.

"You did what you wanted."

"Why are you still wearing that mask, Ferdinand? I know it's you."

"Helps me get in the role," I said. "The role of someone you don't want to mess with." I let my voice rise. "I will protect her to the bitter end and if you don't do what I say, that end really will be bitter, for us both probably, but I've made my peace with that. Have you?"

"She doesn't need protecting. She's stronger than you."

"Everyone has an Achilles heel. And for whatever reason, you're it for her."

"Have you ever lost someone?" he asked, although he must have known the answer.

"Yes."

"Then you know what it's like."

"You were abusive to her too, though, weren't you? Tabby's mum. You were part of why she left. Why she committed suicide. You are a poison and I'm not going to let you ruin the life Tabby has built for herself. I know how much she suffered in those group homes because I was there with her. I was there because I had no choice, because my parents were dead. But you could have sorted your life out and given her a proper home. You could have shown her love."

His voice lowered. "She is loved."

I pulled a ball of paper from my pocket and uncrumpled it. "Does this look like love?"

"That's a gas bill."

I turned it round and rubbed it into his face. "THIS."

I tried to put it into his mouth, which he clamped shut. I balled it up and threw it at the wall.

"It's fair," he said, as he tried to catch his breath. "That's what it is."

I looked towards the door. "Tabby is doing well now. She's normal. She has a boyfriend. She gives excellent advice, professionally even. The world is better because she's in it. You have no right to destroy that."

"I just want to clean the slate."

My tone hardened. "Promise you'll never contact her again."

"No," he said without hesitation and/or deliberation.

I took a step left and checked the front door. No one was coming to his rescue and/or my downfall. This was a surprise. Was this going well, even? I pulled a folded wad of bank notes from my trouser pocket. They smelt of mattress. "I guessed you'd say that. So I brought these." I fanned them for him. "Six hundred and fifteen pounds." I rooted around in my other pocket and found an old bank statement, from happier times, and a silver coin. "And twenty pence. That's the offer."

"That's an insult," he said, his voice rising in indignation.

"It will buy you a lot of alcohol."

"It's... not enough."

"It's all the money I have in the world. And far more than you deserve."

"It's thousands less than I'm owed, shitbird."

"Think about it," I said, holding it towards him. "What it buys you. Think about the alternative, which is no money, since you won't get another penny out of her. Think about the sort of person who would break into your home and do this to you. Think about what Tabby thinks of you since you gave her that bill."

"That's a lot of thinking."

I looked around at the room. "You seem to have the time."

He rocked, fighting against his restraints. "Let me out!" All he could do was spin in a slow, painful, pointless circle. He gave up, grunting from the exertion. "She said *she* would think about it."

"She was being polite. She should have smashed her glass over your head. But she's a good person. That's not because of you, but despite you. Take the money. Destroy yourself with it. But know you can never contact her again."

He was quiet for twenty, perhaps even thirty seconds. "No."

I put the money back into my pocket. "Then we're done."

I bent down and zipped up my bag. His hands shook against the armrests. "You can't leave me like this."

I leaned over him, close enough that I could see the red splotches on his skin. I poked my finger down, my nail just a centimetre from his eyelashes. "Hitting a child is unforgivable."

He turned his head and spat in my face. I leapt back in shock and my left heel slipped on a bottle that had belonged to a woman, perhaps a Spaniard, called Tia Maria. My foot lost its grip and I tipped backwards in slow motion, my eyes as wide as they'd ever been. I landed hard on my neck and shoulders, and my back wrapped around empty bottles in an awkward reverse C. A shooting pain ran down my body.

I cried out.

In response, Craig let out a sick, deep moan of evil laughter.

Then I heard him.

Somehow, he was moving. I couldn't lift my head but I could hear him scrabbling, and I don't mean the board game. He was dragging the chair with him. The gap between us was only a few feet. My back had betrayed me and I was stuck firm, moaning in agony. He drew nearer. I closed my eyes. I opened them as he crashed on top of me, the weight winding me. He grunted again, loudly from the exertion, a mad determination in his glassy eyes, his face just a few centimetres from my own.

"You're mine now, shitbird."

His hands and legs were still restrained, and I wasn't sure what he thought he could do, other than squash me, which, while effective, wouldn't be a long-term solution. I got the answer when he pulled his neck back then slammed his forehead into the bridge of my nose.

The bridge collapsed.

"ARGH!" I screamed as a pain grenade exploded in my brain and my vision flooded with bright light. He grinned sadistically then head-butted me a second time. Blood showered us both. The edges of my vision blurred to black.

I was passing out. I wouldn't get out of this. I had failed yet again. It was as sad as it was predictable.

Nearby was my bag, and in it, kitchen scissors. He struck the third blow, his breathing wild and raspy.

"Sorry," I sobbed. "I'm sorry."

I closed my eyes and my mind drifted. A memory arrived unbidden. It was of a pleasant summer day spent with my parents. We had been for a walk and then stopped to steal carrots from an allotment. My parents were drunk on homemade moonshine, and as I tugged at the roots of the carrots, they danced together to a song my mother sang off-key. I pushed myself between them and soon we were swirling in a circle and I was shouting with glee and perhaps that's why we didn't hear the farmer's gunshot. We escaped, just about, and we ate well that night.

Or rather, we ate carrot soup.

I felt loved.

Music wafted into my memory next, distant yet familiar.

"M-a-n-s field. A field of men. He went there once and he didn't go again."

Then I was in Tabby's room, getting high with her and Cliff in the afternoon light, remembering the way the carpet felt under my neck as I lay on my back. Then I was defacing books in Waterstones, drunk again, but on power. Then ad-libbing with Ricky in his taxi.

It had been little, but it had been mine. I realised how much I appreciated it. I didn't want to die.

I forced my eyes open and saw an object swinging very fast towards the back of Craig's head.

Thwack

Craig slumped onto me and stopped moving. With great effort, I pushed him off. My saviour came into view.

He was holding a cricket bat and wearing a bright-red spandex outfit. Across the chest was a yellow *R*.

"BOOYAH!" he said, and in the process, his voice cracked loudly. "He out? I mean—" He stopped, noticing his voice had changed. It was deep, resonant, timber shaking. "Huh?" he swallowed. "Nice." Adulthood had arrived for my friend, hero, and sidekick.

Craig stirred and moaned and, with great concentration, coughed the word *bllrg*.

Ricky pulled me up, and I sat, albeit with little structural integrity. I took a few deep breaths and tried to compose myself as he took a tissue from his pocket and wiped blood from my face.

"Took time?" I whispered.

"Parking was a nightmare."

"*R*?" I pointed at his chest.

He pulled on his outfit and grinned. "It's an homage to Robin really, only the *R* is for Ricky." He took another look at Craig. "What you done to him?"

"Imperilled and/or imparcelled."

"As long as you haven't impregnated him. Can you walk, buddy?"

I blinked the blood from my vision. "I think he broke my nose."

Craig scowled up at Ricky. "Who are you?"

"Ricky—I mean *Robin*."

We both had a lot to learn.

"What is happening?" Craig asked. He sounded tired.

"I'm helping shaft you," Ricky said, tapping his cricket bat against his leg. He looked camp in his uniform. Even unarmed, Craig would have made mincemeat of him, were he not so thoroughly and, if I'm honest, impressively restrained.

"Let me go," Craig demanded.

"How did you know it was tonight?" I asked Ricky.

"I didn't."

The front door slammed. Fear grew in Ricky's eyes, and he raised the bat and stepped closer.

"No! It's Cliff," I said, when I heard Cliff's breezy steps on the carpet. I'd just given another name away.

Ricky lowered the bat. A mop of blond hair appeared. "Am I too late?" He eyed Ricky suspiciously.

"Our team," I said.

Cliff was dressed normally, had his hands in his coat pockets, and appeared unarmed beyond his face and/or personality. He saw me sitting there, my face smeared with blood, and rushed to hoist me to my feet.

"What you doing here, Cliffffff?"

"I knew you were up to something when you packed that massive bag with bubble wrap. I followed you but lost you, I think behind a lamppost? I only knew Craig's first name. But the boys downstairs helped and then I saw the Vimto can outside and that did the rest. Sorry I'm late. It wasn't as easy as I expected. I should have been better prepared."

"WHAT IS GOING ON?" asked Craig. "I'm so confused."

Cliff looked him over. "You imperilled him too. *Nice.* Did he agree to leave Tabby alone?"

"We were in the middle of negotiations."

Cliff balled his fist. "I'd like to help."

"Take what you want and get out," Craig said, his voice cracking. "Or just kill me or whatever. I'm done."

My sidekicks each grabbed one of my arms as I tried a first, tentative step. "Is Tabby about to walk—" I tried to ask but then wretched from the pain.

"No," Cliff said.

"What about him?" Ricky asked, nodding towards

Craig. "I bought some gadgets I didn't get to use yet." He tilted his belt. "Throwing daggers. Mace. We could just mace him, like, a little bit? It's good mace. Got it from Uncle Sanjay." His voice was still deep and rich like a Brummie soul singer.

"No mace," I said. My initial plan had failed when he rejected the money, but I felt sure we'd made a very salient, threatening point. Several points, probably. Exactly what points I wasn't sure. I think we'd mostly shown him we were very weird and/or unreasonable. If I had no idea what was going to happen next, Craig must have been really confused. You can't negotiate with a madman. Or madmen.

My sidekicks helped me towards the hallway. "WAIT," Craig said.

We stopped.

"Come back."

They shuffled me around in an awkward six-legged circle so I could face him, this lump covered in tape, bubble wrap, and my blood.

"Six hundred and fifteen pounds."

There was urgency in his voice for the first time. He'd worked his right hand almost free of the tape.

"Six hundred and fifteen pounds," I repeated.

He sighed. "Fine."

"Ricky, my trouser pocket." I hadn't worn my anorak. It was too distinctive. Ricky got the money out and fanned it.

"What? Don't pay him," Cliff said.

"I know what I'm doing." While this wasn't true, it was perhaps truth-adjacent.

Cliff considered if he trusted me. He gave a single, short nod.

I looked at Craig. "You agree that if you take this money, you can never, ever contact her again?" It was a pittance for a daughter like Tabby.

He blinked slowly. "Whatever."

"I need a yes."

"Yes." He tutted. "Fine. Fuck. Freaks."

Ricky bent down and put the money on the floor.

"Every year," he hissed. "Six hundred and fifteen pounds and twenty pence. Every year until I die. Or she dies. Or you die."

"That's not the deal."

"It's the deal now, Ferdie, you shitrag. Take it or leave it."

I blinked through tears and blood, looking down at this pitiful creature on his side like a crushed bug. How long would he last? Would I reverse my cash-flow difficulties before next year? The sum was a little over two months' profit from Cliff's exorbitant rent. It was egregious to pay Craig a single penny, never mind six hundred pounds, but it was also an amount I could wrangle. An amount that would hasten his demise, thus solving the problem permanently.

I hesitated but relented. "Okay."

"Good," he said, and smiled. "Now let me out and let's shake on it."

It was my turn to laugh. "Germs." I nodded towards the duffel bag. "Ricky, get the scissors."

Ricky unzipped the bag and put the scissors a metre from Craig, at hand height. This would give us enough time to get away.

We took the lift down. Ricky whooped and hollered the whole way. "That was the bomb!" he said, as they shuffled me towards the car park. "Tarantino shit. We really struck a blow for the good guys."

"Are we the good guys?" Cliff asked. I wasn't sure how much he knew of what Craig had done, or failed to do for Tabby.

"You saved my life," I said, "or at least my face. Not that it's worth much."

"Aah," Ricky said, patting me on the back, forgetting the pain I was in. "Don't mention it."

I was sure he was going to, and often.

"Were you even secretly armed, Cliff?" he asked.

"Nopes."

"What did you think was going to happen?"

"I figured we'd just reason with him."

"Did he seem reasonable?" I asked.

"Eh...? Well, you put him in an unreasonable position. But then you paid him off. I still can't believe that, actually."

We passed those youths still standing moodily around their boombox. "Thanks, guys," Cliff said. "Found him. Them."

"See you around, C-Dog."

"Nice boys," said Cliff. "Bit gruff."

The taxi came into view, parked illegally between two melted shopping trolleys. "Tabby can handle herself," Cliff said. "You didn't need to do this."

"No. I should have done it a long time ago."

They laid me across the back seat. "Why are you dressed like that?" Cliff asked Ricky.

"We're superheroes, sort of. I've had it in the boot for months, actually. It's just I rarely, well..." His voice faltered, and I remembered what a courageous thing he'd just done for me. He'd answered every question I'd ever asked of his bravery. "Where to?" he asked. "Hospital?"

I was now only seeing a single-figure number of stars.

"Or back to my place?" Ricky asked.

I was in no mood for a damp basement. "I'm okay, I think. You got there just in time. Let's go to mine." I looked at Cliff. "Ours."

"Okay, Boss," Ricky said, starting the engine and

opening the glovebox in search of his CD collection. "I'll just find something celebratory."

An upbeat song played and soon both Ricky and Cliff were dancing and raising a metaphorical roof.

Should a heart have grooves? I wasn't sure.

We waited there for a few minutes watching the entrance to the building. Craig didn't emerge to chase us. We had made our point(s). He had made his choice(s). He might have once been a man to fear, but he was now, mostly, one to pity.

32

It had been a day I would never forget and would also perhaps be literally and/or metaphorically and/or figuratively scarred from. I lay down on my bed, shirtless, rubbing my torso with bubble wrap to help me relax. There was a very pleasant squelching sound. Static caused the few hairs on my chest to stand.

I breathed in deeply. It hurt. When I was nine years old, older boys in the group home and one of the staff and two visiting-but-unsympathetic parents, including Craig, locked me in a shoe cupboard for an entire (bank holiday) weekend. The only thing in there was a single sheet of bubble wrap. It was the start of something. A crutch perhaps, a passion certainly, or maybe just a healthy infatuation.

Despite my current pain, I was aroused, exhilarated, still drunk on the power of what I'd done. I also had a terrible, terrible headache and couldn't breathe through my nose, which wasn't broken but was now largely ornamental. And I had a purple eye.

I'd have had much worse if it hadn't been for Cliff and Ricky coming to save me. They had got me into my room without Tabby seeing. Cliff would tell her whatever he would tell her, probably that the Hoodlums, students, or toddlers had attacked me, all of which she would believe.

It felt good knowing Cliff would visit soon to offer kind words and a mug of lukewarm water. He'd agreed to stay up and play computer games until sunrise, monitoring the metaphorical coast to check it remained clear. I had been wrong about him. I had also been wrong about Ricky.

I let the confrontation with Craig replay in my mind's eye. What surprised me most was how important it had been for him to see himself as a good father. At first I'd thought he was lying, but the longer we talked, the clearer it became that he genuinely believed it. He'd changed his memories to fit, allowing himself to be the tortured hero of his own story. I supposed we all did this, but did we do it equally? It was a lot to think about and then, perhaps fortunately, the lids of my eyes became ruinously heavy, and so I let them close.

It wasn't until the following afternoon that I became capable of regular human endeavours. My back was furious at me and I gobbled aspirin and ran a long, hot, regenerative bath and spied on the Hoodlums.

Feeling ready for the stairs, I rewarded myself for the effort with a cool Vimto and two crumpets, put a pie in the oven, then sat down in front of Cliff's personal computer and merged out onto the Internet superhighway. Time ran away from me. I punched a monkey hoping to win a prize.

I missed.

Several hours later, the front door opened, and I turned from Cliff's monitor and the Internet homepage I'd been surfing. It was about eyeball licking.

"Hey, duck," Tabby said, untangling a loop scarf from

her neck and hanging her grey coat on the door without looking at me. She moved closer, saw my face, screamed, rushed over, and then went somewhat hysterical.

"It's okay," I said.

"It's bloody well not."

"It's not as bad as it looks."

"It looks like they did a real number on you."

I still didn't know what Cliff had told her. "You should see their faces."

"Did you see their faces?"

"No."

"Does it hurt?"

"Yes. I mean"—I winced—"not so much, no."

"Did you call the police?"

And tell them that I attacked a man in his own home with packaging supplies? No, Tabby. I didn't call the police. Not that they would have done anything, anyway.

"Of course I did."

"What did they say?"

"Someone came and took a statement."

"That's good then. More than normal, at least. Was it the Hoodlums?"

"I'm not sure. I was hit from behind. Then I was on the ground."

"Where did it happen?"

"In the graveyard."

"There must have been people around?"

"Yes."

Her head lowered. "Sometimes I hate this city."

"I always do."

"I'm sorry," she said, and put her head on my shoulder until I grimaced—not in response to the pain of violence but to the shock of bodily closeness. In the distance, I heard a familiar-sounding engine choking and coughing into life but couldn't quite place it.

"I'm hungry," she said. "Dinner? Shall we order in?"

"I've cooked. Or am cooking. Steak and kidney pie with mash. It's from a tin but a premium tin. Fray Bentos."

"Ah, that's the smell," she said. "Magic."

"How about Cliff?"

"He's not back until late."

"Let's eat in your room?" It had long become the heart of our modest, dysfunctional home.

"Is this fluff?" she asked, thirty minutes later, pulling something from her pie crust as we sat side by side on her couch.

"There might have been an incident on the way here, when I attempted to carry both plates simultaneously. Sometimes my vision is double."

"Your nose is double its size too."

"Then it will match my eyes."

"I'm so sorry," she said, "about everything."

"You already apologised."

"Right. *Right.*"

We ate with the plates on our laps. "Did you hear anything else from your dad?" I asked, feigning innocence.

"No," she said, and sounded relieved. "Do you think about your parents a lot? We don't talk about them much—or ever, really."

"Yes, I guess I do. Not always nice thoughts though."

"Why not?"

"They were gullible and hedonistic and, well, unscrupulous, and I paid the cost."

"At least they loved you."

"Not for long enough."

Outside, an animal howled loudly.

"The wolves are loud tonight," I said.

"Must be full moon."

The howl became a stretched scream. "Agggggiii-iieeeee."

We ran to the window. On his knees—in the front garden, lifting a snapped piece of surfboard—was Cliff. Behind him, his usual parking spot stood empty. He looked up at us, his face contorting in pain. He was being lashed by drizzle. "I'm going to get them!" he cried.

"Who is 'them'?" Tabby shouted.

"The Hoodlums."

Tabby rushed and I hobbled downstairs to console him and stop him from doing anything reckless.

"How do you know it was them?" she asked.

"If it happens around here, it's them," he said.

Tabby called the police and then led Cliff into the kitchen. "She said they're busy tonight but they'll come by in the morning, probably. It's a distinctive van."," she said, taking him into the kitchen. She opened him a cold beer and reheated his dinner as he and I settled ourselves at the table. Above us, the bare bulb cast unflattering shadows on the white walls. "There's a chance, babe."

He rubbed at his head. "I loved that van."

"We know."

I wondered if he'd ever imagined losing it and if that was both helping him in this moment and had helped him appreciate it while he had it.

Then there was jeering. Then ear-splitting music.

"Let's get them," Tabby said, during the next break in the music. "The Hoodlums."

"What?" I spluttered. "How? With whose army and/or expertise and/or weaponry?"

"There's something I need you to see," she said, and walked upstairs.

33

Up in Tabby's bedroom, Cliff was little more than a lump she was moving around. "Sit," she beckoned, and when he didn't, she gently eased him onto the couch.

As he stared despondently into space, she walked the few steps to her corkboard—which held the dates and times of her various selfless civic commitments as well as positive aphorisms about the day and its being seized—and flipped it, revealing a detailed web of white string, sticky notes, and a dozen blurry Polaroid photos.

"I've been watching them," she said, her voice low and full of intrigue. "Studying their operation."

Cliff came back to life. He got up. "Wow," he said, his head tilted. "It's beautiful."

"If the police won't do it," she said, "let's do it ourselves."

I moved in to scrutinise this intricate spiderweb of cunning. Directly above it was a full shelf of romance novels in which women had their bodices ripped off by men who looked like Cliff. The contrast was striking.

Did she really want to rip the Hoodlums off?

She watched our reactions closely. I peered at the

photos and recognised some from my own surveillance, undertaken while binocularing in the bath. At the top and centre of the sticky web was Robin, in his window, shirtless as usual. A needle was in his arm. Ecstasy was on his face.

"Tabby," I said, "you are a brilliant, devious, dedicated mind."

A slow smile spread across her face.

Cliff paced, his steps not breezy but gradually lightening. "Yes. *Yes!* Let's get them. They don't get to win. I get to win. I'm the winner. I win." He pointed at himself with both thumbs.

"Steady on, Cliff."

"It's the body," he said. "That's the tricky part of murder."

"We're not going to murder Robin!" I spluttered.

"Murder's easy," said Tabby. "Just kill him with something edible then eat it."

I took a step backwards. "Who are you people?"

"We're people you don't fuck with," she said. "Or people you used to fuck with but shouldn't anymore, probably."

"We're misfits," said Cliff, with both pride and a cheeky side-smoulder.

"We're not murdering anyone," I said, waving my arms around. "It's excessive. And you two aren't misfits. You might have been once, Tabby, but now you're magnificently functional."

"He robbed you of your savings," she protested.

"Yes, but not of my life."

"And he stole Aggie." Cliff punched his palm. "*My* Aggie."

Tabby pointed at my face. "And his boys did that to you."

I looked quickly to Cliff to see if he would correct her. He didn't.

"You're not a murderer, Tabby. You're a giver of timely pep talks."

She untacked a photo of a young hooligan in a white baseball cap under which she'd written *Twat*. "Do you remember when that guy snatched my bag in the Arboretum last summer? It was one of them." She tapped the photo. of a young thug in a white baseball cap under which she'd written, *Twat*.

"No murder," I said.

"My advice," she said. "We break in, collect evidence, and then make this very, very easy for the police. We'll do what they won't."

"Yes, babe," said Cliff. "Perfect."

"If you're serious—"

"We're serious," said Cliff.

I checked with Tabby, who held my gaze then nodded.

"Then I know exactly who you need."

"Why *you* and not *we*?" she asked. "Don't you want to get them?"

I sighed. "Of course. But I can't be involved. I'm a calamity in trousers. I'll mess it up." I paused, waiting for them to try to convince me otherwise. To tell me they couldn't do this without me. Their eyes met. Neither one said anything. It stung. "Or not heavily involved, anyway," I said, leaving the door a bit open in case they wanted to push it later. "Maybe I can make the tea or something? But anyway, you don't need me, you need—"

"Robert?" Cliff laughed. "Your fifteen-year-old superhero fanboy sidekick?"

"Ricky. And he's seventeen, I think. He's also quite brilliant, even if he's less brilliant than he thinks he is."

I walked downstairs to the telephone before they had a chance to protest.

* * *

Eight, perhaps even nine minutes later, there was a knock on the front door. "You rang, buddy?" He said in his new, deep, pleasing timbre.

It was good to see him. It had always been good to see him. "Left your spandex at home?"

"Nah, it's in the boot. We on a job again already?"

"More you than me," I said, and a wide grin ripped across his face. "But yes."

"Booyakasha!"

As I led him up to Tabby's room, I warned him about Cliff's fragile state, the unknown whereabouts of his beloved rusted eyesore, Aggie, and that Tabby didn't know what we had done to Craig. Tabby's bedroom door was open. They were sitting on the couch, hand in hand.

"This is Ricky, my, err... friend."

"Evening, buddies," Ricky said, bounding in. Tabby gave a meek wave while Cliff smouldered, albeit forlornly, like someone who'd gone to a funeral to seduce the widow.

"This is Tabby and Cliff."

"Do they know about"—he winked at me—"our experiments?"

"Yep, pretty much."

"Good," he said, walking across the room to the window and its uninterrupted cemetery vista. "Cracking view." He turned slowly then whispered in a childlike tone, "'I'm ready to tell you my secret now.'"

Tabby looked at me.

I shrugged. "I didn't know you had a secret?"

"Come closer," he said, but it was he who moved

towards us. He was doing another of his weird bits. I hoped they would overlook this annoying quirk of his personality. "'I... I... *see dead people...* They don't know they're dead.'"

"In your dreams?" I asked.

"No. 'Walking around like regular people.'"

"Might explain why the buses are so full," I said.

Tabby and Cliff giggled and then, not wanting to be socially isolated, I pretend-giggled but too late and too loud and they knew but said nothing.

Ricky's eyes found the corkboard. "A heist! Are we doing a heist? I've always wanted to do a heist! Is it the Hoodlums? I hate the Hoodlums. Oh my god. Are we really doing a heist?"

"Yes," said Tabby, firming. "It is. It's a diabolical heist and I am its mastermind and I am ruthless." She nodded once. "So, there you go."

"Okay, so we need nicknames. Or codenames. He clicked furiously. "How about colours like in Reservoir Dogs?"

"My advice would be to focus on the heist itself, rather than the branding," she said delicately, in her C.A.B voice. Ricky shook his head emphatically. "No no no. That's a total rookie heist mistake. Heists are not about the heist. The heist is almost incidental to the heist itself."

"That's how Cliff feels about surfing," I joked, but he didn't laugh, just continued staring down at the carpet. "I'm pretty sure I could just go and knock on the door and ask for your money and Aggie back," he said, without lifting his head. "I could, you know, like charm them or whatever?"

"Why did they steal your van then?" I asked.

"I doubt they knew it was mine."

"That's not going to work," Ricky said, pulling down the photo of a midlevel Hoodlum. It was one of the men with the neck tattoos we'd seen in town.

"No," I countered. "It probably would, knowing Cliff. Which I do because he lives here."

Tabby nodded. "He's pretty charming."

Ricky tapped his chin. "So he's our confidence man, huh?"

"What's a confidence man?" I asked.

"The team's charismatic front. Their job is to be memorable, but not too memorable. They open the doors and distract people while everyone else sneaks in." The stereo on her desk caught his eye. "Got any heist music, Tabby?"

"What's heist music?"

"I'll take that as a no then." He turned away from it. "Shame. Would have helped us get in the right headspace. I'll bring something next time. *Heat* had a great soundtrack. It has to be one of the top-five heist movies of all time. We should watch that later for research." He clapped. "Okay. If we're serious about doing this, and I think we are, we need..." He counted on his fingers. "A genius, autistic getaway driver, someone coming out of retirement for one last job, someone we hire on a recommendation who turns out to be a loose cannon who shoots first and asks questions later. An explosives expert. An Asian contortionist, maybe. Anyone I'm forgetting?" He shrugged. "No, I guess that's it."

"It's not Fort Knox," Tabby said, sarcastically. "It's a terrace house full of high people whose back door is usually open."

Ricky groaned. "You're underestimating your enemy. Classic heist mistake."

"We went to school with one of them," she protested, pointing at the Polaroid of Pat walking up our front-garden path. "She's a postwoman called Pat with one GCSE, in home economics. She cheated off me on the test."

"We're wasting a lot of time," said Cliff, banging his

knees with his palms. "Aggie is probably halfway to Wales by now."

"I guess I can be the getaway driver," said Ricky. "It's only one street away, so it's hard to see why we need one, but I'm just going to—"

"I already have a rough plan," Tabby said, unpinning a photo of Robin. "His house has the same layout as this one, with my room as his office. Not really an office. We need a more nefarious word than office."

"Den of debauchery?" I offered.

She made a noncommittal let's-keep-working-on-it face. "It's quietest in the morning. And every Friday, Robin goes to the graveyard to meets someone. A guy who looks like he belongs in a budget Mafia movie. Greasy, basically. I think it's his boss. Anyway, within thirty minutes he comes back. But the meeting is reliable."

Ricky tapped his chin. "That's our window. We need to make this case easy for the police. We've got to deliver them wrapped up."

"Bubble wrap?" I said.

Everyone turned.

"Just thinking aloud."

"If we could bug his room," said Tabby, "we could get evidence of their crimes on tape then give that to the police. They'd have to act."

Ricky pulled out his mobile telephone. "Leave the bugs to me."

I closed my eyes for a short moment of personal reflection. So much had happened lately and so little of it seemed to be within my control. It had all just been and now was and here we were and I guess that's how life works until it doesn't.

"We need to draw the rest of them out," Tabby said.

"There will be five, maybe six. I'd suggest diversions. What can they not resist?"

"Heroin," I said, confidently.

Cliff was growing antsy on the sofa. "We're making this too complicated."

"What we need..." Ricky said, pausing dramatically, his hands raised, "is a bouncy castle. No one can resist a bouncy castle. Me uncle has a side hustle renting them out."

"Is there anything Uncle Sanjay doesn't do?"

He scratched his head. "Pay taxes?"

"A party." Tabby nodded. "Booze, women, cake."

"Heroin," I added.

Cliff groaned. "What is it with you and heroin?"

"We could put it in the cake?"

Ricky clapped his hands. "Bangin'. It's all coming together."

Tabby nodded. "We throw the party of the century, draw them out, then sneak you in through the back door. How long do you need? To bug the room?"

Ricky looked at the ceiling. "Fifteen minutes and fourteen seconds."

"That's oddly specific."

"I love it in movies when they have very specific time restrictions and then everyone synchronises their watches."

"For someone who's never done a heist, you seem to know a lot about heists?"

"I've heisted," he said. "In my mind."

Cliff got up and walked through the open door. I thought he was going to the toilet, but then I heard the familiar creak of the back door I'd been meaning to get fixed for the best part of four, perhaps even five years.

"He wouldn't," I said, as Tabby darted out after him. "He would."

We reached the landing window to see Cliff sauntering across the alley, holding his ukulele.

"Cliff, no!" Tabby shouted through the open window, as Cliff opened the Hoodlums' back gate, turned, and waved with an expression that said *Just watch this.*

Ricky winced. "Too breezy."

Cliff positioned himself at their closed back door and played. Imagine. No, really, "Imagine," by John Lennon of the Beatles. Although the song was barely recognisable because the ukulele makes everything sound like a Hawaiian nursery rhyme. And he'd changed the lyrics to suit his predicament.

"Imagine there's no Aggie. It isn't hard to do. Because her parking space is empty. And that's because of you."

"Is he our loose cannon?" Ricky mused, as the door opened. Two Hoodlums appeared.

"Help him," Tabby said.

"It's messed up," said Ricky, nodding in agreement but not action.

"Err," I murmured, still bruised from my encounter with Craig. I didn't want to go a round with the Hoodlums unprepared and unarmed.

"Oh, for god's sake," Tabby said, and stormed off downstairs on her own. This spurred us into action. We chased her. The rest we couldn't see, but we heard some of it, and Cliff filled us in on the rest afterwards.

A conversation occurred and it was reasonably friendly until, seemingly without provocation, a hand reached out from the door, grabbed Cliff's ukulele, and smashed it over his head. A second assailant karate-kicked him down the steps, where he landed in a heap on the concrete slabs of the garden as several beer bottles were launched at his head. Then a very large, very heavy book was thrown from the second-floor window. The word *capital* was misspelt on the cover, which didn't bode well for the contents. I don't know about a Marx, but it sure left a mark. There was a lot of laughter. Then the back door slammed closed and the music was turned up.

"Help me," Tabby shouted, as I reached our gate. She and Ricky had scooped up Cliff, groggy but conscious, and were dragging him back in. I locked the gate behind them and helped hoist him through to his room, where we laid him on the bed.

I rushed off to find an ice pack. "What were you thinking?" I asked, as I placed it on the huge lump on his forehead.

He groaned. "That I'd reason with them. They can't be reasoned with. That was my favourite uke. First Aggie, now Ike the Uke?"

Ricky was silent, contemplating something. He snapped back to life and/or enthusiasm and spun then clapped. "*I get it*. I get what you were doing, Cliff! It's brilliant."

"No," said Tabby, "it was reckless."

"And stupid," I added.

"Well, maybe it was." He batted the notion away with the back of his hand. "But I think Cliff realised a heist can't succeed without an inside man. Technically, you've seen the inside now," he said, looking at Cliff. "Which makes you our inside man. What can you tell us about the layout?"

Cliff whimpered, clutching his head. "S—same as this place. Messier. I saw powder. Baking, maybe? Or coke."

"Did you see Robin?"

"No. A sort of living room. There were couches. People. *Owww*."

"How many people, Cliff?"

"I don't know. Three or four?"

"Was it three or was it four, buddy."

"It was three."

"How many in the kitchen?"

"Just the two that jumped me."

"They proved themselves to be violent," said Tabby, "with little provocation, depending on how you feel about *Imagine*."

"The jury is still out, Tabby." I said.

"I think Ricky might be right," she said. "We need a few more people and definitely a bit more muscle."

Ricky nodded. "And a loose cannon."

"Someone no stranger to violence," she agreed.

"I'm no stranger to *being* violenced," I said. "Does that count? I punched a pigeon once. It was in self-defence, but still."

"Is that why they hate you so much?" she asked.

Ricky's eyebrows knitted. "What was the pigeon going to do?"

"I didn't wait to find out."

"Is that technically self-defence?"

"It is. I defended myself."

"I mean legally?"

"It's a pigeon," I said. "It's not getting its day in court."

"Some days you're the statue, some days you're the pigeon," said Cliff, removing the ice pack and revealing a lump as big as a ping-pong ball.

"He's delirious," I said.

"Do you remember those six-year-olds outside McDonald's?" Tabby asked, tapping her cheek.

My voice softened. "They were on the McFlurry high of their lives."

"There were only four of them, but they gave you a good thrashing."

"They said I looked at them funny. How do you look at a six-year-old funny?"

"Nah," said Ricky. "There's no way around it. Every heist has a loose cannon."

"I guess I'm more of a very tight cannon," I lamented.

We fell silent, contemplating all the worst people we'd ever met.

"How about Albert?" I asked.

She recoiled. "Too loose."

I tilted my head in what I hoped was a classic pose of the contemplation genre. "I think I know a guy."

"Are you recommending him?" Ricky asked.

"I guess... yes?"

"Do you know him well?"

"No. And he might have retired. He was special forces."

"Coming back for one last job?" Ricky grinned. "I'm liking the sound of this."

"But he's violent."

"Whack," said Ricky, and clicked twice.

"I guess he whacks, yes."

"That's it?" Cliff asked. "We're good to go? I want to go. I'd go right now."

"You've already been," I said. "And look what happened. This time we plan meticulously. Or let Tabby and Ricky plan."

"There are still a lot more of them than us," Tabby said.

Ricky rubbed at his neck. "I'd feel better if we had a down-and-out person with an obscure talent that doesn't seem like it would be of any use. Often, it's the idiot younger brother of the confidence man. Anyway, long story short, unexpected events occur that create a need for exactly that skill, and so that person redeems themselves."

"Long story short," I repeated. "Linda."

Tabby and Cliff swapped a look. "The Misfits."

"Yes!" I said, and, in my excitement, punched the air, narrowly missing my own ear. "Cliff is right. This is about us Misfits standing up for ourselves. We need them." I hesitated. "Although convincing them to go to a public library is hard enough, never mind bringing down a ruthless criminal enterprise."

"Who are the Misfits?" Ricky asked.

"Motley Misfits," I said. "It's hard to explain. It's a sort of self-help group, or maybe self-pity. But we need them. Or they need us, perhaps. Either way, there's need."

"What about a femme fatale?" Tabby asked. "We've got a house full of horny young men we need to lure out."

"You, of course," said Cliff, reaching out to stroke her arm. This was love speaking. Tabby was many things, and her everyday homeliness and understated girl-next-door looks could scratch, perhaps even wound, but were they fatal?

She shook her head. "I'm the mastermind. I'll coordinate from the taxi. It's my plan, mostly. It's complicated. But it's there in my head. It'll be ruthless and they'll never see it coming."

"Who then?" Cliff asked.

"Linda?" Tabby suggested.

I laughed. "She might be able to bore them into submission."

"Annie?" said Cliff.

"Maybe ten years ago," Tabby said. "And she'd have a panic attack before she'd even started seducing anyone." Then she grinned. "Esme."

"You've never seen her." I felt defensive of how quickly Esme was being taken from my world into theirs.

"Cliff has filled me in, *in detail*."

"What day is it?" I asked.

"Thursday."

"To the taxi, Ricky!"

34

Ricky slowed to a stop in front of the last house on a long terrace. We were in a part of the city calling itself Forest Fields, but I saw neither. What I did see was soft light emanating from an upstairs window. My heart was beating in my throat. I dried my hands on my trousers.

"You want me to come?" Ricky asked.

"Would you?"

"Of course, buddy."

I believed him but shook my head. "No, this is my pickle."

"Your face might give her a fright."

"She's used to it."

I walked up the path and found a welcome mat that said FUCKOFF. The glass on the door had a bright-yellow sticker:

No salespeople

No canvassers

No tradesman

No junk mail

No religious nuts

Since I was trying to convince her to take part in

Tabby's heist and—I suppose, also—my friendship, I wondered if that made me a salesperson? I knocked quietly, in case her dad was asleep and/or because part of me hoped she wouldn't hear and I could slip back to the taxi and tell Ricky and/or myself that no one was home.

After twenty, perhaps even twenty-five seconds, two locks disengaged and the door opened. "Stab a crab," she said, tightening the cord of her black satin dressing gown. "What happened to you?"

She reached out and turned my face, as if examining a damaged jug. I stepped back to avoid her touch, which was overwhelmingly warm and pleasant. "I... err... there was an altercation, which, well, I lost."

"The Hoodlums?"

My eyes dropped. "It's... complicated."

She tutted. "Okay, well, it's also late, so?"

I stared at the welcome mat. Perhaps more of an unwelcome mat. I hoped the words I'd managed to write on the way over would be sufficient. It had been hard to concentrate, what with Ricky talking nonstop about his all-time favourite heist movies and an idea he had for a Zeppelin nightclub.

Behind me, a group of students stumbled down the road singing a grammatically incorrect song about not wanting to clean. I'd always preferred scrubbing to dusting and hoovering, two things that certainly got no love from me.

"How was the poetry night?" I asked, as they passed.

She watched them go. "*Recital.* There were a whole four people there."

"That's pretty good for Nottingham. Well, for something without nudity or narcotics."

"There could have been *more* people. If those who'd been invited *came.* Although I guess I know now why you didn't."

"That's not the reason," I mumbled. "Well, not the only one."

She tutted again. "Did you just come over here to look sheepishly at your feet?"

"I'm not good at this. Peopling."

"No one is, J. We just bumble through as best we can."

I tried to meet her eyes. "We're all terrible wizards."

Those eyes softened. "That's nice. I'll put it in my next poem."

"Cliff is. Good, I mean. At wizarding."

"You don't see it, do you?" She scoffed. "Cliff is one of the most put-together people I've ever met. He tries so, so hard. Even that breezy walk of his is correcting for a stoop. It's like he's been designed by a committee. A good committee, to give him his dues. People aren't always what they seem. That's kind of the problem. And where I thought you were different."

"Sorry," I said, looking away.

"Stop apologising!"

"Sorry," I said again. "Ahhh. I can't stop."

"How did you know where I live?"

"I have a contact."

"In the government?"

"Worse, Citizens Advice." I pulled a receipt out of my wallet. "I wrote you a poem. An apology poem. You've been nice to me, and very forthcoming, while I've been mostly useless." I cleared my throat and stared down at the scrawl on the back of a Tesco Metro receipt for a six-pack of a certain fizzy beverage. "Life is hard..." I began. My voice faltered. I cleared my throat and started again.

"*Life is hard.*
And it is long.
But not for me.
For I'm not strong.

Or very smart.
Or good at art.
Or ball games.
But I am sorry.
I was scared.
I'm still scared.
We're doing a heist.
No, really...
We need your help.
Please help."

I folded the receipt and put it in my pocket.

"Ball games?" she repeated. "That a euphemism? I'd tell you not to give up your day job, but you don't have a day job."

"It rhymed, mostly."

"Swerved off at the end."

"Can I hear yours now?"

She looked over my shoulder. "Why *is* the taxi driver just sitting there?"

"He's my friend, Ricky. He's being nosy and/or protective."

"He's bouncing up and down in his seat."

"He's irrepressible. We are planning a heist. Mostly Ricky and Tabby. We need your help. Also, to convince the Misfits. We need them too. It's complicated. We're going after the Hoodlums. It might affect the future of the entire East Midlands. Or at least Radford. Or at least my street."

I didn't know if she believed me, but she gestured me inside. "Guess you better come in then?"

My leg began to spasm from fear that if I did, she might want to lick my eyes or other body parts or generally—and, I suspected, also sinfully—sex me up, as the kids were calling it, or so I'd heard on the radio.

"Soon," I said, shuffling backwards. "They stole Cliff's

van, Aggie. We have to plan. We're planning. We're going to shaft them. Probably also ourselves. I'm back-office but anyway, can you come to mine instead?"

Her head tilted from side to side as she considered it. "Can't. I need to keep an eye on my dad."

"Okay." I turned to go. "Soon then? At Motley Misfits, maybe? Soon? I already said soon. We need you. *Soon*. Bye and/or sorry."

35

For the second meeting in a row, I was bringing a new face into the inner sanctum of woe that was the Motley Misfits. We were late because Ricky wasted several minutes finding suitable parallel-parking music.

"Whoa," he said, as we walked down Poetry's last aisle and saw the huddled figures. "A secret club."

Everyone was there except Esme. The size and scope of my sadness at her absence surprised me. I hoped I hadn't scared her off for good with my... self.

"What happened to your face?" Peter asked, as we approached the tables. "I almost didn't recognise you. Lucky you still have your signature eyes."

"I fought a door and lost," I said, pulling out a chair.

"Sure you did. Tricky thing, doors."

"Do doors fight now?" Annie asked, twitching nervously in her seat. "I've always got a bad vibe from my patio door."

"Mm-hmm. Are you going to introduce our new member?"

"Ah, right. This is Ricky. He's my... friend."

"Congratulations," said Hugh.

"He sure is," Peter confirmed, and the others nodded and looked happy for me but with jealous undertones.

"Wassup?" said Ricky. "Nice to meet you all." He looked around and then sat down. "Very, err, secluded?"

"Thanks," said Hugh, proudly.

"Where's Cliff?" Linda asked. "Such a lovely man."

Annie licked her lips, avoiding eye contact.

"Waiting for the police," I said. "That's part of why we're here, actually."

Esme arrived. I heard her before I saw her, her Doc Martens thudding on the tiled floor again. Then there she was, flooding the aisle of books with light. How much she brightened everything around her was extra impressive when you considered how much black she wore while doing it.

"Sorry everyone," she said. "I had to see a man about a dog."

"Me uncle sells dogs," Ricky said. "What sort you looking for?"

She paused, looked at me, then at him, then sat down. "Mr Irrepressible," she said. "We meet at last."

It was the first time I'd seen Ricky blush. I didn't think he had much experience with women, which was something we had in common but that he had an age-related excuse for.

"What's on the agenda?" Peter asked, as Hugh fished through his briefcase. "Whatever it is, I welcome it."

"Me," I said. "I am. We're doing a heist and we need your help."

"Mm-hmm mm-hmm mm-hmm mm-hmm," said a suddenly panicked Hugh, removing a handkerchief and mopping his brow.

"For a second there, I thought you said *heist*?" said Peter, who'd gone almost translucent.

"Me too," said Annie, who was always ghostly white.

"He did," said Ricky.

"I'm already wanted in three countries," said Steven, leaning his chair onto its back legs.

"I did a heist once," said Linda.

We settled in for a story that never came.

"Exhilarating business, heists," said Peter, after a moment. "What's the prize?"

I remembered how I was still being given the runaround by both my bank and the police, who always claimed they were doing something, which was an easy claim to make but wouldn't pay my bills. "Zero pounds and/or zero pence. But you will earn a lot of self-respect. And there will be quite a boost to Radford real estate values, but that might help me more than you."

"Who are we heisting?" Linda asked. "If it's any of my ex-husbands, I'm in. If it's Buckingham Palace, I might be busy. They know my face. Some things went missing. Cake-related things. And a tiara, or so they say, but I mean, what's a tiara between friends?"

"Err..." Ricky frowned, unused to the narrative swerve in Linda's stories. "The Robin Hoodlums. Know the name? I betcha do. They own half of Radford. Or are squatting in it, anyway."

"I live in Hucknall," said Hugh. "Mm-hmm."

"Is it named after a singer?" I asked.

He frowned. "Sorry?"

"I'm busy," said Steven. "I'm training to join the SAS. It's full-on. I shouldn't even be here. It's just that it's on my way to their secret headquarters behind Specsavers." He looked around. "But you didn't hear that from me."

"Mm-hmm," said Hugh. "It's not a strong proposition, all things considered."

"I have to agree with Hugh," said Peter.

I looked to Ricky for help. He was a man, albeit a very new man, who had once convinced me that I had special powers and should use them in a number of doomed and/or hare-brained experiments.

He shrugged and looked at me. "We can do it on our own."

While this was probably correct, I wanted the Misfits involved. If I was standing up for myself, they could too. More than that, they should. Which was why it was such a relief when Esme sprang to life.

"Snare a hare, you lot." She crossed her arms. "I mean, what is this group for? How long have youse been meeting?" She looked from person to person.

"Three years, more or less," said Peter. "The core group anyway."

"And what have you achieved in that time?"

Hugh bristled. "Several of our members have moved on to more prosperous pastures, and I'd like to think because of what they learned here. Tabby, for example."

"The heist was Tabby's idea," I said. "She's the mastermind."

"Think of all the times you've been overlooked, bullied, marginalised, ridiculed," said Esme, pointing at each person in turn.

"That could take a while. Mm-hmm."

"Yes," said Peter. "It could."

"We don't have to be misfits," she continued. "We don't have to cower and hide and make it easy for the world to marginalise us."

"That's easy for you to say," said Annie. "You aren't

really one of us in the first place, if you don't mind me saying. Do you mind me saying?"

"Well, I could keep coming here and feeling sorry for myself for a few years, watching my confidence slowly drain away, and then I would become one of you. But I'm not going to do that." Esme seemed to inflate as she talked. "I'm not giving up. Let's get out of this stuffy library and see what we're made of." She pointed to the window. "Confidence is the most seductive substance in the universe, and even if I don't have it, I'm going to bloody well fake it. Nottingham is not going to become less of a hellhole unless we make it one. So who's with us?"

As I listened, I found myself rising in my seat. I was rousable after all. "Yes," I said. "Exactly. Thanks, Esme."

We swapped smiles, and I felt another tight tug and—I suppose, also—tingle in my loins.

Ricky had been nodding along as well, and he mouthed, "Femme fatale."

"Couldn't have put it better myself," said Peter.

"Anyone's bully is everyone's bully," I said.

"This is your moment," Ricky added, melodramatically.

Was Ricky a Misfit? He had fringe beliefs and odd mannerisms, but he was also full of pep and gusto and verve and other such go-getter substances. You couldn't say that of the others, with perhaps the exception of Esme.

"Self-respect could come in handy," said Annie. "Couldn't it?" Her eyes darted around wildly. "I don't know."

"Mm-hmm," said Hugh, gripping the table's edge. "Heisting, that's, well, that's a young man's game. A braver man. I'm sixty-five. I'm beyond all this. I couldn't even control a classroom."

"I'd love to, of course," said Peter. "But I'm disabled. You all know that."

Ricky cocked his head, perhaps trying to decide where this disability sat within him. Peter ran a clarifying hand up and down his face. "Face blind."

Ricky scoffed. "That a real thing?"

"Of course it is!"

I wasn't sure if it was, objectively and scientifically, but it's best to take people at face value, or non-face value.

"Won't be a problem," Ricky reassured. "Not for this plan."

I turned to Steven, who was gazing up at the ceiling. "Steven, what about you?"

His chair tipped back and knocked into the wall. "I've done a heist already."

"We're not talking about a computer game here."

"Nah, for reals."

"So you're experienced?" said Esme. "Good. We can use that."

"No, it's more like I've already had the experience and I'm actually really busy on... what day did you say it was?"

"I didn't," I said.

"Yeah, I can't make it then."

"It's next Friday."

"Right, yeah. I'm, well, I've got... jury duty."

"Jury duty? Uh-huh. Fine." Esme turned her attention from him to the two women in the group. "Linda, Annie?"

Linda was knitting furiously but I couldn't tell what from its odd shape. She put it down on the table. "Willy warmer," she said, as if answering my unspoken question. "Well, whole thing rather reminds me of a time I robbed that bank in Monte Carlo. It was a gentleman I'd met on a plane who had a moustache like a pencil and a coral-coloured car that was too distinctive to be a getaway vehicle, although we got away, at least from that first one. I'm still on some lists. It's part of why I don't travel internationally now.

There's another story to that though and it would take some time to tell it and I don't want to derail things too much further, what with time being of the essence."

"That a yes?" Ricky asked, cross-eyed. "I got a bit lost."

"It's a yes," she said with a nod. "It will be my pleasure to help destroy your enemies. *Our* enemies."

"I'm finding this all a little overwhelming," said Annie, hiding behind her sleeve. "I didn't even know heists were real. Which has opened a whole new area of concern. Are people planning to heist me? Are they watching me right now? I'll not be able to sleep tonight, I tell you. Come to think of it, I might be heading for a panic attack. You don't walk towards danger. You walk the other way, or hide behind a bush."

"No more hiding," I said, banging my fist on the table. "And we have a plan. A good plan." I would be mostly hiding in the plan, but I left that part out.

"It's too confrontational," Hugh said, his eyes downcast. "It's not who we are."

"I hate to disagree," said Peter, turning to his fellow elder statesman. "But they're right, Hugh. It's about who we *could* be."

"Peter, Linda, Esme, thank you," I said. "Now, anyone else?"

Hugh took a deep breath but then lowered his eyes.

"*Steven?* Last chance," I prodded.

"Can't." He tutted. "It's an important case. Murder. Of a cat, but still, murder is murder. Well, unless the murdered thing is edible."

"Fine. Thanks for hearing us out," I said, moving my chair back. "This group has meant a lot to me. Still does, I guess, is what I'm saying, in a roundabout sort of way. You're good eggs. Fundamentally. Figuratively. Metaphorically, even, perhaps."

“Yeah, you all keep it real.” Ricky said, standing. “Now we’ve got a loose cannon to find and/or convince. James will be in touch in the next days. We know where you live. That’s less threatening that it sounds. Tabby knows, basically. Right?” He looked at his feet. Sweet.” He skipped away.

“Sorry.” I said, starting to follow him. “He gets ahead of himself. Thanks again.”

36

"How do we play this?" Ricky asked, as we walked up the wide alley behind Waterstones. "Your classic good cop, bad cop?"

Several pigeons on a nearby roof had me on edge. I stepped over a dead rat. "What cop would I be?"

Ricky didn't see the rat, and it squelched beneath one of his comically large-tongued, brilliantly white trainers. "Ah, yuck." He shook his foot. "I guess I'd be bad cop? No, I'm too young to pull that off. I'd be good?"

"I don't know if I'd make a good bad cop."

"A bad bad cop then?"

"How about we're just two average cops making the most of their meagre skills and training to make it through the day unscathed?"

"Eh." He frowned. "Not much drama in that, but fine, I guess."

We needed someone who would do the things the rest of us wouldn't dare, whether or not we wanted them to and/or when we least expected. Someone who would shoot first and ask questions later. Or make us ask questions later about why they shot so hastily. I think. This role confused me, but Ricky was adamant we needed it. That without it, our tiger lacked teeth.

And so, we were in yet another alley. "If we get him, we're there," Ricky said, brushing drizzle from the sleeves of his puffy coat. "We'll have the wildest, weirdest crew of misfits since Bruce Willis's gang of asteroid miners."

"How did that end?"

"Courageously."

"He died, didn't he?"

"A little bit, yeah."

"No one dies a little bit."

"What about that Jesus geezer?"

"He a hundred per cent died. Slowly and in great pain."

"Yeah, but he came a hundred per cent back, didn't he?"

"Briefly," I admitted.

The alley widened further. DJ was sitting on the top of three steps, near a loading bay, smoking and staring moodily at nothing. He was in his black Waterstones shirt. He didn't have a coat. I imagined he thought that coats were for sissies. He saw us and leapt to his feet. This had to be the alley he'd wanted to take me to for the almost victimless crime of stickering.

"Where's the rest of him?" Ricky whispered. "Shame he's not Asian."

"Two on one?" DJ said, throwing his cigarette down then raising his fists. "I like those odds."

It wasn't two on one for long because Ricky hid behind me. I put my palms up to my chest in a calm-down gesture. "We just want to talk."

"Never been much of a talker," he hissed.

"We need your help."

"Never been no helper neither."

"Heister?" Ricky said. It would have had more gravitas

if he'd not popped up to shout it then popped back down behind me again.

DJ lowered his fists. "Well, well, well." He laughed, but it sounded more like a howl. "You serious, Janet Snackson?"

"Deadly."

"Not deadly, Ricky," I snapped. "We discussed this and all my various red lines."

"Almost deadly," Ricky corrected.

"Who's the target?"

"Ever heard of the Robin Hoodlums?" I asked.

DJ grunted and looked away.

"You know them?"

"Everyone knows them. Knows *him*." He nodded in Radford's rough direction.

"What do you know about him?" Ricky asked.

"Controls Radford. Had run-ins with his boys when I was working the fairgrounds. They're mean."

"You're meaner," I said.

He bent down picked up the pack of cigarettes from the floor, took one out, and lit it. "Back in the day, maybe."

"You scared?"

He blew a ring of smoke into my face. "Realistic is what I am."

"I get it," I said, wafting it away. "It's a long way from here to Kabul."

I had no idea how far it was to Kabul.

"It's a long way from here to anywhere," he mused, staring off towards a stack of folded cardboard boxes. There was a faint stench of rotten eggs in the air.

"We've got a hell of a plan," said Ricky, which wasn't true. The plan had several large holes and was based entirely on Tabby's surveillance, Cliff's dwindling confidence, Ricky's movie collection, and my wish to make up for almost three decades of lost time.

"What's in it for me?" DJ asked, swapping the grip on his cigarette from a V to a tight pinch.

"Glory," said Ricky, which is what people say when they're trying to distract someone from the answer they wanted, which was always "Money."

"Glory?" he growled. "Glory I've had thanks, Britney Smears. I've been to places you can't even dream of. I've done things you..." His voice faltered. "Can't even dream of."

"I don't know," I said. "Ricky's got an overactive imagination."

My sidekick stepped back out and stood next to me. "I dreamed of Kabul once, actually."

"Well, I'm sure it wasn't accurate," said DJ, dismissively.

"Hot, dusty, mosque-y?"

DJ frowned. "I've retired."

"How would you like to come back for one last job?" I raised my finger. "Not for the money but for honour. For self-respect. For bragging rights."

"You can put that finger down, Andie MacTowel. I have a job. A civilian job. I'm legit."

"Guarding Harry Potter books?" Ricky said mockingly.

"You drive a taxi." So he'd seen us park. He was still paying attention, observing his surroundings.

Ricky's jaw set. "Then I know, don't I? How it feels to be less than you are. You miss it, don't you, the adrenaline? That tingle up your spine. Suiting up. The thrill. The fight. The glory. The celebration after?"

DJ took a long, sullen breath and threw the nub of his cigarette into a puddle. "I'm too old for all that."

"Let me make you—"

I reached out a pacifying arm. I knew Ricky had been

preparing his next persuasion onslaught, which I guessed would be free taxi rides for life. I'd seen few but enough movies to know he was approaching this wrong. "Okay," I said, and stepped back. "Fine. We'll do it on our own. We don't need you. Just pretend we were never here." I ushered Ricky away with a backwards nod. We took a few steps towards the taxi.

"WAIT!"

Smiles rippled across our faces. They had to feel it was their decision. Their idea. "Without me you boys are screwed. You'll get killed."

"We'll find someone younger," Ricky said. "Hungrier."

"I'm hungry."

"It's lunchtime."

DJ hocked from deep in his throat and launched a ball of spit at the wall. "How big is the crew?"

Ricky counted in his head. "Eight, with you."

"All amateurs like you two clowns?"

"Enthusiastic," I said. "And Ricky here is damn irrepressible."

"What did they do to you?" DJ asked me.

"Lately? Well, ruined my street. Stole my life savings. Stole my roommate's van. Spray-painted a penis on my gate —erect. Played loud music every night for the past year. Made all my neighbours move out. Destroyed the value of my home. Probably some other stuff that will happen today. It's early."

"It's lunchtime," Ricky repeated.

We turned away again. Behind us, DJ sucked in a sharp lungful of air. "Read your manifesto, by the way. Once I'd calmed down. Spoke to me, I guess. We are who we are, I suppose." He supposed.

We walked back towards him. Ricky puffed out his chest. "And who are you then?"

"I'm - a - bad - motherfucker," DJ snarled. "That's who I am."

"Prove it."

"I've already proved it to your boy here," he said, nodding towards me. "Got in trouble for it as well. Official warning for 'excessive force'." He air-quoted those last words. "Might even lose my job."

"Sorry about that," I said.

"Prove it to *me*," said Ricky. "Because from where I'm standing, I just see a small—"

DJ strode forwards and poked a finger into Ricky's face, or tried, but made it only as high as his throat. "Finish - that - sentence, Sally Jesse Ring-my-bell. See what happens. I've nothing to prove to anyone." The radio on his belt crackled. "DJ, some brat puked all over the life-size Jamie Oliver. Clear it up, will ya?"

His eyes flitted left and right. "You need me."

"And you need us," Ricky countered.

DJ sighed and his shoulders dropped. "Got a femme fatale?"

"Yep."

"A confidence man?"

"Having a bit of a personal crisis," I said.

"Yeah," Ricky said, prodding me sharply with his elbow.

"A mastermind?"

"The greatest," I said. "You'll love her."

"A woman?"

"It's 1999."

He broke eye contact. "Don't remind me." He tapped his foot then scraped his top lip over his lower incisors. "One last job before retirement?"

"Exactly," Ricky said.

"I don't take orders." He remembered the radio on his belt. He clicked it off. "Tell me the plan."

37

It was Friday. Tabby and I stood shoulder to shoulder at the corkboard admiring what had become a very detailed and/or elaborate plan of multiple and/or perhaps too many moving parts. Tabby rubbed her elbow. She was wearing a blonde wig and heavy make-up.

"I've made the tea," I said.

"That's good," she replied, without looking at me. "What have we overlooked?" She tapped her chin. "There's always something they overlook."

"We're asking a lot of everyone," I said. "Especially Ricky and DJ."

"Are they ready?"

"Esme's finishing up their disguises."

"Esme, James?" Her eyes twinkled with mischief and/or melanoma. "She's—"

Cliff entered the room looking anxious and pale in a curly black wig and shiny gold jacket. He reminded me of a game show host who'd fallen on hard times but was still eager to give away one last fridge-freezer combo. "I barely slept. Not that I sleep much anymore. I guess I'm not feeling very..." He looked away. "Confident?"

"You're our confidence man, Clifffff."

Tabby shot me a look then looked back at Cliff. "You're going to be great, honey."

He hadn't been the same since taking that child's guitar full force to the head. Either that or his time with Tabby and me in the social underworld, not to mention my peril training and the confrontation with Craig, had made him aware of but also paralysed by the overwhelming fragility and casual cruelty of everything.

I was almost proud. "You were born to do this, Cliff."

He brightened. "You think? Really?"

"Absolutely," said Tabby, giving him a tight sideways hug. He broke from that hug to slap himself in the face. "I WAS BORN TO DO THIS."

Tabby thumped him on the back. "YOU WERE BORN TO DO THIS."

He tipped his head back and yelled, "I WAS BORN TO DO THIS." But it seemed his heart and—I suppose, also—other body parts weren't in it.

"I have to go," she said, as a shout came up the stairs.

"James, get your skinny ass down here!"

Esme. She'd set up her disguise studio in my bedroom of many wrapped bubbles. I'd been nervous about everyone seeing it but decided some things are more important than your own self-consciousness, such as destroying your enemies and bathing in their blood.

"I dig it," she said, running a hand across the back of my wrapped office chair. "And it's very easy to wipe down, if you get what I mean?"

"When dusty?"

"I suppose, yeah."

"Or after a spillage of Vimto?"

"That too. Now *sit*," she said, beckoning. "I don't bite. Hard."

I slipped onto the chair and she knelt in front of me and I found myself unable to meet her brilliant, heavily mascara-ed eyes. A make-up kit was next to her on my side dresser. I'd made careful slits in the wrapping so the drawers were still accessible. I had important things in there. Bubble wrap, for example.

"Where did you learn to do this?" I asked, looking down at the make-up bag. Beside it was an open black bin bag of Ricky's disguises.

"Theatre school." She leaned back, tilted her head, and appraised my face, just as she'd done when we first met. "You don't need much," she said. "You've great skin." She dabbed at some kind of powder with a circular sponge. "Very unblemished." She tried to hide the wound on my nose and eye, which seemed not very possible.

"I haven't done much manual labour, even though I'm Amish at heart," I said.

She paused. "Weird, but okay. Your eyes are your signature. If we hide those and your bruises, we're 75 per cent there."

"I fought a door," I said, repeating the lie I'd told the Misfits.

"Sure you did," she said, rooting through her bag. She handed me a pair of sunglasses and placed a baseball cap on my head with the logo of a green grocer's called Apple.

"I always wanted smaller eyes," I said. "They're the source of so much mockery."

"You have spectacular eyes."

"Esme. I..." I faltered.

She slipped a thick gold chain over my neck. "Just because."

Ricky and Tabby had argued that I was too well-known, too facially memorable, and too injured, and so my role in the heist was small and inconsequential, like my life. I would help Cliff and Peter set up the party that would draw the Hoodlums out. After that, my job was to assist as required, staying around the alleys, coordinating with Linda about Robin's whereabouts.

It wasn't much but I'd try my hardest not to screw it up. Ricky appeared at the door, bouncing on his heels. "This is it!" He handed out another earpiece, this one twice the size of the first. New version. Uncle Sanjay's made some improvements. "Tap and hold to talk like a walkie-talkie, double tap and you'll broadcast, like a radio, at least until someone else double taps. They're sensitive, so be careful. Don't lose this one, James. We only have five, so that's you, me, Tabby, Cliff, and Esme."

He handed Esme hers then passed me a small blue walkie-talkie and said Linda had the other.

"DJ ready?" I asked.

"Prowling the garden and chain-smoking."

"Bum a smoke for me, will ya?" said Esme. "I'd ask but he creeps me out. I don't trust him." Her head cocked. "Can we trust him?"

Ricky chuckled. "A man out of retirement for one last job who none of us have ever worked with before and has a violent, uncontrollable nature? No, Esme, we can't trust him. That's the point."

My earpiece crackled. "*I'm in position,*" Tabby said. This meant she was in Ricky's taxi, parked just down from the Hoodlums' lair. "*Windows dimmed.*"

We assembled in the kitchen.

"*Audio check,*" Tabby said. "*Ricky?*"

He reached up to his earpiece and tapped. "Alpha Tango Papa over."

"*Cliff?*"

"I hear you, doll."

"*Esme?*"

"You're damn cool, Tabs."

"James?"

"Present."

"The door's opening," Tabby said. *"Okay, people. Robin's coming out, bang on schedule. Get in position."*

I pushed the button on the walkie-talkie. "Linda, you have eyes on the cemetery?"

"Roger dodger up here at the window in Tabby's room. I've a cracking view of all I survey, James. Reminds me—"

"Great. Over."

A dull thud rang out behind me. I turned to see DJ punching the hallway wall. "Good morning, Vietnam!"

"Who are you again?" Peter asked. Esme had dressed Peter in a striped black-and-white jumper and a red beret. He looked like a French mime.

"DJ."

"Of course. That's obviously who you are."

"Ready for this, Peter?" I asked.

"As I'll ever be, James."

"Okay," Tabby said. *"Remember what this is about. Who it's for. Today the tide turns. Today the Misfits rise up and take over. Synchronise watches. Thirty minutes, starting... now."*

I pushed the button on the fad digital wristwatch Ricky had supplied.

30:00

29:59

29:58

29:57

The walkie-talkie spat static. *"He's on Alfreton Road, over."*

"Cliff, James, and Peter, go start a party," Tabby said.

Peter nodded at me and then we were at the back door and then in the small paved garden and then at the gate, which opened and revealed the Hoodlums' gate, with the green star logo.

Cliff checked the alley. "All clear."

I shivered in the crisp late-December air. In a few days, if we survived this, I'd become thirty years old and there would be much to celebrate. That seemed far away but then everything felt dim and distant, perhaps on account of the sunglasses.

"SHOWTIME," Cliff said, thumping his chest, but his eyes gave him away—his pupils were full of fear and flight. He was becoming a more interesting human, but a less happy and effective one. I hoped I was moving in the opposite direction.

I stepped aside to make space for his Tesco trolley as it rattled out the gate, overloaded with party goods. Then I grabbed my trolley. As I did so, I prickled. I took a moment to enjoy the sensation, threw my head back, howled, and shoved the trolley into the alley after him.

"That's how to do it," Peter said, following me with his own trolley.

We rattled up the alley past fenced-in back gardens before we turned right into a wider passageway—the same one where I'd once hidden in a bin—and emerged at the top of Portland Road. The street behind my street.

"Easy," I shouted, as Cliff hurtled too fast around the right turn and hit a low brick wall. I swerved to avoid dog excrement and my trolley rattled and shook and almost slipped from my clammy hands as I joined him on Portland Road.

It was eerily quiet. Children no longer played here and the elderly shuffled quietly and early as they went about their essential life-maintenance tasks. Even students—those most rambunctious, carefree, belligerent humans—avoided this road. If there had been community here, Robin and his

Hoodlums had destroyed it and today we would destroy him and/or them and win back our freedom and/or self-respect.

Cliff reached the front of their HQ, a home identical to my own. I arrived ten, or perhaps even fifteen seconds later. Standing next to him, in front of it, I was almost disappointed. In my imagination, it was so much bigger. The paving slabs filling their front garden were cracking and had a weed problem. They had set their wheelie bin on fire and its charred remains stood next to several bags of rubbish and a great number of Carlsberg cans arranged in a casual heap that could have passed for modern art, which was a fad, unlike traditional art, which has stood the test of time.

Hanging from the first-floor window, flapping in the breeze, was a faded green-and-white flag with their star logo. A yellow cable ran from the window, above our heads, to the power lines from which they were stealing electricity. Or re-appropriating it, I guess Robin would have argued.

Just a few feet from us, and our trolleys, behind a very grubby, curtainless window, they sat in the living room. Some were sleeping while others were huddled around a video game console.

I felt a rush of heat, as if being toasted. Before all this, I'd not known why a lawbreaking lifestyle might appeal to Robin and these merciless men. That was no longer the case. I enjoyed being sinful.

Peter and his trolley rattled in and knocked into mine. Cliff lunged forward to steady them. We could hear the loud sounds of their game. They didn't seem to have noticed us yet.

"Sorry," said Peter. "Got away from me."

"It does that," I said.

Cliff's trolley held party supplies and a speaker. Peter's was packed with cheap champagne and a small petrol generator. My trolley was full to bursting, holding a giant, strapped mass of green PVC-coated nylon. We'd need to borrow some pavement and a bit of the empty, neighbouring houses paved front gardens, but Ricky assured me the small bouncy castle would fit.

Peter helped me heave it out of the trolley. I unclipped it and rolled it with my foot as he moved what was left of the bin and the rubbish bags to make space. We angled it, diagonally, towards their front door.

Was it true that no one could resist a bouncy castle? We were about to find out.

38

I put two bricks under the trolley's wheels to hold it in place as Cliff hit play on the boombox, brought the microphone to his mouth, then paused.

Our eyes locked. I nodded. He winked in response. We were saying much with little.

I'm here for you.

I'm petrified.

I know.

Me too.

"GOOD MOOOOOOORNING 12 PORTLAND ROAD!" he shouted into his microphone and over the music. "AND WHAT A MORNING IT IS. Don't mind the drizzle."

Peter yanked the cord on the generator, which whirred and clanked and bounced, expelling air that quickly animated the lifeless, limp bouncy castle.

The music Ricky had selected had one message and hit it very hard.

Rhythm, apparently, was a dancer.

"*Ricky and DJ*," Tabby said. We were to keep the

frequency clear for her, unless usage was essential. "Positions at the back gate."

"Couldn't agree more with the start," said Peter, popping the first bottle of champagne.

The front door flew open and a puffy-faced, shaven-headed, confused, pink-track-suited man stormed out looking like an angry pelican. "Get out of here, poofters."

Cliff danced a short jig. "Congratulations, you've been voted Criminals of the Year 1999 by viewers of *East Midlands News*."

It seemed so long ago that they had crowned me Nottingham's Unluckiest Man. Little that had happened since had proved them wrong.

Pelican Paul, as I decided to call him, turned to answer voices from inside the house. "I don't bloody know, do I? This nonce says we've won some award."

Two Hoodlums were at the front door now, blinking out into the light, while two more hovered menacingly, watching on from the living-room window. All wore their parkas.

"Criminal of the Year or somefink," Pelican Paul said, while chewing loudly. He had two gold teeth.

The window opened, and a skinny, wiry man with a hooked nose hung himself out. "This some kind of trick, pretty boy?" he yelled at Cliff.

Peter took a trophy from the shopping trolley and offered it to Pelican Paul. "Something you know a lot about, or so our readers have decided!"

Reluctantly, the Hoodlum took it. It was a footballer kicking a ball on which Esme had drawn a frowning human face with a silver marker pen.

"Your prize, gentleman, is an epic street party," said Cliff, gesturing to the shopping trolleys. "So come on out.

We've got champagne, a bouncy castle, and... drum roll, *Miss Nottingham*."

That piqued their interest. More shapes appeared at the front door as Peter passed out bottles of champagne and a plastic tray of donuts.

"I've never heard of no Criminal of the Year award," Pelican Paul said, but carried on passing champagne bottles down the line.

"True," said one of his criminal colleagues, reaching for a bottle and taking the first bite of a glazed pink donut, "but no reason to look no gift horses in no mouths neither."

Soon each had a bottle. Though they kept eyeing us suspiciously, I sensed they were praise-starved and pleasure-peckish. We offered both. And so they drank. The first few signs of merriment occurred when one sprayed another with champagne, dampening his green parka. The damp one swung a leg at the other but missed and fell over. Everyone laughed.

I kept myself busy with the bouncy castle, trying to avoid their attention. Up close, and in the morning light, the Hoodlums weren't as intimidating as I'd expected. I remembered the Rescue Room and how the scariest place in the entire world is your own mind.

"We did have a good year," said Hook Nose. "Remember those mobile phones we boosted from Dixons, Gav?" He elbowed one of his colleagues in crime. "Now that was a score. Shame what with them being such a fad and all."

"Bit cold for a party, though?" said Pelican Paul, looking up at the clouds.

"Not once you bounce," Cliff said encouragingly, sweeping a hand over the almost-inflated bouncy castle that I was nudging the last folds from with my shoes.

Hook Nose pointed at me. "Does he look familiar? And sunglasses in December? In Nottingham?"

"Get out of there now, James," Tabby ordered.

I turned, bowed, and hurried away, passing the taxi parked on the opposite side of the road. With the windows dimmed, I couldn't see our mastermind. I longed to be back inside it with Ricky, ad-libbing.

"That scuttle," a Hoodlum shouted after me.

I stopped, took a deep breath, slowed my steps, straightened my back, and walked as confidently as I could back towards the alley, feeling immensely guilty that I'd failed at even my minor role in proceedings.

"They're growing sceptical," said Tabby, as the song that had been playing ended. *"Esme, time for our femme fatale."*

"Suck a duck," she said, as I turned into the passageway and found her coming in the other direction. She was dressed to the nines in a black catsuit that plunged at the chest and hugged at the hips, which were swinging on account of her trademark Doc Martens. Black lipstick and an open fur jacket finished the look that said Cruella de Vil wasn't cruel enough.

It wasn't that she was beautiful, conventionally, although she was certainly beauty-adjacent. It was more that she struck with unapologetic female force. Like Uncle Sanjay, she had charisma in spades. She didn't belong here. Life had dragged her somewhere unexpected and she'd grown momentarily disorientated, but she was now finding her footing again. One day, her father would slip from this world and she'd be free.

She was better than this place. I hoped she'd stay anyway.

I moved left so she could pass. "Sorry."

She moved right so we would hit.

I move right so she could pass.

She moved left so we would hit. She grabbed a fistful of my jumper and pushed me against the wall, where she bit me on the neck and I lost my footing and slid down to the ground, my back to the wall, watching her stride wordlessly off to seduce a narrow houseful of local deplorables.

I felt stirred, as if by an invisible spoon. There was prickling, but it was different, centred elsewhere. I shook my head and tried to focus, reminding myself what was at stake.

At the end of the passageway, she turned, cackled, and then disappeared from view. I was supposed to go to the back gate in case Ricky or DJ needed me, but I had to follow and watch her, as soon as my legs were working again.

"Here she comes, boys," said Cliff, sweeping a hand towards her. "Miss Nottingham 1991—" He corrected himself, not wanting to make her sound so old. "9."

There were whistles and jeers and a loud "Coooor blimey."

"Did he say 1991?"

"Trampy vampy."

"The tits and ass are here."

I hung from the end of the alley, on my knees, hiding behind 8 Portland Road's low wall.

Esme walked up to one of the track-suited, parka-jacketed Mafiosi and slapped him across the face. "I am much more than that."

This sent them into a frenzy of whistles and shouts and the last Hoodlum exited the house to get a better view. The Hoodlum she'd slapped went bright red and slunk back from the group, downing the rest of his champagne as the others cheered. They were spilling onto the pavement and down into the road, watching, drinking, growing rowdier, pushing each other closer to the bouncy castle as Esme climbed onto it, took a position in its centre, sank to her knees, and bowed her head.

I unclipped the walkie-talkie from my belt. "Linda?"

"*Howdy doody,*" she answered. "*I'm still sitting pretty up here in the crow's nest. Robin's busy in the graveyard. He just gave a full bag to the guy with the briefcase. I once started a company selling executive knitted briefcases which—*"

"Tell me when it looks like they're finishing up."

"*Eighteen minutes left,*" Tabby said.

Cliff hit skip on the boombox and a new, genteel song built to the sound of galloping horses. There were several neighs and—I think, also—a bugle. Esme pulled off her coat and spun it over her head and then threw it over the back of the bouncy castle, where Peter was waiting to catch it. The Hoodlums cheered. She swung her brilliant red hair counterclockwise. Then she leapt up, mounted an invisible horse, fired an arrow, and galloped around the bouncy castle to the song which was about Robin Hood and his riding through a glen.

I wasn't sure what a glen was, but I was soon nodding along. Esme was excellent at riding an imaginary horse. I saw its every jump, canter, sprint, and bray. The Hoodlums could see it too. They couldn't tear their eyes from her. And that was exactly what we wanted.

She trotted down from the bouncy castle and did laps of the men. On the way she stroked a chin, picked a pocket, blew a kiss, fired an arrow, and sang along to the song, which was a very infectious ditty, if I say so myself, even with my limited ditty exposure.

There was rhythm to her movements, and while they did accentuate her body, the show was more entertaining and/or hypnotic than anything of an exclusively erotic nature.

"What a woman," Tabby said, her voice a mixture of pride and disbelief. *"Ricky, DJ, coast is clear."*

The song looped. For the second round, she grabbed Pelican Paul and put his hands on her hips and together they began an imaginary horse-riding conga everyone joined. Then they were all on the bouncy castle and having a tremendous time. None of it was what I had expected. And definitively not what they had expected.

Esme did not retreat to Sherwood.

Instead, Radford and seven merciless men were hers and—I suppose, also—ours for the taking. While I didn't want to miss what this would become, and what it already was, someone had to monitor Ricky and DJ. I pulled up on the wall and ran for the Hoodlums' back garden.

39

Ricky turned and gave me a thumbs up as I entered the open gate. He'd just finished picking the lock on their back door. His eyes were almost as big as mine, but his were electric. This was the life he wanted. He was more than a sidekick today—he was front and centre.

But he had DJ on his rear, and that I didn't envy.

As they went inside, I crept up to the door to listen. They were dressed in the same Adidas leisurewear and green parkas the gang wore. Theirs lacked the logo, but you could only see that from the back.

"*Just one goon in the kitchen, passed out on a sofa,*" said Ricky, via my headset. There was a loud thump. Ricky activated broadcast mode. "*DJ! No violence. No one should know we've been here. Tabby, DJ is being violent. He knocked one of them out.*"

He sounded like a child telling tales on his younger brother.

"*He was waking up,*" DJ protested. "*Did anyone hear?*"

"*No, the party is in full swing,*" said Tabby. "*They're mid-Macarena.*"

"*He won't remember,*" DJ said. "*Not where I hit him.*"

"*No violence,*" Ricky repeated.

"*It's a violent world.*"

"*We're supposed to be ghosts.*"

"*I'm more of a poltergeist.*"

The song changed. Yes, Nottingham was a gangster's paradise. And today we were its gangsters.

"*A lot of pizza boxes,*" said Ricky, "*and a little blow. And some skunk. Moving upstairs. Shitting myself here, to be honest.*"

"A skunk?" I said. "Don't make it angry."

"*You're doing great,*" said Tabby. "*Make sure DJ keeps to the plan.*"

"*First floor's clear,*" Ricky said. "*Moving up to the second. Shit,* he whispered. *Get back, DJ. There's two guards. Outside Robin's office. We're hiding in the first-floor toilet. How do we get them down?*"

"*The party was supposed to do that,*" Tabby said.

"*I can handle them,*" DJ muttered in the background.

"*That's not the plan.*"

"*The plan was that they'd go downstairs to the party.*"

"Can we send Esme up?" I asked.

"*No,*" said Tabby, "*she's got seven men hanging off her every word and, well, move.*"

"Cliff then?" I suggested.

"*Difficult,*" said Cliff. "*They're asking me questions and stuff.*" All the confidence had drained from his voice. "*Who am I talking to? This headset? For the newsroom,*" Cliff said to a Hoodlum.

"I could go?" I offered, hoping no one would say yes.

"*That could work,*" said Ricky. "*Maybe.*"

"*Pff,*" DJ scoffed in the background. "*What's he going to do? He's just an ugly boggle-eyed dweeb.*"

This, while true, and hurtful, ignored the fact of how he met me. What I was doing. Becoming.

"*No. I can try,*" said Cliff. "*I think.*" He activated broadcast mode, cutting Ricky off. "*Can I use your toilet, sir?*"

"*What?*" said one of the Hoodlums, barely audible for us.

"*Dodgy curry last night,*" said Cliff.

"*We've all been there, fella.*"

"*So, can I?*"

"*I don't know.*" The Hoodlum hesitated. "*It's inside.*"

"*I'll be quick.*"

"*We... the cleaning schedule... Sometimes hierarchy is good, know what I'm saying?*"

"*Not exactly.*"

"*It's rank, basically, fella.*"

"*I'm about to pop.*"

"*Hmm... well, you've a trustworthy face,*" the Hoodlum said. "*Go on then.*"

I heard Cliff's footsteps. He was on the move.

But he had no plan. And minimal confidence. And he'd already risked so much. And Tabby needed him. And he needed Tabby. We had never needed each other, she and I. I had simply needed her. I was expendable. And yet what was I doing? Standing at the back door like a... salmon-spazbucket.

It wasn't right.

I switched off my walkie-talkie, left it on the back step, and darted inside.

Cliff reached the stairs just before me. He was on the third step up when I lunged for him, pulled him down, climbed on his back, and covered his mouth with my hand as he thrashed beneath me.

He saw it was me. His eyes narrowed. I made a *shh* gesture with my finger. Then I pulled the earpiece from his ear and lobbed it over my shoulder to the floor before springing off and up, taking the steps two at a time.

The house was dark and smelt of Ribena and ridicule. It was as cold inside as out. I couldn't believe I was finally in the place I'd spent so much time fearing. It was so much smaller and less *Hammer House of Horror* evil than I'd expected. There weren't even any bloodstains on the carpet.

"*James jumped me and now he's gone up,*" said Cliff. "*I couldn't stop him.*"

"*What?*" said Tabby.

He could have stopped me.

"Leave this to me," I said. "I have a plan."

I had neither a plan nor any of my tools. It was dark. The light was blocked by the flag at the first-floor hallway window. The toilet door opened as I passed. Ricky's head poked through, and he gave a surprised, nervous thumbs up. I grinned and moved down the landing, past a closed bedroom door and a dart board with a picture of Margaret Thatcher on it. The room was a dorm if Tabby's surveillance was correct. Bunk beds. The group home had bunk beds. I pushed a lump of fear deeper into my throat as I crept up the first few stairs towards the second floor.

"*They're getting drunk,*" Tabby said. "*Cliff, Peter, slip back to ours as soon as you can.*"

I angled my head round and up to see what awaited me. There were two of them, on small wooden stools, on either side of Robin's door. One was on his phone. He was narrow-eyed and rat-like, with a long scar across his cheek and cropped gelled hair like Ricky's. The other was bald, gristly, and bearish, a thick gold chain around his neck. I could hear him snoring. They were both in their green parkas, probably because Robin was too tight to pay for heating.

I blew on my hands to warm them up then sat on the step to think.

I knew that they would see me and react negatively,

perhaps lashing out verbally and/or physically. That's what the tests with Ricky and/or my entire life had shown.

The song outside changed. Other people rocked my body, but rarely right. I would love to spend time with happy, young-sounding men in backstreets. Instead, I always ended up in alleys, alone.

I tried to imagine what Esme was doing to this song. Probably teaching them a dance routine of some kind.

Esme.

Ricky.

They hadn't reacted that way to me. Nor had the Misfits.

They liked me.

Respected me.

The well-worn tape playing in my mind squeaked and then stopped with a click. I thought of Craig—imparcelled and imperilled yet still refusing to admit he was a crappy father.

No, I decided, we didn't do it equally, change reality in our minds so we could be the heroes. In fact, some of us didn't do it at all. Some of us, lacking love and guidance, both parents, any living relatives, and a stable home, turned inwards. Became bitter and negative, needing to see ourselves not as the hero of our story but as its villain, loser, reject, weed, and Buster. This role, while unpleasant, became familiar. And familiarity was what we craved more than anything.

Yet, I was in the world.

I was doing a heist.

I couldn't be the person I'd long told myself I was. I had proved myself capable of more. I was having new experiences, common ones, like making friends. I'd watched my friends closely, just as I watched everything closely. I could use the things they'd taught me to gently charm these men and move them downstairs without misfortune befalling them and/or us Misfits.

Roused once more, I stood, took a stupendously deep breath and walked up the stairs.

Scarface looked up from his phone as I reached the top. "Who the fukking fuk are you then?"

"Hello," I said, breezily. "Good day to you both."

"I'll ask the questions," said Scarface, getting up.

"That wasn't a question, buddy," I said, bouncing on my feet.

"Mick, wake up," Scarface hissed. Robin's door was at the end of the landing. I walked a few steps closer.

"Right, yes," I said. "I couldn't agree more. Wake up, Mick. Excellent idea."

Mick's eyes opened. "Who's he then?" he said, in a thick Mancunian accent. He got to his feet and let out a long yawn. If he had a neck under that parka, he was keeping it secret.

"Hm-hmm," I said, authoritatively. "Well, gentlemen, good news. I'm here to take you to the party of your lives. You've been awarded the honour of Criminals of the Year 1999, and we're celebrating downstairs. Which you've heard, no doubt?"

Scarface scowled and ran a finger along his cheek but said nothing.

"We've a bouncy castle, Miss Nottingham, booze," I added. Their indifference remained and so I upped the stakes. "Heroin."

Mick the Mancunian's grey-blue eyes narrowed. "Why would he be wearing sunglasses?" he said, not taking his eyes off me but talking to his partner in crime, literally.

"Disguise?" said Scarface. "Gotta be."

"Why would he need a disguise?" Mick balled his hands into fists and took two steps towards me. A world of pain was approaching and I took a step back, raising my hands as my heel brushed the edge of the top step. This had just started and yet it was not going well.

"That reminds me of a story, actually," I began, wistfully. "About a time I robbed a bank dressed as an Amish man. I never got caught and although a lot of people said I was mad for having a cart as a getaway vehicle, I got away. At least the first time. It's powerful, disguise. I'll tell you the full story over some champagne and heroin out the front, shall I?"

Scarface turned to Mick. "Why's he doing that?"

Mick squinted as if I were far away. "I think our kid here is trying to build rapport."

"My advice, boys—try to be a bit more trusting. Your paranoia isn't serving you. There's this book I'd recommend. It's by Tony—"

"Get him," said Scarface.

"Flog a hedgehog."

"*Run,*" said Tabby.

I turned and made for the stairs. I was two steps down when I felt a tight grip around my right thigh. I tipped forward and smashed my chin on a step. As my head reeled back from the blow, the Hoodlums began pulling me up towards the landing. My sunglasses came off, and I soon lay in a heap at the top, moaning.

It was around then that the kicking started.

"*Help him,*" said Tabby. "*Cliff?*"

"I can't." His voice was quivering now. "I'm sorry."

My plan had sounded so good from the bottom of the staircase. I'd found myself so convincing. I'd been wrong, though. I'd learned nothing. The more I tried, the weirder I became, the worse things went. And now they were lashing out, as expected. This was the reason Tabby and Ricky didn't want me to have an important position in the heist.

I'd only survived the altercation with Craig because Ricky and Cliff had saved me.

I kept my left ear to the dirty grey carpet so they wouldn't see my earpiece. "Look at his eyes," said Mick.

"I hate his face," said Scarface. "It provokes."

"Kicking him helps, I'm finding."

"Looks like someone already has."

"Stop! Argh!"

What were my options now? Being someone else hadn't worked. I could be myself? But what would that even mean? Being weird and mumbling and apologetic? When had that ever helped? I thought about Al, the homeless guy. The right thing to do wasn't the opposite of the wrong thing. It didn't seem like this situation even had a right thing. All the things seemed wrong.

All the things.

That was what had worked with Craig. It wasn't just Ricky and Cliff. It was a combination of us all. That was what had confused him pliant. Confusion. Because I wasn't the only one who wanted to live in a world he understood.

I was curled up, trying to protect my head, as Scarface swung his foot back for the next hefty kick to my ribs. I activated broadcast mode, then took my hands away so he could see me. I turned my head. I smiled.

"Tenner for your ticker!" I shouted. "TENNER FOR YOUR TICKER."

"What?" He looked at his foot and then back at me.

"M-a-n-s field," I sang. "A field of men. I went there once and I didn't go again."

"He's cracking up," said Scarface, who was now looking at me with pity.

"How'd I get past everyone?" I asked.

Mick's foot was still frozen, mid-swing. "Huh," he said,

his tongue probing his mouth. "That is weird, actually. No one's allowed in. But you don't seem brave."

"Or hard," said Scarface.

"Or like you'd win anyone's trust."

"Or their friendship."

"Check my pocket," I said.

I felt Scarface's angry hand rummaging in my trousers.

"Just bubble wrap," said Scarface, discarding it. "Who would come in here unarmed?"

Mick rubbed his stubbly jaw. "No one would be that stupid. I'm confused. This is like one of them whatchamacallits? Riddles?"

"You have to go downstairs." I grabbed his foot. "Robin needs you."

"Liar," said Mick, shaking it free.

"I like a good riddle," said Scarface.

I burst into tears. Real tears. I cried even though it was the last thing any of the action heroes in Ricky's comic books or movies would do. I did it because they wouldn't expect it. I cried because I was in great pain. I cried because boys do cry.

"Take me down," I sobbed. "Please. I can't walk. My ribs."

Mick couldn't even bring himself to kick me anymore. "What a loser."

Scarface looked away and touched his forehead with the back of his hand. "I think I'm coming down with something."

I cried a few more loud, ugly, shoulder-heaving, phlegmy sobs and then activated broadcast mode.

"What do we do now?" said Scarface. "It's not fun to kick him when he's crying like that."

"It doesn't matter," I whispered. "You're shafted." They'd entered my world, and it was a world of pain.

"What?" said Mick. His anger had morphed into intense confusion.

"Your job and/or lives."

"Because of *you?*" he snorted. "You're about as intimidating as a bucket of drizzle."

"You'll see," I said, and sobbed some more.

"Why's he being all ominous?" Mick asked. "Would you be all ominous if you were in his position?"

"No, pal, I bloody wouldn't."

"Something horrific is about to happen to you two," I said. "Because this is a kind of test. And I fail tests spectacularly. And now we're all going to get shafted. But you the most."

"I'm done with him," said Scarface. "Let's throw him down the stairs."

I winced. "That'll hurt you more than it'll hurt me."

"We'll see about that," Scarface said, grabbing me by my collar. Mick took my legs.

I let my body go limp. "You'll fall and end up paralysed while I'll just land on you and dislocate a shoulder, a minor injury I'll blow out of proportion, true, because I'm the only child of a hypochondriac, but still."

"*Everyone, out now,*" said Tabby. "*We've failed.*"

"Wait," said Ricky.

"*No. Go now.*"

They heaved me the few steps to the stairs.

"Trust me," I said. "I've done this a lot."

Confusion had contorted their faces into ugly shapes—wide eyes and slack jaws. "Done what?" Mick asked.

"Failure." I closed my eyes. "We're doomed. It's already happening."

"WHAT IS HAPPENING?" Scarface screamed into my ear. His breath reeked of cigarettes.

"Did I forget to feed the cat?" Mick asked.

"Doom, death, destruction," I said, and let myself go cross-eyed. "TIBBLES!"

"*Baller*," said Ricky. "*I know what he's doing. Everyone stay where you are. I'm going up.*"

They rocked me above the top step.

"1, 2," said Scarface. I braced for impact. There was a shape, and the sound of feet on the stairs: light, fast, closer to a skip.

Ricky walked up, a huge grin on his face.

"Wow," he said, then slow clapped. "Now that was a performance. He threw everything at you two. And yet you didn't budge." He stopped three steps from the top. Other than when Tabby rescued me from the group home cupboard, and at Craig's the other night, I'd never been happier to see someone.

"Put him down, please, and I'll explain," said Ricky authoritatively. Authority came easy to him now with his new, honeyed voice. The two goons dropped me unceremoniously to the ground with a thud. I moaned and scrabbled backwards to get a little distance from them and whatever horrible thing they were planning to do to me next.

Mick rubbed at his bald head. "I'm so confused. Are you a Hoodlum?"

Ricky feigned touching his earpiece. "You're with Robin? Tell him the good news—they passed. He's coming back. They should meet him where? He got them a what? *Wow*. Okay, they'll be delighted to hear that."

I gathered myself and tried to stand with the help of the wall. I hoped we'd confused the Hoodlums enough for whatever Ricky was about to do.

"Great job," I said, between laboured breaths, "you two."

"Who are you?" Scarface asked Ricky.

"Penetration tester," he said. "Hired to test the security here."

I should have thought of it myself. But then again, he was the ideas man. I'd played my part. I'd confused them pliant. They'd rather take any explanation, however illogical, than the chaos.

"I really did need to get in there," I said, pointing behind myself to the door. I wiped my face with my hand. "I tried everything, but I couldn't get you out of the way. Unlike those clowns downstairs, am I right?"

"The party?" Scarface nodded.

"Part of it," Ricky grinned. "Trying to lure you down."

"Smart to come with no weapons, actually," said Mick. "And just being such obvious scrawny wimps."

"Well done," I said. "Both of you."

They high-fived, their palms slapping loudly.

"Robin will probably give us a promotion," said Mick. "Sorry about your face."

"It'll heal," I said, through gritted teeth.

"No, I meant..." He shrugged. "Yeah. Right."

The landing was too small for the four of us and no one knew where to look. "Robin will meet you in the kitchen shortly," I said. "He left a bonus there for you—*if* you passed."

"Follow me," said Ricky, beckoning them down the stairs.

Mick elbowed Scarface in the stomach as they followed. "Prossie. Gotta be."

I looked at them and let my eyebrows bounce in a way that neither confirmed nor denied but perhaps built needed suspense and/or rapport.

"Esme," I whispered, starting down the stairs. "Kitchen."

The first-floor-toilet door was closed. I thumped my feet

as we passed, to be sure DJ would hear. The adrenaline was wearing off and I felt like a potato run over by a monster truck.

"Robin's nearly back?" I asked, as if reacting to my earpiece. "We're coming down now. Tell her to set up in the kitchen."

Mick elbowed Scarface in the ribs and they giggled in delight.

Back in the kitchen, the unconscious Hoodlum that DJ had punched was still out cold on an old sofa covered in burn marks. Ricky slid behind the partially open kitchen door, mouthed, *Wild card* at me, and slipped out once the Hoodlums were distracted by the sight of Esme.

"Well, hello boys," she said, holding a spatula like a whip and glistening with sweat. She licked her lips. The sounds of music and laughter and revelry rang out from the front garden. The song playing claimed that it was necessary to fight for the right to party, which seemed like something better solved by the legal system.

"Sit," she said, but like it was a threat.

I took this as my cue to slip out the back door.

Outside, overcome with pain, disbelief, fear, and uncertainty, I fell to my knees. We had done it. Somehow. We were becoming quite something, Ricky and I. And we were just getting started. Maybe I wouldn't need to find a new job. Not that anyone was replying to my applications.

Insurity Plc
8 Maid Marian Road
Nottingham
NG1 5FD

December 10, 1999

Dear Sir and/or Madam,

I would like to request consideration for the role of Claims Adviser at Insurity Plc, a prestigious firm founded fifty-seven years ago. I would be right for this position because risk is second nature to me. I am constantly scanning my environment, deciding if it's safe for me to pass under that pigeon, snake down the alley behind Maplin where I was once hexed by a gypsy, or eat that day-old tuna sandwich.

I have experience in the insurance industry, most recently at Holloway, Holloway, and Holloway, which I've now heard must move its offices because of extreme subsidence and/or an act of a vengeful God.

I enjoy teams. I think I'm getting a better handle on why they have not always enjoyed me.

I am an experienced user of the Information Superhighway. I have an excellent, mutually respectful relationship with Clippy the talking paper clip.

While limited in formal education, I like to believe I demonstrate formidable casual learning.

I'm very attracted to this position because it pays a regular wage and will allow me to be a productive member of society and/or not destitute.

In my spare time, I enjoy playing Scrabble with my

housemates, Sudoku alone, and researching and perhaps also romanticising the Amish.

I look forward to hearing from you,

James Jones

P.S. I would appreciate it if the interview would be blind.
P.S.S. If hired, I would kindly request not to have to work near any stationery cupboards suitable for non-stationery related activities.

Should I Become Amish? A Pro/Con List:

Pro: Close-knit community.
Con: Few places to hide.

Pro: Very clear rules.
Con: Frequent shunning, although I do have being-shunned experience.

Pro: Will get wife.
Con: Must have many children with this wife, ideally the sooner the better, to reduce the amount of time I'd be doing the manual labour/woodwork.

Pro: Life of clear rules.
Con: Many rules largely nonsensical.

Pro: God.
Con: Older, angrier God who is prone to heckling.

Pro: Impervious to fads.
Con: No Vimto or crumpets, unclear stance on bubble wrap.

Pro: Good chain of custody over food, since you grow it yourself.
Con: Must grow all food. May need to eat carrot soup again.

Pro: Must leave Nottingham.
Con: Must leave Nottingham.

Pro: Self-reliance.
Con: I would be the person upon which I'd be reliant.

Pro: The men wear the trousers.
Con: The men do not wear anoraks.

42

Thirty, or perhaps even thirty-five seconds later, still in their garden on my knees, I stood up and looked up at my home from the Hoodlums' vantage point.

It was nondescript—red bricks, multiple windows, grey drainpipes, a roof, anti-pigeon spikes on every surface.

But it was mine. And I wanted it back. Because no matter what the awful dance music blaring from the front of the house said, yes yes, yes yes yes yes, yes yes yes yes, yes yes there was a limit.

They had pushed me past it. And now I was going to destroy them. I'd already shown I'd do whatever it took. I looked at my bathroom. A yellow duck sat on the ledge.

"*Picking the lock,*" said Ricky, who was up at Robin's door.

Could Esme keep them distracted long enough to plant the bugs?

"*You don't know what you're doing,*" DJ hissed in the background. "*Let me kick it in.*"

"*I'm still here,*" said Cliff. "*I can't get away.*"

"*Just go,*" said Tabby.

"*What if they notice?*" His voice rose. "*More champagne, sir? No problem, I'll just put a call in to the studio.*"

"*One's going inside,*" said Tabby. "*The guy with the nose. Cliff's going after him. He's pretending to interview him. This is getting too close for comfort now.*"

"*One pin left,*" said Ricky.

"*We're behind schedule, everyone,*" she said. "*Five minutes at least.*"

I knew where those minutes had gone. I turned to the back door, picked up the walkie-talkie, and craned to hear which of Esme's many feminine charms were being used to entertain the guards.

"*We're in. He's in. I'm in,*" said Ricky. "*Jackpot, baby. I see money, drugs, and at least a dozen credit cards in different names. One of them's yours, James.*"

I gave a huge sigh of relief, or rather tried to but ended up bent over, winded, and coughing. There were few places their boots hadn't landed. My ribs were in a terrible state.

"*Don't touch anything,*" Tabby said. "*DJ, photograph it. Ricky, get them bugs planted. Four minutes. James, your part is done. You and Esme need to get out—now.*"

"What about the two goons?" I said. "They're going to tell Robin, aren't they? The plan's compromised."

"*It always gets compromised,*" said Ricky. "*It's about how we react. How we work together.*"

I wanted to doubt him but he'd already saved the plan once.

"They don't know you went in," I said. "Maybe there's still a way?"

"*Push them to the party,*" said Tabby. "*Let's get them drunk. Maybe that will discredit them.*"

The walkie-talkie at my belt squawked. "*James? Robin's on the move. He's approaching the entrance to the cemetery.*

I dated a gravedigger once. The bloomin' fingernails. No amount of—"

"Linda," I said, my voice stern but tired.

"Righty-o. You've two minutes, three tops."

"He's on the move," I said into the earpiece. "Ricky? Three minutes, tops."

"We need longer."

"Tough. I'll deal with the guards."

I entered the kitchen and found Scarface and Mick the Mancunian seated at the end of a long kitchen table, quiet looks of earnest concentration on their faces. Esme was standing over them, reading.

"We are not who they say we are.

They lied to us, the rotters.

They called us names.

And played us games.

These lowly, nefarious plotters.

But we have a choice.

We need not fear.

We're all just terrible wizards.

Don't bend your ear.

Or hold your tongue.

Nor give a merry second.

For we owe them nothing.

But ourselves the world.

We are not who they say we are."

Mick dabbed at his eyes with the sleeve of his parka. Scarface nodded slowly, studying the filthy tabletop. I took a step backwards then whispered, "Ricky, DJ, go hide in the toilet until they pass."

"Cliff," Tabby said. *"If you don't leave right now, I'm coming to get you."*

"Okay, fine." He sounded like a bad impression of himself. He was no longer our confidence man, but maybe

he'd faked it for just long enough. I walked back into the kitchen. Esme looked up at me and I winked.

"Where have I been for the last five minutes?" I asked.

"Paperwork?" said Scarface.

I gave a slow head shake. They swapped bemused looks. You could almost hear the cogs turning.

"Ooh," said Mick. "This was part of the test, wasn't it?"

"Yes," I said. "Of course it was."

They jumped up. "The stash!"

"Easy, easy." I raised my hands. "I didn't go up there, but I could have."

Scarface looked to Esme. "Then she's not a reward?"

"This is my colleague Matilda, also a penetration tester."

An incorrect name. Maybe I was learning.

"Blimey," said Mick. "Fine poet as well."

"Not to mention temptress," Scarface added.

She curtsied. "You're too kind."

"I'm still kind of confused, though," said Scarface. "Are we in trouble with Robin? Or did we do good?"

"I mean..." Mick's voice was low and scared. "Nothing actually happened, right?"

I turned to Esme. "What do you think, Matilda?"

"I think there's a door up there and it had better be locked and you'd better be sitting in front of it when Robin gets back."

My walkie-talkie crackled. I'd forgotten to turn it off. "*Robin's turning onto Portland Road,*" Linda said. "*Should I intercept his not-good self?*"

This time there was no stopping them. They dashed for the stairs.

"They're coming back up," Esme said.

"*What?*" Ricky spluttered. "*We're not ready.*"

"No time. Get out."

"How? Where?"

"Lock the door," said Esme.

"Are you crazy?" DJ hissed. *"We'll be locked in."*

We could hear the Hoodlums thundering up the stairs to get back into position and then the thundering stopped. It went silent for twenty, perhaps even twenty-five seconds.

"Finished," Ricky whispered. *"Door's locked. They're outside. You have to get rid of them again."*

"How are we—"

"Jump?" Tabby suggested and/or interrupted.

"It's two floors!"

"Mattresses," I said. "Cliff, Peter?"

"Now's good," Peter agreed. "Absolutely. We're on it."

The music stopped abruptly.

"Robin's here," Tabby said. *"He's out the front. He just slapped one of his men. Now he's trying some champagne. Wait, is that a knife? He's on the warpath. He's just slashed the bouncy castle. Jesus. Get out NOW. Back door or window. That's not advice. It's an order."*

Esme and I rushed out the back door to the garden, where Linda and Peter were hauling in Cliff's mattress. We looked up. Robin's window was open and Ricky was climbing out to the ledge.

We positioned the mattress as close as we could to the wall.

"MIIIIINNNNNNT!" he said as he fell. "Ow," he said on landing, clutching his ankle. Esme helped him to his feet and towards the gate.

DJ climbed out, saw the size of the drop, then dangled there, his firm behind wriggling in the drizzle.

"Jump," I said.

"I can't."

"What? Just let go."

"I'm... too old."

"No."

"I'm washed up."

"You were in Kabul," I reminded him.

"That was a lie. Liverpool. I lived in Liverpool for a while."

"Well, you knocked that guy out."

"I did, yeah."

A mattress thudded into the swinging gate. It was Cliff followed by an out-of-breath Peter. They corrected its path and advanced again. The second mattress was added to the first. I didn't need to ask whose, as its wrapping gave it away.

"And now you need to jump," said Esme.

"*Robin's inside,*" Tabby said. "Get out."

DJ let go. He landed with a perfect knee-bend, followed by a backwards roll, which became a punch of the air. On his face was a mixture of exhilaration and disbelief. "DID YOU SEE THAT?"

"Shh." I grabbed him and pulled him towards the gate. "Go. *Now*. Everyone."

Seconds after we'd placed it there, the second mattress was being yanked back upright and through the gate by Cliff and Peter. Esme and I took the first.

We heard noises from inside as I closed their gate and disappeared behind my own.

We got everything back into the kitchen and spilled into Cliff's room. Ricky mauled me in a sloppy, back-slapping hug. "We heisted those motherlickers."

Had we? It seemed too close for anything like comfort. I smiled meekly. "It appears we did, yes."

Peter wrapped Linda in a hug. "Time for a bloody good knees-up, I say."

"Oh, you old devil."

Someone was missing. I tapped my earpiece for the last time. "Tabby?"

"On my way. Had to wait for a quiet moment. It's like the end of a football match over here. They lost."

I took out my earpiece and put it on Cliff's desk. His room was a mess of people. He was sat on his bed, head resting against the wall, his body language different from everyone else's. He looked shell-shocked.

"Can we switch on the camera in their house?" Peter asked Ricky.

"Sure you can, buddy. Just click connect."

Peter took the mouse and soon there was a loading bar and it was filling. I noticed I was gurgling when I breathed.

"Are you okay?" Esme asked, putting her hand on the small of my back.

"Yes," I said. "I'm used to being kicked while I'm down, although not always so literally."

She wiped her face with one of my wet wipes. "That was quite something. Didn't know I still had it in me."

"You were magnificent," I said.

She looked around at the others. "Is it safe to stay here? We could all can go to mine?"

"There's a lot of heat on us," Ricky said, smiling, hands behind his head, pushing the recline function on Cliff's office chair to its limit. "I don't know if that's true, but I've always wanted to say it."

Linda was on the other end of Cliff's bed, knitting at what must have been world-record-breaking speed. "This is going to be a hell of a story," she said. "I'm looking forward to telling it and in quite some detail, let me tell you."

"One for the history books," Peter agreed, changing back into his leather waistcoat. There was a beep and the screen flickered, revealing a grainy black-and-white video of Robin's lair.

We cheered while Ricky screamed and the chair tipped over, falling to the floor. "IT'S WORKING!"

We could see Robin shuffling on the spot in the centre of his room, his hands on his hips, his head pushed forward, his eyes roaming, drinking it all in.

"Hid it behind his nudie calendar," said Ricky, and instinctively I turned to where Cliff's Women of Surfing calendar had been but where there was now a framed picture of Ike the Uke.

"No one's been in here?" Robin asked Mick and Scarface, who were doing their best impression of normality. Robin moved behind his desk and yanked open some drawers.

"No, Boss," said Scarface.

"And that party?"

"We won an award. But we didn't go, of course. Sat right here the whole time."

Robin went to the door and inspected the lock.

The front door of our house opened and Tabby entered. She removed her earpiece and wig and Esme wrapped her in a bear hug that lifted her off her feet and ended with them crashing onto the bed, which caused a small disruption in both knitting and moping.

"This recording?" Tabby asked, when she'd escaped enough to squeeze next to Peter in front of the computer. The only one not glued to the feed was DJ, who was sitting alone in the kitchen, smoking and/or brooding.

Robin squared up to Mick and Scarface, who were double his size but not half as mean. "THEN WHY'S THERE MONEY MISSING? MY MONEY. I MEAN, EVERYONE'S MONEY."

We all turned towards the kitchen.

Mick gestured wildly at the open door. "We don't have a key. And we didn't let him in. We passed the test."

Scarface kicked him.

"What?" said Robin. "Who?"

"Nothing, Boss," said Scarface, who seemed to have connected several more dots than Mick and recognised that the pattern being formed would not please their boss.

"Why is this open?" Robin pointed to the window. "In this weather."

"Just some light drizzle," said Mick.

Robin kicked a filing cabinet, which banged against the wall.

DJ appeared in the doorway. "Hell of a heist, gang. I'll be off now then."

"Did you steal money?" Tabby asked.

"What? *No*."

A new, bulky shape entered Robin's room. "Where was my party invite then?" I knew that voice. And that uniform.

"We overlooked Pat," Tabby said. "Of course."

"What the hell happened to you, duck?" Pat said, peering at Robin. "You've a face like thunder."

"We got robbed. Sort of."

"What? By who?"

"Good question," he snarled.

"How much did they take?"

"A thou, maybe? But the door was locked. And they left the drugs and cards. It's confusing."

"Inside job then," she said, and turned towards Mick and Scarface, who'd been edging back towards the hallway.

"They wouldn't dare," Robin hissed.

"Are you high?" Pat asked Robin.

"I'm always high, darling."

"You sure you didn't just miscount?"

He scratched his chin. "I'm sure."

She pulled mail from her Royal Mail bag. "Well, I got two new credit cards with your name on. Well, other people's names on, but you know what I mean. Cash me out if you got any left?"

"We got them," Tabby said. "This is it."

DJ went back through to the kitchen. Ricky ran after him. "That's why you wanted me to jump first!" we heard him shout. "You doubled-crossed us!"

DJ pushed past him and back into the room on his way to the front door, but Cliff jumped off the bed and into his way.

They squared up to each other. "Turn out your pockets."

It was the exact line DJ had said to me in Waterstones. "It was lying right there, alright, Heidi Glum? It basically took itself." He pulled two bundles of cash from the waistband of his trousers.

"It wasn't the plan," Cliff protested.

"It wasn't *your* plan."

"The plan you agreed to," Esme said, and took position behind Cliff.

"Plans change. And now I'm leaving."

Cliff jumped on him, knocking him from his feet. "That's James's money."

"Cliff! No!" Tabby shouted.

Esme piled on top of Cliff.

"Or Cliff's money," I said, running and jumping on top of her. At school this was called a bundle. I was always on the bottom and had passed out a few times. Especially when the teachers did it to me. They were heavy. And hateful. I didn't think many of them liked their jobs. They definitely didn't like me. It was something we had in common, then. I was third from the bottom this time. There was ample oxygen. Not to mention a chorus of grunts and shouts until we'd pacified DJ and got parcel tape wrapped around his hands and feet.

"Screw the lot of you," he growled. "You're amateurs. You don't heist the guy without robbing him."

"Shh," said Tabby, looking back at the monitor.

One of the lower-ranking men had been summoned upstairs. "Hell of a party, boss man." His speech was slurred.

Robin shifted on the spot. "I didn't throw it, Gav."

"Yeah, you did. Or so the guy said. The breezy guy."

"The men." Robin made a sucking sound. "Describe them."

"It's blurry," the underling said, scratching his scalp. "The presenter was good-looking. Odd accent. Kind of fake, if you ask me." He swayed and hiccuped as he talked.

"Focus, sunshine."

"Right." He stood a little straighter then hiccupped again. "The rest were normal. Apart from one fella. Scuttled. Face like a smacked ass smacked by a smacked ass." *Hiccup.* "That was funny that, no?" *Hiccup.*

Pat moved nearer. "Any women?"

"Miss Nottingham 1999. Bit arty for my tastes, but she put on a show and I wouldn't kick her out of bed. Can I go to bed?"

"Three of them?" Pat asked, her voice rising in suspicion.

"Some old biker geezer. Goatee. Such a mistake, right? Pedo vibe."

"How dare he," said an outraged Peter. "I don't think I even saw this man. His face is? Oh..."

Pat went to the hallway then came back holding a scrap of something between her fingers. She strode to the window and looked in our direction. Ricky turned from the screen. "She onto us?"

"Let's get out of here," DJ demanded. He'd been sliding towards the door while trying to bite himself free.

"Was she plain?" Pat asked. "The woman. Hair liked

she'd been dragged through a bush backwards? Librarian's glasses? Give advice?"

"Nah."

Pat threw her head back and let out another of her villainous laughs. She raised her hand and extended a finger. "There's more bubble wrap," she said. "In your garden."

My mattress.

Robin moved to the window. "Odd."

"Yeah, he is."

"Who?"

"Ferdinand," she said, and pointed. "It was Ferdinand."

"Boys!" Robin shouted, running out to the hallway and disappearing from view. "Suit up."

43

My gate slammed. "What do we do?"

"I'd suggest running," said Tabby.

"Fine suggestion," said Peter, moving towards the door. "Tip-top."

Esme peeked through the curtains. "Graveyard?"

"It's theirs," I said.

"High Street?" Cliff suggested. "Safety in numbers?"

He still had a lot to learn. There was no safety in numbers, just multiplied danger.

"I see them," Esme said. "Coming from the alley."

They were attacking us front and back. "You need to untie me," DJ barked. "If there's a fight, you ladies need me in it."

"You're the reason for it," said Esme.

"They aren't going to believe that though, are they, Sylvia Faff."

"Is everything locked?" Linda asked. "Doors, windows?"

Tabby nodded.

"Weapons?" Linda asked. "I'm a dab hand with a

nunchuck. Got taught by a nun, actually. Terribly exciting story but perhaps a little long for the circumstances."

There was a loud triple knock on the back door. I'd locked the gate, so they had to have jumped it. I'd known those anti-pigeon spikes weren't high enough. I'd focused on the wrong enemy.

"I'll go," said Ricky. "They don't know me."

His bravery had become something to behold. He went to the kitchen. "Hello?" he said, through the closed back door, after Robin knocked again. "Can I help?"

"It's your neighbour," said Robin. "Can I... err, borrow some milk?"

"Lactose intolerant," Ricky shouted. "Sorry."

"Sugar then?"

"Diabetic."

"Eggs?"

"Vegan."

"A thousand pounds of my ill-gotten loot?"

"Broke, buddy. What you making?"

"Revenge quiche," Robin said, and slammed what sounded like his foot against the door. "Right, I'm not feeling very neighbourly. I'm going to count from five and you either open or we smash windows. Five."

Shapes appeared at Cliff's bedroom window. It had happened again, the sandwich and the peril, but we'd buttered this one ourselves.

"Heavies," said Cliff, closing the curtains. "With baseball bats."

They started knocking loudly on the front door. "Don't make me huff and puff," said Mick the Mancunian.

"Four."

"Three."

I cut DJ free. As I did, he muttered under his breath about how amateur we all were and what a mistake this had been. And then he was free and on his feet, his eyes now more animal than human as he looked around the room for weapons, shaking out his wrists and ankles.

"Two!" Robin shouted.

"Upstairs," he growled. "They can only attack from one side."

"My room has a lock."

We ran for the stairs. Peter, Linda, and Tabby first. Then Esme and Cliff. Ricky turned off the monitor and followed. "DJ," I said, leading him past the stairs into the kitchen. I showed him the secret compartment in my mattress, empty, since I'd given all my money to Craig. "Hide the money here."

"One!" Robin shouted, and began to laugh. He had the power, and probably also the prickle. I felt fear—not for myself, but for everyone I cared about in this world.

"Zero! Smash it."

I was halfway up the stairs when the kitchen window shattered and the thudding and yelling and—I suppose, also—destruction began. I didn't look back. "Hurry!" I screamed at DJ and Ricky, who were ahead of me on the stairs. By the time we'd all bundled into my room, shut the door, and engaged the locks, which, thankfully, I had many of, Scarface, Robin, and Mick the XXL Mancunian were approaching the top of the stairs.

"I've no advice," said Tabby, perched on the edge of the empty bed frame, her head in her hands, her large glasses on her lap. "I was the mastermind. This is my fault."

"We fight," said DJ, cracking his knuckles and swirling his arms to warm up. "To the death."

"No one's dying," I said. "I've been very clear about that."

There was a great thud as they shoulder-barged the door, which bounced on its hinges.

"The window," Esme said, moving to it. "We could jump?"

The next body slammed against the door.

I followed her to the window, opened it, and shouted for help. More of their merciless men and/or Hoodlums were arriving and disappearing inside. They'd smashed Cliff's window. Others were waiting outside. It was too late to jump.

BOOM. CRACK. The wood in the door was giving way.

"Hope is lost," said Peter, who sat down next to Tabby.

Ricky and DJ were searching for weapons. I had no weapons. I was my best weapon.

Linda sat down next to Peter. "Almost called my daughter Hope. Went with Phyllis in the end. I've some regrets."

She'd never mentioned a daughter. Were her stories true? It didn't matter now. We had tried but we had failed. I looked forward to telling my parents about it once I got out of the hospital and/or prison. If we didn't die, of course.

"We were too confident," said Cliff.

We were silent for ten, perhaps even fifteen seconds as the Hoodlums jostled, shouted, and encouraged each other to rain more violence onto my bedroom door. It was reinforced but wouldn't hold much longer. We waited, knowing that the situation was out of our control, and that it would not be merciful.

I wished there were a cupboard I could slip into with a sheet of bubble wrap for company.

"Hello?" said a new, nervous voice.

I looked up. Was I hearing things now?

"Psst?" it said, louder.

"Does anyone hear that?" Esme asked, before there was another great BOOM from the failing door.

"Yes," I said, and looked out the window again.

Two eyes peered out from the bush in my neighbour's front garden. "Sorry to disturb you," the voice said. It was a woman's. Familiar. A hand came through the foliage and waved. "James? Am I too late? I'm too late, aren't I? I'm exactly the sort of person who would rush in at the last minute to help but then only actually hinder."

"Annie?"

"Afraid so. Is Linda there?"

"There's no time, Annie. We need your help NOW. You need to find some police. Try the top of the road."

"I've done that," she said. "I called them. They're coming. Was that right?"

"Who did you speak to?"

"She asked if I was the victim or perpetrator?"

The first panel of wood split in the centre of the door. "Got you now," Robin shouted.

"Thanks," I said to Annie, but moved away from the window towards the others. There was nothing she could do to help. They had too many and/or much weapons, testosterone, and bloodthirst. If there was to be a bath later, it would be our blood filling it.

"We need to fight," Esme said. "DJ's right."

Ricky came out from behind the desk brandishing a hardback book of Amish butter churning recipes.

Peter stood and took off his waistcoat.

DJ pulled up some heavy slats from my bed frame and handed them around. I'd inherited the bed from my parents. They'd inherited it from a nearby manor house whose inhabitants weren't there during the week. He raised the wood above his head. "Show time, ladies."

"Peter," Esme said. "Next time you hear him run towards the door, open it."

Next to the bed was Tabby's black scarf. I remembered

the afternoon we'd spent with Cliff and smiled. All we'd done that afternoon was put a little bit of on-fire plant in our faces, and yet I'd been gifted half a day free of my worst inner-inclinations.

"Why are you smiling?" Peter asked. He was terrified and shaking.

I was calm. At peace, even. "Thank you," I said to both no one and everyone. "For all of it. It helped."

Changing who you are is fiendishly difficult, perhaps even impossible. Changing how you feel about yourself, however? That can be done.

I liked myself now, at least a little. I had friends and they liked me too. Together we were rising up against our oppressors. I'd even played an integral role as a wild card. I was who I was. My manifesto had been right about that, but I no longer wished it was more.

And so I smiled. I was still smiling when Peter opened the door and jumped out of the way. Robin's momentum launched him into the room, where he hit the edge of the bed, tripped, and crashed down into the frame, becoming wedged in the gap where DJ had removed those slats. The baseball bat he was holding clattered to the ground. I jumped onto him. Tabby jumped on top of me. Esme hit the floor and grabbed the bat. And there was suddenly a roll of tape in my hands.

Robin was squirming and fighting. He hadn't expected me to be that good and fast with duct tape. I couldn't see what was happening behind us, but it sounded as if DJ was being very disagreeable, Ricky was backing him up, and even Linda was in on the act, threatening eyes with her knitting needles and raving about everything the nuns had taught her.

It wouldn't be enough. I was proud of them all, nonetheless.

The room lit up: flashing blue lights swirled across the walls and sirens screamed.

"The filth," said Robin, still thrashing beneath me, growling and spluttering, hanging half out of the bed frame.

"Split," said Mick. "Five-o!"

I turned to see the Hoodlums retreating.

"Three cars," Linda said from the window. "They actually came."

"Thwack a yak," said Esme. With a devious smile, she pulled back her leg and booted Robin in the stomach. He howled like a dog.

The first police officer arrived in the doorway. "On the ground! Now! Oh, and 'ello, 'ello, 'ello," he said, dipping his hat.

We put our hands on our heads and dropped to the ground. Robin was moaning and I think also sobbing now, for which I didn't judge him.

"It's him," Tabby said, pointing at Robin. "He broke into our home. This is a citizen's arrest."

"Did I do it right?" Annie shouted from the bottom of the stairs. "I did it wrong, didn't I? I bloody knew I would."

Nottingham Evening Post Exclusive: Radford's Crime Kingpin Arrested
By Jill Scoop

Troubled Radford sleeps easier tonight following the arrest of local crime kingpin Robin Walsh.

Police were called to 12 Cromwell Street, where a vicious neighbourly dispute became a foot chase across an alleyway to 12 Portland Road, the scene of a bizarre street party gone wrong.

After a long, tense stand-off, that property was raided, uncovering a stash of drugs with a street value of over twenty thousand pounds, as well as sixty-seven stolen credit cards and a postwoman called, believe it or not, Pat.

"I hope they throw away the key," said Mrs Smith, a neighbour who claims to have been mugged six times by members of Robin's gang, known as the Robin Hoodlums.

"They were right wrong'uns," said Mr Potts, another neighbour, who claimed the group's love of loud dance music had given him both tinnitus and PTSD. "And I don't care what anyone says—rhythm's a terrible dancer."

"We just complained about the music," said Mr Jones, Nottingham's Unluckiest Man 1999, who, predictably, was being attacked at the time the police arrived. "Don't write that I was being attacked. And I'm not unlucky. It's sensationalised. I'm just uncommon. I provoke."

"No doubt who the perpetrators were," said Police Liaison Natasha Cuffs. "It was a case that utilised the latest in covert surveillance. Our highly trained boys in blue down the station can be very, very proud."

Along with Robin, twelve members of the gang, including postwoman Patricia Eldridge, were arrested by Nottingham Constabulary.

"It's a good day," said Mr Jones, "so far."

Dearest Motley Misfits,

You're cordially invited to the opening party and/or funeral

of

Shaft: Sabotage as a Service and/or James Jones

To be held at 11.40pm (PROMPT), on the 31st of December 1999, at Albert's Public House (and Shaft's HQ).

Dress code: Confused

Irrepressibly yours,

James and Ricky

46

"Albert?" I shouted, from the bar's back door. He looked up from a book he was reading about SAS soldiers stuck behind enemy lines, licked his finger, and slowly turned the page.

"Did the champagne arrive?" I asked, ignoring that I was being ignored.

He half-laughed, half-grunted. "Vimto champagne?"

"No. Opening-party champagne. The party that's happening in"—I looked down at Ricky's digital watch, which had grown on me because, as far as I could tell, you barely ever had to wind it—"one hour and four minutes."

He shrugged. "Maybe did. Maybe didn't." The slightest hint of a smile formed at the corner of his inscrutable mouth. As he returned to his book, the lights of the jukebox began to pulse.

No matter how hard they tried to sell it, I simply did not believe Funkytown was a real place.

"You have some kind of remote for that, right?" I asked.

Albert slowly lifted his head and stared at me for fifteen, perhaps even twenty seconds. "You are remote."

This was my first time hosting a party since my fifth

birthday, when my parents rented the local bowling alley. Although it seemed to be closed at the time. We never got the lanes working, but my mother was nice enough to hover down at the far end with a wide broom. No one else came. My parents told me this was because of a sudden, unexpected plague of locusts in the village. I wondered now if that had been the full truth.

We were holding Shaft's opening party at Albert's because Ricky and I had rented the small, windowless backroom for our shared endeavour. It had its own alleyway entrance and a fold-down camp bed, and permission to tap the bar's inebriated clientele. If they were drinking here, we hoped they had plentiful enemies in this city of rogues, renegades and toe-rags.

Albert had previously used the room to store his pickle collection. You got used to the smell.

A week had passed since the heist. The police had bought into the neighbourly dispute story, or pretended they had. Robin could hardly convince them we'd stolen what he he'd first stolen. We also had video of Pat and him admitting their crimes, edited conveniently for us by Ricky. The police, desperate for a win in this beleaguered city, took the credit for themselves. It was a nice Christmas for them and the papers were full of it.

Soon it was 11pm, and I heard knocking on the back door. I went out past the barrels of glue and opened it cautiously.

"Evening, comrade," said Robin.

I checked over my shoulder to see how far away Albert was.

To try and get his sentence reduced, Robin had put up posters around Radford announcing the end of the gang and offering to help rebuild what his merciless men had destroyed. He also held a public "self-criticism" session that became a riot when half the citizens of Radford showed up armed and in the mood for revenge.

I'd been the only person to request his help so far. I thought the best way to not be scared of him might be to get to know him.

It hadn't worked.

His skin had improved, though, and there was almost a rosiness to his gaunt cheeks. "Give us a hand with this casket, will ya? Barely fits down the alley and me back's killing me."

"Where are your boys?"

"Smoking in the van, lazy sods. Morale's at an all-time low. A lot of them have abandoned the cause."

"Was the cause enriching you?"

"Marxism," he spluttered.

"Ah, right." I tutted. "Of course."

He led me to a small yellow van that wasn't Aggie. In it was a casket. I took one end and, with great exertion, we got it through the back door and onto a table Ricky had prepared in a cleared section of the bar.

"Handsome," I said, when I had my breath back and a chance to look at it properly.

"I don't know," Robin said. "It's been a while since I was a carpenter. Whoever said crime doesn't pay was lying. Although I shared my spoils fairly." His eyes darted left and right. "Somewhat fairly. Can you tell the top was a door?"

I could, on account of the fact it had a handle and the white twelve was still visible. It was his front door. The police had knocked it down. There was still a huge circular dent from the battering ram in its centre. "It adds something to it, I think," I said, in what I hoped was a diplomatic tone. "Is this going to work?"

"Fifty-fifty." He ducked an invisible punch and then bobbed forwards onto his toes. "Maybe sixty-forty against. I followed Ricky's instructions. He's an original thinker, that lad. I wish I'd had him with me in the Hoodlums. But I do wonder if his ideas are a bit above his station?"

"I know what you mean."

"False bottoms? I mean, this is Vegas stuff, in Nottingham."

"What time do you have to report to the prison?"

"No prison can hold me," he said, but then winced. "Now, actually."

"Next time then," I said, thinking that was very much for the best and I wouldn't have invited him to the party anyway.

"You fought well, your crew. But it shouldn't have come to that." He dropped his chin to his chest. "I've been doing a lot of thinking and self-criticism and I'm painting and stuff. Esme has started an evening poetry class that's bloody terrific, truth be told. Everything's easier now I'm not strung out on all that junk. Thanks for giving me this chance to make it right."

"Righter," I corrected.

He held out his hand.

"Germs," I said.

* * *

Annie was the first to arrive to the party, though she didn't announce the fact. I found her hiding behind a large fake palm tree while I was searching for champagne.

"Am I early?" she asked. "I am, aren't I?"

"You're perfectly on time."

"I'm exactly the sort of person who'd be the first person to be here."

"A punctual person?"

"Yes."

"That's a good trait."

"Oh. *Well.*"

"More ice?" I said, nodding to her pint glass of Cocktail.

"We certainly need it," she said. "It's melting. The ice-caps. It's a catastrophe."

"No. I mean. *Yes.* For your drink?"

"Can't." She tutted. "Brain freeze."

I bent down and looked under the next table. "And you, Peter?"

He looked up and blinked slowly, twice. "Are you a friend of James's?"

"I am James."

He squinted. "James old boy, that really you?"

"Yes."

"Didn't recognise you. Did you change something?"

"No."

"Hairstyle, perhaps?"

"No."

"Anorak?"

"No."

"Posture?"

"No."

"Disposition?"

"No... maybe. Come out," I said, and tugged on his ankle. "If you can do a diabolical heist, you can attend a small party."

"Cosy under here, though."

"Come out."

"I'm fine, really."

"COME OUT."

"Excellent suggestion." He crawled out, stood, and brushed the thick dust and/or dirt from his jeans.

"Actually, Annie," he said. "I forgot to ask. What with all the commotion. How did you get the police to come?"

It was the highest I'd ever seen her lift her head. "Well, I called them and I tried telling the truth, but the woman said since I didn't live around there, shouldn't I keep my nose out of it? Terrible really, isn't it? What when we pay their wages and everything. Anyway, I tried to think of the one crime they'd investigate, no matter where it happened. So then I told her I'd found a million pounds in a suitcase outside 12 Cromwell Street. That got them moving. Then they saw the ruckus and so they had to get involved, didn't they, I suppose?"

"Brilliant," I said.

"Spot on." Peter agreed.

"Mm-hmm."

"That you, Hugh?" Peter asked, turning to Hugh, who had just arrived and was standing awkwardly behind us.

"Don't mind me," Hugh said, dabbing at his neck with his handkerchief. "Lovely to see you all. And not in the library. Sorry I didn't make the heist. Mm-hmm. I was scared, I suppose. Mm-hmm. Made a dreadfully poor show of it, really, all things considered. Count me in for the next one?"

DJ arrived and Albert seemed to recognise him, making a point of turning his back, becoming very busy dusting empty bottles. It was the first time I'd seen DJ since the heist.

"You here to apologise?"

"I don't apologise," he said, but handed me an object shaped like a T and wrapped in old newspaper. Unsure whether it would electrocute me, catch fire, or ask me a tricky trivia question, I took it from him.

"Should I wait until midnight?"

"Nah."

I ripped gently at the wrapping, which hung as loose as a mummy's bandage. Underneath was a wooden cross glued on top of an identical wooden cross facing the other direction. It looked like an amateur carpentry project gone very wrong. I held it up and rotated it under the bar's low lights. There was a puzzle here, and I wasn't sure if I had all its pieces and/or if they were supposed to fit together like this.

"Double cross," he clarified.

I laughed. "Clever."

"I had big shoes, you know? What with me being the loose cannon and the one you barely knew and coming out of retirement for one last job. Archetypes and whatnot. It was a lot to live up to." He turned and nodded once sharply. And then he was gone.

The bar filled up. People stood around the weird casket in the middle of the room drinking and eating from the catering provided by Albert: a vat of Cocktail containing Vimto and a collection of pies whose fillings were mysterious. Several people suggested they also contained Vimto.

As we were about to start, the door opened then scraped to a stop. Tabby entered first, sparkling in a turquoise blazer and matching lipstick. Cliff strolled in behind her in a cowboy suit. While it would be Ricky and me working here full-time at Shaft, Esme, Tabby, and Cliff would assist should an assignment call for their specific skill sets.

Cliff doffed his hat.

"We've missed you at home," Tabby said. "You been staying at Esme's?"

"No." I'd been avoiding Esme. But I'd also been reading books about the sexuality of females and—I suppose, also—males, and/or by extension, perhaps, myself.

"Cliff tried to play *spling* last night in Scrabble, triple word. I could have used the support."

"It's what you feel after you've cleaned your teeth," he said, flashing his own. He looked almost back to his old self, minus the smoulder. "When you coming back?"

"Soon. We're nearly ready here."

"Any offers on the house?" She asked.

"Yes, a generous offer. I said no. For better or worse. Mostly worse, but it's where we belong."

Ricky clinked two glasses, reminding me midnight was approaching and I had a speech to give. I climbed up onto the bar via the only stool that still had all of its legs and looked out at fourteen, perhaps even fifteen people.

I cleared my throat. No one turned.

"Let me," said Hugh. "Mm-hmm."

The room quietened. "Ladies and gentleman," I said, then faltered. "Sorry. I'm unused to public speaking. Tonight is bittersweet, so let us begin with the bitter. Those of you that know me know that I find things, well, treacherously difficult. I'm uncommon in my"—I reached up to touch my face—"in everything, really. But combined with Ricky, who's also uncommon, we make stuff happen, basically. Misfortune, mostly. We provoke."

We were an unlikely duo, but one that could effortlessly destroy promising business ideas, flood basements, make homeless people more homeless, get dogs impounded, boost self-help-book sales, kidnap and buy off alcoholic fathers, bring people out of retirement, unite disparate misfits, and destroy ruthless criminal enterprises. Destruction really was much easier than construction. We would start there.

"We're now proud owners of Shaft: Sabotage as a Service. If you need your nemesis thwarted, or at least irritated, we're the people to make that happen. Use responsibly. That said, we're just starting out and really there's no dispute too petty at this point."

There was a light ripple of applause. It was a lot to wrap your head around. I was still trying.

I looked down at my watch. "Okay, I've got to be quick. It's 11.59. And assuming the Y2K bug doesn't end life as we know it, in one minute I'll become thirty years old and assuming all the paperwork's gone through, a new and/or previous person."

Ricky opened the door to my casket. I stepped into it, with his help. I knelt and then lay down on my side. Ricky closed the door and—I suppose, also—lid behind me and started the smoke machine at his feet as Albert hit play on the jukebox's remote.

A song encouraged us to dance like it was the year we were just about to leave. Its singer played fast and loose with the truth and wasn't even a real prince, I'd recently discovered.

As I slid the fake bottom up, revealing a hole in the real one that I then shimmied through, down to the floor. On cue, Ricky would have pushed a button on another of his giant remotes triggering a loud explosion as the roof of the casket blew off and its sides collapsed to reveal... nothing and/or no one. There was a chorus of *oohs* and *aahs* and one solitary *mm-hmm*.

Uncle Sanjay's smoke machine went into overdrive and there was a chorus of coughs as Ricky fought to get it back under control. I was a few metres away scrabbling from the casket on all fours, moving between people's legs towards the back of the bar and our new office.

"It's okay," Ricky shouted to the room. "Probably."

Tabby sprang into action and unplugged the machine from the wall as Albert flapped a tea towel and called us a word you can't repeat in polite and/or impolite company.

Behind the palm tree, I nudged Peter to the side and changed my outfit. The music stopped, Ricky grabbed a disco light and swivelled it towards me, and I popped out in a white tuxedo. "Ladies and gentleman, James Jones is dead. Long live Ferdinand Fairweather!"

I bowed to claps and cheers. I might die in a day, I might

die in a decade, but what I'd discovered was there was no point staying alive if you didn't actually do some living.

It rhymed with shunts, the word.

I glanced at my watch. We'd left little time for the next celebration. "Now, a new millennium in ten." The room joined in.

"Nine!"

"Eight!"

I didn't make it to "one", on account of the fact that someone had pinned me against a wall.

"I nearly didn't come," Esme shouted into my ear, as the room broke into shouts and applause.

"Yes," I said, but looked away towards the toilets.

She grabbed a plastic cup full of Cocktail, downed it, and then wiped away the purple foam moustache forming above her lip. "I'm done with the bullshit, J. Sorry, Ferdinand. Nice name by the way. Got gravitas. Time is precious. I'm not wasting any more of it."

"Esme."

She raised her hand. "I like how you make the world—which, let's be fucking honest, is a pretty mundane and kind of shitty place—feel exciting and novel and really, really terrifying. You are honest and vulnerable and perhaps even deliciously odd. You are also cripplingly shy with women. So I'm going to make this very, very easy for you."

I stood as if held at the end of a very long, very powerful wind tunnel.

She shrugged. "Another snakebite and I'm yours, basically."

I gulped. "Can we take—"

"No." She wagged her finger. Her nails were black. "We're not going to take it slow. Because there's a lot you have to learn and I intend to teach you."

She grabbed my head, pulled it towards her and,

holding my eyelid open with two fingers, bent her head down and licked my left eye. It felt like... it was... all of the things in one confusing swirl: intimate and objectifying; arousing and violating; prickly and pricklier.

She let me go and licked her lips.

"We're going to get you drunk. Sozzled, even, possibly. Enough to switch off that brain of yours but not your body. Then we're going to get into a cab that might or might not be driven by Ricky. That cab will take us to my house. My dad will be very, very asleep. In that house, in my room, you will do unspeakable things to me as I command. Because frankly, it's been too long since a man made me scream, or even moan. Heck, at this point, I'd settle for a yelp. And I like your eyes. And your friends. And they like you, and are loyal to you, and that says a lot about you."

"Foul an owl," I said, as she smiled and slipped an arm around my waist. "Bubble—"

She cut off my question with another deep, filthy, depraved laugh. "Fine by me."

Thanks, and a free book

Hello, it's Adam here.

We've made to what traditionalists call *The End.* I just wanted to take a moment to show my appreciation that you're still here, with me, reading the final page of my first full-length work of ~~lies~~ fiction.

At some point, somehow, about five long years ago, I accidentally became a travel memoirist. I have a series of four gonzo *Weird Travel* books that will take you to some of strangest places in the world, including countries like Transnistira and Liberland, that you probably didn't know exist.

Moving to fiction was a big leap, and I'm glad you jumped with me. I hope you were suitably entertained, and the landing wasn't too rough on your knees. I'm hard at work on the sequel, where Ricky and James and *Shaft* will become embroiled in a plot far larger and nefarious than they could ever imagine. Something that will threaten much more than just Radford.

To be the first to know when it's out, to help me shape its plot and characters, and to get an exclusive free book called *Lost But Not Least*, join my newsletter at - http://adam-fletcher.co.uk

Thank you,

Adam

Printed in Great Britain
by Amazon